ELI HARPO'S
ADVENTURE
TO THE
AFTERLIFE

ELI HARPO'S ADVENTURE TO THE AFTERLIFE

A NOVEL

ERIC SCHLICH

THE OVERLOOK PRESS, NEW YORK

This edition first published in hardcover in 2024 by
The Overlook Press, an imprint of ABRAMS
195 Broadway, 9th floor
New York, NY 10007

Abrams books are available at special discounts when purchased in quantity
for premiums and promotions as well as fundraising or educational use.
Special editions can also be created to specification. For details,
contact specialsales@abramsbooks.com or the address above.

This book is a work of fiction. Names, characters, places, and incidents depicted are a
product of the author's imagination and not based on real persons.

Library of Congress Control Number: 2023936455

Printed and bound in the United States

1 3 5 7 9 10 8 6 4 2
ISBN: 978-1-4197-6912-2
eISBN: 979-8-88707-078-0

ABRAMS The Art of Books
195 Broadway, New York, NY 10007
abramsbooks.com

For Jade and Ender

And God shall wipe away all tears from their eyes; and there shall be no more death, neither sorrow, nor crying, neither shall there be any more pain: for the former things are passed away.

—Revelation 21:4

In Sugarcandy Mountain it was Sunday seven days a week, clover was in season all the year round, and lump sugar and linseed cake grew on the hedges. The animals hated Moses because he told tales and did no work, but some of them believed in Sugarcandy Mountain, and the pigs had to argue very hard to persuade them that there was no such place.

—George Orwell, *Animal Farm*

HEAVEN HOAX

BIBLE WORLD—15 MILES. WE PASS the first in a series of signs counting down to the park's Orlando exit. It's faded, easy to miss among the larger, glossier billboards advertising Disney and Universal Studios. But I recognize it instantly. Purple, with the signature lion and lamb. I'm already regretting this.

Will, driving, reaches over and takes my hand. He glances in the rearview mirror. "Hey, Oliver. See that sign? It says Bible World. We're almost there!"

Our three-year-old cheers in his car seat. "Bible World!"

"And then Disney tomorrow," I say. "Don't forget Disney."

Because Disney's the deal we made. Disney's my reward. The secular dreamland after the Christian nightmare of my youth.

"Who can forget Disney?" Will winks.

Will comes from a Disney family. They bought into the whole magical caboodle: Cinderella's castle, spinning teacups, flying elephants. I've seen photos of him with his sisters, lined up on Main Street, USA, wearing those mouse-eared hats with their names fancy-stitched in the back. Eating Mickey-shaped ice cream in front of a giant golf ball. ("That's not a golf ball. It's Epcot's Spaceship Earth. A geodesic sphere!") He owns a small red autograph book signed by Snow White, Chip and Dale, Pooh.

These were not the characters of my childhood. That place in my imagination was reserved for Biblical figures—Noah, Moses, Jonah. Adam and
Eve and the Serpent. Daniel in the lions' den. The myths we've chosen not
to pass down to Oliver. Prophets replaced by princesses: a new generation
of mouse-eared memory making.

BIBLE WORLD—10 MILES.

"Why'd I agree to this again?"

"Because you love me." Will kisses my hand. "And because it'll be good
for you. And your father."

"He's never going to do it."

"You should give him more credit."

"Says the man who once called him—what was it? Pastor Brimstone?"

"*Brother* Brimstone," he says, like that's much better. It's been an issue
between us, Will seeing Dad as a cliché: the homophobic Bible-thumper.
The truth is he barely knows him. Just from the holidays, when things are
polite, but strained. And only as "your father"—never "Dad." *Dad* was the
one whose Pastor Zeb impression made me and my brothers laugh so hard
we almost peed ourselves. *Dad* was the one who serenaded Mom, dancing
like a maniac, boom box overhead, blasting his *Pow! That's What I Call
Praise!* CD. *Dad* was the one who helped hospice nurses change bedpans
without blinking, who spent hours praying by hospital beds, who taught
me it was okay to be sensitive and a man. That it was more than okay: It
was admirable—to feel what you felt, to do unto others—a kind of grace.
I remember Dad on that terrible day at Bible World, gazing at the tank of
seahorses in the Red Sea Aquarium, promising to take care of me. I haven't
thought of that in years.

"Hate the belief, love the believer," Will teases—my motto whenever
Dad says or does something offensive.

"Oh, so now, when it's convenient *for you*, you can put up with him."

"Come on, E. He's trying. He wants to make amends." Will smirks.
"Pretty good for Friar Hellfire."

"And there it is." I swat his arm. Playfully. Well, mostly. It's hard to stay
mad at him. I turn and look out the window.

We're a caravan on I-75: Abe's SUV, Jake's truck, our car, and the van with all the camera equipment. When Will first broached the idea of the doc, I was vehemently opposed. Will works for our local paper, the *Herald-Leader*, but he's never given up his dream of becoming a documentary filmmaker. His previous projects have all been low-budget affairs on political and environmental issues in Kentucky. His short on mountaintop removal mining found critical acclaim in certain corners of the internet. *Heaven Hoax* is something new.

A few months ago, Will told me Bible World was closing for good. *About time*, I thought. It'd been on its last legs for years, the Heaven Realm the first of many last-ditch efforts to up park attendance. And now the end had finally come for the owner, televangelist extraordinaire Charlie Gideon. The IRS had finally nailed Gideon—or were in the process of nailing him. The legal battles dragged on, but Gideon knew it was time to cut bait. The Charlie Gideon Network aired ads announcing Bible World's final summer, tickets at half price. Will played one for me on YouTube. It was the last opportunity to *take your family on an adventure of Biblical proportions!*

"Good riddance." I slapped the laptop shut. I was glad the place was closing. I wanted it to be demolished. I wanted to forget it ever existed.

"You have to go back."

"What? Are you crazy? No."

"Just hear me out, okay?"

I bit my tongue, waved for him to continue.

"You have a really important story to tell—a *socially relevant* story. If people knew—"

"Will. Spit it out already."

He straightened his shoulders. "I want to make a doc about you."

"Ha!"

"Come on! Aren't you curious? Haven't you ever wanted to go back? It's your last chance to make your prodigal return."

"That's not what *prodigal* means."

"I think it could be really great. Our generation's *Marjoe*."

"Are you kidding me?"

"If you look at the impact *Religulous* had. Or *Jesus Camp.*"

These were all Christian-critical documentaries we'd watched in college, screened at the University of Kentucky by the Atheist Student Union, the club where we first met. Will called them life-changing. I had trouble sitting through them. I have a vivid memory of walking out of the student center after the first twenty minutes of *Hell House*, in which a Texas youth group prepares a Halloween attraction featuring "sodomites" in cages and women forced to relive their coat-hanger abortions for eternity. Will thought I was offended by the fire-and-brimstone stereotypes—but actually, I'd glimpsed something of my brothers and me in the teens hammering sets together, fighting over sinner roles, and I had to get out of there.

"Will," I said through gritted teeth. "I'm your husband, not your subject."

He didn't push, but he did sulk. He was so sure it was a good idea. It was my own fault. I'd seduced him in college with the Heaven stuff.

BIBLE WORLD—5 MILES.

It's all so much smaller than I remember. The highways, the palm trees, even the billboards. I forgot how tacky it was. Oversize surfboards advertising souvenir shops, smiling cartoon manatees, pink-and-purple flamingo hotels. Everything's an "attraction." It feels cowardly to be afraid of this place. What did I think would happen? Charlie Gideon, in his signature cowboy hat and bolo tie, would pop out from behind a palm tree? We'd be forced as a family onto the crosses at Crucifixion Corner? I'd be recognized as the Heaven Boy and hounded by Christian paparazzi? I'm thirty-three now, with a receding hairline, a middle-aged spread, and my first grays. I bear little resemblance to that scared thirteen-year-old in his blinding white suit under the hot halogens on Bible World's megachurch stage.

Will pulls off at the exit with the rest of our caravan.

What had once been lion and lamb topiary are now overgrown, shapeless hedges. The parking tollbooths are closed, and no wonder: The lot's practically empty. Two rows of cars sit near the entry, probably owned by park employees.

We park, and the family piles out. It's quite the crowd. My older brother, Abe, and his wife, Becca, with their three kids—Chris, Hannah, and Jessie.

Dad rode with them. My younger brother, Jake, and his wife, Rachel, with their two—Leah and Ella. Then there's the doc crew, Will's buddies: a boom operator and a camerawoman. Will hops out to help them unload. Everyone's mingling, but I can't get out of the car.

Will turns back. "You okay?"

"Fine."

"Are we going to the castle now?" Oliver whines.

He means the Disney one, but when he says it I think of the Celestial Palace, of its lumpy cloudlike plaster, glittering, misshapen, like a wedding cake melting in the Orlando sun. Angels on zip lines. The drawbridge at the exit of the Holy Roller.

I squeeze the bridge of my nose. "Give me a sec."

Will nods. "Take your time."

I sit and watch my nieces and nephew run around the lot, squirting one another with water guns. The adults gather at the **Shalom!** Welcome Arch, organizing snacks and water bottles, unfolding strollers, pulling tickets up on phones. They glance at our car. My absence is noticed, but I don't care. I'm not ready yet. I turn in my seat and look back at Oliver.

"You going to have fun today?"

"Yeah." He toys with his car-seat buckle. "Can we go in now?"

"Remember what we talked about, okay? How it's just pretend?"

Oliver nods. "Uh-huh."

We get out. Will's framing a shot for park-entry footage, so I'm left to fend for myself with my family. Abe and Jake wave me over for an immediate assault of nostalgia.

"Hey, Eli," Abe says. "Remember how you pulled on Jesus's beard to see if it was real? I was telling Becks how you were *so sure* it was fake."

"That wasn't me. That was Jake."

"And how you wet yourself on the cross at Crucifixion Corner."

"He didn't *wet* himself," Jake says. "He just had to pee really bad."

"Also Jake."

"And that awful white suit Gideon made you wear?" Abe cracks up. "You looked like Colonel Sanders!"

I busy myself applying Oliver's sunscreen. I swore I wouldn't let Abe get to me today. "How about how you punched the plaster kangaroo in Noah's Ark?"

"What?" Abe colors. "I did not."

Jake guffaws. "Did he really?"

"Uh, yeah. He was so mad when he found out the animals weren't real."

"I don't remember that," Jake says.

I wonder what else he doesn't remember. I don't mention the swimming pool.

Oliver starts crying. Crap. I got sunscreen in his eyes. Just what I need. He's the youngest grandkid, and I tend to feel self-conscious parenting around my brothers and their families, who judge us for raising Oliver outside the church. Will tells me I should just let it go, be myself, but easy for him to say. His family's a bunch of ex-Catholic hippies.

"Here. Let me." Suddenly Dad's there making it all better. He pulls one of his ubiquitous handkerchiefs from his pocket, wets it with a water bottle, and wipes Oliver's eyes.

"Thanks, Dad."

"Anytime." An awkward silence stretches between us. "You okay?"

I guess I'm going to have to get used to people asking me that today.

"I really don't want to go in there," I admit.

"Can't be worse than last time," he says, which is true.

The kids are getting impatient now, pulling on their parents' arms, jostling one another at the park entrance.

"This place is lame," my nephew, Chris, complains. "I wanna do the *Star Wars* rides."

"Stop it," Becca warns. "This place is important to Daddy. And your uncles. We'll do *Star Wars* tomorrow." She smiles apologetically at Jake and me, but I agree with Chris. This place *is* lame. I don't want to be here either.

But this might be Will's—as they say—*big break*. By the time I said no to *Heaven Hoax*, he'd already applied for a grant—and then he had the audacity to go and win the dang thing. Fifty thousand dollars from the Gil Bright Foundation for the Advancement of Humanism in the Arts and

Sciences. More money than he'd ever had for a project. More money than our bank account had ever seen.

And the money issues in our household were all my doing: my student loans, my car note, my credit card debt. Will had gone to college on a full ride. His parents had bought his car. He owed nothing. It was all my expenses dragging us down—and that was *before* the mortgage and the surrogacy. ("Isn't it kind of gauche to put a price tag on a baby?" "Well, if it bankrupts us, at least we'll be poor and happy." "Sometimes I think I'd rather be rich and miserable.")

As angry as I was that Will applied for the grant before asking me, how could I say no after he won? When I was the one preventing him from investing in his documentary career in the first place?

"I know what you're thinking," Will said. "That they only picked my project because of your history with Bright. I'm not an idiot."

I had, in fact, been wondering if Amelia was on the foundation board, whether she'd been a judge. But it hurt to see his moment of glory stolen by my past. Gil Bright was Will's hero. This was a huge honor. I couldn't take that away from him.

"Don't be silly," I said. "You sent them samples, didn't you? This award is in recognition of your work. You earned it. I'm proud of you."

☦

Before we enter the park, Will takes out release forms and puts himself through the wringer one last time. "Now I know you're all hesitant, but please hear me out . . ."

It's pointless. And kind of embarrassing to watch. When he first asked the family to do the doc, it did not go well.

"We're not going to be part of some atheist propaganda flick," Abe had said.

We were hosting everyone for a BBQ. Will didn't eat meat, but my brothers are pure carnivores, so he'd gone all out and ordered steaks, brats, and chops. He could barely look at the packaging while stocking the freezer, so I was the one manning the grill.

"That's not what it is," Will said.

"Right." Abe rolled his eyes.

Will put a hand to his heart. "I swear it's not. Look. Do I have my issues with religion? Sure. You know that. But this isn't my story to tell. It's your family's. A chance for you to go on the record about what happened with Gideon."

"Don't act like you're doing this for us."

Will looked to me for support. I pretended not to notice, flipped a burger. After all, Abe had a point. If it wasn't Will's story to tell, then why should he be the one behind the camera?

"What about you, Jake?" Will said. "Simon?"

"I don't know," Jake said.

"I'll have to give it a think," Dad said.

That was a no. Even when Will promised to give them the final cut: "If you don't agree with it in post, no one will ever watch this film. I promise." Still no.

I thought it was over. Will would simply have to apply the grant money to another project. Surely the foundation would allow that.

Then, a few days later, Abe announced he was taking his family on vacation to Bible World. Apparently, the doc was a no-go, but the idea of returning to the park had stuck. It wasn't long before Dad was on board. Then Jake and his family. My brothers clearly didn't feel the same as I did about the place. They wanted to share it with their kids before it closed.

"I can't believe them!" Will ranted. "Are they seriously going to go just for vacation? How fucked-up is that?"

"This is what Abe does," I said. "He steals people's thunder. Just forget about it."

"No." Will shook his head. "He doesn't get to make this into some kind of triumphant return. He doesn't get to *celebrate* that fucking place. We're going with them."

"Why would we ever do that?"

"We'll do the doc without them."

"Will. There is no doc without them."

"But you'll do it, won't you? You're the one that really matters."

It was too late for me to back out now. I'd already committed to the role of Supportive Husband. "Don't you think it'll be a little one-sided?"

"Maybe. But who knows? Once we're there, they might still come around."

✝

"I'm not signing this." Abe tears the release in half. "Neither're Becks or the kids."

"Don't be a dick," Jake says.

"What? I'm here for a nice family vacation. That's all."

Will changes tactic. He tells Abe that's fine. Anyone who doesn't want to be on camera doesn't have to. No biggie. The group can split up in the park or they'll shoot and edit around them. He turns to Jake next.

Of all my family members, Jake has always been the nicest to Will, but he draws the line at being humiliated on camera.

Will tries not to look disappointed. He tells Abe and Jake to go ahead with their families, so he can interview me alone.

But then Dad surprises us. "What about me? Aren't you going to ask me?"

We all turn and stare. I'm shocked. Is he serious?

"You really going to be part of this?" Abe says.

Dad glances at me. "It's up to Eli. I'll do what he wants."

I can't believe it. I don't know what to say. I just nod dumbly.

Abe grumbles while Dad signs the release. Will beams, shoots me a thumbs-up.

I force a smile.

While his boom operator and camerawoman get ready, Will positions Dad and me beneath the giant **Shalom!** It's been two whole decades, but already this feels all too familiar. Before I can shake off the déjà vu, we're rolling and Will's lobbing questions.

"So, guys, how's it feel to be back at Bible World?"

I look at Dad; Dad looks at me.

"I don't know," I say. "Weird, I guess."

"How so?"

"Everything's . . . smaller than I remember."

Dad chuckles. "Well, you're bigger."

"Yeah, I guess that was a dumb thing to say."

"There are no dumb things to say," Will says. "Just say what you're feeling."

"What if what I'm feeling is I can't believe my husband's making me do this?"

Will offers a thin-lipped smile. "Perfectly valid. Say more."

I don't know what to give him. I know what he *wants*. A dramatic return to the site of trauma. Confrontations of sins past. Catharsis. But I don't feel any of that.

"Debbie always wanted to bring the boys to Bible World," Dad says.

"Oh?"

Dad tells Will how he and Mom planned the trip, how excited we all were for our favorite Biblical Realms. Listening to him, I go numb. I close my eyes and shake my head and that's when I see it. The Throne Room. Jesus in the gold chair. Flecks of makeup in his beard.

"You okay, E?" Will says. He's asked me a question and I missed it.

"Sorry. What?"

"Anything you want to share before we go in?"

"I—I think—Dad covered it."

There might be no dumb things to say, but I can tell I've already disappointed Will. When I try to apologize after the camera's off, he reassures me: "Don't worry. No need to force it. We have a long day ahead of us. We'll get it. Ready to go in?"

Never.

The security guard checks our bags. "What's with all the camera equipment?"

Will provides the paperwork. It's a marker of how far Charlie Gideon has fallen that the nominal fee Will paid CGN was enough for them to grant permission for him to shoot a doc that goes against everything Bible

World stands for. I guess with the park closing and Gideon's creditors come to collect, money speaks louder than any dogma.

This time around, there's no Jesus tour guide to welcome us. The Harpos aren't VIPs anymore. Just a rowdy group of tourists. I've never been more relieved not to be special. I hold fast to Oliver's hand, take a breath, and enter the park.

PART ONE

THE CALLING

1

NEW JERUSALEM

Eli sat up in the hospital bed, my brave little boy. I was a nervous
wreck, we all were, but then he smiled and said, "Don't cry, Daddy.
Jesus heard you pray, so he sent me back."
"Back?" I said. "Back from where?"
There was a mischievous twinkle in my son's eye. He waved me
closer so he could whisper in my ear. I thought he was going to tell
me one of his usual "secrets." Something silly like I have to pee *or*
Abe farted. *Not a revelation that would, ultimately, test my faith*
and rock our family to it's [sic] core.
—from *Heaven or Bust!*, "Answer to a Prayer," ch. 3, p. 16

THE DAY I WAS RECRUITED for Bible World began like most Saturdays—
with Dad and me sharing my Heaven story. That particular Saturday we
were at the New Jerusalem Nursing Home. Our rounds were not only to
nursing homes but also to hospitals, retirement communities, the houses of
people on our church's homebound list. Dad called what we did the Calling.
He said this half-jokingly, as in *Sorry, can't this weekend—line's busy, we*
got the Calling. I always thought of it as Hospice Duty.

This was November 2007. Trees clinging to Crayola leaves. Christmas
on the radio. Outside the old-folks facility, there was an oak, red as sin,

loud as a shout. From the back of our van, Dad unloaded three boxes of books. *Optimistic*, I thought. I offered to carry two, but he said he had it. I was thirteen, still treated like I was three.

The first thing you notice entering a nursing home is the smell. Of urine and disinfectant, cigarettes. Old-man farts. Old-lady perfume. And under all of this: decay.

A nurse in pink scrubs signed us in and led us to the TV room. There was a vintage set with wooden panels and rabbit ears, but not much furniture. A single couch in a floral design, a yellow armchair. An empty birdcage stood in one corner, a plastic ficus in the other. The rest of the room was a wide, open space for the residents to park their wheelchairs. The light was stale and made everyone look anemic.

I shifted the box in my arms. Usually we had a table to set up on.

"Just put it down here." Dad dropped his two boxes next to the TV and I set the third on top.

The nurses wheeled in the last of our audience. Heads lolled. Mouths drooled. Hands twitched in laps. Dad kept up the pep—waving hello, making small talk. I nodded along. We waited to be introduced, but the nurses wandered off without a word.

Dad clapped for attention. He spoke in his Minister Voice.

"Good afternoon, New Jerusalem! Praise the Lord! My name is Simon Harpo and this is my son Eli. It's an honor to be here with you today."

During his opening spiel, I liked to busy myself with the books. I'd set up a display on the table: build a pyramid or a staircase. When I was little, my job was to just stand there and look cute. Hospice Duty started when I was seven—freckle-faced, gap-toothed, pudgy, but in that still-adorable, baby-fat way. That day at the nursing home I was acned, bespectacled, and teenager obese. Red hair buzzed to a crew cut, fuzz on my upper lip, self-conscious and fleshy-chested. I cracked open a box and started piling books on the TV.

The cover of *Heaven or Bust!* was sky blue and featured me, age three. The photo had been taken at a Sunday school picnic in the yard behind Creation Baptist. The kids were tossing around a beach ball and I was just about to catch it. Dad photoshopped the ball out so my arms looked like they were raised in prayer. Then he added graphics of a halo and angel wings and the title in a bold calligraphy font. Since he designed the cover himself, without help from the art department, he got a discount from the Cincinnati press that printed the book.

The book tower on the TV collapsed and the room's attention shifted from Dad to me. I scrambled to pick up the merchandise. Dad chuckled and said why didn't I hand out books, so everyone could take a gander?

The New Jerusalem residents happily accepted copies of *Heaven or Bust!* They fondled them, flipping through the pages to the photo insert. I placed copies gently in the laps of those who were asleep.

One old woman jerked upright and snatched my hand. "You the boy who went to Heaven, right?"

"Yes, ma'am."

"They got Salems there?" She mimed smoking a cigarette.

"Uh . . . I guess."

Satisfied, she let go. I moved down the row. Dad was in the middle of our story.

"When Eli was just four years old, our family had quite a scare. He was playing in the backyard, wrestling with his older brother, and suddenly he was screaming in pain. We didn't know it then, but he had a hole in his heart, and my wife—"

"I thought he was in a car accident," a resident interrupted.

"Yeah," said another. "Weren't you paralyzed? How can you walk?"

"It's a miracle!"

"No, no," Dad said. "Eli had to have an emergency surgery, and when he went under, he had a bad reaction to the anesthesia."

"But in the movie—"

"*What* movie?" Dad said. "There is no movie."

"We watched it last night. Friday night is movie night."

Dad sighed and removed his glasses. He ran his hands down his face. "I believe," he said, "you are mistaken. That movie is about Levi Livingston. A boy who admitted to *lying* about his trip to Heaven. And frankly, I find it upsetting they'd show you such a fraudulent film, allowing you to believe it a faithful account from a servant of the Lord."

Three years ago, when *A Tour of Heaven* topped all the bestseller lists, Dad went out and bought a copy like he was on a mission. He came home and sat down at the kitchen table with the Bible, a highlighter, a red pen, and a pad of sticky notes. He read the entire book straight through, marking passages, annotating in the margins, crossing out misquoted Scripture. By the end of the day he'd proven—incontrovertibly—that Kyle Livingston and his son Levi were frauds. When the movie came out two years later and we went to see it, Dad spoke through the entire thing, pointing out inaccuracies. Others in the theater were sobbing, they were so moved. But Dad never doubted the Livingstons were scamming the public. A few weeks before our visit to New Jerusalem, when Levi released a YouTube video recanting his Heaven testimony and coming clean, Dad was finally vindicated.

Now he took a breath. He put his glasses back on. "You know what? It's fine. Forget the movie. You ready to hear a *true* testimony of Heaven?"

The residents just stared.

He began to explain about the heart surgery. How I flatlined on the table and the angels came. That was my cue to unbutton my shirt and show my scar. When I was younger there was always an awkward moment in which I struggled to get my tee over my head and then stood cold and bare-chested, feeling completely naked. Dad was perpetually swatting at my arms because I kept crossing them to cover up. It got easier when he came up with the idea to dress me in a button-down, so I could open it but keep the shirt on.

I unfastened the top button, fingered the next one down, then stopped.

The week before, at Lambkins—that was our youth group—Pastor Micah served carrots and celery sticks on the snack break. We used to get potato chips and cookies. He delivered a mini-sermon on gluttony and the Perils of Childhood Obesity in America, and while he talked, every eye in the church basement slid toward me.

I was a whale. I knew this because later that night Chase Brinkley claimed he heard someone crying for help, and even though no one else heard it, he made the Lambkins search all over Creation until he located the shouts . . . coming from my stomach. *It's Jonah!* he announced, poking me in the gut. *He's trapped in there.*

Dad reached for my shirt, but I stepped back. He stumbled and several people laughed. My father was a brilliant man; he knew the Bible better than anyone. But being a minister requires a degree of showmanship and he never could deliver. At home or among small groups of church friends, where he was most comfortable, he had us in stitches. But this rarely translated in front of an audience. He was not a charismatic performer: His movements lacked grace, he had poor stage presence, and he was a mediocre orator at best. He stuck too strictly to the script in his mind, leaving little room for improvisation. And when he became overexcited, which happened often, he rambled incoherently. This was only just becoming apparent to me as a teenager; when I was little, I'd always thought he was the funniest, smartest guy in the room.

He left my shirt alone and moved on with his sermon. He began talking about being known as you are known.

"In Heaven, no one is old. You are once again your true self. Won't it be wonderful to be young again?" He took the hand of a woman draped in a purple afghan. "These age spots? No more!" To a bald man, he said, "No need for Rogaine. You'll have a full head of hair!" He asked another patient to remove his Coke-bottle glasses. The man obliged.

"How well can you see?"

"Blind as a bat."

"Well, in Heaven you'll have twenty-twenty vision. When you go to meet our Lord and Savior Jesus Christ, you will see every strand of hair in his beautiful beard with perfect clarity. How's that?"

Squinting, the man nodded.

"Think back and answer me this. When, out of all your life, were you your most true self? Won't it be great to be the star quarterback again? The prom queen? To have your health fully restored. No more heart monitors, no more oxygen tanks, no more chemo!"

Dad opened *Heaven or Bust!* to the photo insert and showed them the two pictures of Memaw. In the first, taken on her last Easter, 1995, Memaw was sixty-five. She stood in her garden in a floral dress, holding a bouquet of lilies. The second was her wedding photo, taken on May 25, 1952. She was twenty-two. Dad told them the story of how I met her in Heaven. When he asked which Memaw I saw, it was my job to point to her younger self.

Q&A was my turn to talk. It was the typical stuff:

"Where do people live in Heaven?"

"In Heaven, everyone lives in their own mansion."

"Alone?"

"No! With their family and with Jesus."

"*Everyone* lives with Jesus?"

"Yes. Heaven is like one big happy family. Jesus is like your big brother and God is like your dad."

"They got animals there?"

"Yes. They have *all* the animals. In Heaven I played with lions. I saw an elephant. I even got to pet a unicorn."

Oops—I wasn't supposed to mention the unicorn. It used to be the cue for Dad to talk about the animals that didn't survive the Flood. How even though they didn't make it onto the Ark, they weren't forgotten by God. They were in Heaven. But one time I'd mentioned it at a church we were visiting and the minister had laughed in my face. He apologized, but couldn't stop snorting. Dad had gone on with his Noah sermon. Later, when we were leaving and the minister shook my hand goodbye, he bent down and whispered, "Were there dragons, too?"

Dad told me never to mention the unicorn again.

"But I saw one!" I insisted. When I closed my eyes I could see it. Ivory, luminous. We were in the Meadow, Jesus by my side. I reached out my hand and—

"Talk about the lions more," Dad said.

At New Jerusalem, I hurried to correct myself. "But there are also cats and dogs and birds and all the regular animals, too."

Dad cleared his throat. That was the signal for me to stop. He led us in prayer. The old men and women of the New Jerusalem Nursing Home closed their eyes and bowed their heads. I peeked. I always did. I looked at them with their sunken eyes and neck flaps, their blue hair, and I tried to imagine them as they would be in Heaven. Known as they were known. Their youthful bodies returned to them. I tried to strip away the years, but I couldn't see beyond their earthly bodies, wasting away in front of me.

The nurses returned to wheel the residents back to their rooms. The old ladies kissed me goodbye. A few of them weren't wearing dentures and their mouths collapsed inward. It was like being kissed by a wet sock puppet. The old men shook my hand. Their skin was tissue-thin. They were all so desperate to be touched.

"The books are twenty-four ninety-nine," Dad announced. "We're happy to take cash, check, or credit card."

On the ride home to Canaan, Dad was quiet. We'd sold two books—one to the Salem-smoker and one to the nurse who'd signed us in. She said she was hard up for reading material, but I think she was just being nice. This barely paid for the gas it took to drive out there. Dad insisted sales weren't the point, but I knew he used them as a kind of spiritual barometer for how many souls we'd Saved.

"What happened back there?" he said finally.

"I talked about the lions, I did."

"Why didn't you show your mark?"

Outside my window we passed the sights of rural Kentucky: silos, ponds, a stretch of limestone bluffs bisected by the highway.

"Look, Big E. Words can only do so much. It's actions that count! And when you show your mark . . . it's like the marks on Jesus's hands and feet. The scars tell the real story. It's an important part of your testimony."

"I know."

"Then what?"

What could I tell him? That I was fat and hated it? That I didn't want to show off to a bunch of old biddies what Chase Brinkley recently pointed out were boobs bigger than his sister's? That the other Lambkins called me King Eglon and thought the Calling was a joke?

"I get it. You're a teenager. Everything's embarrassing at your age."

"Were you? Embarrassed?"

"You kidding? With my four-eyes, buckteeth, and giraffe neck? No, never. I was the most popular kid on the block."

I tried to imagine Dad at thirteen. Couldn't. He just seemed so . . . old. Not old-old. Not like the residents of New Jerusalem—they were ancient. But middle-age old. The weird thing is, at that time he was only forty-two. Not much older than I am now.

"It's not easy being the Messenger, but God wouldn't have chosen you if He didn't think you could handle it. And that means putting others before yourself. Even if it is embarrassing."

I thought he might skip our special treat, but he still pulled into McDonald's and bought us fries and vanilla shakes. This was our usual reward after Hospice Duty; part of me felt I hadn't earned it that day. But I'd said I was sorry and I was. I promised to show my mark next time. I wouldn't let him down again.

2

CHARLIE GIDEON

After Eli's surgery we struggled financially. The medical bills piled right up. Debbie suggested I look for work outside the church, but I couldn't turn away from the Lord now. Not after he'd just given us back our son.

We had a terrible argument after she tore up the tithing check. I wrote out another. The money went right back into our bank account anyway when our church family took up a collection for us. It wasn't enough to cover our debts, but it was a start. God would provide.
—from Heaven or Bust!, "Spiritual Bankroll," ch. 10, p. 54

WHEN WE GOT BACK FROM New Jerusalem, Charlie Gideon was on our porch. On our crummy concrete stoop, sitting in the last unbroken lawn chair—famous televangelist Charlie Gideon. Sipping iced tea from a wineglass with a miniature umbrella left over from Creation's luau party—*the* Charlie Gideon. Chatting away with Mom, Abe, and Jake like it was nothing.

Dad and I were starstruck. We watched Charlie Gideon's sermons on *The Charlie Gideon Hour* every night of the week (except Wednesdays, which were church nights). CGN, the Charlie Gideon Network, was the most frequented channel on our TV. I'd grown up with Saturday-morning cartoons on that station. My favorite, *Bible Tales*, featured a time-traveling brother and sister who rode dinosaurs with Adam and Eve, roasted marshmallows on the burning bush with Moses, and brought back Chick-fil-A for the Last Supper. At the end of each episode, Logan and Emma recounted their adventures in the form of Bible book reports, only to be chided, once again, by their Sunday school teacher, Miss Persnickety, for making up stories.

"Howdy." Gideon stood, holding his signature white cowboy hat. They say celebrities look shorter in person, but Gideon, six-three, loomed. He ran a hand through his silky black hair. He was in a brown leather coat, a navy-blue pin-striped suit, and hand-stitched calfskin boots.

I remember he did this move on his show where he'd keep a Bible in his belt like a gun in a holster. He'd pace during his sermons and when he needed to quote Scripture directly, he'd whip out the Bible like a gunslinger in a Western. Abe and I used to practice this move with our own Bibles. Gideon was originally from Texas and split his time between his family's ranch outside Lubbock and his ministry in Orlando; the cowboy attire was less shtick than his critics presumed.

"Simon," Mom said. "This is—"

"I know who he is, Deborah!"

Gideon chuckled. "Nice to meet you, too, Simon. You have a lovely home."

Our house was anything but. It was a one-story two-bedroom, with beige vinyl siding. Mom used to garden in front but stopped after she got sick. All her flowers were dead. Our neighbors' to the right was still decorated for Halloween—faux cobwebs in the hedges, a witch on her broomstick splattered to the front door, pumpkins miraculously unsmashed—and the house to the left was early with their Christmas lights. We didn't celebrate Halloween and Mom insisted we wait until December before hauling out the holiday decorations, so ours was the least festive house on the street.

Gideon offered his hand and Dad shook. I thought he might faint. I thought *I* might faint. I glanced at Abe, sixteen then, dressed in his grease-stained Chick-fil-A uniform. I shot him an incredulous look—*Is this really happening?*—and he just smirked like Gideon was a prank he'd sprung on us. Jake, six, wasn't any help either: He sat cross-legged on the stoop, engrossed in a game on a Nintendo DS. We didn't have a Nintendo DS.

"And you must be Eli." Gideon turned and beamed the full wattage of his fame in my direction. It was like being caught in a searchlight. "Wow. I've only seen pictures of you as a little boy, but you're practically a man! Put 'er there, fella."

"I've never met anyone who's been on TV before," I said.

"And I've never met anyone who's been to Heaven. So there. We're square."

Dad invited Gideon to dinner, but Mom protested. "Simon, I didn't know he was coming. I didn't make enough—"

Dad waved her off. "Eli and I just had McDonald's. I'm sure there's plenty." He held the screen door open. Gideon thanked him and stepped inside. Before following, Dad reached out and touched Mom's hand. "Why don't you go put on your wig?"

She had on her favorite green bandana. Before she shaved her head for chemo, Mom was a redhead, like me. The wig was long, blonde, and curly. It itched and she regretted buying it, but Dad liked it. She wore it only in public, but lately she'd given up even that.

"No thanks," she said.

An exchange of looks passed between them. *Be nice*, his said. *I'm* always *nice*, hers answered. They followed Gideon in.

"Hey." I tugged on Abe's sleeve. "What's going on?"

"I don't know. He just showed up. He was telling us about how he interviewed Mel Gibson on his show."

"I can't believe it. Why do you think he's here?"

Abe shrugged. "You're the Chosen One. You tell me."

⁜

Gideon could not have been more out of place in our living room, with its mismatched armchairs and water-ringed Goodwill coffee table. I wanted to run around and hide things: Abe's GED study book; the wicker basket where we kept bills and junk mail; Jake's Biblical action figures scattered about the rug Memaw had braided, its colors long faded; awkward family photos, especially the one in which Abe said the expression on my face looked like I was mid-fart. I imagined Gideon's beach home and his ranch-mansion to be palaces. He belonged to the world tinkling inside the word *chandelier*. The word we lived in was *Podunk*.

He stood up from the couch and wandered over to the bookshelves—filled mostly with encyclopedias from the eighties—pointed at a display of Delicate Twinklings, and remarked that his wife had a set just like them. The comment, aimed at Mom, who was refilling glasses with tea, flew wide of its mark. She hated those little pieces of bisque. That's what she called them: *bisque*. Like the soup. There was a family story that went along with them, how on their first Valentine's Day, Dad had given her a rectangular box with a red ribbon. She thought it was perfume, but instead unwrapped a porcelain cherub. It was playing a flute.

"Uh, thanks?" She'd held the little statue out on the palm of her hand, then pecked Dad on the cheek.

How romantic! her friends joked. *All I got was a gold locket . . . a dozen crummy roses . . . a bottle of Chanel No. 5 . . . Debbie got bisque!*

They were married for three years before she told Dad how she really felt about the gift. By then she'd amassed more than twenty Delicate Twinkling figurines from anniversaries, birthdays, Christmases. (She would eventually inherit fifty more after Memaw passed. Memaw, who'd advised Dad on what to get Mom, was the true collector.) When Mom finally came clean, Dad laughed and said, "Well, good night, Debbie, you could have told me sooner. I might have ended up buying you the whole catalog."

"I didn't want to hurt your feelings! Or your mother's."

It became an inside joke: Dad's early ineptitude at gift-giving. He'd set wrapped presents in front of her and we'd all guess what piece of bisque it was—a rocking horse! A hot air balloon! A nativity set!—before she opened what was inevitably jewelry or perfume (he'd learned). The original cherub was close to a holy relic in our family and got prime positioning in the display.

"Oh?" Mom said to Gideon. "Yes. They're very . . . delicate." She offered him a strained smile and announced that it was time to eat.

Gideon sat next to me at the dinner table. Dad said it would be an honor if he led the prayer. Gideon politely declined: No, no, Dad should, of course, it being his home. This turned into what Mom called a Humbattle. *You should . . . No, I couldn't, but you . . . Oh, no, really . . .* until Mom snatched up her silverware, banged it on the table like a hungry toddler, and said, "God is good. God is great. Let us thank Him for our plate. Amen." She took a bite of green beans. Gideon laughed. Dad frowned, but made no remark.

We ate. I was still hungry despite the McDonald's, but Mom had served me a small plate. Gideon cut his pork chop into little bites and moved them around with his fork. I didn't see him eat but three pieces, yet he kept saying how delicious it was. He wanted to know all about my trip to Heaven. Nodding along to my answers, pretending to chew, wiping his mouth with a paper napkin. Dad interjected his own commentary. At the time, we ate this up: Dad and I were finally getting the recognition we deserved! When I consider this now, it seems so obviously calculated. The Calling blinded us with a false sense of self-importance.

Mom, at least, knew something was up. She brooded through the entire meal. Eventually, she couldn't take it anymore. She looked right at Gideon and flat-out asked, "What do you want from us?"

"Deborah," Dad warned. "Don't be rude."

"No," Gideon said. "That's okay. I'm sure you're all curious. I didn't want to spoil the meal with shoptalk, but now that you've asked." He turned back to me. "God has sent me a challenge, Eli. I believe He's testing me like He did Job. I've come here hoping you might help."

"Of course we will," Dad said. "We're servants of the Lord."

"Simon," Mom said. "Let the man speak."

"What do you think, Eli?" Gideon said, and I was glad he didn't take Dad's answer for my own.

"What do I have to do?"

"Do you know who Levi Livingston is?"

The moment the name left Gideon's lips the room went cold.

"We're not supposed to talk about him," Jake said.

"Oh? Why not?"

"He stole Dad's book."

"He's a liar," Abe said.

"It's true," Dad said. "He's a copycat. Got the idea from *Heaven or Bust!*—had to."

"I don't think he *planned* to be in a car accident," Mom said.

"You know I mean after. In the hospital."

This was one of their frequent arguments. Abe and I braced for it.

"Well, he's clearly confused."

"I told you we should have gone after them. I told you."

"However it happened," Gideon interjected, "the boy admitted to lying. His confession has been a huge headache for our team. It's a PR nightmare. We should've looked into his story more before we signed him to CGN. We've had to pull the books from the shelves, remove the film from the network's schedule, release a statement of apology . . ."

"Terrible," Dad said. "Just terrible."

"And our plans for Levi at Bible World are obviously ruined."

Jake's attention snapped up from his plate. Abe and I glanced at each other.

"Did you say Bible World?" Abe said.

Jake squirmed in his seat. "I wanna go to Bible World!"

"Hold your horses," Gideon said. "You mean you boys never been?"

The three of us shook our heads.

"Some Lambkins have," I said. "But not us."

"We always planned to take them," Dad said.

"Lambkins?" Gideon said.

"Youth group," Mom explained. "We never could affor—"

"Find the right time," Dad said. "Something always came up."

Only the most affluent families at Creation Baptist could afford vacations to Bible World. They brought back souvenirs for the other Lambkins—pins, buttons, refrigerator magnets, bracelets, candy, stickers, socks—all with the Bible World logo. Abe and I'd had a Bible World park map tacked to the corkboard in our room since before Jake was born. It was an artist's rendering of the park with each ride and attraction color coded by Biblical Realm. Back then we would have *killed* for a trip to Bible World. We told Mom the tickets could count for both our birthdays and all of Christmas. We were obsessed.

I blame CGN advertising. On every commercial break they played ads for the amusement park, each featuring a Biblical figure welcoming visitors into their Biblical Realm: Noah lifted a girl in pigtails so she could pet a pony in Noah's Ark; Adam and Eve, tastefully covered in leafy costumes, seated a couple at a candlelit table in the Garden of Eden; Moses pointed with his staff and a blond boy's jaw dropped in awe at a giant stingray in the Red Sea Aquarium. All spots ended with the same tagline, glittering in silver and gold: BIBLE WORLD, THE MOST SPIRITUAL ADVENTURE ON EARTH!

Gideon clicked his tongue. "No childhood's complete without a trip to Bible World."

"Can we go?" Jake whipped his head from Dad to Mom to Dad. "Can we? *Please?*"

"What would you say if I could get you in *for free?*" Gideon said.

Jake cheered. Abe's eyes widened. I couldn't believe it.

"You came here to offer us free tickets to Bible World?" Mom said.

"Not only that, Mrs. Harpo. Bible World is building a new Biblical Realm and—would you believe it—we want to base it off Eli's trip to Heaven!" Gideon clapped his hands, clearly expecting a *hurrah!* at this announcement. He was met with a confused silence.

"But Eli's not in the Bible," Dad said.

"Well, no. But Heaven *is* a Biblical Realm. Some might say the most important realm of all. And Eli visited it himself. We want to showcase that at Bible World."

Dad slapped the table. "Wow! You hear that, boys?"

Mom wasn't convinced. "You want to . . . build Heaven? In your theme park?"

"Biblical immersion facility."

"What?"

"Bible World is a *Biblical immersion facility*. A living history museum, where the Bible comes to life."

"It has rides, doesn't it?"

Gideon smiled politely. He had a strict aversion to the words *amusement* or *theme park*, believing what went on at Bible World was of a holier caliber than Disney.

"The point is not only would Eli get to share his story with a wider audience; his testimony would be interactive! You'd get to experience everything he did—the angels, the Celestial Palace—all of it, firsthand. He'd be a kind of—"

"Mascot?" Mom said.

"I was going to say *guide*. A guide to the afterlife."

"Like the Grim Reaper," Mom deadpanned. "'Welcome, ladies and gents, to Heaven on Earth!'"

"Exactly." Gideon smiled.

"'Here, hold my sickle.'"

Gideon's expression changed to puzzled annoyance.

"Deborah." Dad forced a chuckle. "Always joking."

"'Why wait to die when you can visit Orlando, Florida!'" Mom performed a sarcastic jazz-hands number.

"I'm sorry." Gideon sounded anything but contrite. His face was red and blotchy. "I can see you're uncomfortable with the idea." He scooted his chair back. "It was a lovely dinner. Thank you, Mrs. Harpo."

Dad scrambled after him. "Mr. Gideon! She's kidding."

"I was not. I think it's absolutely ridiculous. You can't just swap Eli for Levi."

Dad glared at her. "I'm sure it's more complicated than that."

"Of course," Gideon said. "We want to do right by Eli's story."

"Why don't we move to the living room and talk?" Dad said. "I want to hear more about this Heaven Realm." He ushered Gideon out of the kitchen. Abe, Jake, and I followed, but as soon as we reached the door, Dad stuck his head back in. "Boys, dishes."

"Aww," Jake whined.

"I do trash and lawn," Abe said. "It's Eli's—"

"Don't care," Dad said. "Do it. All three of you."

"Simon," Mom said. "I really think we should talk."

"Debbie, I swear, if you ruin this for us—"

"Oh—you *swear*, huh?"

Dad backpedaled. He was against all forms of swearing, even if he did slip up at times. "I'm sorry. I didn't mean it like that. Just—please. I could really use your support right now. I mean—good night—it's *Charlie Gideon!*"

"I know who he is, Simon."

"We'll talk after he leaves. I promise."

Mom sighed and nodded. She started to follow him into the living room, but he stopped her. "Coffee."

She raised an eyebrow.

"Please, Debs."

The door closed behind him. This is how things were done at church, too. Women and kids in one room, men in the other, making all the decisions. We eyed the dirty dishes, but Mom held a finger to her lips, waved us over to the cabinet, then handed us each a drinking glass. We jockeyed for position at the wall by the jelly cupboard until each of us had claimed territory: glass to wall, ear to glass. Mom cleared the table and brewed the coffee.

"They're talking about agents," Abe said. "Gideon keeps saying *your agent.*"

"What's that?" Jake said.

"Dad is pretending like we have one," I said.

"Of course he is," Mom said.

We didn't have an agent. *Heaven or Bust!* had been printed by a small vanity press in Cincinnati, run by the cousin of a member of our church. An editor at a Christian publishing house had considered purchasing the rights, but then Levi Livingston and *A Tour of Heaven* happened and she wasn't interested anymore.

"Now it's about a contract," Abe said. "Something about lawyers."

Mom arranged cups and saucers onto a tray. "He better not," she mumbled to herself. The coffeepot hissed. Mom added a pot of cream and the sugar bowl.

"I think he has a piece of paper," I said.

"What!"

"Dad asked for a pen."

"He didn't sign it, did he? He didn't—" She flew across the kitchen and burst through into the living room. We put our glasses down and went after her.

Dad was kneeling by the coffee table, hovering over a stack of papers. He held a gold pen. Mom lunged across the room and slapped it out of his hand.

"What the heck, Debbie!"

Abe, Jake, and I gasped. We'd never heard Dad curse like that before—not a real curse. And especially not at Mom. She was breathing heavily, her bandana askew.

Gideon cleared his throat. He was obviously annoyed, but he didn't push. "This is a family matter, of course. Everyone should be on the same page before you make any commitments. Why don't you hold on to that and you can go over the terms together?"

"We'll do that," Dad said, through gritted teeth.

"You don't want to sign something you haven't read forward, backward, upside down, and with a magnifying glass. Right, Mrs. Harpo?"

Mom straightened her bandana. I could tell it took everything in her power not to scream at Dad. She smoothed her hands down her jeans.

"How do you take your coffee, Mr. Gideon?"

"Black, with lots of sugar. I have a bit of sweet tooth."

Dad blathered his apologies. Mom retreated into the kitchen.

Gideon pointed at the rug near my feet. I picked up his pen. It was heavier than I'd expected. I held it out to him, but he shook his head.

"Why don't you hold on to that, Eli?" He winked. "Just in case."

✠

We did the dishes. Abe scraped, I scrubbed and rinsed, Jake dried. Mom served the coffee in the living room. This time she didn't come back into the kitchen. She didn't trust Dad alone with the contract.

"Are we still going to Bible World?" Jake said.

"They'd be stupid not to take that deal," Abe said.

"You don't even know what the deal is," I said.

"I know it's better than nothing, which is what we've got now."

I couldn't argue with that. Besides, I wanted them to take the deal, too. But I also didn't want to upset Mom. Why was she so dead set against it? Ever since she got sick, she'd become a mystery to me. I shook drops from a pan and handed it to Jake to dry.

"Are you going to be famous?" he asked.

"No," I said, just as Abe said, "Probably."

"Don't tell him that."

"He's the Chosen One, Jakey. It's his destiny."

Jake giggled.

"Shut up." I splashed them. Jake whipped the dish towel at me.

I'd long given up fighting Abe on this Chosen One stuff. In the fantasy novels we read there was always a prophecy about a boy or girl, a witch or wizard, a prince or princess. Sometimes it was the Seventh Son of a Seventh Son or some other convoluted lineage. The so-called Chosen One always had to go on a quest and accomplish great deeds only he was capable of—slay the dragon, infiltrate the underworld, sacrifice himself on a stone altar. At some point this had become Abe's metaphor for my trip to Heaven.

To their credit, our parents never banned books in our house. They let us read whatever we wanted, trusting us to tell fact from fiction. How unbelievably naive we were. A man walks on water, heals the sick, and raises the dead: bona fide miracles. But a boy waves a wand and levitates a feather? Utter fantasy. Didn't stop us from loving both stories, of course.

"Boys!" Dad called. "Come say goodbye to Mr. Gideon."

They were standing at the front door, Gideon in his brown leather coat. Mom handed him his white cowboy hat. He thanked her.

"Now, you're sure you can't stay the night?" Dad said. "We'd be happy to have you."

A look of horror crossed Mom's face. I didn't blame her. It was one thing to serve Charlie Gideon dinner; it was quite another to put him up. I couldn't picture him—televangelist extraordinaire—sleeping on our fold-out couch with *Bible Tales* sheets.

"I think he'd be more comfortable in a hotel," she said.

Gideon nodded. "I already have a room."

"Had to offer," Dad said. "*Do not neglect to show hospitality to strangers: for thereby some have entertained angels unawares.*"

Gideon chuckled. "I'm no angel. Just a shepherd tending his flock."

"Thank you for fellowshipping with us this evening," Dad said.

"My pleasure. Church tomorrow?"

"Creation would love to have you. I'll tell Zeb you're coming."

"No need to make a big fuss."

Charlie Gideon in our ramshackle church? I couldn't imagine a bigger fuss at Creation Baptist.

"Boys." Gideon tipped his hat.

"Bye, Mr. Gideon," we chorused.

And out he went. There was a black town car waiting for him on the street with a driver—a *chauffeur*. We waved from the porch. He stuck a hand out the back window and then was gone.

☦

The moment the car was out of sight, Mom turned on Dad.

"I can't believe you."

"I wasn't going to sign without discussing it first."

"Tell it to the birds."

"What's wrong with you? We should be celebrating! Charlie Gideon's opening a door for this family—"

Mom scoffed. "More like the purses of little old ladies."

"—and here you are, saying you don't want to walk through!"

"The wallets of senile men!"

Jake started to cry. Abe picked him up. I glanced down the street: mercifully empty.

"I thought you were a better Christian than this," Dad said. "Here comes an angel knocking, and do you offer him hospitality? Do you give him a warm bed? No! You slam the door in his face and make him sleep at the Days Inn."

"Dad," Abe said.

"An angel!" Mom laughed. "More like a devil cloaked as an angel of light."

"Could we go inside?" I begged.

"That man goes on TV and makes promises he can't keep," Mom said. "I never liked his show. He's *fleecing* people. And now he wants to use Eli to do it!"

Before Mom got sick, she used to watch *The Charlie Gideon Hour* with the rest of us, though she'd always complained about the showiness of the megachurch stage and how a toll-free number constantly flashed across the bottom of the screen for donations. After her diagnosis, though, she'd stopped watching it altogether, retreating to her room with her library books while Dad and we boys continued to camp out in front of the TV every evening.

"His church needs money just like ours," Dad said.

Mom snorted. "You know it doesn't all go to his church."

"The man doesn't even make a salary! He lives on the sales of his books and DVDs alone. He told me."

"I don't care!" Mom was yelling. "It's a cover-up, Simon. Levi Livingston embarrassed him and now he needs Eli to fix it. I won't have it."

A light came on in our neighbor's house.

"This could pay off your treatments!" Dad shouted.

Another light, across the street.

"It's not about the money," Mom said.

"Or for the boys' college," Dad said.

Mom stopped short. All she ever talked about was us going to college, like she and Dad never got to. She'd been pressuring Abe with brochures, all for in-state schools—he'd have to take out loans even for those—but he was more interested in making money at the Chick.

"No." Mom shook her head. "Not like this."

Jake sobbed louder. Sometimes, if he got their attention with tears, their fights fizzled.

"It's not just the money," Dad said. "It's the *Calling*, Debs. God's ringing and it's time to pick up."

"God can leave a voice mail for all I care."

I winced. It was scary hearing her say things like that. God could strike you down for it in a heartbeat.

"Don't you see? This was His plan all along! He wants Eli to take His message outside Canaan."

"God does? Or is it you?"

"It's not our decision to make. It's in the Lord's hands."

"Oh, we'll see about that." She marched inside and we stampeded after her.

Back in the living room, she snatched the contract from the coffee table and waved it, threatening to rip it up. "Whose hands is it in now, Simon?"

"Don't . . . you . . . dare." Dad edged one way around the table; she moved the other. They feinted left—right—left.

She made the first tear at the top. He launched himself *over* the table and snatched her wrists before she could do any more damage.

"Let go of me." Mom tried to shrug him off.

Dad held fast. "Drop it."

Mom curled her lip. "No."

They fell back on the couch together, wrestling with the contract. There was a loud ripping noise and they came apart with half pages.

"Oh, Solomon's Judgment!" Dad yelled.

It was such a silly, if Biblically accurate, substitute curse, Mom couldn't help it: She laughed. She balled up her half pages and threw them at him. The wad bounced off his forehead. "Solomon's Judgment, indeed."

Dad laughed, too. Then they were laughing together. The green bandana had come off in the melee. Mom's bald head shone round and oblong. Dad kissed it. She shoved him away playfully, tried and failed to look stern.

"I'm still mad at you."

"Well, you're being ridiculous."

"Hey," I said, before they could start up again. "Charlie Gideon asked *me*. Shouldn't I get a say?"

"Yeah," Abe said. "Eli's the one he wants."

Dad stood up from the couch. "I think that's a great idea." He retrieved the paper ball, uncrinkled it, and smoothed it out on the table. "Eli's old enough to decide for himself." He put the two stacks together and held them out to me.

"Okay," Mom said. "We'll do whatever Eli wants."

"Agreed."

I took the damaged stack of papers.

"But you should know something first." Mom held out her hand to me.

I hesitated. She looked serious. Determined. Steeling herself to deliver bad news.

Dad frowned. "What are you talking about?"

She ignored him, sat me down on the couch. "Abe, why don't you take Jake to bed?"

"What? No. I want to hear."

"Me, too!" Jake said.

"I thought this was a family meeting," Abe insisted.

Family meetings were big in our house. Dad called them whenever we had to make an important decision, usually one that involved money. He was all about open communication, even with us kids. We all looked to him, but he looked to Mom.

"Fine," Mom said. "Family meeting."

We settled in. Jake on the couch with Mom and me, Abe in the armchair. Only Dad remained standing, perplexed.

"Well, go on."

Mom was still holding my hand. She squeezed it, took a breath. "Listen. After your surgery, I talked to your doctor."

Dad groaned. "Aw, come on. Not this again."

"What about my doctor?" I said.

"Are you really going to dredge this up?" Dad said.

"You bet I am." Mom set her jaw. "I should have said something a long time ago."

"It doesn't matter what that doctor said. Eli knows what he saw." Dad turned to me. "You know what happened to you. You know, don't you, Big E?"

"I—I don't know." Dad's face fell and I rushed to add, "I mean, I know what I saw. I don't know what the doctor said."

"And I'm *trying* to tell you." Mom glared at Dad.

He unlocked his arms and threw up his hands. "You know what? Go ahead. Tell him whatever you want. It won't make a difference. We know, don't we? Don't we, bud?"

I nodded, shifting in my seat. Dad hadn't called me *bud* in years.

"Would someone tell us what on earth you're talking about?" Abe said.

"Maybe this would be easier if you left the room," Mom told Dad. "So I could talk to the boys alone."

"Not on your life."

"Fine."

"Fine!"

Silence.

"Would you just tell me already!" I said.

"Okay," Mom said. "After your surgery you said you saw angels. Your dad was very excited to hear about this."

"Well, who wouldn't be!" Dad said.

Mom shot him a look. He zipped his lips and waved her on.

"He asked if you met Jesus and you said yes. Then you told us about your trip to Heaven. Your dad was pleased, but I wasn't. I didn't like to think about you dying, even if it was such a beautiful experience."

"It was scary for *all* of us," Dad said. "We almost lost you."

"Your father wouldn't stop talking about it. When I didn't want to hear any more about Heaven, he told the nurses and other patients and their families."

"They asked to hear about it! They wanted to know."

Mom rolled her eyes. "He started recording your conversations. When you were recovered enough to get out of bed, he wheeled you around the hospital so you could visit patients and tell them about meeting Jesus in Heaven. Sure, some people thought it was cute, but others were bothered by it."

"You can't Save everyone," Dad said.

"Eventually, the doctor told us to please stop talking about Heaven. Your dad asked to speak to him out in the hall. I could hear them yelling, and your dad was very angry when he came back in."

Dad was angry now, too, or at least embarrassed: He was turning red in the face. "He didn't know what he was talking about. He had no idea—"

"What did you fight about?" I asked him.

"It doesn't matter."

"Your dad kept recording your testimony, but he stopped taking you on patient visits. Two days later you were well enough to go home."

"So?" I knew most of this already. "That's it?"

"That's not it." She seemed to be bracing herself for what came next. "I was still upset. I was having nightmares about you dying. What if it happened again in your sleep? Only this time you didn't come back?"

"Aw, Mom," I said.

"Your dad said I was being silly."

"You were," Dad said.

"He said you were fine."

"He was!"

"And he was right. Your doctor had told us your surgery was a success. The valve had been fixed. There was nothing to worry about."

"Exactly."

"But I couldn't stop myself. All that talk about Heaven. It was like you were one heartbeat away from leaving us."

"Mom, I'm fine."

"On the morning we were taking you home, I was in the cafeteria getting coffee and I ran into your doctor there. I went right up to him."

"I can't believe you did that," Dad said. "They'd already discharged us."

"I'm glad I did!" Mom said. "Or I'd never have known. I'd still be worried. When I asked your doctor if it could happen again, he told me no, your heart was fine. There were no complications in the surgery. But this time he also said your vision of Heaven was likely no more than a dream, a reaction to the anesthesia."

"Stop it," Dad said. "He doesn't know what Eli experienced."

"But I died," I said. "My heart stopped . . . didn't it?"

"No." Mom shook her head. "You never died in surgery, Eli. That's what the doctor said. Your heart never stopped. Your EKG was regular—no flatline. Not even a blip."

"My heart never stopped?"

"That doesn't mean anything," Dad said. "You going to let a machine decide for you? All it takes is a microsecond. Less than that. An infinitesimal moment can stretch to infinity in Heaven. A moment so small a man-made machine couldn't read it."

"Enough," Mom said.

"You had a transcendent experience—one nobody lives to tell about—and you want to deny it? Because what? A doctor says it's not real?"

"You had a dream," Mom said. "It was a dream, honey."

"God gave visions to Jacob in dreams," Dad said. "He saw a ladder that stretched between Heaven and earth. Does it make any difference how you entered the spiritual plane? What you saw was real. That's all that matters."

"Really, Simon?" Mom said. "Some dreams are Heaven-sent, but others are just dreams?"

"Of course. The difference is pretty clear when God speaks to you—"

They devolved into bickering again.

I was more confused than ever. Then, suddenly, I was angry. "You *lied* to me."

"I know, baby. I'm sorry." Mom hung her head. She looked truly repentant, but I didn't care.

"You should have told me!"

"I know. I made a mistake. But I'm telling you now. Come here, honey."

She reached for me, but I shoved her away and jumped up from the couch. "You're a liar and I hate you!"

"Hey," Dad said. "Don't talk to her like that."

"It's fine," Mom said.

"No, it's not. He knows better than to disrespect us like that."

"Disrespect *you!*" I yelled. "What about me? You're the ones fighting over *my* experience. Telling me what did or didn't happen *to me.*"

"Enough," Dad said. "No one is disrespecting you. We already said you get to decide."

"Yeah, so are we going to Bible World or not?" Abe said. "Who cares what the doctor said?"

Jake, who'd fallen half-asleep, jerked upright. "Bible World!"

"Come on, Big E," Dad said. "What's it going to be?"

"I know you're mad at me," Mom said, "but surely you see why you can't accept now?"

They were all looking at me. Jake, now bouncing on the couch. Abe, fidgeting in his Chick-fil-A polo. Mom and Dad, avoiding each other's gazes. I shuffled the papers in my lap. I could feel Gideon's gold pen in my pocket. "I don't know, okay?" I was tired and upset and didn't like being put on the spot. "Can you all just leave me alone for one second so I can think about it?"

Mom nodded. "Take your time. It's late anyway. We should get to bed."

As if to illustrate the point, Dad yawned and stretched. "Big day, y'all."

We went to the bathroom and brushed our teeth, then to our bedroom, where Dad tucked Jake in the top bunk. It'd been years since he'd done the same for me, but tonight he bent down and planted a kiss on my forehead.

"Pray on it, bud."

✢

Of course, the moment the three of us were alone in our room, our tiredness left us. We were too keyed up to sleep. Abe read in his bed. I sat with Jake on the top bunk of ours, watching him play a game on the Nintendo DS he'd had on the porch.

"Where'd you get it?" I asked.

A few kids at Creation had handheld video games. I'd seen them but had never gotten to hold one. Mom and Dad thought they were too expensive and encouraged laziness. They said we watched too much TV as is and were constantly sending us out to play in the backyard.

"It was a present for you." Abe didn't look up from his book. "Gideon just let him open it."

"You mean—it's mine?" It was, by far, the most expensive gift I'd ever received.

"Duh." Abe turned the page.

Jake shied away with the game.

"It's fine. You can play with it."

Heathen Holdup involved baptizing the unSaved with a holy squirt gun. We sat side by side, dousing cartoon characters until their souls changed from red to white, pretending not to listen as the fight continued across the hall in our parents' room.

"You shouldn't have gotten between them," Abe said, from his own bed. "Now you have to pick a side. That's how custody battles start."

"It's not like that."

"If they get divorced it's your fault."

"Shut up."

"Occupational hazard. Bearer of responsibility. Comes with the job, Chosen One."

"I said shut up!"

Abe was always exaggerating about divorce when Mom and Dad fought. I never took him seriously. Sure, Mom and Dad had their differences, but I never doubted their love for each other.

"What should I do?" I said.

"Duh," Abe said again. "Take the deal."

"What about what Mom said?"

"Mom's crazy. You know it was real."

"Yeah." I was pissed at Mom, but beneath the anger, I also felt kind of bad for her. She'd been acting weird lately, but it was beginning to feel like we were ganging up on her and I didn't like it. Even so, there was no way I was saying no to Charlie Gideon. I just had to figure out how to break it to her and keep the peace. "I can't believe we finally get to go to Bible World." Abe scoffed dramatically. "Bible World's for kids."

"You used to *beg* to go to Bible World."

"Yeah, when I was like five."

"You don't have to go," I said. "You can stay here with Mom."

"I just meant Bible World's not even the cool part. You're going to be famous."

"Really?"

"Duh. We all are. But you most of all."

This was the thing about Abe. He craved attention, sought it out, while I shied away from it. He would have made a much better Heaven Boy than me. I always knew he was jealous and I often wished we could switch places.

We were both quiet, dreaming about the future. Mom's insistent voice swelled through the wall. Then Dad's. The inane rodeo song on *Heathen Holdup* played on a loop, punctuated by splashing sounds and cheers of *I'm Saved!*

"Turn it off," I said eventually. "It's time for bed."

Jake fell onto his pillow and I climbed down to my own bunk. I lay wide awake, listening. Abe's breathing slowed in minutes and I knew he was drifting off.

"Abe," I whispered. "Hey, Abe."

He mumbled unintelligibly.

"I think they stopped."

With the fight finally over, I thought I'd be able to go right to sleep, but I couldn't. I closed my eyes and imagined our vacation at Bible World. Boarding a raft and drifting through Jonah's Whale. Rising high above the park for the best views on the Drop-Tower of Babel. Marching out onstage for *The Charlie Gideon Hour*, the congregation clapping and cheering as my family waved.

When sleep did come, it was fitful. I was with Jesus in the Meadow. We were grooming the unicorn together, his hand on mine, guiding the brush over the fur of that majestic white horse, and when I turned, I saw that he was shirtless, and I was, too, my mark exposed. And when he reached up the long, sleek neck, he pulled me with him, our fingers laced, his strong, broad chest warm against my back, stroking, stroking, stroking, and all was beautiful, all was wonderful . . . until I woke, hot and sticky and ashamed.

Under the covers I changed out of my wet boxers and into the dry ones I kept under my pillow for this purpose. Abe and Jake slept on, oblivious. I reached under my shirt and pinched and pinched and pinched until all the pain concentrated on the scar there and I could finally fall asleep again.

3

NOT EXACTLY FOOTLOOSE

*Eli's birth was much easier than Abe's. Debbie and I knew better what
to expect the second time around. Even still, I worried about divid-
ing our love between our two boys. What if we were spread too thin?
But a parent's love doesn't work like that. It is not a finite resource.
It grows and grows. It knows no bounds. They put my second-born
son in my arms and the love I felt holding him was as strong as the
love I felt holding my firstborn.*

*My love for Debbie and Abe only feeds the love I feel for Eli. And
vice versa. And the same with our third son, Jake. For all human
love is but a mere reflection on the surface of the infinite ocean that
is True Love: God's Love.*

—from *Heaven or Bust!*, "Meet the Harpos," ch. 1, p. 2

THE FIRST TIME I SAW Will was at the Get Involved! Club Fair in the
student center at the University of Kentucky. This was in 2011. I was a
freshman; he was a sophomore. We didn't officially meet until spring
semester, but by then I already had a huge crush on him. At the fair,
he stood at a table with an ASU banner and asked everyone the same
question.

"Can you guess what one group in America will never have a member elected president?"

He was short, dark-haired, and built, but not in a show-offy way.

"Like, never? It's impossible. More than any other affiliation?"

He had the longest, thickest eyelashes I'd ever seen. Later, while snooping through his apartment, I kept a lookout for a tube of mascara, but one never appeared. I eventually confessed this to him and he laughed and told me they were naturally dark. He was self-conscious about his nose, though, which I admit was quite a schnoz, but it only heightened his appeal to me.

"Go on, guess."

Gays? Feminists? The trans community? Illegal immigrants!

"Atheists," Will said. "More than any other group, America views atheists as moral degenerates. Many people ignorantly believe that to be a good person, you must believe in God. Well, the ASU is here to prove differently."

This led to some heated debate:

"Are you really saying atheists are more discriminated against than Black men in this country? Just because Obama . . ."

"Yeah, but look at Hillary. She's earned the presidency ten times over."

"Seriously? You honestly believe a genderqueer person could get elected before . . ."

This, of course, was the point. It attracted people to the table and, hopefully, into the club—the Atheist Student Union. But this strategy didn't work on shy, introverted freshmen (like me) who were intimidated by being on their own for the first time in the "big city" and preferred to admire such displays of intellectual exchange safely at a distance.

I kept seeing Will around campus, though. He was perpetually manning a table somewhere—in the halls of the White Hall Classroom Building, the quad by the statue of President Patterson, the lobby of the William T. Young Library.

"Always be hustling," he liked to say. "That's what America is. One big hustle."

He wasn't just in the ASU, but also in the Gay-Straight Alliance, the Kentucky Young Democrats, and the UK Film Club (he was a media arts and studies major). In his free time (*what* free time?) he volunteered in the Office of LGBTQ Resources. I wasn't stalking him exactly, but I may have looked him up online.

I happened into the ASU by accident. In the spring of freshman year, I was studying in my dorm's lounge when an impromptu ASU meeting formed around me. I was about to take my chemistry textbook to my room when I heard a familiar name.

". . . but Bright's brand is more intellectual than political. He doesn't address the underpinning socioeconomic factors that divide skeptics from believers."

"Oh, come on! You've got to give him more credit than that. *Fallacy of God* is foundational—it's as close as you can get to atheist scripture."

"After *Origin of Species*, of course. Bright is second to Darwin—"

"Can we help you?"

I'd been openly staring. Standing with my textbook hanging over one arm, blatantly eavesdropping on their conversation.

"Sorry. I was just leaving." I turned to go and ran smack into Will.

"Or . . . you could stay?"

God, those eyelashes.

"I—uh, got to study."

"Hey—aren't you in my Renaissance lit class?"

"Yeah," I said, my face growing warm.

"I'm Will."

"I know. I mean—EJ. I'm EJ."

It was a dumb, cliché move: thinking you could change who you are by changing your name. Like getting a haircut and proclaiming yourself reborn. But as soon as I got to college, I worked hard to hide who I was. I went by my initials. I swam laps at the Lancaster Aquatic Center to lose weight. I got contacts. I grew a beard—or tried to. It was really just amber stubble, but it hid some of my freckles. When asked where I was from, I said small-town, western Kentucky. The asker would hold out his hand so I could point geographically (Kentucky is roughly the shape of the inside palm of your right hand, held out for a handshake; people use it as a map in conversation—it's a thing), and I'd gesture vaguely. If asked what my father did, I said sales. If asked about my mother, I said she died when I was a kid. It was easier that way. I didn't have to talk about her and I could shrug off looks of pity, say I never really knew her.

Until I met Will, I only ever saw my past identity—the Heaven Kid—as a liability. I lived in fear that someone in my dorm or classes would recognize me on the "Heaven Boy Homo!!!!!!!" YouTube video. It was three years old, and buried under millions of tweets, memes, and God-knows-what other flotsam and jetsam in binary, but still—the internet is forever. You never know what's going to surface.

"We were just about to go to lunch," Will said. "Come with."

Fall Semester Eli would have said, "Sorry, but thanks for the invite!" then skulked back to his room, beating himself up for the next three hours for not going. But Spring Semester Eli was willfully trying to be more social, so I pushed myself and went.

We sat at a table in the dining hall with other ASU members. They were all friendly. Things were shockingly not awkward until the Gil Bright critic, David, asked me, point-blank, "So, what religion are you?"

I hesitated. It wasn't just that I was afraid to say the wrong thing—I was—but that I honestly didn't know the answer. Not anymore.

When I got to UK, I'd stopped going to church. At first I'd had every intention of joining a congregation in Lexington, but whenever it came down to it, I just couldn't. I slept in on Sunday mornings. I skipped the Christian Student Fellowship's luau party for new members. When Dad called—every Sunday afternoon, like clockwork—and asked how this week's service was, I lied. He thought I was trying out new churches and got a kick out of my tour through the offerings. I'd half-heartedly collected a bunch of pamphlets from various Christian organizations at the same club fair where I first saw Will and I used these for inspiration to make up things I was learning about the different denominations.

"Did you know women can be ordained in the United Methodist Church?" I said, staring at a photo of a woman minister. "In fact, one in four pastors is a woman."

"Really?" Dad said.

"The one this morning gave a sermon about, uh . . . women overlooked in the Bible."

"Wow. That's so interesting."

I felt guilty. Dad would have *died* at that club fair. So many options! He'd have visited every last church group on campus, out of simple curiosity and a burning desire for fellowship. And there I was unable to drag myself to the Gospel Sing-Along Cookout I could hear on the lawn right outside my dorm.

That day at lunch with the ASU, I was quiet for a long time, groping for an answer to David's question. They were all staring at me.

"No pressure or anything," Will said, and the table laughed.

"I'm a recovering Presbyterian," one member offered.

"And I'm an ex-Jew," David said.

"He's still a Jew."

"Oy vey. Such a Jew."

"Okay," David said. "*Culturally* a Jew. Will's the only one of us born into atheism. His parents are Communist quacks."

"I have Catholic lineages in my family," Will said. "On both sides."

"Your parents don't even celebrate Christmas," David said. "They think Coke invented it and it's all one big capitalist conspiracy."

"Well, they did. And it is."

David was obviously in love with Will, and Will was obviously uncomfortable with David's flirting. He later told me he never knew what to do with David's feelings toward him and felt bad about not returning them. At that first lunch, he deflected David by focusing on me.

"The point is, EJ," Will said, "you're not defined by the family you're born into. Everyone here knows that. You choose what to believe."

"Baptist," I admitted.

"Ooooh!" David said. "Southern or American?"

"Southern."

"Thought so. You have an evangelical way about you."

"What's *that* supposed to mean?" the Presbyterian asked.

"Yeah, David," Will said. "What *do* you mean?"

"I just—he has a kind of brooding intensity. That's all. It's a compliment, really."

"Ignore him," Will said. "Do you still believe? No judgment, I swear."

"Judgment?" David said, mock-offended. "Never. Except for the Jesus Freaks. We *love* to judge the Jesus Freaks. Are you a Jesus Freak, EJ?"

"Well . . . I haven't been to church in a long time."

David snorted. "Oh my God. He's adorable. Isn't he adorable?"

Will batted his lashes. "He is."

My college meet-cute with Will was nothing compared with Mom and Dad's. Mom and Dad met where all Canaanite couples meet: Canaan County High. But they weren't high school sweethearts in the typical sense. Mom's high school sweetheart was Doug Purdie, now a senior loan officer at Canaan Bank & Loan. He was the one Mom and Dad worked with for their mortgage, which was weird. I even met him at the bank once. I hated him because he was much better-looking than Dad and I didn't like the overly familiar way he talked to Mom. The lollipop he gave me tasted like cough syrup.

Mom and Doug had dated since they were freshmen. Mom was pert and pretty and popular; Doug was buff and charming and a bit of a prankster. Everyone expected them to marry and have the best-looking offspring Canaan had ever seen.

But in June 1984, the summer before their senior year, tragedy struck: Mom's family went from a family of four to a family of two when her brother, Michael, died in a motorcycle accident and not two weeks later her dad dropped dead of a heart attack while playing basketball at the YMCA. Mom had been close with her brother; they were Irish twins—born eleven months apart—and each other's best friend. Mom was also a daddy's girl; she'd learned all about cars, fishing, and *The Godfather* from her dad, the grandfather I never knew. She had never gotten much along with her own mother, who did hair and nails in a beauty salon and kept a pristine house and liked her soaps—both the rose-scented ones on the little porcelain dish in the bathroom and the *you-slept-with-my-evil-twin!* kind on TV—and never understood Mom's tomboy ways.

Suddenly, cruelly, it was just the two of them, stuck together in mourning, pitied by all of Canaan, screaming their heads off at each other for nothing, for no reason at all—for merely continuing to exist when their dad and brother, husband and son, did not. My grandmother took a hiatus from hair spray and started day-drinking: parked herself in front of the tube, watching characters fall into and come out of comas, while downing a steady diet of gin and ignoring calls from the high school, because Mom was always playing hooky. Sometimes with Doug, sometimes her friends, often alone, at the mall or a diner or movie theater but mostly in the cemetery, listening to Michael's Journey tape on his Walkman and snapping photos of dead leaves with her Polaroid, alternating between their two graves. A grief picnic all her own, if the weather was nice.

She ditched class, but still went to the football games, the school's social events. She needed the distraction. The Sadie Hawkins dance that year was Wild West themed. They did the gym up like a saloon with swinging doors, wagon wheels, and WANTED signs. There were barrel tables topped with rustic lanterns. Hay bales. A prop bar, down which the bartender would slide you a root beer. Most of the decorations came from the set of *Oklahoma!*, last semester's musical. Beneath the bleachers was a makeshift jail where the sheriff would lock up arrests, guarded by his deputy. Boy prisoners only. The bail? A kiss from their date.

Doug Purdie was in a foul mood that night, because when he went to pick Mom up, he found her not in a hoopskirt or prairie dress, but in jeans, boots, and a fringed leather vest.

Mom's Polaroid flashed in his face. He swatted it away.

"You look like a stable boy," he grumbled. He'd about reached the end of his patience through the past months of Mom's gloom and doom—it was their *senior year*, and she'd been a major buzzkill, even when she was pretending to have a good time. Everyone tiptoed around her the best they could. The teachers cutting her major slack, classmates casting consoling looks in her direction. But none of them had to deal with her like Doug did. Mom said he'd probably have broken it off with her already if there'd been a way to do it without looking like a tool—which there wasn't, and he was.

Mom ignored him. She'd been dreading the dance and was sick of Doug, too, but she didn't want to stay home either and was determined to forget her pain, if only for an hour. She didn't like to drink—watching her mom deliberately enter an alcoholic fog before noon every day was enough of a deterrent—but before Doug picked her up, she'd taken a few swigs of Maker's from her father's flask, the one with his initials, a tenth-anniversary gift from her mom, and that helped a little.

At the dance, her outfit was a hit. Especially the holstered toy guns. They were metallic so they looked like the real thing, although all they did was make a sound. She'd draw like an expert gunslinger and—*pop! pop!*—one of her friends would clutch his chest and fall over dead on the dance floor. They all got a kick out of that. Mom snapped their photos to collect a record of her kills. See, Doug? She could still be fun.

But Doug was also the jealous type, always had to be the center of attention; he soon took to harassing the sheriff so he could be arrested, then call out for Mom to come post his bail. She was game for a while. Sauntered over and puckered up. The deputy granted Doug his freedom and he'd return to calling the sheriff names, stealing his plastic gold star, or spilling drinks on his boots. Mom was soon fed up with the shtick—"Oh, let him stew in there"—and danced on with her friends. That was, until Doug started belting out "Every Breath You Take" by the Police, the stalkeriest of all love songs; appending every *I'll be watching you* with shouts of "That means you, Debbie!" He got through ten renditions before she finally caved and went and pecked him. The drunker Doug got, the sloppier the kisses. A peck wasn't good enough. He made a show of it, dipping Mom back so the whole jail watched. After they came up for air, he plopped his ten-gallon hat on her head. "There's my cowgirl!"

Mom wiped her lips with the back of her hand. She locked eyes with a skinny boy leaning against the back wall. He wore no cowboy costume other than a sad, faded handkerchief tied like a bandana around his neck. He'd been trapped in jail all night. No girl had asked him to the dance; he had no date to kiss him. At one point, the deputy made a plea to the public: "Come on, ladies! This fellah's hard up. Got a spare smackeroo to post his bond?"

The girls all giggled and dared one another to kiss him. No one wanted to. They all thought he was a weirdo. A Jesus Freak.

The deputy eventually took pity and offered to release him on good behavior, but Dad said no. On this point in the story, my parents loved to disagree.

"You *wanted* me to kiss you! It was all a charade."

"No, I was just following the rules. I didn't mind it under there. I had a good view of the dance floor."

"It was entrapment!" Mom accused, and Dad would raise his hands innocently, then wink at us boys.

"This is the last time," Mom warned Doug as the deputy let them out.

But Doug couldn't stop himself. Back into jail he went and this time Mom kept her word. He bellowed out for her like a hound dog, but she just kept on dancing. It soon got back to her that Doug was taking get-out-of-jail smooches from any girl who offered. And, unlike for Dad, they lined right up.

Mom spotted Doug perched on a barstool, circled by all his bail bonds-women. Half of them were in cancan dresses: his own personal brothel.

"Aw, don't be mad at this little jailbird," Doug said.

Mom drew her gun and placed the barrel against his temple. She pulled the trigger—*pop!*—but Doug didn't flinch. So she holstered her weapon, marched into the jail, and dragged Dad out by his tattered hankie. She planted one on him right in front of Doug and the whole school. Dad turned bright red. He almost fainted.

"You did not," Mom said.

"It was my first kiss! I didn't have a Doug."

Mom rolled her eyes. "Count your blessings."

Doug threw a fit. Yelling and spitting and flinging barstools. Mom knew he had a temper, but she'd never seen him that far gone. She grabbed Dad's hand, snatched up her purse and Polaroid, and together they skedaddled out of the gym and into the night.

She skidded to a stop in the parking lot. "Where's your car?"

"Don't got one."

"What!"

Dad shrugged. "I walked."

"You mean of all the guys I coulda kissed, I chose one *without wheels*?" We'd all say this line with her, like we were quoting a movie.

The gym doors flew open and Mom tugged Dad down. They crouched behind a bumper until Doug and his buddies gave up looking, piled into his truck, and tore off. The disappointed spectators wandered back inside.

"Sorry," Mom said, once she and Dad were alone.

"For what?"

"For, you know, using you like that."

Dad blushed. "I didn't mind."

Ever the gentleman, he insisted on walking her home. They'd been in school together since they were kids but had hardly spoken two words to each other. Mom thought of him only as a quietly brooding, born-again believer. Dad thought of her as a pretty, but ditzy, redhead. They were not a match made in Heaven.

"Sorry about Michael and your dad," Dad said, after they'd walked quietly for a bit.

Mom noticed he'd said Michael. Most people shortened it to Mike, which her brother always hated. "You go to that Baptist church, right? The one with the funny marquee?"

It featured corny puns the whole town made fun of:

SON SCREEN PREVENTS SIN BURN.

LIFE IS FRAGILE. HANDLE WITH PRAYER.

WANTED: SINGERS. INCHOIR WITHIN.

"I help do those."

"Oh yeah? Which ones are yours?"

"NEED HOME IMPROVEMENT? BRING YOUR FAMILY TO CHURCH."

Mom snorted. "Wow."

"My dad works at Canaan Hardware, okay?"

"No, it's good. I like that sign. It makes me laugh."

The conversation waned and they passed silently under streetlights. But it wasn't unpleasant. Lately, Mom had been used to long awkward pauses in which no one knew what to say after *Sorry for your loss*. Dad exhibited a seriousness, a softness, she'd not often encountered in the male gender; with him, the quiet was comfortable.

"I'm surprised you were at the dance," she said finally. "I thought your church might have banned it."

Dad laughed. "It's not exactly *Footloose*."

Mom looked away. She was a big fan of that movie, had seen it three times in theaters with Michael. She had a major crush on Kevin Bacon.

"We sing and dance in church all the time," Dad said. "It's how we praise Him."

"You know that's not the kind of dancing I mean."

Dad shrugged.

"I'm not sure I even believe in God," Mom said.

"Well, He believes in you."

"Or *She*," Mom amended. "Or *It*."

"I don't know about that," Dad said.

"Do you *really* believe . . ." Mom trailed off. Before Michael and her father's deaths, she hadn't thought much about God. Her family were lapsed Catholics who went to church only on Christmas and Easter. Their lack of religious devotion had never really bothered her until the family's loss. When Mom once tried to broach the idea of an afterlife, my grandmother scowled and said, "Don't go believing in no angel parties. Your father and brother belong in only *one* place and that's here with us. They're not anywhere but in the ground, you hear?"

"Go on," Dad said. "Do I really believe in what?"

"I don't know." Mom rolled her eyes. "Heaven and all that."

"Course," Dad said. "It's where Michael and your dad are now."

There was something in the matter-of-fact way Dad said it that gave her pause. It wasn't a condolence. It wasn't pity. It wasn't just something you said at a funeral out of politeness. He really, sincerely, believed it.

"But they weren't religious."

"I'm sure they had Jesus in their hearts. That's all that matters."

Dad began telling her about Heaven, how beautiful and pure it was, how at peace they'd be there. Mom was surprised to find that, for the first time in weeks, she felt a little better. She didn't know if she believed it, but she wanted to.

They walked by a gas station. A pop song drifted out a car window. Dad started to sway to it.

Mom stepped away, horrified. "What are you doing?"

"Gotta show you us Baptists can dance."

Another line we loved to quote.

Dad has never been a good dancer, but what he lacks in grace, he makes up for in commitment. His swaying soon turned into a little jig. He threw in some jazz hands.

"I'm not with him," Mom said, laughing, to the people who stared. "You're crazy."

But Dad kept dancing. He looked so silly. Mom took his photo with the Polaroid. He finished out the song.

They were in her neighborhood, two streets from Mom's house, when Doug Purdie's truck veered over the curb, nearly running them over. The driver's-side door swung open and Doug stormed out. "What the hell, Debbie!"

"Jesus Christ, Doug!" Mom shoved his chest. "You could have killed us."

"You with this Godwad now?"

His buddies in the truck bed whistled and catcalled.

"He's just walking me home."

"Why you being such a little bitch?"

"Hey," Dad said.

"Stay out of this, creep."

Doug had a good fifty pounds on Dad, but Dad stood his ground. Lifted his chin and said, "*Think not that I am come to send peace on earth.*"

"Yeah, okay, pal."

"I came not to send peace, but a sword."

Doug called to his buddies: "You hearing this?"

"I will laugh at your calamity; I will mock when your fear cometh."

"This how your new boyfriend talks?"

"Leave him alone," Mom said.

"When your fear cometh as desolation—"

"My fist is the only thing that *cometh*." Doug snatched Dad's shirt.

"—and your destruction cometh as a whirlwind—"

Before I go on, let me say this: I don't believe in fate. At least not anymore. When my parents told the story of how they met, this was the moment that carried the weight of destiny and for a long time I, like my brothers, believed it proved my parents' marriage—and by extension, our existence—to be preordained by God. That kind of magical thinking is more than a little embarrassing to me now, but I do still believe in coincidences, and what happened next, you've got to admit, makes a good story.

The night before the Sadie Hawkins dance there had been a torrential storm in Canaan, one that downed power lines and toppled fences. Tree branches littered lawns all over town. It just so happened that one of the broken branches on the giant oak Doug had parked under was balanced precariously overhead and an instant before Mom's high school jerk of a sweetheart meant to clobber Dad, right when Dad said that word—*whirlwind*—just enough of a gust came through to tip the scales and that branch came crashing down on Doug Purdie's truck.

Ka-boom!

Thankfully, none of the guys in the bed were hurt, but the truck's roof dented inward and the windshield spider-cracked. After the initial shock, all anyone could do was gawk at the damage, like God had personally struck Doug Purdie down.

Mom and Dad slipped away in the ensuing chaos: Doug yanking frantically on the branch, screaming at his buddies to help lift the thing off.

"That was crazy!" Mom said, panting. They'd run all the way to her doorstep.

"I warned him," Dad said.

"Oh, come on. You don't honestly think—"

Dad just grinned. "Mysterious ways. I hope you have a blessed night, Deborah."

"Wait." She grabbed his arm. "You know you don't have to go to jail to kiss me."

"I know."

"You don't want to?"

"Of course I want to. But you're already with someone."

"And if I wasn't?"

Dad considered this. "Why don't you come to church on Sunday?"

Mom balked. Some first date that would be. What would her friends say? "Doesn't it ever bother you? What other people think of you?"

"There's only one opinion that matters," Dad said.

In bed that night she turned his invitation over and over in her mind, like a stone in her pocket. She'd dress up and her mother would ask, *What's the occasion?*, and she'd say Sunday. Just that. Sunday. She could hear their argument now.

"I don't want you getting involved with those zealots."

"At least they *feel* something. At least they're connected to something bigger than themselves!"

So she went to church with Dad that Sunday—partially out of curiosity and attraction, but mostly in rebellion against her mother. It was the first step down a long road of wanting, trying, sometimes pretending to believe. Mom always said Dad was a better person than her. Less vain, more self-less. He healed her in a way no one else could. There was a kind of magic that night of their first kiss. How her heart leapt when the branch fell. How he moved, blissfully, to the music at the gas station. How sure he was that Michael and her father were somewhere good, somewhere better. He was nothing like Kevin Bacon. Only one opinion mattered.

"You're crazy," she'd told him. He was.

4

CREATION BAPTIST

*In my darkest hour I suffered doubts: How could a child so young
be entrusted with such crucial information? Why would God choose
to speak through a vessel so naive?*
    *But don't you see? That's just it. That's exactly why. Psalm 8:2.
God ordains strength out of the mouth of babes and sucklings. Only
through the innocence and wonder of a child is the glory of Heaven
to be believed.*
—from *Heaven or Bust!*, "The Divine Suckling," ch. 13, pp. 74–75

AT THIRTY-NINE, MOM WASN'T SURPRISED to find a lump in her
breast. Her grandmother, great-aunt, and three cousins had all died
from breast cancer. A fourth cousin had survived and went pink-ribbon
crazy every October. Mom knew she had the genes. What surprised her
wasn't the diagnosis, but how it made her feel, how it closed one world
and opened another.

Most people diagnosed with a terminal illness become more, not less,
religious; they look to God for answers, for comfort. But Mom? When Mom
got sick, she lost God for good. She'd gone through the motions of prayer,
services, and Bible study all through our childhoods. At the best of times,
Dad's faith carried her. At the worst, she felt like a fraud. She liked to direct
her prayers to Michael and her father more than to God; she believed if her

dead family members were listening, God was likely there, too. But after the diagnosis, God up and disappeared on her like a fair-weather friend. It was an epiphany: *Oh. Church is a game we play to make ourselves feel better about the things we can't control.* And she didn't want to play anymore.

Mom's bucket list included no scuba or skydiving, no trips to Paris; the only tourism we could afford was of the armchair variety. So, instead, every Saturday morning, Mom wheeled the red wagon she used to tote us around in as kids to the Canaan Public Library, a five-minute walk from our house. She used to work part-time there until she got sick. All the librarians loved her. While Jake looked at the magazines and Abe and I picked out fantasy and mystery novels in the YA section, Mom filled the wagon with books on any topic: French history, Egyptian hieroglyphs, Gaudí architecture, black holes, the *Titanic*, biographies of Caravaggio, Elvis Presley, and Audrey Hepburn . . . her curiosity knew no bounds. On Sunday, in lieu of church, she'd camp out in the living room, books piled high on the coffee table. She skim-read to get through at least a little of everything, then carted them all back the following Saturday and returned home with a new haul. She once checked out a world atlas and spent hours flipping through maps at the kitchen table. Another time it was an encyclopedia of dog breeds. Our homeschool lessons became less structured. She'd deviate from the textbooks for our respective grades and would ramble on about whatever had recently struck her fancy.

Her absence was noted in church, where everyone was praying for her. Dad used her illness as an excuse. The first month after her diagnosis he fought with her every Sunday, trying to get her to attend again, but she was stubborn and eventually he gave up. She hadn't been to church in over a year, but the morning after Gideon's visit, we came into the kitchen to find her cooking pancakes in her Sunday best. A blue-and-white flowered dress, sensible navy pumps, her blonde wig. Pearls even.

"Glad to see you'll be joining us," Dad said. He didn't sound glad.

Mom put on her church smile. "It'll be good to be back."

She fooled no one. We all knew she was only coming to stand between Dad and Charlie Gideon.

✢

"Eli, let me fix your tie," Mom called.

Most Sundays, we wore polos to church, but that day Dad dressed us in sports coats. He'd tied our ties and I thought mine looked fine, but I trudged into the bathroom, where Mom was finishing her makeup. This routine used to be familiar: She was always last to get ready; Dad always lectured her in the car about being late; and we always arrived plenty early. She snapped her compact shut, reached past me, and closed the door so that we were alone.

"Is this about Bible World?" I crossed my arms. I was still mad at her. "Because I haven't decided—"

"Do you remember when you asked me if Santa was real?"

"What? No."

She pulled my arms apart, then tugged at the already-straight tie. "One of the kids at Sunday school said something, so you asked me."

"Mom, you're choking me."

She loosened the tie, messing up the knot, then shook her head and yanked it apart completely.

"You looked up at me with these big innocent eyes. I was about to say what any parent would say. *Of course he's real, sweetheart.* You were only five."

She flipped up my collar and crisscrossed the tie ends.

"But you saw it. You looked at my face and knew. You said, 'You wouldn't lie to me, Mommy. You wouldn't lie to me, would you?'"

"I don't remember that."

"And so I caved. I told you it was a game we played. The mommies and daddies put out the presents. Santa was just for pretend."

Dad was calling us now, from down the hall. Mom ignored him.

"You were such a skeptical child. Not like Abe. Abe believed in Santa until he was a teenager. He'd probably still believe if your uncle Wade hadn't blabbed."

I suddenly remembered finding presents in her closet: a miniature basketball hoop, a Nerf gun, a set of walkie-talkies. It must have been a few years after she'd told me. Some kids at church had teased Abe about believing in Santa. He wouldn't give in. It was embarrassing. So I went looking for proof and I found it. I was going to show him, but then couldn't bring myself to do it. I let him keep believing.

"Why are you telling me this? Who cares about Santa?"

"Because I see it in you. What you saw in me, when I was going to lie about Santa."

"What? Wait. You mean—about Heaven?"

She pulled the knot tight on my tie and sighed. "I can't help but get the feeling the person you're trying to convince is yourself."

"That's dumb," I said. "And I don't care what the doctor told you. I know it was real."

"Eli, please. Listen to me."

"Why didn't you say anything? If you thought I was lying all this time? How could you just sit there and let me go on and on—"

"I *did* say something! I tried to talk to your father when he was writing the book. But he was so *happy*, Eli. You don't know how bad it was before. How depressed he got when they made Zeb pastor instead of him. You gave him *purpose*. I thought, *What could it hurt? It's just a hobby. It'll never get published.*"

"But it did!"

"I know. We paid for a printer, but no one bought any—they sat in our garage for years."

"What are you talking about? We sold them. I helped sell them!"

"Well, yes, but only to the nursing homes. That was harmless. And the hospice work is so meaningful . . ."

"You should have told me!"

"I was going to. I was! When you were eighteen, before you left for college. That was always my plan. I was going to tell you then and you could stop talking about Heaven. For good. Or, you know, maybe just on holidays, when you came home. For your father."

"I can't believe you."

"Okay, so I'm not a perfect mother. No surprise there. I should have put an end to it a long time ago, but I expected it to blow over. I never, not in a million years, would have thought that Charlie Gideon, of all people, would—"

Dad knocked. "What's taking so long?"

"I don't care what you say," I told her. "I'm not the liar. You are."

I flung open the bathroom door and showed Dad my tie. She'd made a mess of it, bunny-eared the ends like a shoelace.

"Could you fix this, please?"

✢

Before Charlie Gideon, our family was hardly appreciated at Creation Baptist. Many on the church board saw *Heaven or Bust!* as a peculiar sideshow of Dad's and tolerated it only as part of his duties as pastor to the homebound. Pastor Zeb, the senior pastor, and Pastor Micah, the youth pastor, were the more public faces of the church. Their wives, Candace and Kelly, were music ministers. Their kids were all best friends.

It's not that either of them was a particularly good pastor. Pastor Zeb stole sermons off the internet, which Mom discovered one Easter when he kept referring to "the fecund bunny of the soul" as a symbol for the infinite love of Our Lord and Savior Jesus Christ. *Fecund?* Mom wondered. *Where's he getting this?*

Google, of course.

This upset Dad, but there was little he could do about it. Dad spent hours writing his own sermons at the kitchen table. He practiced them on us in our living room. We were his congregation on the couch. This was material he'd use when ministering to the homebound and small Bible groups, and on his YouTube channel, Simon Says. We all knew he harbored hopes that he might one day fill in for Pastor Zeb and address all of Creation. But when Zeb had a family emergency or was sick, it was Micah who delivered the sermon.

What Pastor Zeb had that Dad didn't was simple: charisma. They were about the same age, but Zeb was far better-looking, with a sharp jawline and a cleft chin. He worked out obsessively: His body was a temple and that temple was stacked. It wasn't so much *what* he preached as *how* he preached. His sermons would be stuffed with sawdust but clinked like gold. It was his booming voice. Abe called it Morgan Freeman voice. The voice of God Almighty. Dad used to do an impression of Zeb, drop an octave and bellow out sentences in words of one syllable. He sounded a bit like the Terminator: *GOD'S—SON—WILL—BE—BACK*. This never failed to drive us into a fit of hysterics.

Pastor Micah wasn't much better. He was always hitting on teenage girls in Lambkins. He did this subtly, with double entendres. You couldn't take offense without being accused of having a dirty mind.

"How often do you get on your knees?" he'd ask, ostensibly referring to prayer.

And the girls, playing innocent, just tossed their hair and giggled.

Zeb and Micah used *Heaven or Bust!* as an excuse to make Dad do the jobs they didn't want: visiting the sick and dying, attending funerals, comforting the bereaved. Dad did this without complaint. He always told me being pastor to the homebound was a privilege. The work Zeb and Micah did—leading worship, singing songs, planning activities for the youth—was important, but the *real* ministerial work came in counseling church members during the hardest time of their lives. It earned him little respect from Zeb or Micah, but the congregation, especially those who had suffered loss with Dad at their side, loved him.

Then Charlie Gideon was a guest at Creation and *Heaven or Bust!* was no longer a joke. As always, we arrived early to set up. Mom ignored the whispers about her sudden return and brewed coffee in the church kitchen. Jake sprawled out on a pew with the Nintendo. Dad, Abe, and I were usually the sound guys, which meant Micah's wife, Kelly, ordered us around while we plugged in speakers and Zeb's wife, Candace, warmed up the choir. But when we headed toward the music supply closet, Pastor Zeb stopped us.

"No need to worry about that today, fellas. We got it covered."

Zeb's and Micah's sons—neither of whom had ever worked a sound board in his life—appeared around the corner, extension cords looped over their shoulders. They nodded amicably at us as they passed.

"Why don't y'all come to my office?" Zeb beckoned to Dad and me.

Abe followed, too, but Zeb stopped him. "Not you."

"What am I supposed to do?"

Zeb shrugged. "Take a load off. Grab a doughnut."

"Keep an eye on Jake," Dad said.

As Dad and I were led away, Abe mouthed *Chosen One* at me. I rolled my eyes.

We followed Zeb to the senior pastor's office. Inside, Charlie Gideon and Pastor Micah were laughing. Gideon was again in cowboy dress; this time his suit was tan.

"Simon!" Micah said. "Man of the hour! Charlie here was telling me about your upcoming press tour."

Dad frowned. "He was?"

"And your new attraction at his theme park," Zeb added.

"Biblical immersion facility," Gideon corrected.

Zeb patted Dad on the back. "We always knew *Heaven or Else!* was going to make it big!"

It was like we'd stepped into another dimension. A parallel universe in which Zeb and Micah actually *liked* us. It was *Invasion of the Body Snatchers*.

"You should be proud of your old man," Zeb told me. "He wrote one heck of a book."

I flinched at the curse, but no one else seemed to notice.

Dad was confused, but nodding along. "I'm . . . glad you think so."

"And you, Eli," Zeb said. "You are going to reach so many people. Praise the Lord!"

"Amen," Micah said.

"And that's not all," Zeb said. "Mr. Gideon has promised Creation a sizable donation. He knows how much the two of you do here. He wants to compensate us for the time you'll be away. That means we can finally afford the renovations we've been saving up for. Get that new roof. Isn't that great news?"

Gideon beamed. "The least I could do."

Dad cleared his throat. "Well . . . we haven't actually, ah, signed yet."

"What's the problem?" Zeb asked.

"Debbie needs some convincing."

"I'm sure you'll bring her around."

"She has her doubts."

"Even those of the strongest faith are bound to stumble," Gideon said.

"How about jewelry?" Micah said. "That always works with Kelly."

Even after years of being around my mother, of making small talk with her at countless church events, these men clearly had no idea who she was.

"I don't see what the problem is," Zeb said. "*The husband shall rule over his wife.* First Corinthians."

"I believe that's Genesis," Dad said. "*As God said to Eve—*"

"The husband is the head of his household," Zeb said, "as Christ is the head of the church."

Gideon chuckled. "If only it were that easy, pastor. You should meet my ex-wife."

The men guffawed, slapping their knees. Dad shifted uncomfortably in his seat. He'd always chafed at the way Zeb and Micah talked about their wives. He and Mom might have fought a lot since her diagnosis and falling-out with the church, but he still admired her willfulness and doted on her.

After they settled down, Gideon said, "Joking aside, I'm sure Simon will find a way to talk sense into her."

"Debbie's sense is fine," Dad said. "She's just a little hardheaded, that's all. But I can persuade her."

Pastor Zeb clapped. "This calls for a toast!"

He went to his mini-fridge and brought Dad and me Ale-8s.

"To *Heaven or Else!*"

"Bust," Dad corrected him. "*Heaven or Bust!*"

We clinked bottles. I felt weirdly grown-up. I wondered if this was what it was going to be like now. Chauffeurs and sizable donations and toasts. I could get used to this.

"I'm very much looking forward to your sermon," Zeb told Gideon.

"Oh?" Dad said. "He's giving the sermon?"

"Of course. You can't expect us to host a legend like Charlie Gideon and not offer him the pulpit."

Micah lifted his drink. "Give the people what they want."

"You know what?" Gideon patted Dad on the shoulder. "Why don't you let Simon take this one?"

Zeb and Micah frowned.

"He doesn't usually . . ." Micah said.

"I don't know if he's ready for that," Zeb said.

Dad was ebullient. "I just have to get my notes from the car!"

"Great." Gideon rubbed his hands together. "It's settled. Zeb can introduce me, I'll give the welcome, then turn it over to Simon."

The pastors grudgingly concurred. Outside, we could hear the congregation milling about the foyer, filing into the chapel. Zeb ushered Dad and me out the door. "Be sure to sit in the front pew where everybody can see you."

⚜

"I thought I get to decide," I said as we left the office.

"You do," Dad said.

"You told them you were going to convince Mom."

"We are. You're going to say yes, right?"

Of course I was going to say yes. I just wanted him to include me in the decision. But he was too distracted by the sermon that had fallen into his lap. He rushed out to the car to retrieve the Bible and the note cards he kept in the glove box, in case Zeb and Micah were ever sick and he got to fill in for them. Mom was in the vestibule, arranging doughnuts on a platter.

"Where's he off to?"

"He's doing the sermon," I said.

"Wow," Mom said flatly. "His big break."

"Why do you have to ruin this for us?"

"Eli." She sighed. "You were four years old."

"So?"

"So do you remember anything else from when you were four? Does anyone?"

Before I could answer, the door to the parking lot opened and in, with a sharp gust of cold air, strode Chase Brinkley and his family. Black leather jacket, blue sweater. He had the cutest dimples and his hair was always gelled to perfection. He nodded coolly to me as they passed. "Eglon."

"What did he just call you?" Mom was raring for a fight. I wouldn't put it past her to pop Chase a good one. King Eglon was the fattest guy in the Bible. Book of Judges. He was so fat that when he was stabbed, the sword got stuck.

"Mom—don't. Forget it."

"I don't like that kid."

"He's not so bad." I was blushing, I could feel it.

She looked at me curiously, with that studious head tilt of hers. I felt my face grow even warmer, my mouth dry up. I yanked at my tie knot.

Dad came back in then and let out a loud *brrrr!* In his hurry he'd neglected to retrieve his coat from the closet. But he had his Bible and his note cards and the biggest grin. We made our way down the center aisle to the front of the church, where Abe and Jake were waiting. The chapel was abuzz with rumors about a special guest. Word was out that it was a celebrity, but no one knew who. The mayor? The governor? The University of Kentucky head basketball coach? It was kind of exciting to know something no one else did.

Soon Candace led the choir in the opening number and we all stood and sang while Pastor Zeb made his entrance.

When the song died down Zeb gestured for us to sit.

"Praise God! It's good to be here today. I feel so much of Jesus's love in this room. Don't you feel it? Wow!

"Now, I know you're all wondering who's here to fellowship with us today and I hope we don't disappoint. You just *might* have heard of him. He's a pastor from a church in Orlando, where he also owns and operates a television studio and theme pa—ah, a *Biblical insertion experience.* He's written numerous bestselling books about how to achieve your most spiritual self. But you probably know him best as the host of *The Charlie Gideon Hour.* Please welcome our brother in Christ, Pastor Charles Gideon!"

Everyone cheered and applauded. Gideon entered the chapel sheepishly. He poked his head in between the back doors and Zeb waved him up to the stage. Gideon walked modestly down the aisle, nodding casually to his bug-eyed, jaw-dropped audience. Zeb held out his hand, but Gideon brushed it aside and embraced the pastor. The congregation let out a delighted sigh—*awww!*—at the spectacle. Gideon took the microphone from a rather ruffled-looking Zeb.

"Thank you for that warm welcome, pastor! I'm delighted to be here at Creation today. I'm delighted to be in Kentucky, for that matter. Your church is beautiful and so is your state.

"But I want to be clear that I'm here for selfish reasons. Just as He spoke to Moses, God has given me a glimpse of His Great Plan. Our Heavenly Father has come calling and I *must* answer His Command. I'm talking about *destiny*, people. I mean *fate.* And no—I don't mean my own. Eli Harpo, would you come up here, please?"

Oh God. I slumped down.

"Eli?" Gideon said.

Abe elbowed me. Dad raised his eyebrows and jerked his head. Mom groaned and dropped her head in her hands.

"That's *my* brother!" Jake yelled, and everyone laughed.

"Eli?" Gideon repeated.

We were in the front pew. There was nowhere to hide.

I stumbled up. Climbed the stairs to meet him. Gideon clapped a hand on my shoulder and my knees nearly buckled. The eyes of the entire congregation were on me. I'd never seen the church from this angle before—center stage. Three rows behind my family, Chase Brinkley sat with his folks.

"Let me tell you something," Gideon said into the microphone. "This boy is extraordinary. He has met Jesus. He has seen the face of God. He has been to Paradise and come back to tell about it. Now I know you know he's special. Eli and his father have been sharing this message with you for a while now. But it's high time for Eli to answer a higher calling. I'm here to offer Eli and his father a chance to take their book on the road. The Harpo family will be guests of honor on my show and at Bible World for the opening of a new Biblical Realm based off Eli's visit to Heaven!"

The congregation cheered.

"God is knock-knocking on your door, Eli. You going to say yes and let him in?"

What else could I do? I nodded dumbly.

I tried to move back down to the pew with my family, but Gideon steered me to a chair onstage. I sat.

Mom was livid. She kept motioning for me to get down and rejoin them. I looked away.

Gideon was announcing Dad now to give the sermon, but I wasn't really listening, because Chase Brinkley was staring right at me. I tried not to stare back, to look anywhere else, but each time I glanced over, he was still staring.

Dad's legs shook as he moved to the pulpit. His forehead was shining. He took the note cards from his breast pocket. I wondered if he'd give the Known as You Are Known sermon from Hospice Duty. He didn't need the cards then; he was comfortable around old people (many of whom were deaf) and confident in his Simon Says YouTube videos. But this was live and in front of all of Creation. This was his chance to finally prove himself. He had to get it right.

Before he began, he set the cards down to wipe his hands on his pants. Somehow he missed the podium and the note cards scattered at his feet.

If this had happened to Gideon—which it wouldn't, because Gideon never used note cards; there was a teleprompter on his show—but if it *had*, Gideon would have turned it into a bit. He'd make a remark like: *good riddance!* He didn't need note cards (wave of the hand). It was all up here (tapping his temple). He was going to speak from the heart (palm to chest). The note cards would have been *blank*—a ruse to emphasize his spontaneity. What Gideon would not have done, what Gideon would never do, is scramble around onstage, scooping up note cards, apologizing over and over, making the entire congregation wince.

Dad performed a mortifying circus act in which he juggled the cards on the podium to get them back in order. Once he had the cards ready, he began reading from them, word for word. The delivery came out rote, robotic. He spoke too quickly, all in a rush. He had a nervous tic of clearing his throat and wiping his brow with the sleeve of his jacket. He'd also glance up quickly from the note cards to look out at the congregation (I remember Mom coaching him once: *Don't forget to make eye contact!*), bobbing his head like a meerkat poking out of its hole. He punctuated his sentences with "Amen!" and "God is good!" as he'd seen ministers do on TV. He flipped to a passage in his Bible and read it directly in that same droning monotone.

"Can I get an *A*-men!" he said at one point, pausing for dramatic effect. I could imagine it, written on the card: *Pause Here. Ask for Amen.* But Dad said it at hyper-speed, coming to a sudden halt: a sprinter at the edge of a cliff. The congregation didn't realize he required a response. They'd been lulled into a state of semiconsciousness, tuning him out. What followed was an awkward silence in which he waited for an *Amen!* and the congregation waited for him to finish and put them out of their misery.

Despite everything to come, I still think of this as one of the most painful moments of my childhood. Dad's dream was finally within his grasp and he was *bombing*. Gideon furrowed his brow. Chase Brinkley was cracking up. He wasn't the only one.

Kill me, I thought. *Please, God. Just kill me so this moment will be over.*

At some point, Dad must have realized it was going poorly, but instead of correcting himself and adjusting his delivery, he tripped faster over his words to get through to the end. Then he flipped a note card and the wrong one followed. He faltered. He shuffled through the cards like a deck—there was a card missing. It must have fluttered down off the stage when they slid off the podium. Again, I wished he'd been like Gideon, or even Zeb, who would have adapted, leapt over the missing anecdote and wrapped things up.

But Dad froze. He was a deer in headlights—his mind caught in a feedback loop: no card, no sermon; no card, no sermon.

Five seconds. Ten. Fifteen.

Finally, I couldn't take it anymore. I stood up.

I didn't know what I was doing, but as I strode forward, instinct took over, and I shucked off my suit coat and dropped it onstage. Everyone was looking at me, but I couldn't think about that. I loosened my tie, slipped it over my head like a freed noose, and cast it aside. My fingers worked at the buttons of my dress shirt. Halfway down, I unbuckled my belt to untuck the rest.

The chapel was stirring now. Zeb moved from his chair to stop me, but Gideon waved him off. I couldn't look at Chase. I wouldn't.

By the time I had the dress shirt off and was down to my white undershirt, the church was in an uproar. I pulled the tee over my head, clearing the cotton fabric just in time to see Dad turn. He stared at my bare chest. Relief dawned on his face. He raised his hand and I went to him.

"My son," he said, "bears the scar of his journey. He has been touched by Jesus, by God." He pressed his hand against the knotted skin over my heart. He knelt before me.

Then he did something he'd never done before.

He leaned forward and kissed my mark. I flinched. He was weeping. I loved my dad—always have, even after our falling-out, after everything got so much worse—but this was too much. It took everything in me not to shudder, not to pull back or push away. I knew everyone was watching, Gideon especially, and I didn't want to ruin our big break. So I did not wipe the tears that fell on my stomach, trickled down, and pooled in my belly button. I stood there rigidly, waiting for the moment to pass.

"As God gave His son, I give mine, so that you might not fear death, but embrace it and know your Heavenly reward."

Dad stood and took my hand. He led me over to Gideon, who followed suit, bowing his head and clasping his hand to my chest. The tension in the church released. Confusion turned to understanding. Discomfort into elation. We went down the stairs and were embraced by our church family. I was Dad's offering. All of Creation wept over me. They traced the outline of my scar. They pressed their lips to my skin. They felt the beating of my heart, warm against their palms.

I might or might not have died once. I might have gone to Heaven, but I was alive now. That was the miracle in that room. That was what they could all feel.

The evidence in their hands.

☩

After, all I wanted was a shower. I'd never felt dirtier in my life. My chest had accumulated a layer of grime from so many hands and mouths touching my scar. The worst was Mrs. Jacobs, whose mother had just died after a long, painful struggle with Alzheimer's, and who was crying so hard a strand of snot flew from her nose onto my left nipple. Shirtless, I had no choice but to wipe it away with my bare forearm.

But when the service was finally over, there was no sudsy respite. Dad stationed me in the lobby to shake hands—anticlimactic, you'd think, after what just happened in the chapel—while the congregation mingled over coffee and doughnuts. He'd given me his suit jacket to wear so I wasn't completely uncovered. It still sucked. The families who'd lost loved ones, whom Dad and I had comforted before—the Cruises, the Stepkas, the Goodins—seemed genuinely proud, and I didn't mind them. But most of the congratulations that day irked me to no end.

We always knew you were special! was the gist.

No! I wanted to yell at them. *No, you didn't!* But, as Dad always said, we didn't do the job for personal recognition. Our work was not for any earthly reward. Our rewards would be eternal. One day we would lay our crowns at Jesus's feet and our good deeds would sparkle up at Him like jewels. So I played the good pastor's son. I smiled and nodded, nodded and smiled. By that point, I'd settle for a wet wipe.

Gideon came up to us, ecstatic. "Wow! Just . . . wow. I've never seen that kind of audience participation before."

Dad beamed. "We could do it on your show, just like that."

"Genius. Absolute genius."

"It's just a scar." Abe had joined us. "The doctors did it, not Jesus."

Jake was there, too, fiddling with his clip-on tie.

"Where's Mom?" I wondered if she had any hand sanitizer in her purse.

"He could do a healing," Gideon told Dad. "For mourners. A kind of reverse laying on of hands."

"I have one on my elbow," Abe said. "From skateboarding."

"Can I go to the bathroom, Dad?" I asked. "Please?"

"We could do it in the Celestial Palace," Gideon said. "The Throne Room."

"I love that," Dad said.

"*Dad,*" I said.

"Jake!" Abe said. "What are you doing?"

He had his shirt off and was running around, swinging it over his head, playing helicopter. Dad caught him.

"What?" Jake pouted.

"Put your shirt back on," Dad said.

"Eli did it!"

"Yeah, well. Eli's special."

"He's the Chosen One," Abe said.

"What the hell was that!" Mom came bustling up with my clothes in her arms. She'd almost trampled the Stepkas, who shared scandalized looks with the Brinkleys. She might have been mad, yelling—*cursing!—in church!—was she insane?*—but, boy, was I glad to see her. With Chase watching, I was dying to cover up. She shoved my shirt and jacket at me. "Come on. Get dressed. We'll talk about this at home."

"Debbie, please," Dad said with pleading eyes, begging her not to make a scene.

"Was that *your* idea?" Mom rounded on Gideon. "Turning my son into a holy stripper?"

Chase snickered.

"No, ma'am," Gideon said. "I was just as surprised—"

"That was all Eli," Dad said. "But I'm glad he did it."

"Your son was naked in church!" Mom shouted.

"It was just his shirt. He has to show his mark—"

They were at it again. People were staring, and not just the Stepkas.

"I'll just . . ." Gideon slipped away.

Abe and I tried to break it up, but there wasn't much we could do. Even with Jake crying. It was absolutely mortifying. Mom had never lost it in church quite like this. And Dad had never fought with her so openly in public, especially not in front of his congregation. It made both of them look bad. It made *all* of us look bad. Chase was getting a real show.

"Good job," Abe whispered to me.

"I didn't mean to."

"Sure you didn't."

I pushed past him and down the church's side hall. Ducked into the bathroom.

Finally—a sink! Water! Soap!—but Gideon was in there, too.

"Oh. Hi, Eli." He was washing his hands.

For some reason I couldn't clean myself up with him watching. I moved into a stall and latched the door. I could hear him drying his hands with a paper towel.

"You did great out there," he said, on the other side of the stall door. "I forget that it's a lot. After so many years in front of a camera, you get used to all the attention."

"My mom and dad are fighting. And it's because of you."

Gideon sighed. "I'm sorry to hear that. But I don't think that's my fault."

"Of course it is! If you never showed up—"

"They never fought before?"

"Well, no. I mean, yes. But not like this."

"That must be hard."

I sighed. "Would you please just go away?"

"If that's what you want. Say the word and I'll leave."

"Okay. Then go." I peeked out a gap in the stall door. He was facing the mirror, running a wet comb through his hair.

"You sure?"

I wasn't sure about anything. I still wanted to go to Bible World. I still wanted to make Dad proud. But at that moment all I cared about was getting my parents to stop fighting and getting to that sink.

"You mean you'll leave us alone for good?"

"Yes, Eli. Just say the word and I'll go. I'm not here to make you do something you don't want to do. And I can't stick around forever. I have a life to return to."

I wasn't sure whether to believe him. Would he really back off if I just asked him to? I'd never had that kind of power in my family's decision-making. Even though they'd said it was up to me, it sure didn't feel that way. And although I wasn't ready yet to admit it, I was confused about what Mom said about the doctor. And my chest felt so gross. I was glad I'd saved Dad from complete embarrassment, but I never wanted to have to do that again. Not at Bible World. Not anywhere. If I was going to tell Gideon to get lost, now might be my only chance.

"What about Bible World?" I meant the free tickets, but he took it another way.

"Don't worry. We'll find someone else."

"How?"

He shrugged. "Move down the list."

"What list?"

Gideon shook the comb and returned it to his pocket. He pulled out his cell phone. It was unlike any phone I'd seen at that point, a first-generation iPhone, practically futuristic. He tapped the screen a few times, then came over to the stall. I backed away from the door.

"Molly Picket, eight. Tucson, Arizona. Drowned at the neighborhood swimming pool. Sam Fox, eleven. Portland, Oregon. Electrocuted by a robotic Christmas Santa. That was a weird one. Thomas Redding, two. Salva, Texas. Heatstroke. One of those locked-car cases. Jennifer O'Neill, nine. Trenton, New Jersey. Choked on a gobstopper. Got lodged right in her windpipe. No one around to Heimlich her. She turned blue and—"

"They all died?"

"And came back. That's the part that counts."

"Oh."

"Did you think you were special?" He returned his phone to his breast pocket. "Sorry. That came out wrong. You *are* special, Eli. Just not one-of-a-kind." He went back to the sink to examine himself once more in the mirror. "I can't have another Livingston on my hands, so if you and your family are having doubts, and you clearly are—not to mention *your mother*—I think it's time for me to move on to the next candidate." He straightened his bolo tie. "A shame, though. Cancer Mom. Pastor Father. Adorable small-town family. And that book! Absolutely ripe for plucking. Plus, the thing with your scar. Should have known it was too good to be true." He returned his cowboy hat to his head. "Have a nice, unremarkable life, Eli. Don't worry. I won't be back to bother you again." And with that, he was gone.

I counted to ten before opening the stall door. It was over.

"You fucking idiot."

Chase Brinkley swung out of the stall next to mine. The F-word detonated in my chest like a bomb. At that point in my life, I'd only heard it once or twice. Abe once said *Goddamn it!* after slamming his thumb in a drawer and was grounded for a week. Chase went to public school, where kids used language like that freely.

"Hi, Chase."

"You're just going to let him leave like that? I always knew you were ugly, but I didn't think you were dumb."

My heart pounded, my palms itched. Chase Brinkley could say the meanest things to me and all I could do was watch his Adam's apple bob in his beautiful throat.

"That guy wants to make you famous and you're just like, *Um, no thanks?*"

"My mom doesn't like him."

"Who cares? She's got, what? Like a month to live?"

I swallowed. "She's in remission," I lied.

"Whatever. Look, Eglon. You and your dad give everyone the creeps. You always have and you always will. But I don't know. Maybe you're onto something."

"Thanks, Chase."

He'd cornered me in my stall. I could smell his deodorant. We were breathing the same air. I'd always thought I was jealous of Chase's popularity, his good looks, his family's wealth and status in the church, that he got to go to public school and "be normal." But now it struck me: I wanted him to kiss me. I wanted to run my fingers through his hair. I wanted to press my body against his. This was more than a little alarming. I could logic myself out of the fear that came with the Jesus sex dreams: No one else knew about them and dreams were all nonsense anyway, right? Right? They didn't mean I was . . . Surely I wasn't . . . I couldn't even say the word then. Not even to myself. But with Chase closing in on me in that tiny cubicle, this was the first time my attraction to boys made itself physically known *in the light of day*—and that scared the crackers out of me.

I was becoming aroused in my khakis. I glanced down and discovered similar evidence in Chase's own. He caught me looking and turned beet red.

"You're too fat for TV anyway."

☩

I washed my chest, splashed water on my face, and dressed. I was shaking in the mirror over the sink. I couldn't look at myself.

I came out of the bathroom confused on so many levels. About how I felt about Chase. About what he'd said about Gideon's deal. Maybe he was right and I'd blown my only chance. Maybe there was a way to go to Bible World and be on the show without having to debase myself by taking my shirt off. It was hard enough doing it for Hospice Duty. Like most fat kids my age, I was self-conscious going bare-chested even in normal situations. If Abe hadn't given me grief, I would have worn my tee into the pool every summer. The idea of revealing my pale, pudgy belly on live TV was physically nauseating. But if I could get them to drop that part, maybe it wouldn't be so bad. Why was I so afraid of Gideon's offer? Who cares what some doctor said? Did I not want my family to be successful? After years of being ignored, did I think we didn't deserve it?

I looked for Gideon in the vestibule, which was crowded with church members putting on coats and scarves and gloves before heading out to their cars. He wasn't there.

I moved into the chapel. It was mostly empty. A few stragglers. No Gideon. He must have left. If I hurried I could catch him in the parking lot—

"Oof!" I ran smack into Dad.

"Big E! Where've you been! Come on. We're going to Ramsey's to celebrate."

"There's nothing to celebrate." Mom came hustling up in her pink coat. "That stunt doesn't mean anything. Eli still has to decide."

Dad scoffed. "Oh, please. Tell her, Eli."

"I'm hungry," Jake whined, pulling on Mom's purple-gloved hand.

They were all bundled in their winter-wear, ready to go. Abe tossed me my jacket.

"Is Gideon with you?" I asked Dad.

"What? No. He's meeting us at the restaurant. Now would you please tell your mother you meant it? That you would not *lie* in front of your church family."

"I don't know," I said.

"Ha!" Mom said. "What'd I say? He was caught up in the moment."

"But he said *yes*. We agreed. Whatever Eli decided—"

I broke away down the aisle.

"Hey!" Dad yelled after me.

"Eli!" Mom called. "We have to talk about this!"

Back through the vestibule, then out the church doors. A freezing gust of wind slapped my face and my eyes watered instantly. I put on my jacket. The parking lot was clogged with its typical post-service traffic jam, cars lining up to exit. I moved down the rows, looking for Gideon's black town car, his ten-gallon hat. I didn't even know if I wanted to be his Heaven Kid. But I was afraid I no longer had the option.

I'd never been one to pray for signs. Dad always said it was wrong to demand God reveal Himself for your own selfish purposes. It was not for us to decide when or how He showed us the Way. All we could do was ask for guidance. But as I bustled about searching those cars, hot in the face, breath heavy, it started to snow—the first snowfall that year, early for the season—and I couldn't help but feel God was speaking to me. He was mourning my denial of the Calling. My refusal to accept fate, destiny, whatever you called it. I stopped and looked up and the sky was a swirl of white flakes. Maybe He *had* Chosen me. Maybe He'd brought me to this moment so I could find Gideon and say yes and everything would be good again. Maybe this was it, my tree branch falling, this was my moment to—

A car honked. I jumped, startled.

The driver laid on the horn again. He waved angrily—*get out of the way!*

I moved aside, the car rolled past, and I came back to my senses. I saw myself for what I really was: not Chosen or Called, just this frantic fat kid in the middle of a parking lot, gawking up at the snow. Somebody about to get run over if he wasn't careful, if he didn't pay attention and watch what he was doing.

5

ASK AGAIN LATER

Heaven is one big reunion. And it's not just the people you knew in life—it's the people you were meant *to know, too. My mom died before my kids really got to know her. I've always regretted that. When Eli told me about their time together in Heaven, he delivered more than a great comfort to me personally. He brought with him a promise, direct from God.*

So when you're missing your Loved Ones most, remember: It all works out in the end.

Well, after *the end.*

—from *Heaven or Bust!*, "Meeting Memaw," ch. 16, p. 89

THE SNOW DIDN'T STICK. IT let up after lunch. There was no celebration at Ramsey's. We went to the restaurant and waited over an hour. Dad refused to be seated until Gideon arrived, but he never showed. Dad tried calling, but apparently, the phone number Gideon gave was the office line to his megachurch in Orlando, and the receptionist refused to give out his cell. Dad was too distraught to eat, so we went home.

Mom made tomato soup and grilled cheese sandwiches. Dad barely touched his. He kept checking his cell under the table.

"Simon, please," Mom said.

"What if there was an accident? It must have been an emergency. I'll ask Zeb if he's heard from him."

He sent a few texts, then put the phone on the counter. He circled his spoon in his bowl of cold soup, glancing over every so often, like a lovelorn teenager, waiting for a crush to respond.

It rang a few minutes later. He scrambled up, then took the call in the garage. It had to be Gideon, telling him he'd moved on to another Heaven Kid. Dad was going to be heartbroken. I couldn't stand it. I felt sick to my stomach.

I shouldn't have been surprised to find out about the other Heaven Kids. Of course Gideon had backups! That there were others who'd died—or almost died—and gone to Heaven had never bothered me. In fact, it gave me a sense of relief to have what I thought I'd experienced corroborated. Not long before Gideon and his list, my brothers and I had watched a History Channel special on near-death experiences. They were interviewing all these people with different NDEs—from car accidents and head trauma and even heart surgeries like mine—and what they described was all the same. Rising out of their bodies. Dark tunnels. The blinding white light.

"Looks like I'm not the only Chosen One," I told Abe.

One of the most memorable interview subjects, my favorite at least, was a scuba diver whose oxygen tank had malfunctioned. He would have drowned—well, he *did* drown, but it would have been permanent—had his friend not saved him.

"It should have been the scariest moment of my life," the diver said. "I mean, it was at first—when I realized I couldn't breathe. But then eventually I stopped resisting. And I let go. And all I felt was warmth and kindness and peace."

They showed a reenactment of this. An actor underwater, suspended, like an astronaut free floating in space. Then blackness. Then that beautiful light.

After watching that, Jake turned and looked at me. He was absolutely thunderstruck. It might have been the first time he ever really understood what I was meant to have gone through.

"Was it really like that, Eli?"

I felt so close to the diver, it didn't feel at all like a lie. "Yeah, Jake, it was." And telling him that, feeling his immense awe, made it real for me, too. "Exactly like that."

✢

Sunday afternoons were for homework, which meant coming up with innovative ways to distract Mom from making us do homework. This took little effort that day, as Mom was already distracted by Dad's call. Abe, Jake, and I put our dishes in the sink, then went to watch *Bible Tales* tapes in the living room. I was too upset to focus on the episode's plot. I'd seen them all a million times anyway.

Dad came in from the garage. Mom demanded to know who he'd been talking to.

"Business matter."

"I swear, if you told Gideon—"

"It was Wade, okay?"

Wade was Dad's cousin. A lawyer. He'd been entangled in Mom and Dad's fights before, after Dad met with him about suing the Livingstons. Mom was livid when she found out. She'd stormed into the garage, where Dad was editing one of his ministry videos, and slapped a bill down on the laptop.

"Why is your idiot cousin charging us two hundred dollars?"

"Don't be mad. It was just a consultation."

"Are you kidding me?"

"Wade thinks we have a case."

"How could you not tell me?"

"I knew you'd be unsupportive."

"Darn right."

"What kind of language is that?"

"Simon. Those people didn't steal Eli's story."

"You bet they did." He went over to his bookshelf and located the dog-eared, Post-it-noted copies of *Heaven or Bust!* and *A Tour of Heaven*. "Thirty-seven similarities! I've cataloged them all."

"We can't afford a lawyer," Mom said.

"Sure we can. Besides, Wade said they'd probably settle out of court."

"What does *Wade* know about copyright law?"

"Intellectual property."

"Same thing! Simon. He deals with car accidents."

"He's a personal injury attorney," Dad said. "He knows more than you think."

At the time, Mom had talked him out of wasting our savings on a retainer for Wade. It was no wonder why she was so mad to hear Dad was involving him again.

There was a break in the argument, then Dad came into the living room. "Let's go, Big E."

"What? Where?"

Mom clomped in after him, arms crossed. "You're not taking him to see Wade."

"We're going to visit Memaw."

Mom's arms loosened. "Oh."

"I want to go," Jake said.

"No you don't," Abe said.

"Maybe next time," Dad said.

"He can go," I said. "I'll stay and watch TV with Abe."

Dad cleared his throat. "Get your coat."

✢

We tossed the rake and yard bags into the back of the van, then stopped at Kroger for flowers. They were out of lilies, so we bought white roses instead.

Cemeteries have never been scary to me. This was probably because of the number of funerals I attended as Creation Baptist's Child Emissary of Heaven. I always thought cemeteries were beautiful, peaceful even. They were just parks, but with an important spiritual component. Holy ground. You could feel it.

Memaw's grave was a plain granite headstone among many. *Eleanor Beattie Harpo: February 17, 1930–November 22, 1995.* The last flowers we'd left there had shriveled. I had the honor of replacing them.

Dad rested a hand on her stone. "Hey, Mom. I brought Eli to see you." He waved me forward and I put my hand next to his.

"Hi, Memaw. How's Heaven?"

I didn't know what else to say. Dad always wanted me to open up to her, like she was my guardian angel or something. He thought we'd had a heart-to-heart in Heaven. But in Heaven all she did was bake me cinnamon oatmeal cookies, her specialty. Or that's all I could remember.

Dad raked and I collected the leaves. It didn't take long to clear the plot. When we were finished it stood out like a green door in the ground. Dad lingered, staring at the stone.

"Mom," he said. "Your grandson's in need of some guidance. He's at a spiritual crossroads. I thought maybe you could help him look into his heart and see which road to take."

He nodded at me. "Go on. You can ask her."

"What?"

"Tell her about Gideon. She'll listen."

"Uh, Dad?" I had to tell him. About the list of Heaven Kids. That Gideon had already moved on. I'd blown our only chance. But when he looked at me, his eyes were soft and eager.

"What is it?"

"Never mind." I stepped forward. "Hi, uh, Memaw? I guess, what I want to know is . . . do you think we should sign with Charlie Gideon?"

"Good," Dad said. "Now close your eyes, look into your heart, and see what God answers."

I thought, God or Memaw? But I didn't press the point. Sometimes praying felt like consulting a Magic 8 Ball. There were three possible answers: Yes, No, or Ask Again Later. I closed my eyes, and when I saw her, she was taking a cookie sheet out of the oven. She wore a light blue dress and a flowery apron. She looked like a 1950s housewife. She was young, of course. But when she came toward me with the cookies, her teeth fell out.

I shuddered.

"What did you see?" Dad thought I'd had an epiphany.

"She was wearing dentures. They fell out."

"Oh." He was disappointed. "Try again. Listen for the voice in your heart."

I closed my eyes again and this time I listened. Rustling leaves, chirping birds, Dad breathing beside me. I never heard a voice when I prayed, but sometimes I felt a presence. I felt no longer alone. Was that God? Or was it wish fulfillment? Maybe it was a delusion. Or just a heightened sense of awareness. It could be comforting, but it gave no answers.

I opened my eyes.

"Well?" Dad said.

"I think I'm supposed to wait."

"Wait?"

"I can't just ask God to tell me. I have to be patient."

"Ah. I see." He didn't push further.

Dad led me over to one of the stone benches. He sat and checked his phone. No calls. The day was cold but sunny. I sat next to him and we watched the wind in the tree, leaves drifting down.

"Did I ever tell you about when I was first Called to the ministry?"

"You mean when God spoke to you in the storm?"

The story went like this: Once, long ago, Dad was a telemarketer. Every day he sat in a cubicle and sold magazine subscriptions over the phone. It was hard to picture: Dad, in an office building, by a watercooler. He hated that job, and every day he thought about quitting. But he had a wife to support and they were having difficulty getting pregnant, so there were fertility treatments and that was expensive. Eventually there were two sons, back-to-back, to provide for. Quitting clearly wasn't an option. He was miserable. Sometimes God speaks to the miserable.

And, yes, not to be dramatic, but it was during a storm. A freak one that accumulated suddenly in the middle of what was supposed to be a sunny day. It hit right at noon and Dad was on lunch duty. He'd meant to slip out around eleven to pick up everyone's orders, but he got caught on a long call, so he was running late. The radio in his car announced a flash flood warning. Everyone was supposed to stay inside. Dad didn't listen, though. His co-workers were counting on him. He'd brave a hurricane to bring someone a cough drop.

When he pulled back into the office park it wasn't raining yet. He got out of the car, walked around to the passenger side, and fumbled to get all the bags of soups and salads in one go. He slammed the door with his hip, turned, and caught a rare sight.

The sky behind his office building was a malevolent purple. Lightning flashing. Thunder rumbling. Clouds roiling in. But—weirdly—the storm hadn't quite arrived and the sky directly overhead was the calm blue of a spring day.

Stranger yet was the sensation Dad felt when he caught sight of his co-workers, framed in the windows above him, foreheads against glass. On this side of the building, they couldn't see the storm. Only he could see it. And that's when God spoke to him.

"And do you know what He said?"

"He said it was your job to warn them about the storm. To lead the blind to Jesus. And that's why you quit your job."

"No."

No? What did he mean *no*? That was how the story went.

"Well, yes. That's how I've always told it. Mostly because of your mother. Think about it. I came home and told her I'd quit my job and there she was with two little boys to take care of. She was so mad at me."

"So . . . God didn't speak to you?"

"He did. But he only said one word."

"What?"

"He said, 'WAVE.'"

"'Wave'?"

"Yes, 'WAVE.' They were all looking down at me, the storm moving in. And I heard this voice inside of me and it said, 'WAVE.' So I put down the lunch bags and I waved. And they waved back."

"Oh." I didn't get it.

"You see, I was waving at all of them. At each and every one of them, with that one wave. And that's how I knew I had to go into the ministry, where I could reach everyone, all at once. And that's what you can do, too."

He nodded his head profoundly.

I'd never have admitted this then, not even to myself, but I thought that was kind of . . . dumb. I'd always thought God had spoken more directly when Dad was called. Like to Moses in the burning bush. WAVE? What was *that*?

We went to say goodbye to Memaw. Dad bent down and picked up a few stray leaves that had blown onto the otherwise spotless grave.

"Tell me again."

So I told him. About meeting Memaw in her mansion in Heaven. How she baked me her cinnamon oatmeal cookies. How happy she was, living with Jesus. How much she missed him, her only child. He'd heard it a million times and never got sick of it. It was a kind of power I had, the ability to console him.

Dad sighed. "I can't wait to see her again. Do you know how blessed you are? Don't you want to share that with the world? Don't you think Memaw would want that for you, too?"

✣

"My spirit simply does not commune with this man's," Mom announced when we got back. She was on the couch, reading one of Charlie Gideon's spiritual self-help books. There was a pile of them on the coffee table. This one was called *Faith, Freedom, Fortune*, the title embossed in gold letters.

"Gideon gave those to *me*," Dad said.

"They were a gift *for the family*."

"That doesn't mean you can write in them. Or rip them up!"

She was pulling a Dad, highlighter in hand, pens, Post-it notes at the ready. And, yes, she'd gone one further: torn out pages and tacked them to the corkboard wall in Homeschool Corner, the section of the living room with our desks, where our classwork and Jake's drawings were displayed.

"I'm just doing my research." She stood up, waved us over to one of the pages pinned to the wall. "Come here. Listen to this."

"I don't want to hear it." Dad stalked right past her, through the kitchen, into the garage.

I tried to retreat to my room, but Mom wasn't having it. She sat me on the couch, went back to what would eventually become her Wall of Scandal, and read the passage aloud in her most sarcastic voice.

"*If you love God, God loves you back. The more you show your love to God, the more he shows His love back. The more riches you give to God, the more He gives back.* He means money, you know. The more money you give to Charlie Gideon, the more money God gives you. Prosperity gospel, if I ever heard it."

"Money's not evil," I said. "We need it."

"Of course. If money's evil, we're a bunch of saints. It's not the money itself, Eli. It's what you'll have to do to make it."

I didn't want to go into this again. "Where's Abe and Jake?"

"Studying. Don't forget—you have an algebra quiz tomorrow."

"*Mommmmm.*"

"Just because Charlie Gideon wants you to be on his TV show doesn't mean you can fall behind in your schoolwork. He might be impressed, but I'm not."

I got up to go, but she sat me back down. "How was Memaw?"

"Still dead," I said.

"*Eli.*"

"What? It's true."

"What did you and your father talk about?"

"What do you think?"

"And have you decided?"

"No." Like it mattered now that Gideon had moved on to his backups.

"Take a look at this face." She held up the book.

From his author photo, Charlie Gideon beamed his most radiant smile. He looked photoshopped: There wasn't a blemish on him.

"Does this look like a man you want to be beholden to? Just look at his suit. Those gold cuff links. His capped teeth. This is the face of a worldly man. His spirit is corrupt."

"Just because he's rich, doesn't mean he's a bad person."

"Easier for a camel—"

"Do you think Dad will be mad if Gideon doesn't want me anymore?"

"Did Gideon tell you that?"

"No. I don't know. Maybe."

"Hey." She patted the cushion next to her. "What is it? You can tell me."

"You won't tell Dad?"

"Not unless you want me to."

I sat down beside her. "Gideon said there are other Heaven Kids. I'm not the only one. I think he's going to ask one of them instead."

"Oh." I thought she'd be relieved, but she wasn't. She almost looked disappointed.

"Dad's going to kill me." I started to cry.

"Hey. Come here." She tossed the book aside. If anyone else had been in the room—especially Abe—I wouldn't have let her baby me, but we were alone and so I scooted down the couch and into her arms.

It was different hugging her since her surgery. She'd once been bigger, full-bodied. Abe and Jake had inherited Dad's lean build, but I somehow ended up with Mom's fat gene. Only on her it wasn't fat, but curvy. You could rest your head on the shelf of her breasts. Now there was nothing, just a sunken spot in her chest.

"Your father will always love you, no matter what."

✢

Three days passed. Not a word from Gideon. Dad called every morning and left a message with the receptionist at Bible World's megachurch. The first day he called four or five times until the secretary finally chewed him out. She had his contact info and she'd pass it on to Mr. Gideon, now would he please *stop calling*. He couldn't. But he did limit himself to one call every morning thereafter. The rest of the day was spent sulking around the house in sweatpants and a bathrobe, carrying his phone from room to room.

"Why don't you make a new Simon Says video?" Mom suggested at breakfast on Wednesday. "You haven't done one of those in a while."

"I don't understand," Dad said. "Didn't he like us? He liked us, right?"

I glanced at Mom and she shook her head almost imperceptibly.

"What's up with you?" Abe said, watching Mom and me exchange looks.

"Nothing," I said.

"If you hadn't been so rude that night at dinner," Dad told Mom.

"You're right," she said. "I wasn't nice enough to Charlie Gideon. I scared him off. I'm sorry. Now can we *please* move on with our lives?"

Dad stood up from the table. "I'm calling Zeb again."

"He already told you he hasn't heard from him," Mom said.

Dad ignored her and went out to the garage.

✛

The packages arrived that afternoon, during homeschool.

We weren't always homeschooled, and it wasn't for religious reasons like most people assumed. Abe and I went to Canaan County Elementary until Abe was in third grade and I was in first. Our parents pulled us out when the teachers wanted to hold Abe back and skip me a grade. Abe had been diagnosed with dyslexia and my parents weren't confident with the school's ability to accommodate him. At the same time, I was bored in class, already reading at a fourth-grade level. Homeschooling was the best solution. It allowed for us both to learn at our own paces—and without the embarrassment of Abe being in the same grade as his little brother.

This was the official reason at least. But I suspect there might have been personal reasons for my parents' choice, too. Dad had bad memories of public school because of bullying. And Mom hated sending us away every day. She was lonely at home by herself. Her part-time job at the library wasn't enough to keep her occupied and when Dad suggested she might look for full-time work, she realized the main job she wanted to do was be our mother. Since her own mom's death a few years previously, she had no other family she was close to and homeschooling gave her a way to keep us boys close. This makes her sound needy and she'd probably never have admitted it, but I saw how she moped around, trying and failing to cover up how much she missed us when we went to school those first few years. She was happiest when we were home with her.

It was science hour. Jake was growing a lima bean plant and filling out a worksheet. I was learning about natural selection. Abe was answering practice earth and space questions for the GED—or was supposed to be. He was always doodling in his notebook when Mom's back was turned, then randomly filling in bubbles on the multiple-choice answer sheet. Mom had been lecturing him lately about applying to colleges. She'd ordered brochures and recruitment packets and flipped through them with him, trying to get him interested. Abe couldn't have cared less. When I think of this now it's obvious Mom was dreaming of college more for herself than for him. I saw the way she went all misty-eyed, reading over lists of majors and class electives. If we could have afforded it, she would likely have gone eventually, earned a library science or education degree. But she put us first: If they were budgeting for tuition, it would be ours, not hers. Still, she loved learning, and she always made homeschool fun.

The book I was reading was *Evolution Now* by Gil Bright. Dad was a creationist, but he also believed in evolution. He did not see these as mutually exclusive systems of belief. He did not believe the Earth was only six thousand years old, as many at Creation Baptist did. Instead, he interpreted the seven days of Genesis metaphorically, as epochs of time. One "day" to God stood figuratively for millennia in the eyes of mankind. In fact, evolution was potential *evidence* for intelligent design. How could such an intricate form of species differentiation exist without a divine entity behind it?

Since her cancer diagnosis, Mom had become much more radical than that. Among the library books she loaded into her red wagon were books that outright opposed our religion. She deliberately hunted them out and passed them on to me, asking for my take. Gil Bright, a geneticist who wrote popular-science bestsellers and was a sort of atheist spokesperson, was her latest fix. She'd finished *The Unholy Gene* and *Evolution Now* and was currently reading *Fallacy of God*. When Dad caught me with Bright's book, I thought he'd be upset, but he only said, "Be a filter, not a sponge.

Your faith is meant to be challenged. Combating the notions of the ungodly can only make it stronger."

The doorbell rang.

Jake's head perked up like a dog's. "I'll get it!" He darted from his desk, across the living room, and to the front door.

Mom followed. "What's all this?"

Abe and I wandered over. A deliveryman stood on our stoop. His uniform was fancier than UPS brown—a personal-courier type. Instead of cardboard boxes, the stack of presents in his arms were pristinely wrapped, in glistening white paper, with silver ribbon and gold bows.

"Christmas comes early!" he announced.

Mom reached forward curiously and took the top box from the stack. She examined it for a label. Not finding one, she handed it off to Jake; Abe and I took the other two. The courier held out an electronic signature pad, which she signed with the stylus and gave back to him.

"Happy holidays!" he said cheerfully and turned to go. "Oh! Almost forgot." He reached into his jacket and extracted a purple envelope. "Here you are."

"Thank you." Mom took the envelope and closed the door.

Dad came in from the kitchen. "Who was that?"

"Santa!" Jake yelled.

"Charlie Gideon more likely," Mom said.

"He was here?" Dad rushed to the door and pressed his nose to the window glass.

"He sent gifts," Abe said.

"He sent *bribes*," Mom said.

"That means he still wants us!" I said.

"Can I open this one?" Jake was bouncing up and down, pointing to the largest present Abe had put down on the couch. Mom checked the tag tied to the bow.

"To: The Harpo Boys, From: The Grinch."

"It does *not* say that." Dad marched over and looked for himself. "They *are* from Gideon! Should have known he'd make the grand gesture."

"Your boyfriend asking you to go steady?" Mom said.

Dad made a face. "Deborah, don't be obscene."

"Gross, Mom," Abe said.

Mom glanced at me. "I don't think it's obscene. Or gross."

I pretended not to notice. "Come on, Jake," I said, and the three of us tore into the present.

"Whoa!" Jake said. "PlayStation 3!"

There was a smaller present taped to the top of the box. Abe peeled it off. It was a video game: *Raptured! VII*. The cover featured a bearded Jesus look-alike in army fatigues, running through a postapocalyptic city, wielding a spear-tipped crucifix.

"Holy crap!" Abe grabbed the game from Jake.

"Abraham," Dad said. "Language."

"This is the one where Zeke tracks the Anti-Christ to the City of the Beast and gets his Mark removed."

"Sounds violent," Mom said. "I don't know if I want you boys playing that."

"Paul's only got up to *Raptured! VI*. I don't think this one's even out yet."

"It'll give you nightmares," Mom insisted, hand out.

Abe clutched the game to his chest. "Paul and I played the others. They're fine."

"Listen to your mother," Dad said.

"This is so unfair." Abe forked it over.

"Rated M-16," Mom read on the back of the case.

"See?" Abe said. "I *am* sixteen! It's age-appropriate."

"We'll see," Mom said, which we all knew meant *no*.

"Which one's next?" I asked.

Jake pointed at the midsize present. I looked at the tag. "It's for Dad."

He came forward shyly. "For me? Gideon didn't have to do that." He checked the tag himself, set the bow aside, then carefully removed the ribbon. He detached the paper at the seams.

His eyes lit up. "A digital camcorder! With a collapsible stand."

"For your YouTube channel," I said.

"No duh," Abe said.

"How . . . thoughtful," Mom said.

"Can I do this one?" Jake rattled the smallest present. *"Pleeease."*

Abe checked the tag. "It's for Mom."

"Have at it," she said.

Jake showed less restraint than Dad in opening the gift. He was like the *Looney Tunes* Tasmanian Devil: a wrapping-paper tornado.

"What is it?" Abe said.

Jake shrugged. He couldn't tell from the box, which was brown cardboard without labels or pictures. He tried to open it for nearly a minute, but soon became impatient with the tape sealing it shut.

"I don't like this one."

"Give it here." Dad took out his pocketknife and made short work of the tape. He held out the present to Mom.

"Gideon meant it for you."

Mom rolled her eyes and took the box. She opened the flap and pulled out a mass of bubble wrap. She broke the tape on the end, unrolled the bubble wrap, removed the tissue paper around the gift, and revealed . . . a Delicate Twinkling.

It was a little clown boy. He was dressed in a circus suit: red-and-blue checkers with fluffy, oversize buttons, ruffles at the collar and cuffs. His face was painted white with teardrop eyes and the signature red clown nose. He was topped with a curlicue orange wig and a miniature jester's cap. In one hand he clutched a yellow balloon, suspended overhead on a piece of twine. In the other, held behind his back, was a cream pie.

Dad nudged Mom with a grin. "The perfect gift to woo a lady, right, Debs?"

"Ugh. Men," Mom said, but she was smiling, too.

"If anything's giving me nightmares," Abe said, "it's *that*."

"No kidding," Mom said.

"It looks a little like Eli." Abe smirked.

"Does not!" I punched him in the shoulder.

"Don't," Mom said.

"It's the hair." Abe punched back.

Mom was shaking her head. "I don't like the message this sends."

"What?" Dad said. "It's a kind gesture."

"He thinks we're clowns."

"That's ridiculous."

"Hey—you dropped something." Jake held out a little white card. It must have fallen out of the bubble wrap.

Mom took it. "Pffft. It's just his business card."

"There's writing on the back," I said.

She flipped it over and read: "*D.H.— Hope you enjoy rare, limited edition Twinkling. His name is Barnabas. —C.G.*"

"See?" Dad said. "How generous."

"Maybe I can sell it on eBay."

"That's it?" Jake said.

"Looks like it," Mom said.

"What about the letter?" I said.

"What letter?" Dad asked.

"Oh, right." Mom looked around. The room was a mess of wrapping paper, ribbon. "Where'd I put that?"

"Deborah!" Dad chided, and we began the search.

"It was in a purple envelope," I said.

"It looked important," Abe said, unhelpfully.

"Can I play PlayStation now?" Jake asked.

Dad was tossing wrapping paper willy-nilly. Mom went into the kitchen, came back with a trash bag, and began collecting the scraps. I spotted the envelope on the coffee table, wedged beneath the PlayStation box. I picked it up and presented it to Dad.

The front of the envelope was addressed in gold ink to *The Harpo Family*. On the back was a wax seal, stamped with the Bible World crest: a lion and lamb lying together between the capital letters *BW*.

"Oooh!" Dad held it up before opening it. "How fancy."

He pulled out a letter on thick stationery and unfolded it. Something fell out.

At first I thought it was more business cards, but when I bent to pick them up I saw they were longer, flashier. There were five of them. Purple and white, with gold lettering and the same crest as the wax seal.

Dad peered over my shoulder. "What is it?"

"Tickets," I said. "To Bible World."

Jake shrieked with delight. He zoomed around the room, screaming his head off. "Bible World! Bible World! We're going to Bible World!"

It was right out of their commercials, like the one where the parents hide the tickets in Easter baskets at the church picnic and when their kids pick them up to go egg-hunting—surprise!—and then the choir shouts *Hallelujah!* and sings the Bible World jingle and the kids go berserk.

"Calm down." Mom caught hold of him, but Jake's elation couldn't be contained. He leapt up and down in her arms, spinning like a top. Mom laughed. A six-year-old's joy can be very contagious. Soon she was bouncing and chanting along, too. "Bible World! Bible World! Come on, Eli!"

I waved the tickets and jumped in with them. "Bible World! Bible World!"

"Amen!" Dad flung up his arms and started dancing with us. "*A*-men!"

Abe rolled his eyes. "You guys are *so* embarrassing."

"Get in here," Mom said.

"No way."

"Come on! You've wanted to go since you were a little boy!"

"Key words: *Little. Boy.*"

"Oh, stop. You're not too old to dance with your mama."

She took Abe into her arms and he swayed back and forth with her—reluctantly. But he couldn't completely hide his excitement.

"Oh! Oh! The letter!" Dad was still clutching it in his hand. He cleared his throat dramatically, the celebration died down, and he began to read.

"*Harpo family, I'm very happy to present you with five free passes to Bible World.*"

"Eeeeeeeeeeeeee!" Jake squealed.

"You may attend CGN's Biblical immersion facility whenever you like—excluding holidays, peak season dates, and only until next year's end: see expiration date."

"Huh?" I said.

"Hmm," Mom said.

"But what about the grand opening?" Abe said. "Eli's Realm?"

"It was a pleasure meeting you . . ." Dad's voice trailed off. He looked up from the letter, crestfallen.

"Well?" Mom said. "What does it say?"

"Wishing you a blessed life. In Christ, Charlie Gideon."

"That's all?" I said.

Dad flipped the letter over and glanced at the back. It was blank.

"I don't understand," he said.

"What's wrong?" Jake asked. "What is it?"

"It's a pity gift," Abe said. "A freaking booby prize!"

"Hey," Mom said. "Calm down."

Dad was blinking weirdly. He took off his glasses and rubbed his eyes. Was he going to cry? I couldn't believe it.

Mom reached for him. "Simon—"

"I, uh . . . the garage," he mumbled and left the room. Mom went after him.

"I can't believe this," Abe said. "What a fake! He bought us all this stuff out of guilt. He's just trying to buy us off."

Jake started to cry.

I pulled him to me. "Hey—it's okay."

"What happened!" he sobbed.

"Gideon broke up with us," I said. He sniffled into my shirt. I rubbed his back. I felt awful. I'd never seen Dad like that.

"Hey, Eli." Jake rubbed his eyes and looked up at me. For a second I thought he was going to say it wasn't my fault, it didn't matter, he was going to comfort me, too.

"Yeah, Jake?"

He wiped his nose with his sleeve. "We still get to go to Bible World, right?"

✛

I had to do something, so that evening I went to the junk drawer in the kitchen and dug around for the Scotch tape. Then I went down the hall to our room and closed the door. I reached under my mattress and pulled out the torn contract. Laid the pieces on the floor, fitted them together like a jigsaw puzzle, and began taping.

Mom was soon calling me to dinner.

"Just a second!"

When the contract was intact, I went back and felt around under the mattress until I found the gold pen. This time I didn't hesitate. I signed.

That night, I snuck out of bed and down to Dad's workstation in the garage. I took a photo of the contract with his digital camera. Then I logged into his heavenorbust@gmail.com account. I attached the photo to an email and filled in the address from the business card that came with Mom's gift.

Dear Mr. Gideon, I wrote.

What next? "Please reconsider"? "Don't do this"?

I settled on: I won't let you down.

Typed out my name, tapped send.

It would probably go to his secretary just like Dad's phone calls, but I closed my eyes and prayed it would reach him.

If there is a moment I could go back to and change, this would be it. If I hadn't sent that email it would have all been over. Gideon would have moved on to the next Heaven Kid on his list, instead of returning for Mom and Dad's signatures. Dad would have sulked a few days more, but he'd have eventually gotten over it. We wouldn't have been happy, exactly. But at some point the cloud over our family might have passed—if I hadn't brought Charlie Gideon back into our lives.

PART TWO

HIGHWAY TO HEAVEN

6

RAPTURED!

When I first met Elijah Harpo, I knew there was something about him. I sensed it immediately. A Spiritual Magnetism emanated from the boy. He was, as they say, Touched—not merely by angels, but by the Hand of the Almighty Himself.

Humanly speaking, he was just a child. But Spiritually? Spiritually, he was attuned, with every fiber of his being, to the Unseen World. That Eternal Dimension that surrounds us, that permeates all of Space and Time. Few in this life are granted the strength of spirit to witness it firsthand.

With all my years serving the Lord, I thought I knew a little something about the sovereignty of God, but after meeting such a dynamic messenger for Jesus Christ, I was truly humbled. Elijah had a lot to teach me and I was ready to learn.

—from Charlie Gideon & the Heaven Boy!, *"Introduction," p. x*

WILL AND I DIFFER ON the story of how we finally started dating. In his version, he was attracted to me from the moment we met and, soon after, he made the first move. "*I* asked *you* out," he insists, which is technically true. But I know the tru*er* story, which is that *I* seduced *him* with my past identity as the Heaven Kid.

That spring, the semester I became a member of the ASU, I wouldn't have called myself an atheist per se. I was a work-in-progress. I used the word *agnostic* once.

Will didn't like that. "Do you really want to be a line-straddler, EJ? Better to pick a side and go all in than hedge a bet."

I saw his point, but it was never as easy as he made it out to be. It was always so obvious to Will. I'd go to ASU meetings and they'd all make valid points. They'd say things that sounded perfectly reasonable:

"We've got to destigmatize atheism. Rituals and traditions are important, but you don't need God for them. We can form community and celebrate the human experience without superstition."

I agreed. But then on the weekends I'd talk on the phone with Dad or my brothers and it was like another planet, strange yet familiar.

"We sang 'It Is Well' in church today," Dad said. "It was always your favorite."

"Eli, I get to be a disciple at Easter!" Jake, breathless with excitement.

"Hey, bro. How's college?" Abe sniffed dramatically. "Do I smell Pine-Sol? Is that lemon-scented? They get all your lobes nice and shiny yet?"

This was Abe's new shtick. Brainwashing, brought to you by libtards.

"Ha," I said flatly. "How's the Chick?"

"Same. Except I cut back my hours."

"Why?"

"Dad didn't tell you? I'm an assistant youth minister now."

"Oh. Wow. At Carpenter's?"

"Yeah. They pay me and everything."

"That's—that's great, Abe."

"You can visit at Easter. I'll show you my office."

"Can't wait."

But I didn't go home for Easter. I made up an excuse about midterms. And instead of moving back that summer, I stayed on campus. I took summer classes and got a job as a tour guide for prospective students and their parents.

"Are you *ever* coming home?" Jake whined. This was in June. They'd called to wish me a happy birthday. Since leaving for college, I'd been home only once—over winter break. They were only two hours away.

"Soon," I promised.

All through this time Will and I were getting closer. But we couldn't quite find the way to go from friends to more-than. He later told me he'd had trouble asking me out because he was just out of a six-month relationship. That, and he didn't want to hurt David, the culturally Jewish ASU treasurer who was crushing on him and always around when we were hanging out. On my end, I was super intimidated by Will. He'd had lots of boyfriends and my lack of sexual experience held me back. I was what Will and I now refer to as a "baby gay." I'd come out to my friends at UK, but not to my family—not yet—and navigating those two worlds, my two selves, even just in my head, took a lot of mental and emotional energy.

But in the fall, when I'd heard David had finally gotten up the courage to ask Will out *and Will said yes* ("What? He was a nice guy! I thought I should at least give him a shot!"), I knew I had to do something. So after the next ASU meeting, I invited Will back to my dorm to watch *Man on Wire*, his favorite documentary, which I'd never seen. My roommate was staying over at his girlfriend's—I hardly saw him anymore—so we had the room to ourselves.

We sat together on my bed, the laptop and a bowl of popcorn between us. The movie was good, I could tell, even though I could hardly focus with Will on the mattress next to me. Eventually, I asked about his date with David.

"It was okay. We're going out again next weekend."

"Oh. Really? That's . . . cool."

"You think so?" He raised an eyebrow.

It was an opening, but I just nodded. I was pathetic. I had zero game.

When the movie ended and nothing had happened between us, I was disappointed. He was getting ready to leave and I didn't want him to go. There was only one way I knew how to win him over. It was risky and dumb, but it was what I'd been taught made me special.

"Will, wait. I need to tell you something."

He turned in the doorway.

"I swore I'd never tell anyone this," I said. "But I don't want to hide anymore."

"You can tell me anything, EJ."

"Actually, it's Eli."

I reached under the mattress and pulled out the books. I held the first up so he could see the cover: *Charlie Gideon & the Heaven Boy!* He came back into the room and the door swung shut. He sat next to me and I showed him.

"Wait—is that *you?*" He touched the face of the child model on Gideon's lap.

"No, but this is." I passed him *Heaven or Bust!* Compared with Gideon's version, the design and production quality were laughable, but part of me still felt sentimentally attached to it. All those years schlepping it around, peddling it in hospitals and nursing homes.

Will examined the cover, looked up and down from the photo to me. I was hoping he might say, *This looks nothing like you*, but my transformation from small-town Baptist to big-city atheist wasn't enough to cover up the resemblance.

"You were a cutie."

"Uh, thanks."

"Still are."

"Yeah, okay."

He flipped the books over and read the jacket copy.

"Is this for real? Because it feels like some kind of prank."

"My life is the prank."

I turned to the photo insert in *Heaven or Bust!* and showed him the family portrait. Mom, Dad, Abe, Jake, and me, all in our Sunday best. Then the picture of me in the hospital bed. I was shirtless, wearing the angel wings a nurse had fashioned out of a coat hanger and coffee filters, pointing to my scar. I pulled off my shirt and showed him. He reached out and touched it.

"Tell me," he said, and I knew he was mine.

✢

Once the contract was signed, things moved quickly. That December, Gideon sent a PR lady, a CGN photographer, and a flock of Christian news reporters to our house. They took pictures of everything: our mailbox, our van, our bunk beds—us included.

Especially me.

I'd never liked having my photo taken. I was self-conscious about my weight. Since we signed in November, Dad had put me on a new diet, took me jogging in the mornings, and bought me my own set of dumbbells so we could do workouts together in the garage. I hated those early mornings, the endless arm curls and squats. By the time the reporters came, I'd lost only five pounds. Whenever I faced a camera I couldn't stop blinking, so in most pictures I came out with my eyes closed. They posed me on the couch in the living room, at my desk in Homeschool Corner, sitting at the kitchen table pretending to read my Bible.

They asked me a million questions about Heaven.

Gideon hired a ghostwriter to update *Heaven or Bust!* and in March we got the first advance reader copies in the mail. The title had been changed to *Charlie Gideon & the Heaven Boy!* and the cover featured a photo of Gideon sitting on a gold throne with a redheaded boy on his lap—a dimpled actor who, besides the hair (so red it looked dyed), looked nothing like me at age four. The blurb on the back cover mentioned how Gideon was a family friend who had shepherded us through our darkest time.

"What a liar," Mom said. "We're in bed with a liar, Simon."

It was obvious Dad was wrecked by the changes made to his book, but in the end he insisted they were superficial—cosmetic, really. So what if Gideon inserted himself into our family story? If he plastered his face on the front cover? His star power would help us reach a wider audience, take our story to the people God wanted us to Save. The story of my trip to Heaven—the part that mattered—was still intact.

"You'd sacrifice the integrity of this family for a little media attention," Mom said.

"Don't be melodramatic," Dad countered. "Some sacrifices are necessary. You weren't so high and mighty when we cashed the check."

Dad had been responsible with the money from the advance and the licensing of my name and story to Bible World. Even so, it had evaporated quickly. He paid off medical bills, part of the mortgage on the house, and the loan on our van. He'd wanted to put some in savings, but after those payments and the tithe for Creation, there wasn't much left. His one indulgence: a new computer and printer for the family.

The photo of Gideon and my proxy soon showed up on the CGN website with a countdown clock and a flashing announcement:

COMING SOON! NEW BIBLICAL REALM! ELI HARPO'S ADVENTURE TO THE AFTERLIFE! VISIT HEAVEN JUNE 7.

☦

Soon, it was May and we were packing. While Mom slept, Dad sorted through her dresser drawers for clothes to add to their suitcase, crumpling her underwear and scarves, fumble-folding her summer dresses in the hopes he could convince her to wear them to the churches we visited. She'd refused to do so since her breasts had been *axed*, as she dramatically put it—all she ever wore after her surgery were T-shirts. She had good days and bad days. There were an increasing number where she never left the bed. Others she was up, working on her Wall of Scandal. What had started as a few pages torn from Gideon's books had grown into an enormous collage of anti–Charlie Gideon research. Our living room looked like an FBI investigation from TV; all that was missing was red string.

During the spring leading up to the grand opening at Bible World, Charlie Gideon had become embroiled in a number of hot-button issues. Levi Livingston's recanting video was turning out to be the least of them. Mom added to the Wall: a printout about Bible World's unfair tax breaks, filed in the name of religious freedom; articles on CGN's recent endorsement of the Prayers First Foundation, which advocated that doctors prescribe prayer as a supplement to medication; and editorials in response to Gideon's sermons in support of the anti-evolution, pro-creationist agenda in the education reform bill making its way through Congress. All of this, though, was nothing compared with the reportage on sexual harassment allegations against Gideon from six different women, either employed by CGN or members of his congregation. When news of that broke, Mom had to take down our collage of family photos to expand into the hall, which was soon wallpapered over with the faces of Gideon's accusers.

While Mom collected the evidence of these public outcries, Dad heard none of it. He was always ready with a defense. So what if Gideon found a way to avoid paying taxes? It was good business sense. And what sick person *wouldn't* want extra prayers along with the drugs for their illness? Prayer works! Regarding the education bill: Dad wasn't a strict creationist, but he believed evolution, like the rest of the natural world, was guided by God's hand and should be taught alongside a Biblical understanding of the world. Finally, and most importantly, the sexual harassment lawsuits were all either tied up in litigation or settled out of court. Besides, there was no proof—the cases were all he said, she said, and the women could easily have misunderstood Gideon's gestures of affection (*"Misunderstood* an ass-grab?!" Mom shouted) or be outright lying, looking for a quick payday.

Mom made sure I was intimately familiar with her Wall. "Eli!" she'd call at any hour of the day. "Could you come help me with this, please?" Then she'd hand me a new addition, hot off the printer. Once, it was just a meme: a photo of Charlie Gideon's face with the words LIVE LONG AND PROSPER . . . BUT ONLY IF YOU LOVE JESUS.

"Very scientific," I said.

"The Wall could use a sense of humor." She pointed to a blank spot she couldn't reach. "Pin it there, please?"

I did as she asked, patiently waited out whatever lecture followed, then retreated to my room. She'd become increasingly erratic, and if I'm being honest, I was a little scared of her. I'd never heard either of my parents say *ass* before and sometimes she'd grip me by the shoulders and kind of shake me, mostly during her "believe women" rants. I tried to chalk up her escalating attack on Gideon to a kind of cancer-induced dementia, but even then, I sensed some of it might be deserved. Much of what she drilled into me about his depravity was disturbing. Maybe not the political stuff—at thirteen, I didn't understand a lot of it, and most of it bored me, really. But I couldn't just ignore the fervor with which Mom defended those women.

The Wall, though, wasn't the most confusing thing for us kids. We'd gotten used to Mom and Dad's opposing opinions about Gideon, but Mom's constant flip-flopping on our impending trip to Bible World often took us by surprise. She was filled with contradictions, vacillating between bouts of outrage, reluctant acceptance, and manic enthusiasm. Take Easter. Instead of plastic eggs filled with candy, she'd bought us all summer vacation gear: Hawaiian shirts, tank tops, swim trunks, fanny packs, visors, beach towels, sunglasses, inflatable beach balls, plastic shovels, sandcastle buckets.

"It's going to be the best family vacation! My best memory with my boys."

We all grew uncomfortable when she talked like that. What we heard wasn't *best*, but *last*. The remission we'd all held out for hadn't happened, and unlike our deal with Gideon, our hopes for the chemo couldn't be reclaimed. The cancer was worse. It had spread to more vital organs: her lungs, her liver. The doctors told her she had two options. One: She could do another round of chemo, which came with all its nasty side effects—the nausea, vomiting, muscle atrophy, fatigue. It might buy her a year, but her prognosis wasn't much longer and it would certainly prevent her from going on the road trip. Or two: She could forgo treatment and maintain some facade of physical health her last few months—until her insides killed her.

She chose the latter. No more chemo. Her hair slowly grew back. Even without the chemo, the doctors were skeptical about her going on the trip. They said, technically, travel was AMA—against medical advice—but if provisions were made . . .

So Dad got her the wheelchair and oxygen tank they suggested. There was even an umbrella with a special clamp for the Florida sun. Mom locked them away in the coat closet. She swore she'd never need them and for a while we thought she might not: Sure, she slept a lot, but she was still mobile and had a healthy appetite, which were good signs. She held out until one night in April when she fell on her way to the bathroom and lost her breath and Dad made her use the oxygen for the first time. It was scary,

seeing her like that. I wasn't just scared *of* her, but *for* her. She was beginning to resemble the end-of-life patients Dad and I were used to visiting.

Thank God for Dad. I don't know how any of us would have survived
without him. Dad was the consummate caretaker. Sometimes I think he
missed his true calling and could have done more good in the world if he'd
become a hospice worker, instead of a minister. We couldn't afford an actual
live-in nurse, so he did everything for Mom: helped her in the bathroom,
doled out her meds, cleaned up her messes. He had perfect bedside man-
ner, knew exactly when to be upbeat and get Mom out to the lawn chair in
the backyard for fresh air. When to be more lenient and soothing and baby
her in bed with her library books and soup. Our house filled with the herby
savor of Dad's homemade chicken and wild rice soup—Mom's favorite. Abe
and I picked up some of the slack in the housework with our chores, but I
know the brunt of it still fell on Dad. I honestly don't know how he did it
all. It's enough trouble for me to keep the house clean and my son fed, much
less care for a chronically ill spouse, take over the homeschooling for three
different grade levels, wake up early every morning and exercise to help
your son get in shape, plan an upcoming publicity tour with a Christian
television network, and continue to make routine visits to the houses of
homebound congregants.

He must have been going insane, but he did his best to remain positive and hide the strain from us. The only time I remember him breaking
down was after an all-nighter at the hospital, where he'd kept vigil with
the family of Mr. Watkins in the old man's last hours: also dying of cancer,
but at seventy-six, nearly double Mom's age. I'd been there with Dad earlier, praying bedside, telling my Heaven story. The soon-to-be-widowed
Mrs. Watkins loved Dad and wanted him to stay until the very end, so he
arranged for one of our nurse friends to drive me home after her shift.

I'd always been a light sleeper. I heard Dad as soon as he came in. He
was in the kitchen with his head in the refrigerator. Just standing there.
Staring at the food. His shoulders were shaking and I thought he was
laughing, so I asked, "What's so funny?"

He jumped and I saw there were tears streaming down his cheeks. I'd never seen Dad cry before.

"Sorry, Big E." He took off his glasses and wiped his face with his sleeve. "Didn't see you there."

"Did Mr. Watkins . . ."

"He's with the Lord now." Dad had said this many times before, always with a smile—never a quivering lip. He collapsed into a chair at the table and dropped his head in his hands. "Oh, Eli."

"Was it bad?" I said.

"I know it's selfish. I know it's God's Will. Jesus will take care of her. But I don't want her to go like that. I can't stand it. I love her so much."

"Mom," I said.

He reached out to me. "Tell me. You were there. She'll be happy?"

I took a step back, nodding dumbly. It wasn't like comforting him about Memaw. I couldn't do it the same way, I wasn't ready to think about Mom like that.

"She'll be with your uncle Michael and granddad Joe?"

It was weird hearing him talk like I was supposed to know them, since they'd died before I was born. I hadn't met them in Heaven. Just Memaw. But I nodded anyway.

He hadn't eaten, so I busied myself making him a bologna sandwich. I prattled about how we should play Elvis at the Watkins funeral, since everyone knew Mr. Watkins was obsessed with the King. We sat, listing Elvis songs, while he ate.

"Is it good, Dad?"

He tried to smile, chewing through tears. "Thanks, son."

✣

Three weeks before our trip, I suffered my own breakdown about Mom. It happened after I'd walked in on her smoking pot. Dad was out filling her prescriptions, Abe was working at Chick-fil-A, and Jake was playing at a friend's down the block, so it was just the two of us in the house. She thought I was working on schoolwork in my room, and I had been, but she'd been nauseous all morning (we had only one bathroom and you could hear *everything*) and I knew that Dad's chicken and wild rice soup helped settle her stomach, so I heated two bowls for us for lunch. I took it to her room on a tray with crackers and a ginger ale like she always did for me when I was sick with the flu.

She sat on the bed, reeking in a cloud of smoke, looking at old Polaroids. She had shoeboxes full of them, stacked in her closet. Her Polaroid camera wasn't so much vintage as a relic. It was her first camera, the one she'd grown up with. She'd used it at her high school graduation, her wedding, each of our births. She distrusted the advent of screens (Gideon had gifted us all first-gen iPhones, practically futuristic in 2008, which we barely knew how to use); she always wanted a photo she could hold in her hand, not trapped in a device. She liked the instant gratification, the suspense of watching the film develop in real time. She didn't have the discipline or the desire to keep photo albums, so the pictures were pitched into boxes willy-nilly, landing, with any luck, in the ones labeled with the right decade. She'd dump these in piles on her bed and pick through them for hours.

"Boy, this is a reversal," Mom said. "I always thought it'd be me walking in on one of you with this stuff."

I turned to go, embarrassed, like I'd caught her in her bra.

"Hey—come back!" she called. "I'm starving."

I put the tray down on her bedside table, then pinched my nose closed. "It stinks."

"I always thought it would be Jake." She inhaled—no cough. "Abe's too pious."

"Smoking gives you cancer," I said, but the point was undercut by the whine in my voice.

"Lung's my favorite kind," Mom said. "*Once you pop, you can't stop. Gotta catch 'em all.*"

She was turning into a different person. A person who smoked in bed and mixed up product slogans for the sake of black humor.

I let go of my nose. "It's not funny."

"Relax. This isn't tobacco, honey. You want to try it?"

"What is it?"

"Grass."

"Ew. Grass?"

"You know, Mary Jane. Dope. Weed."

"Oh. Isn't that . . . illegal? Where'd you even get it?" I imagined her on a street corner with a guy in a trench coat.

"Esther Riley."

"Wait. *Mrs.* Riley? From church?"

"She wanted to put it in brownies, but I wouldn't let her."

"Jake's Sunday school teacher is . . . a drug dealer?"

Mom laughed. "You wouldn't expect it of her, would you? With the beehive."

"I don't believe you."

"And that priest-stones necklace."

"You're lying."

"I'm not!" Mom snickered. "She put it in a little wooden box and everything. It's right there, on the vanity."

She pointed at a box resting on a pile of torn tissue paper, a green bow.

"She gift wrapped your weed?"

"She gift wrapped my weed! What a sweetheart. I had her all wrong."

Mom sat up on her pillows, snatched a Polaroid from the nearest pile on the bed, and held it out to me. "Look how cute you were!" It was a photo of me in nothing but a diaper and her red high heels.

I crossed my arms, unwilling to be won over. I was holding my breath as much as I could. Weed smelled like dead skunk.

"If Abe's too pious, then what am I?"

"I shouldn't have said that. Abe takes after your father, that's all."

"Okay, but you said it would be Jake. Why not me?"

"I don't know. Jake's a little spoiled. It comes with being the youngest."

"What comes with being in the middle?"

Mom puffed pensively. "Independence."

"Yeah, right."

"I'm serious. One day, you'll never look back." She offered me the joint again. "Or I could just blow a little at you? That's called a secondhand high. Thirteen's a bit young. I first tried it when I was fifteen. But you're almost fourteen and it's not like I have time to wait . . ."

I shook my head in disgust. "You're supposed to be my mother."

"Come on! I never got to be the cool mom. Too busy baking apple pies. Help me be cool. Come get high with me."

"You've never made us an apple pie."

"I meant figuratively. Metaphorical apple pies."

"What are they a metaphor for?"

"You're not going to smoke this roach with me, are you?"

"Ew. Mom."

"What? I know how they say it."

I couldn't stand to be in the same room with her anymore, so I went back to the kitchen and sat at the table with my chicken soup. But I'd lost my appetite. I didn't even know I was crying, just like Dad, until there they were: tears dropping into yellow broth. The soup was cold anyway. I dumped it down the sink.

The day before our road trip, Abe, Jake, and I helped Dad Tetris suitcases and boxes of *Charlie Gideon & the Heaven Boy!* into the back of the van.

"Hey, Eli." Jake pointed to a black backpack. "Can you get that one?"

I reached down, grabbed the strap, and nearly ripped my arm off. "Ow!" I toppled over, caught myself.

Abe and Jake were in a fit of hysterics. "Told you he'd fall for it," Abe said. They high-fived.

"Not funny, guys." I rubbed my shoulder, then rolled it to see if it'd popped out of socket.

Still giggling, Jake unzipped the backpack to show me what was inside: my dumbbells.

"Come on," Dad waved. "Bring 'em here."

I groaned. "Are we really taking these?" I'd been hoping we'd give up the exercise routine once we hit the road.

"Course," Dad said.

"Don't you know training with a mentor is part of the Chosen One's quest?" Abe said.

"Can't quit now, stud."

"Da-*ad*," I complained, although I secretly loved it when he called me that. I lifted with my legs, carried the backpack over. Jake "helped." Dad wedged the weights in.

That's when Chase Brinkley rode up on his bike.

"Hey, Eglon. Came to say goodbye."

My mouth went dry. "Hi, Chase."

Things had changed between Chase and me. As soon as everyone knew I was going to be on Gideon's show, my social status skyrocketed at Creation Baptist. Chase was the real reason why. He was fame-hungry and thought it was *so cool* I was going to be on TV. It's not like he was suddenly my best friend, but he started hanging out with me, mostly at church events, and the Lambkins who'd always picked on me fell in line. At some point he began texting me. On nights when we stayed up late on our phones, I kept wondering if there was something more to his newfound interest. I thought about that time in the bathroom a lot.

Then came the church lock-in. What had always been a dreaded event— I typically brought a book and sat in a corner, willing myself invisible— turned into an unforgettable night. After the chaperones, Pastor Micah and his wife, Kelly, went to sleep, there was always a surreptitious game of spin the bottle. I'd never been invited to partake. I just watched the popular kids sneak off to play, leaving me behind to fantasize from the safety of my sleeping bag about what it would be like to be in a dark, enclosed space with Chase.

That night, for the first time, I got to play for real. Chase nudged me awake and I tiptoed with the others up the stairs, out of the church basement, and into the dark chapel. We sat in a circle outside the AV closet. It was boy, girl, boy, so there was a girl between Chase and me.

Too shy to kiss out in the open, Lambkin teens played the Seven Minutes in Heaven version of the game, in which couples were locked in the AV closet while everyone speculated about what they were doing in there. The closet provided enough privacy (and mystery) to maximize gossip and minimize the chance of anyone actually having to do anything.

"Hey—he's already been to Heaven!" someone joked when I sat down.

The first few spins went by in a daze. The couples came out of the closet sheepishly: hair mussed, lip gloss smeared. It was done in such a way that it was obvious nothing had happened except they'd deliberately mussed their hair and smeared lip gloss with their fingers. The pairs who'd more likely done something came out looking flushed, but otherwise unruffled. I felt a little bad for the girls. Mom's lectures had started to rub off on me. I noticed the guys were unanimously cheered, but there was no winning for the girls. It was either: "What a slut." Or: "Prude. You know she didn't do anything."

Then it was Chase's turn. All the girls sat a little straighter. I remember his pajama bottoms had a print of little pineapples wearing sunglasses. He scooted forward, reached out, and spun the empty Ale-8 bottle. It was pointless—they'd never put two boys or two girls in the closet together— but inside I was all: *me, me, me . . . land on me.* And, miraculously, it did.

Chase and I locked eyes. I couldn't decipher his expression. That signature smirk of his—unreadable.

"Do-over," Sarah Beth Hardy announced and Chase spun again.

Me . . . me . . . me . . .

It happened again! What were the odds? But this time Crystal Chambers, who was sitting beside me and leaning strategically, jumped up and claimed victory. I waited for someone to point out the bottle was clearly pointing at me, but no one did.

Chase and Crystal disappeared into the AV closet. Those seven minutes were unbearable. Everyone knew Chase was experienced.

"Think they'll go all the way?"

"You know Chase has gone all the way."

"But I don't think Crystal would go *all* the way."

If someone said *all the way* one more time, I'd scream.

Seven—million—minutes later, Chase and Crystal emerged. Shy grins. Mussed hair. Chase's lips: pink with Crystal's cherry lip balm. I started to doubt my earlier conclusion that such blatant markers were staged and they'd done nothing. *Had* they done nothing? Or had they . . . gone *all the way*? Crystal lifted her tank top strap up her shoulder and Chase adjusted himself, discreetly, in the pockets of his pajama bottoms. Everyone teased them about how cute their babies would be. I thought of Mom and Doug Purdie and how wrong they were for each other, even though they looked the part. I was so lost in those thoughts, I hadn't noticed the entire circle was looking at me: It was my turn.

I didn't want to go. I was hoping they'd skip over me or just forget about me or I could pass, but Chase was watching and waving me forward, so I crawled to the center. It was humiliating. Sure, my social stock had risen—I was *in* the circle, after all—but I was still a nervous, fat kid and I could tell none of the girls wanted to kiss me. They all shrank inward and back, trying to make themselves as small as possible, in the hopes they'd be spared.

For the third—third!—time that night, the bottle matched Chase and me. Inside I was yelling: *It's fate! A sign! God* wants *this!*

But what did Chase think? That dang inscrutable smirk!

"Do-over," Sarah Beth said.

"No." Chase shook his head.

For a moment, I thought he was actually going to do it: get up, take my hand, and lead me to the closet. Then he said, "It's closest to you."

He was talking to Sarah Beth, seated at his left side, and, yes, the bottle was clearly on Chase, but angled more to his left than his right.

Sarah Beth protested. "It's not, like, *pointed* at me. Do-over."

Chase and Sarah Beth fought over this for a good two minutes. All I could do was sit there, dying inside, while they went back and forth. I would have offered to spin again, but Chase was adamant and the group's opinion swung to his side. He told Sarah Beth she could either play by the game's rules or quit. Sarah Beth gritted her teeth, rose indignantly to her feet, and stormed into the closet in a huff.

"Are you coming or not!" she yelled at me.

Not clearly wasn't an option. I'd rather have been anywhere than locked in that closet with Sarah Beth Hardy—anywhere *except* in a circle of disappointment after letting Chase Brinkley down. Did he really want me to kiss her that badly?

The AV closet was lit by a single hanging bulb. It smelled like cedar. The door snicked shut.

Sarah Beth was rigid as a statue. "I don't care if you're going to be on TV or whatever, I'm not kissing you."

"That's fine." *Thank God.* "You don't have to."

"Everyone's just being nice to you because Chase is."

"I know."

"I don't even believe you went to Heaven. My dad says you made it up for attention."

"Okay."

We stood there in silence, waiting. Sarah Beth was on her phone the entire time. She was probably texting the other girls how unkissable I was. I took my phone out, too, but I never knew what to do with it—unless Chase had just texted me. I opened the weather app. Cloudy. I flipped through my photos, which were mostly of Jake making funny faces. Phones were most useful in awkward situations like this, when you didn't want to pay or be paid attention. Staring at the screen was a kind of social camouflage.

Our time was almost up, but I didn't want to leave it this way. I wanted to make it up to her, the mortification of having to do this with me. I tried to think of something nice to say. Something authentic. I could have complimented her hair (mouse brown) or her smile (braces) or her arms (toned from tennis), but none of those felt right. And I didn't want her to think it was a come-on. I felt not an ounce of physical attraction for Sarah Beth Hardy. The only thing I really liked about her was how she was always so confident, so unafraid—or at least seemed that way. So that's what I blurted out in our seventh minute of purgatory.

"I really like your confidence, Sarah Beth."

"What?"

"I like your . . . um, confidence?"

"God, you are weird."

The door opened and Sarah Beth stalked out. At the catcalls that followed our exit, she held up a hand like a traffic guard. "Don't even."

✢

This would have been just another embarrassing memory had what happened later that night not happened. What happened later that night was this: Chase took me into the closet (!).

The entire encounter felt like a dream. His foot nudging my sleeping bag. ("Shhh! Quiet, Eglon.") His hand pulling me through the dark. The blind stumble through the maze of snoring adolescent bodies. At first I thought we were all playing again. Round two. But then it was just Chase and me in the dark chapel. Cedar again and the soft snick of the door. I was so hard it hurt.

"This doesn't count, you know," Chase said.

"I know."

"It's just practice."

I knew I should have felt guilty and sinful about kissing Chase, but instead I felt euphoric. Not only was it my first kiss, but it was with the most popular boy at Creation Baptist! I couldn't believe it. Sometimes I still can't. It's funny remembering this, and not just because it took place in a *literal* closet, but because my excitement had little to do with the quality of the make-out session. Chase was a terrible kisser. (Then again: What did I know about it?) Teeth were a major part of his repertoire. Chase didn't kiss. Chase nibbled. It was like making out with a rabbit.

I later got up the courage to ask if he'd actually kissed Crystal Chambers. By that time, the AV closet had become our special place. Dad had a key to the church, and when Chase texted, I'd steal it off its hook, then bike to Creation Baptist to meet him. I don't know why we never did it anywhere else. It just became a habit, without either of us really deciding on it.

"Nah," Chase said. "We just messed up our hair and I put on her ChapStick."

"That's what I thought." I should have been relieved, but I wasn't sure I believed him. Had he chewed off her lips, too? I had a feeling he wasn't as experienced as everyone thought. "Why'd you make Sarah Beth go with me?"

"I thought it was obvious? I could tell you didn't want to, and out of all the girls, she wasn't going to do anything. I was saving your ass."

I blushed at the word *ass*.

That spring, we *practiced* a lot. My lips were constantly bruised. We even did it once with our shirts off—Chase tracing my scar, like that day in church—but neither of us was ever brave enough to go below the belt. Our sessions often ended abruptly, with Chase ducking into the church bathroom and me stiffly walking my bike home. I knew he was, you know, taking care of himself, but I didn't know how to do that, and even if I did, I doubt I would have committed that particular sin. My Jesus dreams became more vivid, though, and I danced my nightly boxers dance.

We were never officially caught, but something must have happened, because a few weeks before our family road trip, Chase stopped texting me. He didn't respond for days. My digital prodding piled up until, finally, he sent, unambiguously: STOP TEXTING ME. I was heartbroken. I even looked up his address in the church directory and biked to his house, but he wouldn't come out. I approached him after Sunday services, but he gave me the cold shoulder. I tried to distract myself with preparations for the trip to Bible World, but he was all I could think about. Had his parents found out? Was he in trouble? Or maybe he hadn't been caught and meant what he'd said. It was just practice and he'd practiced enough. He'd realized that despite my impending fame, I was still fat and ugly and—duh—*a boy* and he was *Chase Brinkley*, for goodness' sake. He had his pick of whom to kiss. He'd moved on to girls like we were supposed to. And I should—I *would*, I told myself—too.

But I was way too miserable to move on. Moping around the house. Pinching my scar. Locking myself in the bathroom, one of the few places you could find privacy to cry. Mom and Dad knew something was up, but when they tried to talk to me about it I said I was just nervous about Bible World. Dad bought it; Mom didn't. They reassured me the best they could.

Eventually, my chapped lips healed. I thought I might not see Chase again, at least not until after our Florida trip—but then he came to say goodbye.

"Chase," Dad said, surprised. "What are you doing here?"

"Wanted to tell y'all good luck."

"Well, that's nice. Thank you."

"Why don't we—" I wanted to go somewhere private, but Chase wasn't having it.

"Have fun on your trip, Eglon." The barb had become sort of a pet name the past few months, but now I wasn't sure how he meant it.

"Wait." My eyes stung. He turned and looked at me, but I didn't know how to say what I wanted to say. All I could get out was: "What happened?"

Dad, Abe, and Jake were pretending not to watch us. I moved toward Chase and he jumped back like *I* might bite *him*. Ha.

"No," Chase said. "No more . . . practicing."

"Practicing?" Abe said.

I opened my mouth, but nothing came out.

"For Gideon's show," Chase said. He was always a better liar than me. "It's the big-time now, huh?" I couldn't stand the false cheer in his voice. "Well. See you on TV, I guess." He swung a leg over his bike and rode off.

"Bye!" Jake waved.

"You boys get in a fight or something?" Dad said.

"Probably jealous," Abe said. "It's not your fault you're famous and he's not."

✠

I never really got over Chase until college. When I finally made it to public school and joined the ranks of Canaan County High, he was always in the halls with some girl on his arm. We were made partners in physics once and our rubber-band catapult won both the distance *and* accuracy challenges. I was thinking we made a good team, but then Wes Dixon made a joke about how he thought Chase wasn't my type because he was clean-shaven and didn't I only like, like, bearded messiahs? And the only way for Chase to save himself was to riff along, so he said I was taken anyway—didn't they know my boyfriend, the Prophet Muhammad?—and everyone laughed, but he said sorry with his eyes and I didn't even blame him.

Later, my junior year at UK, when I was home for Christmas, Chase and I had a run-in that made me reconsider all that had happened between us. By that time, of course, my family had changed churches. After the disaster at Bible World, we were booted from Creation Baptist and had to go "church shopping." We didn't have many options. Canaan's a small town and the Bible World scandal stuck to us. It was hard for a while. The stares we suffered through services, the whispers. We finally ended up at Carpenter's Way, a large storefront church in a defunct Home Depot. Mom and Dad had always thought Carpenter's was too oversize for their taste. Our family preferred a congregation that was just that: a family. Small, close-knit. We didn't have megachurches in Canaan, but of all the limited options, Carpenter's was the closest to it. You could get lost in a congregation that size. But you could also hide. Which was exactly what we needed for things to settle.

Christmas was always a big to-do at Carpenter's—a Christmas service, a Christmas pageant, and a Christmas potluck party. It was exhausting. Everyone wanted to talk to me about college and life in the "big city," which meant lecturing about staying true to Canaan and prying into my (assumed to be heterosexual) love life:

"Meet any nice young ladies?"

"We're your community, remember. Can't forget your roots."

"When you going to bring a gal to church?"

Abe, one of three assistant youth ministers at Carpenter's, was helping set up the pageant backstage and Jake was playing one of the wise men, so it was just Dad and me out front. He filled me in on all the gossip as the congregants came in and took their seats. I was only half paying attention, nodding along, when Chase Brinkley walked in with his very married, very pregnant wife. I did a double take.

"Oh, yeah," Dad said. "Thought you knew. Your old friend Chase."

"Is it—is that—*Crystal Chambers*?" I barely recognized her. She was enormous.

"Yup. Twins."

Chase caught me gawking and I looked away. "What are they even doing here? Why aren't they at Creation?"

"They changed churches a few months ago." Dad hesitated, then added, in a whisper, "Right after they got married."

A few months ago? But Crystal looked ready to pop. The implication was clear. If Chase had knocked Crystal up and they'd shotgunned a marriage, it would have been easier to start fresh at Carpenter's and blend into the large congregation as an expecting married couple than to hide their sin at tiny Creation Baptist when the babies came "early." There was never a shortage of scandals at Creation.

All through the service, I brooded on Chase. Not in a romantic way. In fact, I was pleased to discover I was no longer attracted to him. I imagined Will beside me, sizing Chase up: *Really? Him?* Chase had gained weight since I'd last seen him, but that wasn't even it. College had changed me. Chase was still trapped in a world I'd left behind. He was a glimpse at the life I might have lived and I felt relieved, elated even, to realize I wouldn't have to—I'd already escaped it. The funny thing was, all while I was thinking this, I could feel Chase looking at me the way I used to look at him.

I've never had a good handle on my own attractiveness. Will always says I have more charisma than I give myself credit for. I always felt that I was fat, ugly, and awkward as a kid—and I still think that's somewhat true—but how much of that was my own self-consciousness? After all, Chase had kissed *me*. Chase had taken *me* into the closet. He'd made the first move. And, sure, maybe it was because he thought I was going to be famous. Or because, without any real friends, I was an easy mark—who was I going to tell? But also maybe, just maybe, I was a little cuter than I'd thought. Maybe Chase hadn't used me. Maybe he'd actually *liked* me—he'd just been a scared, closeted kid in a too-small, too-conservative town that would never let him be his true self. One thing was for sure; that day at Carpenter's I knew he was lusting after me. Not just EJ, but Eli, too. The college boy *and* the Heaven kid. A little of both.

We exchanged pleasantries at the potluck. It couldn't be avoided. Crystal told us the names they'd picked out for the twins—Abigail and Delilah—and that launched Dad into his Samson bit. Abe broke in to say the Brinkleys should stop by the Chick sometime for lunch, on him. Jake, twelve, and still in costume, bowed and thanked them for complimenting his performance. He really was the best of the wise men, with his jaunty beard and sheikh's turban. Through all this, Chase was awkward, halting. He kept biting his lip. I felt a phantom pain in my own, remembering his nibbles. I told them about applying to pharmacy school next year.

"Sounds great," Chase said. "College suits you."

"Thanks." I couldn't help myself: "I'm getting pretty good at it. I've spent a lot of time *practicing*."

Chase choked and coughed. He went red in the face. Crystal patted him on the back. "You okay, honey?" He nodded and cleared his throat, eyes watering. Tried to say something, shook his head. They really should be going anyway, Crystal said. Her ankles were swollen, she had to pee *again*, and they needed to get home to set up before her parents came over for Christmas dinner. They made their goodbyes and left.

"What was that about?" Abe said.

I played dumb. "What?"

✢

The night before we left for the Bible World press tour, everyone was exhausted from packing, but I couldn't sleep. I lay on the bottom bunk, listening to Abe snore and Jake wheeze. I'd texted Chase—I couldn't stop texting Chase, but there was never any response. I tossed and turned on my pillow, wondering what he was doing, what I'd done wrong, what tomorrow would bring. I'd never been out of Kentucky before, barely ever left Canaan except for Hospice Duty at a few nearby towns.

I must have eventually drifted off, because I kept hearing these noises. It was like I was dreaming in sound. There were no images, just the dark and what sounded like a radio, muffled in the distance.

I sat up. I wasn't asleep: The sounds were real, seeping under the bedroom door.

I got up, careful not to wake Abe or Jake, and tiptoed down the hall. In the living room the TV emitted an eerie green light. On the screen was a bearded army man jumping up and down, trying to grab hold of a dangling fire escape ladder. Over his shoulder, a horde of ravenous zombies raced at him down an alley overgrown with vines.

"Jump, you dolt! Jump!"

Mom jerked the controller. The zombies were getting closer. They moved fast for zombies.

Finally, she nabbed the ladder, but Army Man was still dangling and one of the zombies caught his leg. A bar appeared, flashing at the top of the screen: KICK HIM OFF! Mom pressed a button over and over until the bar filled and Army Man booted the zombie in the face—a chunk of rotten jaw went flying.

"Too violent, huh?"

Mom screamed, clutching the controller to her chest. "Eli! You can't sneak up on people like that. You could have been an unrapt!"

She was wearing her nasal cannula. It had been a couple of months, but I still wasn't used to seeing her use oxygen.

"Oh, this," she said. "I don't really need it. I just get overexcited playing."

I sat on the couch next to her. "What's an unrapt? The zombies?"

No, she told me. Not a *zombie*. The unrapt were left behind after the Rapture. They all bore the Mark of the Beast: 666 in bright red letters burned into their foreheads. They wanted to stop Ezekiel "Zeke" Shepherd, who'd been mistakenly Marked, left behind on accident by an angel's clerical error. His mission? Track down and defeat the Anti-Christ before the Second Coming.

"How long have you been playing?"

"I had to see how violent it was before I could let Abe play it."

"Mom."

"Just a little while. On nights I can't sleep."

"*Mom.*"

"A few months, okay? I've tracked the Beast to the Citadel. I might beat it tonight."

"Wow." And I thought she'd been sleeping through the day because of her illness.

"Don't tell your father."

"Only if you let me watch."

"Deal."

The next part of the game involved fighting, level by level, down the Citadel—an enormous warehouse overrun by unrapts—to reach the Beast in the Underground. The Beast's Lair was an all-white room with a throne at its center. Jesus was there, in a white silk robe with gold embroidering, a crown tilted on his head.

"My son!" Jesus held out his arms. "Come, kneel before me, and I shall remove your mark."

"Where's the Beast?" I said.

"It's a trap," Mom said. "That *is* the Beast."

Zeke lashed out with his Crucifix sword and struck Jesus's hand. The Beast retreated, holding the wounded limb, which had become red and scaly. Five more hits revealed a curved horn, a forked tail, two hooved legs, and a line of dragon scales across the Beast's chest.

"Now you know me in my true form."

It began to laugh. Then, without warning, it went into berserk mode, flashing around the Underground lair like a red comet—straight through Zeke's abdomen. Whenever Zeke Shepherd died there was a gratuitous slow-motion replay. This time his body split in half at the midriff, the top half sliding off the bottom, intestines spilling out like ramen noodles.

I'd never seen such violence in my life. We rarely watched PG-13 movies in our house, much less R-rated slashers. This was the closest I'd ever been to blood-and-guts horror on-screen. My ears pounded, my feet tingled, my neck grew warm. It was like watching porn for the first time.

"Mother fudging fudge on a sundae!" Mom threw the controller.

I picked it up. "Can I try?"

She snatched it back.

"Who braved the Lake of Fire? Who collected the Trinity Nails? Who defeated the Horned Lamb, hmm? When you do those things, you can *try* to beat the Beast."

"Okay. Sheesh."

"I'm sorry, baby. I didn't mean it." She took several deep inhales to catch her breath. "Now watch Mommy slaughter the Anti-Christ."

An hour later, we were no closer to beating the Beast. Mom was tired, but determined. We took a break. I helped her to the bathroom, then made us popcorn. We energized ourselves with Ale-8s.

"Dad said Chase was over," Mom said. "To say goodbye?"

"Oh. Uh, yeah."

"That was nice of him."

"I guess." I could feel tears trying to surface, but I fought them.

"I heard you're friends at church now. Have you two gotten close?"

It was an opening. She was fishing and I stonewalled her. I hate to think about this now. How she was trying to give me the space to crack open the closet door, and I just couldn't. I held it shut. She knew we didn't have the luxury of time, but I wasn't ready to come out to myself, much less to her.

"I want you to know you can tell me anything. I love you no matter what."

"Okay, Mom. Jeez." I used the game to distract myself from how I was feeling about Chase. "Are we going to play or not?"

This time she let me try. I was terrible, died almost immediately. Three times in a row.

Mom took over again. She put on the Shroud of Turin and fired pieces of the Crown of Thorns using David's Slingshot. She drank from the Holy Chalice only when her life was at its final 5 percent. When the Beast's life bar dipped below 50 percent, it began to cajole Zeke, tempting him with promises of power and glory.

"If you stop this now, you can join me. An army of unrapts will be yours!"

At 25 percent its tone took on a new urgency.

"You were not Left Behind by mistake, Zeke. There was no error. They're only using you to get to me."

Mom was sweating, tapping buttons like mad, her thumb frantically swiveling the joystick. Zeke's life was down to 7 percent and there was no Chalice to restore him. The Beast, at 10 percent, shape-shifted into other characters from the game.

A leggy blonde in a dress patterned with cherries. "Zeke, honey. You're *hurting* me."

An older woman with an oxygen tank. "Why, Zekey? Why?"

A towheaded child in overalls. "Daddy! Stop it! You're being mean."

With each of the Beast's shifts, Mom didn't hesitate. She struck again and again.

7 percent . . . 5 percent . . . 3 percent.

And now the Beast had taken its final form: Zeke Shepherd himself. There was a moment of confusion, a strange doubling. The Beast's and Zeke's lives were each at 3 percent.

"Would you sacrifice yourself?" the Beast said in Zeke's voice. "For their crusade?"

Zeke raised the Crucifix. The Beast-as-Zeke raised its own Crucifix and when the two met they shattered. The Beast rushed Zeke, locked its hands around his throat, and began choking away the last of his life.

"You cannot beat me," the Zeke-Beast said. "We are one and the same."

Mom panicked. "What do I do?"

"Use that gold cross on the chain."

"That's not a weapon. Zeke had it before the game started. It's part of his costume."

"Then why's it in your inventory? You used all the other stuff. You should be able to *use* it."

Mom pressed two buttons: "item" then "action." The real Zeke, who was going purple, used the last of his strength to take out this final item—the gold cross on its chain—and put it around the Beast's neck. The Anti-Zeke shuddered and let go. The cross began to glow against its chest. The Beast's life dropped to 1 percent and the Anti-Zeke illusion sloughed off, revealing nothing but a cockroach twitching on its back, unable to right itself.

Mom tapped the joystick. Zeke stepped forward and there was a satisfying *crunch!* beneath his combat boots.

Zero percent.

The Beast was dead.

"You did it!" I cheered.

Mom collapsed back on the couch. She was too tired to do more than smile.

"You okay?"

"Watch." She pointed at the screen.

The game had shifted out of play mode into a video sequence: An angel descended, flapping her wings in applause. She dove down, hovering next to Zeke. Then she bent forward and kissed his forehead. The camera view swiveled, so we could see the 666 mark dissolve. His feet left the ground and he began to rise with the angel. They were immaterial and passed through the ceiling—up, up, up, until they left the Underground, then the roof of the Citadel, then the Earth completely. They ascended into the starry night until they were beyond the clouds, the atmosphere, the moon, faster and faster, light-years beyond. At the edge of the universe, they passed through a glowing barrier and everything went white.

The television was white for so long, I thought that was it. It was over. But then the screen blinked—that is, Zeke blinked—and we were in first-person, seeing through his eyes. And what we saw was a blurry figure approaching from the distance. It was a speck, then a dot, then a shape. As it drew close, it clarified, and I could see that it was Jesus—the real Jesus— Our Lord and Savior. He was blond and beautifully bearded, in a plain white robe, and when he reached us, he held his arms out for an embrace.

"Welcome home."

✢

All through the credits, Mom cried—whether out of happiness or sadness, relief, triumph, exhaustion, I didn't know. I moved down the couch and put my arm around her.

"This stupid game." She sniffed. "I hate this stupid game."

"But you won."

"So did they get him right?"

I knew what she was asking, but I didn't answer. Dad had asked a million times. *What did he look like? Like this or this?* He'd shown me painting after painting, the work of Christian sketch artists, computer-generated facial images that supposedly used data from historical documents. It was like a police lineup. *Who's our guy?* None of them were quite right.

"They didn't, did they?" Mom said.

I shrugged. I was noncommittal on the exactly-what-did-Jesus-look-like thing. The problem was I'd been exposed to so many representations of him—from shows and movies on CGN, in the literature at Creation, the "tests" Dad gave me—they'd blurred in my mind with my actual experience. This is what I told Dad when he became frustrated with my failure as an eyewitness. What I didn't tell him was that sometimes, only rarely, I *could* still see him. Only in dreams did he come to me—the real Jesus, the one that matched my memories of Heaven. Burly, barrel-chested, with a square jaw and a perfectly groomed beard. Caucasian, but with a deep tan. Movie star teeth. I could see him distinctly, I knew it was him, but what happened in those dreams—brushing the unicorn together, lying down naked in the Meadow—wasn't something I could ever, *ever* tell either of my parents.

"Tell me," Mom said. "What's it going to be like?"

"You know what it's like."

"I'm going to live in a mansion with Jesus, right?"

"Yes," I said.

"I'll get to see Michael and your grandma and grandpa. And they'll be young."

"Yes."

"There'll be angels and cloud palaces and I'll get to look down on you and everything will be beautiful . . ."

"Yes," I said. "Yes, yes, yes."

But I was crying and shaking my head. And she was crying at her own need to hear it from me. I couldn't lie to her. I couldn't tell her those things. I wasn't sure I still believed them. Ever since she told me about the heart surgeon, I'd felt this doubt growing inside me. And I kept pushing it down. I tried to ignore it. I *did* ignore it. I could ignore it with everyone—except her. She'd uprooted my belief in myself and in my memory and in Dad and I hated her for that, but I hated that she was going to die more.

"What do we do now?" I said. "We signed a contract. How do we back out—"

Mom did a double take. "Back out? Who said anything about backing out?"

"I mean, we can't go now."

"Why not?" All while the doubt she'd planted was sprouting in me, she'd been changing her own mind. "Listen. Last fall, I convinced your father and Wade to get Gideon to add a new term to the contract. He's agreed to pay for your college tuition. I wanted him to pay for Abe's and Jake's, too, but he's only agreed to yours and we'll take what we can get."

"But that doesn't matter anymore."

"Of course it matters! You're going to college, Eli. You'll be the first Harpo to go."

"Mom. I can't do it. I'm not . . . sure anymore."

"It's a few interviews. A tour of the park, a ribbon-cutting—that's it."

"But you hate Charlie Gideon." I gestured at the Wall of Scandal.

"I do. God knows, I do. But I was wrong about the money. If Gideon can make a truckload, why can't we? Then you can get out of here and make something of yourself."

"I can take out loans."

"No." She shook her head. "No more debt. I've sunk this family far enough."

"Mom, it's not your fault."

"The least I can do is help us climb back out."

"You're sick."

"Exactly. And if I told you this was the last thing I ask of you?"

I winced. "Don't. That's not fair."

"Eli, please. Your father was right. Chances like this don't come around often."

"What about what the doctor said?"

"Forget the doctor, okay? I'm sorry I told you."

"But . . ."

"What, honey? What is it?"

"Do you think I went to Heaven or not?"

She sighed. "It doesn't matter what I think. I want you to do this."

"It matters to me."

I needed her in my corner. If she just told me yes, she believed it; yes, it was real—it would all be fine. I could go through with it. But we couldn't lie to each other anymore. We couldn't tell each other what we wanted to hear, just because we wanted to hear it.

"You know I don't," she said. "I thought I did, but I don't. I'm sorry, honey."

"So . . . you want me to *lie*?"

"No. I don't know. It could still be true."

"But you just said—"

"Look. It doesn't matter what I believe. Or what your dad believes. Or even what you believe. It matters what you *do*. And your family needs you to do this. I need you to do this."

"I'm not going to lie."

"It's not . . . exactly a lie, if it could be true. Think of Heaven like *Raptured!*—it's a game we play. It's just a game. It makes people feel better, eases their pain. What's wrong with that? You said it yourself. Gideon has others. If you quit, he'll just replace you. So why not us?"

"Don't make me. Please don't make me."

"Come here, baby." She rocked me against her pancake chest. "You can do this. I know you can. I have so much faith in you."

7

CHRIST TALK

At times Eli had difficulty describing what he saw in Heaven. The experience was too complex for his limited vocabulary. He often spoke in superlatives. Everything was beautiful, incredible, wonderful (bootiful, incwedbul, wodduhful). Sometimes he'd get frustrated, flapping his arms with a desperate "I dunno how to say!" or else shut down completely.

"That's okay," I reassured him. "Some things are just ineffable."

He perked up. "What's that?"

"It means you can't put it in words."

Eli smiled. From then on, that word was like a superpower. Instead of throwing a tantrum when struggling to convey some aspect of Heaven, Eli would simply shrug and say, "It's ef-bul, Daddy. It's ef-bul."

—from *Heaven or Bust!*, "Eyewitness Testimony," ch. 12, p. 60

THE NEXT MORNING, A FEW hours after Mom and I went to bed, Dad woke everyone up with his boom box blasting his *Pow! That's What I Call Praise!* CD at max volume. It was the *Deluxe Edition: Famous Hymns Sung by Today's Top Artists, 1990–2000.* The portable player was a piece of plastic junk that ran on six C batteries and looked like a giant, mutant ant's head. He carried it, room to room, on his shoulder, dancing and singing along. He did this every time we needed to be up at some ungodly hour, like the sunrise service on Easter.

You could *feel* Madonna's "Amazing Grace" (#1) reverberating through the walls.

That was Phase One.

By the end of the third song, he expected to see movement, which meant jockeying for the bathroom. If you hadn't rolled out of bed and into the fray for the shower by the time Snoop Dogg started to rap "Nearer, My God, to Thee" (#4), he moved into Phase Two. This involved standing by your bed with the boom box held directly over your head.

"No!" I begged, burrowing under my pillow. "Please!"

He turned up the volume on NSYNC harmonizing in "Holy, Holy, Holy" (#5). It was like our room had been invaded by a gang of vociferous eunuchs.

"I'm up! I'm up!" I swayed woozily, clutching my pillow to my chest.

Mom once called Dad's up-and-at-'em! shtick romantic. That was because he got it from *Say Anything* (1989), when John Cusack wins his girl's heart by standing under her window with a boom box playing their song. Mom's favorite pop-hymn on the CD was the Phil Collins rendition of "How Great Thou Art" (#9). Whenever it played, Dad made sure to go to her and hold the player over his head—a bodily declaration of love. Mom always made a big show like it embarrassed her, but we all knew she couldn't get enough of it.

Not today.

"For Pete's sake! Would you shut that doggone thing off!"

Mom stumbled in and threw a hairbrush at him. She had perfect aim, but it bounced off the boom box without a dent. "Jeez Louise. Some of us are trying to sleep." She wandered out again in a daze, down the hall to their bed.

"We're hitting the road in an hour, whether you're dressed or not!" Dad fired back.

"I choose not!"

"Me, too." I fell back into the covers.

Dad cranked up Vanilla Ice's "I'll Fly Away" (#6), and I groaned myself vertical once more.

✢

An hour later we stood in the drive while Dad made last-minute adjustments in the overpacked van. He was trying to fit one final box in the back. Abe helped him shift things around—toiletry bags, CD cases, the mini-cooler. Meanwhile, Jake hopped around in the yard like a caffeinated bunny, humming the theme song to *Bible Tales*. Mom and I swayed on our feet like a pair of willow trees, yawning. Still in her nightgown, she'd chosen sleep over hygiene. I'd snuck in a five-minute shower and put on sweatpants. We both clutched pillows, yearning to rest our heads against the windows of a moving vehicle. Our late-night *Raptured!* marathon was beginning to take on the aspect of a fever dream.

"Oh, would you just leave it?" Mom said. "You've got a trunkful of them. How many more do you need?"

It wasn't just the trunk. Mom's wheelchair and the suitcases took up a lot of room in the back, so he'd had to stack boxes of *Charlie Gideon & the Heaven Boy!* between the seats, too. That way no one had any legroom and everyone would be adequately uncomfortable for the long ride.

"It's tapes and DVDs, not books," Dad said. "You know how Jake needs his *Bible Tales*. And Gideon told me to bring all our home videos. He said we might be able to use footage from when Eli was little on the show. And clips from Simon Says, too."

"Of course he did."

"What? You don't believe him?"

"He's just flattering you. You really think he'd give up the limelight and show one of your sermons?"

"It's not about who gets the attention, Debbie. It's the Message that counts."

"Don't get your hopes up. That's all I'm saying."

Dad slammed the back shut and Mom lined us all up in front of the van for a family photo. She snapped one of Dad and us boys with her Polaroid.

Then Dad took one with her and us boys with his iPhone. I don't know what happened to the picture on Dad's phone, but I still have the Polaroid in a shoebox, with many more she took. They've faded over time. I love that Polaroid like I love the others, because they help me remember her, but I also kind of hate it—because of what happened later, sure, but mostly because she's not in it. She's barely in any of them. She was always the one behind the camera.

After the photos, everyone piled in. Dad popped the *Pow!* CD into the van's player and skipped ahead to the song he'd left off on—MC Hammer, "What a Friend We Have in Jesus" (#15). Mom snapped it off. He reached forward and calmly turned it back on. Eventually, they compromised and he turned it down to half volume.

Once we were all buckled, Dad backed out of the drive and we waved goodbye to the house, then drove through our sleepy town to Billy Joel belting out "Crown Him with Many Crowns" (#16). Mom fell asleep instantly. I thought I would, too, but leaving home was too momentous for me—it kept me awake.

The sky was that dim sort of dark—just a touch of light before dawn. I'd never seen the streets so empty. It was strange to be in the world before it had roused for the day. It was like the whole town had come under a spell. We stopped at red lights, waiting for them to change while no traffic moved through the intersection. We passed neighborhood subdivisions, the post office, Fifth Third Bank, the Kroger shopping center where we bought groceries, the Canaan County library, where Mom used to work and loaded books into her red wagon. We passed Creation Baptist and waved goodbye to the church.

The first stop on the Heaven Boy Publicity Tour was a radio station in Knoxville, Tennessee. Gideon got us a spot on *Christ Talk*, an interview in which we were supposed to announce the new realm at Bible World— *Eli Harpo's Adventure to the Afterlife! Brought to you by CGN and* The *Charlie Gideon Hour!*—as many times as possible. *Christ Talk* was a non-denominational radio show, targeting all types of Christians. The host was a good friend of Gideon's, Reuben Hawker. My family had never listened to *Christ Talk*, but Hawker was something of a celebrity at Creation. Many members of our church swore by his program, listened to him every morning and evening to and from work.

We merged onto the highway, Dad following the directions announced by the GPS. This was another of Gideon's gifts. His PR department had programmed all the stops on our publicity tour into the device.

Dad turned on the radio until he found *Christ Talk*, catching the sultry tones of Reuben Hawker mid-sentence.

". . . if prayer was still allowed in school. That's all I'm saying. Our forefathers would be horrified at the rampant secularization . . ."

"Has this guy even cracked an American history book?" Mom said.

"Shhh!" Dad said. "Hang on, did you hear that? He's talking about us!"

"Later this morning, we'll have a very special guest—Charlie Gideon's Heaven Boy. That's right. The boy who died and went to Heaven. We'll hear his testimony in just a few hours, so be sure stick around. I'm Reuben Hawker and this is 94.1, *Christ Talk*."

✠

An hour later, I woke to the GPS announcing our exit. Dad pulled off.

The radio station was a squat redbrick building overshadowed by enormous satellite dishes. We parked in the lot and got out. It felt good to stretch outside the musty van; after only two hours, it already reeked of cardboard and morning breath.

"You can't go in like that," Dad told Mom—still in her nightgown and slippers.

She glanced down at her outfit. "Well, I don't see why not. It's *radio*, not TV. Might as well be comfortable."

Abe, Jake, and I sat on the van's bumper, waiting out the spat. It was almost nine A.M.—our time slot was scheduled for the back end of the morning rush hour—and the summer sun was already bright in the sky.

Mom put on tennis shoes, a jean jacket, and a floppy beach hat. She refused to take off the nightgown.

It was much cooler inside the station. The receptionist at the front desk greeted us warmly. "You must be the Harpo family."

"That we are." Dad bowed and waved his hands to present us, like a reality TV host.

"Come on back."

She led us past a wooden door, through a maze of offices, to the recording studio. We squeezed into the control room, where the *Christ Talk* producer was manning the soundboard with its array of knobs and dials. Through the glass window into the recording booth, we could see Reuben Hawker lounging in a La-Z-Boy recliner, his microphone extended to reach him. The lights on the recording panel lit up as Hawker spoke.

". . . just like the Sermon on the Mount. We'll be right back with our very special guest, after a few words from our sponsors."

The producer signaled to Hawker they were good. Then he turned to us. "Heaven family!" He rubbed his hands together. "It's great to have you here. I'm just going to check in with Reuben and then I'll get you all set up." He pointed to a table with coffee and doughnuts, told us to help ourselves, then ducked out.

"Cool!" Jake eyed the audio console. "We're famous!"

I didn't feel famous. Just tired and anxious. I was really regretting staying up last night. I'd spoken in front of church congregations before, in nursing homes and Christian bookstores, but it was always in person and to a small group of people. This would be broadcast live to thousands.

The producer stuck his head in. "I need Heaven Boy and Dad in the sound booth."

"What about me?" Jake said.

"Mom and brothers can have a seat here and listen in."

Jake's face fell. Mom squeezed his shoulder.

"Only the Chosen One gets interviewed," Abe said.

I started panicking. "I can't. Please, Mom—"

"It'll be fine, Eli," Dad said. "Just tell your story like you've always done."

"You can do it," Mom said.

The producer seated me in front of a microphone with giant headphones, then left to check our sound levels. We spoke into our mikes—how weird to hear your own voice, amplified in your ears—and he gave us the thumbs-up behind the glass partition. He reached over and clicked a button, and his voice hummed in our headphones.

"Sounds great, guys. Reuben will be in soon and we'll go from there."

Dad shifted in his seat. "Won't we meet Mr. Hawker before?"

The producer shook his head. "Reuben hates rehearsed interviews. He prefers the first time he meets a guest to be on-air."

"Shouldn't we at least go over the questions?"

"No. Sorry. Reuben likes the interactions to be authentic, spontaneous. Don't worry. He's been briefed. Just be your Heavenly selves."

I glanced at Mom, Abe, and Jake, seated behind the producer in the control room. Mom smiled and flashed a thumbs-up. *You got this!*

Dad turned to me. "Remember—"

"No unicorns."

"Right. And don't forget to mention Bible World. Gideon wants you to talk about how excited you are to have your own realm. The grand opening is June 7."

"And *Heaven or Bust!*, right?"

"It's *The Heaven Boy* now."

"Oh, right."

"Don't be nervous." He cleared his throat.

A moment later Reuben Hawker came in. Dad stood up to shake his hand, but the cord of his headphones leashed him to the mike and yanked him back. Hawker raised a finger to his lips and motioned for Dad to sit.

Instead of returning to his recliner, Hawker slid cockily into the office chair across from us at the interview table. He snapped his headphones on, then swiveled around to face the control booth. The producer held up three fingers, counting down: *Three . . . two . . . one . . .* Then he pointed at Hawker and flipped a switch. The sign over the window lit up red—ON THE

AIR—and Hawker whirled around to the microphone: "Annnnnd we're back on *Christ Talk*! This is your host, Reuben 'The Hawk' Hawker, and I have here with me two very special guests. The famous Elliot Harpo, a.k.a. the Boy Who Went to Heaven, and his father, Tim. Welcome, Harpos."

Dad and I were both too stunned by the mistakes in our names to say anything. At first I thought it was a joke, a shtick—like the dramatic entrance or the Hawk nickname—and at any moment he'd laugh and correct himself.

"Come on, fellas. Don't be shy. You're on the air. Say hi."

"Hi," I said.

Dad cleared his throat again. "Hello."

Hawker said, "Elliot is famous for his near-death experience in which he purportedly traveled to Heaven and back. Why don't you tell us about it, Elliot?"

I was still off-balance by the name. Should I correct or ignore it? I looked at Dad for a cue, but he was still recovering, too. We Harpos were not ones to point out the mistakes of others. We'd rather let things slide to avoid any awkwardness, and so—wishful thinking—I prayed Hawker would catch the error on his own.

"Elliot?" he prompted.

"I was four." I told him about my heart defect, the episode I had in the backyard.

"So you had open-heart surgery," Hawker said. "And you were only *four* years old? Wow. Now, Tim, that must have been very stressful as a parent."

Dad leaned into the microphone. "Yes, it was. It was our worst nightmare. You can read about it in my book—"

"Then what happened, Elliot?" Hawker said. "On the operating table?"

"I went to Heaven."

"You mean your heart stopped? You flatlined?"

I hesitated, looked at Dad.

"He left his body," Dad said.

"You had a vision?"

"It wasn't a vision," Dad said. "It was real. His soul was hovering over—"

"Okay, Tim. But our listeners want to hear from Elliot. Could you see the doctors operating on you?"

"Yes," I said.

"Yikes! That must have been scary."

"No. It was . . . peaceful."

"Really? You must have been a brave little boy! I mean—good night alive!—I know if I ever found myself floating over my own body, looking down to see my chest cracked and my heart not beating, I'd have crapped my pants. Metaphorically speaking, of course. I'd have spiritually crapped my ghost pants."

I didn't know what to say. No one had ever put it like that. The sight of my own still heart . . . I shuddered. It *did* sound scary.

Dad was frowning. "*Those who walk uprightly enter into peace; they find rest as they lie in death.* Isaiah 57."

"Sure, Tim," Hawker said.

"*Rest* in death," Dad repeated. "Peace and rest—not fear."

"It might have been a little scary," I said. "At first. But then the angels came."

"What did they look like, Elliot?"

"They were beautiful."

"Could you be a little more specific?"

"They wore white robes with colored sashes. They had huge wings. And they were . . . beautiful."

"Halos?"

"No, but they glowed."

"What do you mean?"

"They glowed, their bodies."

"So they were corporeal?"

"Huh?"

"They had bodies? They were physical beings?"

"Yes. I mean, no. They were spirits. They were made of light."

"Oh? Like a hologram?"

I wasn't sure what that was either. I felt the first twinge of tears. I pressed on.

"They flew me out of the hospital."

"Now hold on, Elliot," Hawker said. "Back to those wings. Were they feathered? Like a bird's?"

"Yes. They were white. The purest white I've ever seen."

"So . . . like a duck?"

"No."

"A swan?"

"Um, maybe?"

"But if they were made of light, why did they need wings to fly?"

"I—I don't know."

"The Bible describes three species of angels with wings," Dad said in his Minister Voice. "The seraphim in Isaiah, the cherubim in Ezekiel, and the four living creatures in Revelation. Now, most people believe angels only have two wings, but the cherubim actually have four and the seraphim and each of the four living creatures have *six*. The cherubim and the creatures are also covered in eyes—all over! Even under their wings. They see *everything*." Dad forced a chuckle. "You don't see that in the movies."

An awkward silence. Hawker blinked at Dad, stretching the dead air. It couldn't have been more than five seconds, but it was excruciating. I shifted in my seat. Dad cleared his throat for the third time. The producer waved his arms frantically in the control room, like—*Somebody say something!*

"And were *your* angels covered in eyes, Elliot?" Hawker finally asked.

"Um, no."

"The angels Eli saw were likely from a lower order than the cherubim—"

"Sorry to interrupt, Tim, but I bet our listeners out there would appreciate it if we got the story straight from Elliot. So we can hear exactly what he remembers."

"Eli," I said. "I go by Eli."

If there was ever a time for Dad to politely correct Hawker about his own name this was it. But he just stewed.

Hawker smiled. "Eli, then. Please continue."

"They flew me out of the hospital and up to Heaven."

"The holograms?"

"The angels."

"Yes, all right. So they flew you to Heaven. Up through the ceiling like a ghost? Or out a window like Peter Pan?"

"This isn't a joke." Dad was getting huffy. "What happened to Eli wasn't some . . . fairy tale. It was a truly sacred experience. He transcended—"

"Okay, Tim. I meant no offense. I'm only trying to get the details straight."

"The ceiling," I said.

"You flew through the ceiling?"

"Yes."

"To Heaven?"

"Yes."

"In the clouds?"

"Yes. I mean, no. Heaven is not *in* the clouds. Heaven is . . . another world."

"Like Narnia? Or the Matrix?"

Dad snorted.

"I'm speaking in analogies, of course," Hawker said. "I only meant it sounds like Heaven is an alternate dimension, a new plane of existence."

"Yes!" Dad said. "Exactly. A parallel realm, God's dwelling place. When it descends to the New Earth, the Holy City will be made of gold, pure and transparent as glass. It will have twelve angels at twelve gates of pearly white. The walls will be decorated with every kind of precious stone—jasper, sapphire, agate, emerald, onyx, ruby—"

"Tim," Hawker said, exasperated. "Tim, I want you to do something for me, okay? Could you stick out your tongue, please? Go on. There you go. Great. Now put this finger on top and your thumb on the bottom . . . and *hold it*. Excellent. Thanks."

Dad hadn't moved a muscle. He just sat there, flabbergasted, but Hawker made it sound like his orders had been followed to a T.

"Now, Eli. What did Heaven look like *to you*? Aside from all the jewelry."

"It was beautiful."

"Ha!" Hawker barked. "There's that *beautiful* again."

"Sorry."

"Again, if you could just be a bit more specific?"

Specific! I berated myself. Specific!

"It was filled with meadows and lakes. Everybody lived in mansions. Jesus was there and he took me to the Throne Room."

"What's that?"

"It's in the Celestial Palace, where God and Jesus sit on gold thrones and look down on the world. It's beaut—"

"Beautiful, we know. What did God look like? Besides beautiful, I mean. Was he like Michelangelo painted him on the Sistine Chapel? Old man, white beard?"

"I couldn't see his face."

"It was covered?"

"No, he was . . . too big."

"Too big?"

"Yes. He was huge! He reached way high up into the clouds." This was truly how I'd experienced God. Or how I'd told people I'd experienced God, over and over, so many times it'd *become* how I'd experienced God.

"He was a giant?" Hawker said. "Like Jack and the Beanstalk?"

Dad grunted, but said nothing.

"He's so big he can hold the whole world in his hands," I said.

"Hmm . . . But what does that mean? What does that even look like? He reaches through the Heavenly dimension and cups the Earth from . . . space? I'm sorry, Eli, but I'm having trouble picturing it."

I was at a loss. I was describing it as I always had. No one had ever questioned it before, but he was looking at me like I was crazy. I *sounded* crazy—I could hear that now.

"Is there anything else you can tell us?" he asked.

"There were animals in Heaven. Lions. But they don't try to eat you or anything. They lie with lambs. You can play with them."

"Wow. I don't know if I'd ever be brave enough to approach a lion like that. Even if I was—you know—already dead."

"It was . . . fun."

"I bet." Hawker held up a hand before I could respond. "An extreme petting zoo! Fascinating stuff. We'll be back in a moment to hear more from Eli Harpo and his father, Tim. That's after the break."

☩

The red ON THE AIR sign went dark. Hawker snatched off his headphones, elbowed the microphone out of his way, and dug around in the pockets of his skinny jeans.

"Great job, kid. Riveting. Just riveting. That stuff about the lions? *Priceless.* Throw in a giraffe next time, yeah?"

"Ah, Mr. Hawker," Dad said. "Could I speak with you, please?"

"Sure, Tim. But make it snappy. I need a smoke."

"Well, first off . . ."

"*First off?* Jiminy Cricket! Spit it out!"

"My name's not Tim. It's Simon."

"What! Well, why didn't you say something? I've been calling you Tim for the past fifteen minutes."

"I thought it best to wait for the break."

"You thought wrong. If you'd told me the first time, I could have covered it. If I correct myself now, I'll look like an idiot." Hawker had extracted a lighter from the vise of his jeans. He patted the pocket of his flannel shirt, removed his pack of cigs. "That it?"

Dad was clearly worried the name issue hadn't been addressed enough, but moved on anyway. "It seems you're being less than cordial to me and my son."

"What's that? Some kind of jam?"

"No, I mean, you're being quite—perhaps *antagonistic* is too strong a word . . ."

"How about *yanking your chain*? Does that work? I mean, it's not even a fair fight. He's practically doing it for me."

"Excuse me?"

"This is how radio works. You play devil's advocate or else there's no drama."

Dad looked horrified at the idea of playing the "devil's" anything.

"Look," Hawker said. "You want me to ease up?"

"Yes," Dad said. "Thank you."

"Well, that's too bad, because we're just getting started. Gotta make sure Gideon gets his money's worth."

"Gideon?"

"That's what I said." He patted Dad on the shoulder and went out to smoke.

"Dad?" I said.

"Not now. I'm calling Gideon." And out he went, phone to ear.

Mom, Abe, and Jake came in from the control booth.

"Don't worry, honey," Mom said. "You're doing great."

Who was she kidding? I was being humiliated on national radio.

Abe and Jake were in better spirits. Abe didn't have as much of a problem with the Chosen One being the only one on the show after seeing how Hawker treated us. He echoed Mom sarcastically—"Yeah, great show!"—then lifted Jake into my chair and helped him try on the headphones.

"Hello, people! I'm the radio man," Jake said into the mike.

"How about . . ." Abe cleared his throat. "Welcome to the Jake Harpo show! You're on with Jake the Rake. How can I insult you this morning?"

Abe was good at voices. He'd nailed Hawker's sultry timbre.

Mom laughed. "Not bad. What do you think, Eli? You foresee a broadcasting career in your brother's future?"

I wasn't in the mood for goofing. "Can we just go? *Please.*"

"You know we can't do that. Let's get a picture." She made the three of us pose around the mike, then snapped a Polaroid.

Dad came in, grumbling. "Three different numbers and still can't get hold of him."

"Gideon?" Mom said. "I thought he gave you his cell."

"He did. Straight to voice mail!"

"Well, did you leave a message?"

"Of course I did. But that means he won't get back to me until *after* this nightmare is over. Much good it'll do then. I was hoping he'd talk some sense into the DJ."

"He's not a DJ," Abe said.

"Here's the plan," Dad said to me. "The next time he picks on you, cry. That's sure to stop him. And it'll win us the sympathy card."

"Simon!" Mom said.

"I don't want to do that," I said.

"Why not? Oh, I know." He beckoned to Mom. "Do you have any of that Visine in your purse? He can squirt some in his eyes—"

"Honestly," Mom said.

"You're right. Forget it. It's radio. We don't need real tears, just the sounds. Why don't we practice? Come on, Eli. Give us a sob."

But before I could produce so much as a hiccup, Hawker was back in the room, reeking of nicotine. He stopped short when he saw Mom, Abe, and Jake. "What're y'all doing in here? We've got thirty seconds before we're live again. Out!"

They scrambled from the room. Dad and I sat down at our microphones.

"Ready, fellas?"

The producer counted us down and we were back ON THE AIR.

"It's time to take some callers for the Harpos," Hawker said. "For those of you dying to ask the Boy Who Went to Heaven your questions, this is your chance! You've got a direct line with a Heavenly Tourist."

He rattled off the station's phone number and the producer soon patched a caller through. The first voice that spoke to us sounded snide. He gave Hawker his name and the town where he lived, but I don't remember either. I wasn't used to being directly attacked and was hurt to hear from someone who just wanted to tear us down.

"Yeah . . . so what I want to know is if *this* Heaven Kid knows about the *other* Heaven Kid—the one who made it all up? If *that* Heaven Kid lied and got away with it, why should we believe you?"

"For the listeners who don't know," Hawker clarified, "I believe our caller is referring to the boy from *A Tour of Heaven*. Levi Livingston recanted the story of his own trip to Heaven last fall by posting a YouTube video in which he apologized for having deceived so many people."

"That boy has nothing to do with us," Dad said.

"Well, now, Tim, I think it's only natural for the public to compare your two cases—Eli's and Levi's, I mean."

"Even their names sound alike," the caller pointed out, with the air of conspiracy.

"And there are certain similarities between their stories," Hawker said.

"*Let he who is without sin cast the first stone*," Dad said. "It is not man's place to judge others. But I will say this. Levi Livingston is a liar. He will have to atone for that in this life and the next. It is not our job to determine his punishment. That's up to God. But my son is nothing like him. Eli's telling the truth. He and I stand by his story one hundred percent."

"Eli?" Hawker said. "Care to comment?"

This was it. A chance to come clean, to make it all go away. *I might have lied, too, I'd say. Maybe. On accident. I can't be sure. I didn't mean to. And my dad didn't either. He really believed it. Still does. We're not bad people. Honest, we're not.*

Only—no one would believe us. There wasn't a world in which Reuben Hawker forgave us on the air and everything went back to normal. We'd be villainized like the Livingstons. Gideon would fire us. Mom would hate me for losing the money. We'd be in debt forever. I'd never go to college. I'd never get out of Canaan. I couldn't do it. The only way out was through.

"It's like my dad said. He lied, I didn't."

The caller scoffed. "These Heaven Kids, you know what they are? Products of internet culture. Their need for attention is insatiable. It's *pathological*! No wonder they make up stories about angels and rainbow unicorns and cloud castles. They'll say anything to get noticed. It's all these damn cell phones and MySpaces and YouTubes. These Heaven Kids are symptomatic of a generation of narcissists with short attention spans and no respect for—"

The line went dead. The producer had cut him off mid-rant.

"Oops," Hawker said. "Looks like it's time for our next caller. Hello! You're on the air with Reuben Hawker of *Christ Talk.*"

"Yes, hello." It was a female voice this time, sounding much warmer. "I was wondering if the boy could tell me—what did Jesus look like?"

"Eli?" Hawker said.

Oh, the dreaded question. Specific, I reminded myself. Specific!

"Jesus was tall with a beard and blue-green eyes."

"Was he white?" Hawker said.

"He was . . . tan."

"Of course," Hawker said. "From all that time in the desert."

But the caller was becoming animated. "Yes, yes! That's *exactly* how he looked to me, too! Exactly as you described him."

"You died and went to Heaven, too?" Hawker said.

"No, no," the caller said. "He comes to me in dreams! In visions! Prophecies. I know they'll come true. And he looked just like the boy said."

Encouraged, I said, "And he has the brightest smile and the whitest teeth."

"And dimples!" the caller added. "He has the cutest dimples."

I wasn't sure about the dimples, but I made a noise like I concurred.

"We've been on the lookout for an authentic portrait of Jesus," Dad said. "We've searched many paintings. Eli has yet to make a positive identification, but—"

"Did he have those bulging arms?" the caller said. "Muscly in all the right places?"

"Yes," I said, although my throat had gone dry. "He's, um, very strong."

"And washboard abs? And that juicy butt!"

I flinched. Flashed on Jesus in the Meadow. Closed my eyes and shook it off.

"Sorry?" Hawker said. "Are you saying Jesus comes to you *naked*?"

"The way God intended."

Dad blushed. "That's *not* what God intends."

"Why should he need clothes?" the caller said. "He exists in a realm without sin, like Adam and Eve before the serpent's temptation."

"Yes, but Adam and Eve's clothes were designed not by Satan, but by God," Dad said. "As a symbol of His love and protection."

"Only *after* their fall from grace," the caller said. "Jesus *is* that grace."

"He wore robes in Heaven," I said, desperate to close the book on this subject. "And a gold crown. And sandals."

"He's quite big, too," the caller said matter-of-factly.

"Yes," I agreed. I thought she meant his height.

"You know, down *there*."

Dad looked like he was about to explode out of his seat.

My face was on fire. It was like she'd been in my dreams. I had to talk myself down: *No one knows about what happened in the Meadow. It's just a coincidence.*

Hawker cut the caller off and went to commercial.

✞

The next caller I will always remember. She was Helen Gallagher, an octogenarian from Alva, Oklahoma. She made a big speech on the air:

"Almost three years ago my husband, John, passed. Ever since he died, I've been having trouble at work. I'm distracted, see. And I get these headaches. My doctor said it was just grief, that it would pass with time. He prescribed me an antidepressant, but it only makes me sleepy. Then a friend of mine told me about your book."

I had a very vivid mental image of Helen from her voice alone. It was raspy and warm—grandmotherly. I pictured her in a bathrobe with pink curlers in her hair. She was standing at the stove in her kitchen, making tea in a kettle, and speaking into one of those landline phones with the long curlicue cords that could stretch all across the room. The phone was mint green. Her robe was coral.

"Now, I never once doubted my John had gone to Heaven. He was a good man. A good husband. And a good father. Only, you know how they say, he's in a better place? Well, I don't know if I really believed that. I felt like the best place was here, with me. But after I read your testimony, about all the things you witnessed, I realized how selfish that was of me. John is in this beautiful place and all I can do is mope around the house wishing I had him back. And that helped me find peace. So don't you listen to anyone who makes you doubt what you saw. And that includes Mr. Hawker. You hear me, Mr. Hawker? Shame on you for grilling that little boy."

"I—I wouldn't exactly call it *grilling*," Hawker said.

"Don't play coy with me. We all heard you."

"It's okay," I said uncomfortably.

"Maintaining faith in the miraculous can be a challenge." Dad smiled at Hawker. "For some people."

Hawker glared at Dad, but before he could defend himself, Helen spoke up again. "John lost an eye in Korea, so my question is . . . you said in the book that in Heaven people are young and whole again. Do you think that means he's got it back? Do you think John's eye grew back and now he can really see?"

I was dumbfounded. I didn't know how to respond. Here was a woman—a stranger—who existed hundreds of miles away and she had gotten hold of our book? And it had meant that much to her? I felt terrible for Helen, alone in her kitchen, with no one to care for her—with no one to care for. Maybe her kids had all moved away and wanted to put her in a home. Maybe John was all she had and now that he was gone, she spent all her time in front of the TV or a romance novel. Maybe she hadn't mastered the art of cooking for one and she refused to go the microwave dinner route. The least she could do was stand at the stove, gosh darn it, and cook herself a proper meal. But now her fridge was filled with Tupperware containers brimming with leftovers she'd never have enough appetite to eat—her appetite was so low these days—and she'd have to throw it all out before it began to mold.

It wasn't selfish to want John back. It was natural. It was the only human response. But here she was convincing herself she should be happy for him and his reconstituted eyeball.

"Eli?" Hawker said. "He's speechless, Helen."

I might have been, but Dad definitely wasn't. "God bless you, Helen! Your words are touching. Just touching. The good news is you are absolutely right. Rest assured. John is looking down on you right now with two perfect eyes."

The sound that followed was like a goose honking: Helen Gallagher was getting choked up. Dad got the tears he'd wanted, just not from me.

Helen wasn't the only caller like that. Just the first. Call after call the producer patched through, people were thanking me, sobbing over their grief. It was the most cathartic hour of radio you've ever heard. A man who'd been recently diagnosed with pancreatic cancer said he was no longer afraid to die because of me. He used to have insomnia. Now he lays his head down every night, fully expecting to wake up to angels. A woman converted her parents on the air by making them open up to me about Jesus. A minister put his youth group on speakerphone and they all cheered for me. I never would have thought there were so many people counting on me. The calls came in and the overwhelming message was: *Thank you. You have given us something to believe in. Something to hope for. We love you, Eli Harpo.*

It was Hawker's turn to be dumbfounded. Even after his best attempts to mock Dad and me, to poke holes in my story, the people knew, in their hearts, the truth of our message.

Dad swelled in his chair. At the end of every call, he said, "Don't forget. June 7. Bible World. Hope to see you there."

The five of us sat—stunned—in the van in the radio station parking lot. Our reversal of fortune, from having our credibility questioned by Hawker to being showered with praise by adoring fans, left us speechless.

Or—most of us. Jake was bouncing in his seat, chanting, "We're famous! We're famous!" over and over.

"Don't let it go to your head," Mom warned. I couldn't tell if she was talking to Dad or me or Jake. "We're still the same people we were before."

But we weren't. That show on *Christ Talk* was the first sign that what was happening to our family was a phenomenon bigger than any one of us, bigger than the lie I'd never meant to tell, bigger than our love for one another—and far outside our control.

"This is it." Dad started the van. "We're finally reaching people."

We'd barely pulled out of the lot before Dad's phone was ringing. He fumbled it out of his pocket. "How do I—?"

Mom took the phone from him and put it on speaker, so he could focus on driving. We'd merged back onto the interstate and were heading south toward our hotel.

"Yee-haw!" came Gideon's voice from the phone. "Now if that wasn't the most fabulous radio interview on the planet, I'll eat my shoe!"

No one said anything.

"Simon. You there?"

"I'm here," Dad said. "Just wondering why you paid Reuben Hawker to heckle us on the air."

Gideon chuckled. "He tell you that?"

"Did you?"

"Well . . . it's not quite that simple."

"What then?"

"Look. Did I pay him to get you on the show? Yes. Hawker does Christian celebrities and—let's face it, Eli isn't exactly that well-known yet. We need to increase his profile before the Bible World opening and there's not a lot of time."

"So you didn't tell the DJ to give us a hard time?"

"Well."

"Well!"

"I *might* have suggested he test Eli a bit."

"What's that mean—*test him*?"

"Calm down. Hawker's a shock jock. It's what he does."

"I don't see why we couldn't go on a more wholesome program."

"Why are you so upset? Eli did a fine job. Not that I don't have a few pointers . . ."

"Pointers!"

"Have you forgotten *why* you got this gig in the first place? I don't need another Levi Livingston on my hands. I have to know Eli can handle the pressure. He's going to be under intense media scrutiny from here on out. Just wait until the liberal media catches hold of your story and runs with it. Not a lot of stations are as fair-minded as Fox News."

"I don't know if the kids should be hearing this," Mom whispered.

"Well, you might have warned us," Dad said, ignoring her.

"Warned you!" Gideon chortled. "Hawker's prodding is the only reason you got noticed in the first place. The public *thrives* on scandal. It's the only entertainment. The way that caller took up for Eli—do you think she would have done that if Hawker hadn't been poking him?"

"Next time, a heads-up would be nice."

"Here's your heads-up," Gideon said. "Whoever told you fame was fun lied. You're going to have to learn to take flack, because you're going to get a hell of a lot of it. Your kid claims he went to Heaven, for Chrissake! I need to know that no matter what's thrown at him, you've got him under control. So can you handle your kid or not?"

Mom's eyes grew wide. Dad reached for the phone in her hand, to switch it off speaker, or maybe to just hang up. The car swerved. A trucker beside us blew his horn in warning and Dad overcorrected. The tires, crossing over the line onto the highway shoulder, made a loud, angry thrum. Mom and Abe and Jake and I were all yelling, bracing in our seats for an impact—whether with the truck on one side or the guardrail on the other . . .

But Dad righted the car back in the lane, easing over this time with his arms locked in front of him, both hands back on the wheel. It took a second for us to realize we were all safe and alive and the car was still moving forward down the slow right-hand lane, no worse for wear. The truck passed us on the left.

"Sounds like you have your hands full," Gideon said. "Talk later."

The line went dead.

"This is Reuben Hawker, playing . . ." Mom reached forward and turned the radio off. We drove the rest of the way to our hotel in silence.

8

GIL BRIGHT

No one can say with any definitive proof that there is an after. Even near-death experiences, the kind with a tunnel of light, life review, or religious encounters of any faith—even those have scientific explanations. Which begs the question: Why live your life pretending to know things you can't? *That kind of magical thinking might ward off existential dread or serve as a palliative for grief, but it can also lead to a dangerously distorted worldview. It is far better to embrace a truthful state of not-knowing than to delude oneself into believing something that is unknowable.*
—from *Fallacy of God,* "On Death and Dying," ch. 10, pp. 396–97

AFTER THE SPEED BUMP OF Hawker's radio show, the next part of the publicity tour went without a hitch. We visited church after church in Tennessee, rounds and rounds of the same Q&A, selling out more books than ever before. No one questioned my credibility like Hawker, but then again we were playing to our audience—not so much Saving new souls as satisfying old ones. They all loved us. I'd never seen Dad happier. Mom was faring well, too. There were days she stayed at the hotel to rest, and she had given in to using the wheelchair at the churches she did attend, but her spirits were up. We were on a family vacation *and* making money—what more could we ask for?

Only it didn't feel like a vacation to me. My family was happy, so I should have been, too, right? But what I was, was physically, spiritually, and emotionally exhausted. The congregations, the adoration, the public face were catnip for people like Dad and Abe—not so much for me. I didn't hear the word *introvert* or *extrovert* until I got to college, and it was obvious what side I fell on. The truth of the matter was: I was quickly discovering that I hated being famous. Not like: Oh, there are mild inconveniences, but, ultimately, it's worth it. No. I *loathed* being famous. Being the center of attention, having to constantly perform . . . it was a self-conscious chore. We'd come back to the hotel at night and my face would literally hurt from all the smiling. I would have given anything for a day off—time alone to recharge, to watch TV in bed or lounge by the hotel pool with a book. I was sick to death of being adored by strangers. It was suffocating. The worst part was that in a room with Dad and Abe, this opinion was not only unacceptable, but untenable, *unfathomable*—everyone wanted to be famous!—so I couldn't complain. When I did, I sounded spoiled, unappreciative. Selfish. *Why can't you just eat your cake and be happy?*

Well, I was trying. I really was. Dad had continued our exercise regimen on the road, which mostly consisted of climbing flights of hotel stairs with my hand weights. Every morning and night, as I huffed up and down, red in the face, I imagined a slimmer, more devout version of myself emerging. Things went on like that for two weeks that felt like two years and likely would have continued that way.

Enter: Mom's favorite atheist, Gil Bright.

Three years before our publicity tour, long before I read *Evolution Now*, Gil Bright had been diagnosed with stomach cancer and, at his family's urging, stepped back from his genetics research and writing. After surgery and chemo, he went into remission, but then the cancer returned and spread to his lymph nodes and liver. His doctor suggested he forgo treatment to enjoy the short time he had left. I'd say his cancer story was similar to Mom's, if there weren't thousands of other cancer victims and families going through the same thing. All of this was shared on Bright's website in a heartfelt letter to his fans. At the end of the letter, Bright indicated this would be his last post online. He planned on spending his final days with family and friends, unplugged from the distractions of the digital world.

Knowing full well Bright wouldn't see it (or, at least, couldn't respond without going back on what he'd written in his farewell letter), Gideon began releasing videos on the *Heaven Boy!* website about a potential deathbed conversion. He likely assumed this would fall on deaf ears, since Bright's PR department had gone dark—which meant easy, free publicity for *Heaven Boy!*, the Charlie Gideon Network, and Bible World. Within an hour of the first video's posting, there were hundreds of comments from both sides of the Heaven debate:

> Eli Harpo has seen the LIGHT. There's still time for Gil Bright!
> If anyone can knock the Heaven Kid from his cloud, it's Gil Bright.
> Bright vs. HK Showdown!!! Arm wrestle for deathbed conversion!!!

Soon the campaign to get me and Bright in the same room ignited on the internet, from both Christians and atheists alike. At all my events, I was constantly being asked when I was going to convert him. Unlike a newbie celebrity like myself, and a minor Christian one at that, Bright was used to this kind of harassment. He wasn't easily provoked and as a matter of principle refused to do formal debates with leaders of any religion, claiming his books outlined his stance in sufficient detail and that agreeing to appear at a podium across from a spokesperson of any faith would only lend credibility to their delusional worldview. He did engage on the internet, though, where his posts about religion were typically facetious. He had a puckish persona online and after the success of *Fallacy of God*, he posted a series of videos on YouTube entitled "Gil Bright Presents . . . His Hate Mail." Each featured a parody of a TV-series host. In one he stepped into an Alfred Hitchcockian silhouette ("Goood eeevening"). In another, objects floated across a starry night sky—a pot of boiling water, a tomato, an erupting volcano—all in black and white.

Voice-over:

There is an emotion beyond that which is rational to man. It is an emotion as hot as anger and as ignorant as a Holocaust denier. It is low, low ground, lower than the fossil record that proves evolutionary theory; it is the low ground of no science, all superstition; and it lies beneath the pit of hell— *metaphorical* hell, that is—filled with the intolerant: racists, sexists, homophobes, and the idiots who truly believe global warming is a hoax. This is the emotion of self-righteousness. It is an area that we call *The Hate Mail Zone.*

Cut to:

Bright in a Rod Serling suit and tie.

The *Masterpiece Theatre* spoof had Bright in a velvet armchair by a crackling fire in a Victorian parlor. He wore a smoking jacket and held a pipe between his teeth. His husband (well, not legally; North Carolina wouldn't recognize same-sex marriage until 2014, years after Bright's death, but his husband nonetheless) appeared in a *French maid costume* with a letter on a silver platter. Years later, when I first saw these videos in college, I about died. Bright made a great show of slicing the envelope open with a silver letter opener. Doing his best Alistair Cooke impression, he read his hate mail in a faux British accent, deliberately mispronouncing the misspelled words and correcting misquoted Bible verses with his own giant leather-bound King James, which he kept at hand on a tea trolley, complete with silver tea set.

The hate mail videos belied his true reclusiveness. He was highly selective about when he appeared on camera. At some point there'd been an interview with a creationist advocacy group disguised as a *Nature* documentary crew, and when the resulting footage was released, edited for creationist purposes, Bright became even more tight-lipped, preferring to express himself solely in print or videos of his own making.

Which was why it was all the more surprising when Gil Bright posted

an official invitation for the famous Heavenly Tourist Eli Harpo to come
visit him in North Carolina for an open discussion of the beyond.

✥

"I don't like this," Mom said. "Not one bit."

"I thought you'd be happy to meet the man," Dad said. "You read his
books."

The GPS announced the next exit in 2.5 miles. Dad changed lanes.

"At a book signing, sure," Mom said. "But as missionaries for Charlie
Gideon? No thank you. The man's a scientist, Simon. A genius. We're lambs
to the slaughter!"

"Don't be ridiculous."

"I just don't see how this can go well."

"I don't see how it can go *wrong*. Either we Save the man and win one
more soul for the Lord or he dies and goes to hell and we know we did the
best we could for him. You can't lose when God's on your side. Besides, it's
good PR."

"Good PR, good PR," Mom mocked. "If I have to hear one more time
about good PR."

She had a point. Those days you got the sense that whatever came out
of Dad's mouth had come from Gideon's first. That said, if anyone honestly
believed our visit to Gil Bright had any hopes of swaying him toward salva-
tion, it was my father. To Gideon, to my mother, to everyone really, this was
only ever going to be a PR stunt. But Dad *believed*. And I wanted to, too.

Dad took the I-75 exit onto a rural highway, and the road weaved up
into the Appalachians, through towns that were little more than a gas station and a Walmart.

"Just think of how many people will follow him," Dad said. "How many
eternal souls we'll Save through this one man."

✥

We came around a bend in the road and there on the shoulder, next to
the gravel drive, was a crowd of television vans topped with satellites

and protesters from both sides—evolutionists to the left, creationists on
the right—waving picket signs and shouting behind wooden barricades
manned by police officers to prevent people from wandering onto Bright's
private property.

"Wow," Jake said.

"Looks like the circus is in town," Mom said.

"Death Eaters," Abe said. "Called by the Dark Lord."

To my older brother, Gil Bright was only ever a villain I was meant to
defeat. He was Voldemort, Sauron, Darth Vader. I was determined to pick
up the wand, the ring, the lightsaber—and do Abe proud.

Dad pulled the car up to the gate and rolled down his window to speak
with the officer in charge.

"No rubbernecking." The cop waved us on.

"Simon Harpo," Dad told him. "Here to see Gil Bright. The scientist."

"You can park down the road, then take a side. No crossing the property line."

"You don't understand. My son Eli—"

"Move along," the officer said.

"We were invited."

The officer peered through the driver's window, to the middle seat. His
gaze fell on Jake. "You the Heaven Kid?"

"Yes," Dad said. "That's us. Say hi, Eli."

"Hi," I said.

The officer glanced at me and frowned. "You're not a kid."

"I grew up," I said.

"He grew up," Dad said.

"They tend to do that," Mom said.

The officer laughed. "I should know, got two of my own. Well, folks, I'm
going to need some identification before I can let you in."

"Oh, sure." Dad unbuckled and reached around to his back pocket for
his wallet. He'd just about fumbled out his driver's license when the officer
stopped him.

"Not yours. *His.*"

"I'm sorry?" Dad said.

"He's only thirteen," Mom said.

"Almost fourteen," I said. My birthday was in June.

The officer shrugged. "We've had three kids claiming to be the Heaven Kid show up just this morning. He's not getting in without ID."

"Eli, pass up a book," Dad said. I handed him one from the box at my feet and he showed the cop the photo insert inside, the family portrait. "See? That's us."

"Sorry. I need an official, government-issued ID."

"Will this work?" Mom leaned over. She'd extracted a small piece of paper from the wallet in her purse—my Social Security card.

"What are you doing, carrying that around?" Dad said.

Mom shrugged. "Always be prepared."

The officer took the card and examined it, said he had to make a call. He told us to wait in the vehicle and left.

"This is ridiculous," Dad said.

The protesters on one side of our car were waving posters with the Jesus fish on them. On the other side, the fish had legs. Chants of *Bright to the Light! Bright to the Light!* were answered with *Heaven boy is all a ploy! Heaven boy is all a ploy!*

As the officer returned, he was speaking into a walkie-talkie, nodding.

"Sorry about that. Had to be sure you're the real deal. Eli, if you could come with me, please."

"It's all right, we'll drive up," Dad said.

"Can't let you do that. Only your son is allowed on the premises."

Dad scoffed. "He's a minor."

"I understand that, sir. But I only have the authority to let Eli in."

"Well, that's . . . that's . . ."

"Simon." Mom touched his arm. "Maybe we should just go?"

"You know what?" Dad said. "You can tell Gil Bright he can see Eli *with his father* or he won't see Eli at all."

The officer stood his ground.

"Go on." Dad waved him away. "Tell him."

"Dr. Bright was very clear," the officer said. "My instructions are to deliver your son to the house. If he requires a guardian to accompany him . . ."

"What?"

"Then the invitation is rescinded."

"That's absurd!" Dad looked furious. "If you think I'm going to let him go *alone* up to that house with that man, you're out of your mind."

Mom put a hand on Dad's shoulder. "You're right. It doesn't seem safe."

The officer's walkie crackled. He turned from the car and spoke into it. "No, they're not coming. The father refuses."

I snapped off my seat belt.

Dad turned in his seat. "Put. That. *Back.*"

I opened the car door.

"Eli! Don't you d—"

I stepped out. I was immediately blinded by flashes. Cameras clicking. Shouts of "Heaven Boy!" The officer beckoned me forward. Into his walkie, he said, "The unicorn is over the rainbow. I repeat, the unicorn is over the rainbow."

"Eli!" Dad called. He was hanging out the car window. I thought he was going to stop me, but then he changed his mind, nodded with resolve. "I have faith in you, son."

"We'll be right here when you get back," Mom promised.

"I want to go, too!" Jake whined.

"May the Force be with you!" Abe shouted.

The officer led me through a side entrance in the gatehouse. On the other side of the perimeter wall, a golf cart awaited us.

"Climb in," he said.

We whizzed away, tires kicking up gravel, protest chants fading in the distance. There were several woodsy bends in the drive before the house came into sight. I don't know if it was being apart from my family for the first time in days (the confines of the car, the monotony of I-75, church after church after church) or the wilderness around us (blue mountains, bird talk, that loamy smell) or simply because it was the first time I'd ever ridden in a golf cart—whatever the case, it was exhilarating. It was a taste of freedom, an adventure all my own, a feeling of independence that made me almost light-headed with delight—one I wouldn't experience again until the day I moved out of my family's house and into my college dorm.

"Dr. Bright's an oddball type. Doesn't invite many people inside. Count yourself lucky."

I felt like Daniel, just before he was cast into the lions' den. I was curious about Bright. His book hadn't made much sense to me. I'd read it and mostly felt angry and confused. I'd tried to do what Dad said: to filter, not sponge. Bright's prose was rapturous about science. He wrote about evolution how Dad spoke about God. I liked the parts about how miraculous it was that we existed at all. There was this one passage I still remember about the infinitesimal odds—one in four hundred trillion, statistically negligible, i.e., impossible—of *that* sperm fertilizing *that* egg at *that* exact time and yet . . . here you are! But on the same page he'd be openly hostile against God, and I'd find myself angry and confused again. What better proof did Bright need of God's existence than the miracle of each and every human created in His image?

The house was a massive wooden lodge with a huge porch, facing out on a cliffside view of the mountains. The entire structure seemed to stand on stilts, blending into the landscape: an enormous tree house. Three evenly spaced stone chimneys, a wraparound deck, blue solar panels glinting on an A-frame roof. The officer parked the golf cart next to a walkway leading to a flight of wooden stairs.

"Go on. He's waiting for you."

⚜

I was expecting Gil Bright to be on his literal deathbed. I knew what to expect from those. I imagined a pale, bony figure between thin hospital sheets, hooked up to machines beeping on either side of him. A glass of water with a straw on the bedside table. Bouquets of flowers covering every available surface. A patient with barely enough strength to prop himself up with pillows, much less partake in a lucid discussion about the existence of life after death.

But Gil Bright was not in bed. The Gil Bright that awaited me on the deck was busy toying with a mechanical device that looked like a giant bug on the picnic table before him. I don't know why I assumed he'd be sicker than Mom, but I was taken aback. I waited for him to notice me, to welcome me, but he just began humming to himself as he tapped on a remote control next to the gadget. He didn't look up for a full minute.

"Hand me that battery," was the first thing he said to me.

He pointed to the deck chair. I did as he asked. No *please* or *thank you.* I watched him attach the battery to the bug's body.

"You know," he said, fiddling with a screwdriver, "you're awfully quiet for a missionary. I've had all kinds. Mormons, Jehovahs, Muslims. Most of them talk your ear off. Yet here you are—the Boy Who Went to Heaven— and not a peep."

So I said, "What *is* that?"

"A quadcopter prototype."

"Oh."

"A drone," he clarified.

I had no idea what that meant either. Commercial drones weren't really a thing at the time, but they soon would be. Gil Bright was always ahead of the curve.

Bright put down his tools. "The way I see it, we have two options. Number one: You tell me about your trip to Heaven and how I'm going to hell if I don't accept Jesus Christ as my Lord and Savior. Then I explain to you why it's preposterous to believe the Earth is only six thousand years old. We proceed to volley verses back and forth—yours Biblical, mine Darwinian. Neither of us will really listen to the other, neither of our foundational beliefs will change, but a whole lot of air and energy will be spent, both of which I'm in short supply of these days."

"Or?"

"Or we can fly this drone together."

"It *flies*?" I said, and he laughed.

I blushed, ashamed of my ignorance. Of course it could fly. The robot bug reminded me of the Egyptian plague of locusts. According to Dad, they would return after the Rapture.

"All right," Bright said. "So we're agreed, then. Option number two?" We shook on it.

Bright lifted the drone off the table, along with the remote, and we walked to the center of the deck. There was a bounce in his step. For a dying man, Gil Bright seemed awfully chipper. Suddenly, his humming burst into song:

> Let's go fly a drone! Up to the highest zone!
> Let's go fly a drone! And send it soarrrrring!
> Up to the atmosphere! Up where the air is clearrrrrr!
> Oh, let's go . . . fly a drone!

Then again, maybe *chipper* wasn't the right word. Maybe *nutty* was.

On the other side of the deck, there was a circle of lounge chairs, a covered hot tub, and a table with an umbrella. A plate of chocolate chip cookies and two glasses of milk had been set out for us. Bright put the drone down on the hot tub cover. "Our launchpad," he said. He handed me the remote. "You do the honors."

The remote had a video screen that showed a front-camera view. At that moment, it was mostly trees, with some of the deck railing at the bottom. In the corner was a smaller square that showed the camera view from the drone's bottom: the solid blue of the hot tub cover.

"I don't know how," I said.

"It's easy." He pointed to the launch button, and I tapped it.

The drone began to whine, a high-pitched shrieking, as its four propellers whirled and it rose steadily into the air.

"Houston, we have liftoff!"

The drone hovered three feet over the hot tub. Bright took over and showed me the controls: up, down, left, right. Then he stepped back and let me go at it alone. At first I kept looking to him for permission. *Is this okay? Am I doing it right?* He just cheered me on. Eventually, once the drone was beyond the limits of the porch, I forgot about him completely. I was whizzing through the forest, dodging trees, spotting deer. It was like the golf cart earlier. A thrill came over me and I lost myself at the chance to explore on my own. I'd never had the chance to play with motorized cars, boats, or planes before. It was the most fun I'd had all trip.

But I couldn't enjoy it for long. At one point, I was laughing and he smiled at me and I stopped short. Flew the drone back. I wasn't stupid. I knew what Gil Bright was doing. He was treating me like a child. Distracting me with a toy and cookies. I should have been offended he thought I was so easily manipulable, but I was secretly grateful for the out. I was sick of telling people about Heaven. And I didn't want him to laugh at me again. I knew my faith was supposed to make me strong, I was supposed to feel Jesus in my heart and share His word with others, but I felt hollow inside. I touched my chest, felt my scar through my shirt.

"What's wrong?" he asked.

"Nothing." I dropped my hand.

"Come on, why don't you take her *really* high."

I meant to land the drone back on the hot tub cover, but he kept encouraging me to go higher, so I flew it up and up and up. The image in the corner of the screen retracted. Bird's-eye view. As the camera pulled back, two figures appeared and then shrank below. It took me a second to understand: They were us.

"This must be what God sees," I said, forgetting who I was talking to.

But it didn't faze Bright. "Yes, like the Greeks. They believed the gods looked down on us, mere mortals, from the Pantheon on Mount Olympus."

"Yeah, but those are only myths."

"Of course. Myths are the bedrock of any religion. The flood myth, for instance, occurs in many cultures, all around the world—from the *Epic of Gilgamesh* in Mesopotamia to Manu and Matsya in Hinduism. There are versions in many Native American tribes, too. The Chickasaw have one. And the Mayans. The Incas, too."

I had a feeling he could go on naming flood myths for days without getting to Noah. I pretended not to catch his drift, focusing instead on navigating the drone. But I knew what the implication was and I hated him for thinking it. For making me think it. I thought we'd called a truce. This was what Dad meant by the cult of the intellect. Cold, philosophical talk that did nothing more than blow out the flame in your heart, leaving only a puff of smoke. In that moment I hated Gil Bright. I didn't want to Save him. I wanted to push him over the deck rail and watch his body crumple in the underbrush below.

"Are you even dying?" I said.

I'd meant the words to wound, but Bright was delighted by them.

"Don't be fooled. Doctors tell me I have a month, two tops. The tumors are growing inside me—little ticking time bombs—but as long as I refuse treatment the rest of me stays hearty and hale. It's a deception, though. I'll be dead before Halloween."

"My mom has cancer."

"I'm sorry to hear that."

We were quiet then. The drone was so high I could see the lake of blue solar panels on the roof of the house. The undulation of the mountains. The serpentine gravel drive. I followed it like a river, winding above the trees, until I came to the gate and the road and the protesters.

"We draw quite the crowd," Bright said, looking over my shoulder.

I touched my scar again.

"What's that? The sign of the cross?"

"What?"

"I thought you were Baptist, but that's a Catholic gesture."

"I just do that when I'm nervous."

"Oh."

"I don't know what to tell them when I go back," I explained.

"Tell them you gave it your best shot, but I'm a stubborn old fool," Bright said. "Or you laid hands on me, but the tumors wouldn't shrink because I'm such a heathen. Or—I know!—tell them you baptized me in the hot tub."

"You really want me to say that?"

He shrugged. "Doesn't matter what you tell them. They'll believe what they want to believe in the battle for my soul."

"I could tell them I read the Bible to you."

"I've read the Bible, Eli. The King James. Several times. I explicated much of it in *Fallacy of God*. No—say you exorcized me, but it didn't take."

"You could tell them you showed me some fossils or something."

"Ha! Maybe." He brought over the platter of cookies and I took one. I dipped the drone down, skimming over the crowd until I found my family. Abe and Jake were sitting on the hood of the van. Mom was taking their picture with her Polaroid. Dad was speaking to a reporter. I could imagine exactly what he was saying. He looked so proud. He had no idea I was eating chocolate chip cookies and flying a mechanical bug with the man I was supposedly Saving.

The chocolate turned cloying in my mouth. I thought suddenly—irrationally—that it might be poisoned. I thought of Eve in the Garden of Eden, the serpent offering her the apple. That first bite might have been sweet, but I bet it turned to ash on her tongue. I went over to the railing and spat out the cookie.

"You okay?"

I wiped my lips with the back of my hand. "Why don't you believe in Heaven?"

"I thought we agreed not to talk about that."

"But we have to. If there's no Heaven, what happens—"

"*Poof!*" he said.

"Poof?"

"Poof."

"But aren't you scared? Aren't you afraid to die?"

"Of course."

"Then why—"

Bright sighed. "Yes, Eli. I'm afraid. We're all afraid. It's what makes us human. But that fear doesn't give us permission to abandon all reason. Especially when the alternative—belief in a delusion—distorts how we live the one life we've got."

"I don't know," I said.

"What don't you know?"

I took a breath. "I don't know if I went to Heaven."

As soon as the words left my mouth, I wanted to take them back, but instead I couldn't stop. It was like turning on a tap. It just came pouring out. All of it. Charlie Gideon wanting me to fill in for Levi Livingston. Mom telling me I never died in surgery. Dad saying it was a vision from God. I told him everything. I hadn't realized how much I'd been holding inside until I had someone to talk to without my family present. And now, when I had a minute alone with a stranger who showed me a little kindness, who let me just be a kid for a moment, who *asked* how I felt for once instead of *telling* me, all of these doubts I'd been pushing down were suddenly overflowing in the most embarrassing way. By the end of it, I had to catch my breath.

Bright whistled. "I'm impressed. Here I thought you were going to be this little evangelical-in-training, but you have a mind, Eli. You have a *mind.*"

How could a single comment make you feel both insulted and flattered at the same time?

"Do you mind if I write some of this down?" Bright picked up a yellow legal pad from the table with the umbrella.

"What? Why?"

"It's what I do. I take notes. It helps me keep track of my thoughts."

"Notes about *me*?"

"Of course. You're very interesting to me."

"Ha!" I couldn't help it. The idea that *I* was the interesting one!

"Well, it's true. I wasn't sure it was worth meeting you, but I was curious. I'm always curious. It's my natural state. That's scientists for you. My family insists I give up my work and I've tried. Really, I have. But dying is so *boring.* I'm glad I invited you. I think I can help."

"What do you mean?"

"We'll tell the truth. Together."

He said it so confidently, like for him the truth wasn't a slippery thing. But I was more muddled than ever. "Huh?"

"I'll interview you, then write an essay about our meeting. About how your parents groomed you to believe you went to Heaven."

"What! No." I'd never heard that word before, but it was obviously wrong. It sounded awful. "They didn't—that's not—"

"Isn't that what you just said? About your father ignoring the doctor?"

"No. That's not right. That's not what I meant."

"Look, Eli. I don't believe in mollycoddling, so I'm going to tell it to you straight. It's emotionally abusive, what your parents are making you do. It's child abuse. It's not your job to take care of them. To tell lies to make them money."

I took a step back, shaking my head. "It's not like that."

"They were raised in a fallacious belief system. You were, too. You don't get to choose the family you're born into, Eli. But you *can* choose to leave."

I wanted to throw the drone remote at him, but instead I took a deep breath and looked down at the camera screen—at Dad, Mom, Abe, and Jake. I saw them through his eyes: ignorant, deluded, naive. They were none of those things. They were good people. I loved them.

"Listen to me, Eli," Bright was saying. "I don't have to write the article. But if you want, I can make a few calls. I have a good lawyer. And a few contacts in social services. They might be able to help."

"Help what?"

"Help you leave."

I still didn't understand.

"Your family. Help you leave your family."

"What? No." I'd backed away so far I hit the rail. "You're crazy. I'm not going to leave my family. They're my *family.*"

Bright sighed. "Are you sure?"

"Leave us alone," I said. "It's none of your business."

"Hmm . . . isn't it?" He shook his head. "Eli, so much of my work has been about educating the public out of a fallacious mindset. It started as a lark, a break from my *real* writing. But then it sunk its hooks in me. It became a much more emotional endeavor. I've met so many people who have survived traumatic religious upbringings. Most of them don't escape until they're adults, and by then the damage is done. I wish we could help them earlier. It's the children born into it I feel most keenly for. They don't choose it." He sighed. "Sometimes it feels like I've been arguing into an echo chamber. I haven't changed people's minds. I haven't truly helped anyone. But I'd like to help you. Let me help you."

I didn't know what to make of any of that. All I could think about was him asking me to leave my family. "Don't do it. *Please.* Don't call anyone."

"Only if you ask me to. It would only work with your support."

I shook my head. "No. Please don't."

"Okay then." He looked disappointed. "I won't." He put the legal pad down and checked his watch. "Fly the drone back, please. Our time is up. It was good meeting you, Eli. I wish you the best."

He turned to go inside.

"Wait," I said. "That's it?"

"That's it."

I didn't know what more I wanted from him, but I couldn't leave it like that. "You don't want to help me. You never did. You just want to write an article about how you're right and I'm wrong. It's all PR."

Bright laughed.

"Stop laughing at me!"

He cleared his throat. "Sorry, Eli. You're not wrong. It's in my own interest to have my version of this meeting down on paper. But that doesn't mean I can't help you, too."

"Yeah, right. You're making fun of me."

"No, I'm not. Really, I'm not. It's just—what teenager talks about PR? Where's that coming from, your father?" He looked at me curiously. "How . . . do you feel about him sending you up here alone?"

"He didn't *send* me. He didn't even want me to come. I *chose* to."

"And he let you."

"So?"

"So he's privileging his cause over your well-being."

"You don't even know him."

"True. But I've met many people like him."

"That's not the same."

Bright sighed again. "You're right. It's not. But it does give me *some* insight. My next book—if I finish it—is on fanaticism. Open versus closed systems. The science behind changing one's mind—or one's inability to. Perhaps your father is an exception to the rule, but I doubt it." He seemed suddenly tired. "Maybe this was a mistake. I shouldn't have invited you after all."

"And I shouldn't have come," I said.

"I guess not." Bright chuckled. "What a mess! I typically avoid fanning the flames of fanatics, and of course that's likely all this will end up doing."

"We're not *fanatics*."

"I wasn't referring to you or your family specifically. But they are out there, among your followers. I've had many death threats over the course of my career, especially after my statements on religion as child abuse. In many ways that's been the most controversial of all my arguments. But I stand by it. I have a feeling our meeting will play right into—"

Bright paused. He put his hand to his side.

"Eli," he said calmly. "Could you get help, please? I'm not feeling well."

Before I could react, he sat down on the deck and sort of slumped over.

I dropped the drone remote and ran. I didn't know where I was going, but I huffed through the door and into the cabin, shouting for help. There was little time. I knew how fast death could take someone. I was in a study. I passed through. About the third or fourth room was a hallway with many doors. I stood there screaming until someone came.

The woman who appeared was alarmed, but efficient. "Where is he?"

"Hurry!" I said. "Please hurry!" I led her back through the maze of doors. On the deck, I helped her lift Bright onto a lounge chair.

"I'm all right." He waved us off. "It's passing." She was in the process of dialing 911 on her cell. He told her to stop. "I said I'm fine. Just bring me a glass of water." He turned to me. "Eli, I see you've met my daughter, Amelia."

"I think we should call someone," she said.

"Where's Dad?"

"The fundraiser, remember?"

"Oh, right."

"I'm calling him."

"Amelia, there's no need."

But she'd turned her back on him and was dialing again.

"Water!" he barked as she walked away. "Stubborn girl," he said to me. "An artist. She can do complex integrals in her head and she wants to paint! Skulls! Of all things . . ."

"They're *memento moris*!" she called through the open porch door.

"It's morbid all right. I think she does it to spite me. She'd make one hell of an engineer."

"Are you okay?" I said.

"I won't be dining with Beelzebub tonight, if that's what you're worried about."

"Who?"

"Lucifer? The Prince of Darkness? *Satan*."

"Oh."

"Eli." Bright reached out and took my hand. I startled at his touch. "Before you go, I want you to know that even if you don't leave your family, you can still quit this Heaven con. I'm sure it'll be hard, but you can stand up to them. You can say no."

"It's not a con," I said. "And even if I didn't go, that doesn't mean it's not real."

"Come on, Eli." Bright tutted. "Don't do that. You're twisting yourself into knots. Lying not only to others, but to yourself. You can't make something real just because you want it to be."

"But it *could* be. You don't know. You're not dead yet." I clapped a hand over my mouth. "Sorry."

But Bright smiled. "No, not yet. Unfortunately, I won't be able to come back and reveal what's beyond the veil. No one can. And that includes you."

Man was he frustrating! I hated how right he sounded. But maybe it didn't matter if it was real or not. It was like Mom said, after we played *Raptured!*—that was it. So that's what I told him: "But they want to believe me. It helps them. It makes them feel better."

"Of course it does. Death is a very scary thing—the scariest—and Heaven is the supreme palliative. But sooner or later you'll have to decide whether to keep telling the lie that comforts or to face the truth that hurts."

Before that could really sink in, Amelia Bright returned. I hadn't had a good look at her until then. She was in her early twenties, wearing jeans and a white blouse. She handed Bright a glass of ice water.

"Dad's almost home. He left early."

They kept saying "Dad," which confused me. Wasn't *Bright* her dad?

"What are you doing out here anyway? You should be in bed."

"We're flying a drone!" Bright said.

The drone. In the suspense of the attack, I'd forgotten it. I picked up the remote I'd dropped and checked the screen. It was dark.

"I crashed it," I said.

"That's okay," Bright said. "It's just a toy."

"A *toy*?" Amelia said. "What happened to *an expensive prototype of a*—quote, unquote—*gamechanger*? If I broke it you'd be livid! Wait." She turned to me, realizing something. "You're the Heaven Kid."

Bright introduced us. "Amelia, Eli. Eli, Amelia."

"Mel," she amended, shaking my hand.

"Eli's here to Save my soul," Bright explained.

Amelia—Mel—snorted. "Like you have one. We all know where you stand on the mind-body problem." At my blank expression, she said, pointedly, "Hate to break it to you, but you're *a brain*."

"Amelia." Bright shook his head. "Don't."

"I was just leaving," I said.

Mel glanced around. "Where are his parents?"

"Waiting in the car," Bright said. "They weren't invited."

"You mean they let him come up by himself?" She turned to me again. "Thrown to the wolves, huh?"

Lions, I thought, remembering Daniel. Close enough.

"I bet *that* goes in your great defense of the child abuse theory," Mel told Bright. Then to me: "You're just a case study, you know."

"That's enough," Bright said. "Eli and I were having an open and honest discussion. He's been perfectly civil. You're the one being rude."

"You both got what you wanted, then? The farce over?"

"Pay her no mind," Bright told me.

But Mel would not be ignored. "It doesn't matter what you write about him. You know what they're going to say. About you meeting with him? They're going to say he converted you on your deathbed. He made you throw out decades of work over some bullshit about angels."

"Let them. They'll drag my corpse to their side no matter what. But before I go, I'll have my say."

"Ugh!" Mel threw up her hands. "Would you just give it up already? You said you'd stop working. Don't drag this poor boy into some anti-afterlife article. He's clearly got enough problems as it is."

"Exactly! That's my point. How can we even *begin* to help kids like Eli, if we don't get people to admit there's a problem? If we don't illuminate the issue with cases like his, they'll never stand a chance."

In the years after our meeting, I often wondered how earnest Bright was about this. Did he really care about "saving" me or other evangelical kids? Or was it all just about winning an argument? Will believes that Bright truly cared about secularizing the world: freeing people, kids especially, from religion that was holding them back with centuries-old dogma. I tend to agree. But in my darkest moments, I feel Bright was no better than Gideon—just on the opposite end of the political spectrum. What he really wanted was to use me as a rhetorical device—an anecdote to buttress his theories. Up until he died, I scoured the internet for his take on our meeting, but if he ever did write it with the limited time he had left, it was never published.

"Oh, Daddy." Mel was crying now. "You dummy. There's no convincing them. Haven't you learned that by now? Aren't you tired? You've got to be tired. *I'm* tired."

"I know, love." He held out his arms and Mel climbed into the chair with him, laid her head on his shoulder, and wiped away her tears.

"I'm tired of being the daughter of that mean ol' atheist."

"The godless man," Bright said.

"The loathsome heathen."

"The vile infidel."

"Darwin's Chihuahua."

"Hey," Bright said. "I thought I'd been upgraded to poodle."

Mel laughed. "Fine. Darwin's poodle. Happy?"

They'd forgotten me. I just stood there, embarrassed.

"Gil? Gil!" someone was calling from the house.

"We're out here!" Mel yelled.

A slim man in a tuxedo rushed out onto the deck. "What are you doing out here? You're supposed to be in bed."

"That's what *I* told him!" Mel said.

"You see how they baby me?" Bright said to me.

The man in the tux turned. "Who're you?"

"He's the Heaven Boy!" Mel said. "He's come to smite us all."

"Gil," the man said. "Why is the Heaven Boy on our deck?"

"I invited him." Bright turned to me. "Please excuse my husband. He's *very* rude."

Husband! The word clanged like a bell in my chest.

The husband said, "I thought we decided—"

"*You* decided. You never let me decide anything anymore."

Mel and the husband exchanged glances.

"I see you!" Bright said. "I know what that look means. *Daddy's gone senile. His illness has turned his brain to mush.*"

The husband sighed. "Mel said you fainted."

"I did not! I was parched, that's all."

"Let's get you inside. It's blazing out here." He helped Bright to his feet. They swayed in each other's arms.

"You look quite dashing," Bright said. "I haven't seen you dressed up in ages."

"Compliments will only get you so far."

They kissed. I looked away.

How can I describe what I felt in that moment? Even after what happened with Chase, I'd never seen two men do that before. And so casually! Right out in the open! I knew what I was supposed to feel, what Dad and Abe would have felt, but it looked nothing like a sin. This wasn't *practice*. This was what husbands (*husbands!*) did. It came so naturally to them. It opened up something in me I couldn't yet face. And when I eventually did, it didn't come naturally. Not for a long time. While dating Will, while engaged to Will, while *married* to Will, it took years before I could casually kiss him in front of another person like that.

"Your gayness is freaking out the Heaven Boy," Mel said.

She was right. I was freaking out, but it wasn't just the kiss. I looked at Bright with his daughter and his husband and I couldn't help but imagine another life for myself. A universe in which I *did* leave my family, in which I was adopted by the Brights and flew drones and attended fundraisers and painted skulls, in which I was raised to live for this world, not the next. I didn't know what that version of Eli Harpo—Eli *Bright*—would look like, or if I would want to be that me, or if that me was even still me. I had only the one self. That one in four hundred trillion. I was the me standing there, terrified, because Gil Bright was Amelia's father and this man's husband and part of me still believed he was going to die and go straight to hell, because he didn't believe in it. He didn't know the danger that awaited him. I could not envision this man burning for all eternity in a lake of fire. This man with his soft brown slippers, his easygoing laugh, his twinkling eyes. He seemed so . . . so . . . *genuine*. I liked Bright. I couldn't imagine him damned, but I believed it. I believed it and it scared me and I had to do something to stop it.

So before they could send me away, I fell down on my knees and I begged him to accept Jesus Christ as his Lord and Savior and get baptized before it was too late. What could it hurt? Do it for me, I said. Do it for your family. What did he have to lose? If he was right, it wouldn't matter—nothing mattered—he'd said it himself. *Poof!* But if he was wrong, if there was the slightest possibility he was mistaken, he had everything to gain.

"We wouldn't have to tell anybody. I'll tell them you said no. I promise.

But Jesus would know. God would, too. And you'd be Saved. You wouldn't have to be afraid to die. You'd be safe."

I was sobbing, begging Bright to reconsider, breaking my promise, giving him a chance. I still cringe remembering this. When I first told Will about meeting his hero, I left this part out. I told him about flying the drone, about the skull-painting daughter and the dashing tuxedoed husband. When I eventually came clean, he looked so embarrassed for me. He told me it was okay, that I was a kid and it was my family's fault. But he looked really uncomfortable. He looked the way the Brights looked in that moment.

All three of them stared at me, shocked.

Then Mel snorted. The man in the tux rolled his eyes. Bright looked at me with great pity. He felt sorry for me.

"Get up, Eli. It's time to go home."

✢

Only I wasn't going home. Back to my family, but not home.

I was no longer Daniel, but Moses, coming down from Mount Horeb. I was supposed to bring something back, but I had nothing to show for it. No stone tablets. No voice of God.

I hadn't defeated the villain; I'd been corrupted by him. Recruited to the Death Eaters. Seduced by the One Ring. Turned to the Dark Side. That's how Abe would see it.

I could hear the protesters chanting before I could see them. My family would be waiting for me. They'd all want to know.

What could I tell them? That Gil Bright thought I was a victim of child abuse? That I'd seen two men kiss and my heart sung? That in a moment of weakness I wished I could trade places with Amelia Bright? I couldn't say any of that.

So I told them Gil Bright said he'd think about it. He'd read his Bible and do some soul-searching. That was the most we could hope for. I did not tell them we prayed together or that I converted him. I did not say how he and his family made me feel. They did not know, they had no idea, that it was me, not him—I was the one who'd been changed.

9

SIMON SAYS

When I asked Eli about what happened in Heaven, I was very careful never to ask leading questions or fill in any blanks. I approached his testimony with a skeptical mindset, vigilant against flights of the imagination or any signs of exaggeration. I even tested him, deliberately trying to trip him up—only to have his account authenticated by the Bible again and again. For instance, when he told me about the lions, I said, "Oh, well, I hope they have plenty of steaks for them to eat."

Eli giggled like I was being silly. "Lions don't eat steak *in Heaven, Daddy."*

"They don't?"

"No!"

"Then what do *they eat?"*

"Grass."

"Grass? Like in our yard?"

"No, the yellow grass, Daddy!"

"Oh. Okay. So strictly vegetarian, then?"

At age four, Eli didn't yet know the word for hay *and his exposure to the Bible was limited to the classic stories retold in his children's books: Adam and Eve, Noah's ark, Jonah and the whale. He certainly hadn't read Isaiah, where it explicitly states:* The wolf and the lamb shall feed together, and the lion shall eat straw like the ox.

I was continually awed by my little man. Everything he told us he'd
witnessed firsthand matched Scripture perfectly.
—from *Heaven or Bust!*, "God's Menagerie," ch. 18, pp. 103–104

WE DROVE TO OUR HOTEL in Atlanta. We were all tired from the
drive, but I did three sets of weights up and down five floors without
complaint. For once, the muscle ache felt good, like a kind of atonement
for my failure with the Brights. After I showered I was ready to crash, but
Jake, who'd napped in the car, was bouncing off the walls. Mom tucked
him in next to me and he kept tossing and turning, kicking me beneath
the sheets. Finally, Dad hooked up the VCR he'd brought from home and
put in a *Bible Tales* tape.

"Just one episode, then bedtime," Mom said.

Soon Jake settled down and everyone fell asleep to the sounds of Logan
and Emma summing up their latest Biblical time-travel report. Everyone
but me. My body was aching, but my mind was alert. I couldn't stop thinking about Gil Bright and his husband. I was also obsessively checking my
phone. In a moment of weakness I blamed on the Brights, I'd texted Chase
I missed him. No response.

The *Bible Tales* episode ended and Jake begged for another. I took the
keys from Dad's bedside table and hobbled out to the van. Dug around all
the *Heaven Boy!* boxes in the back until I found the one with the tapes. I
picked out a few favorites and reached up slowly to close the hatchback,
careful with my sore arms, when I spotted the box marked *Simon Says*.

I opened it.

DVDs, neatly labeled in Dad's handwriting: *Simon Says 2008, Simon
Says 2007, Simon Says 2006 . . . HoB! 2005, HoB! 2004, HoB! 2003 . . .*

Beneath that: VHS tapes. I pulled one out.

Eli #13 (8/12/99).

Back in the hotel room, Jake had fallen asleep, the TV emitting a blue
screen. I put the box down on the bed, arms aching, and sorted through it

until I found the earliest tape: *Eli #1 (7/20/98)*. The date was a week after my heart surgery. I removed the tape from its sleeve, fed it into the VCR, and lowered the TV's brightness and volume to not wake anybody. I hit play.

On-screen appeared a little redheaded boy with freckles. He wore blue jean overalls and was seated at a card table in front of a white wall with a wooden cross. I recognized it: Dad's workstation in the garage.

"Okay, Eli," Dad said, off camera. "You comfortable?"

Four-year-old Eli fidgeted in his seat; it was a lawn chair I recognized. The lime-green one. Only it hadn't rusted yet. It looked brand-new.

Eli stared directly through the screen. It gave me chills, making eye contact with my younger self.

"Don't look at the camera," Dad said. "Look at me."

Eli's gaze shifted upward.

"Good. Now I'm just going to ask you a few questions, okay?"

"Uh-huh," Eli said.

"Okay good. Let's start. Can you tell me what happened at the hospital, Eli?"

"I went to the hospital," Eli said.

"Yes, good. You went to the hospital and what happened there?"

"I got to eat a banana pudding and in the banana pudding they have the crackers . . . And the cookie crackers, they're on the top."

"You mean vanilla wafers?"

"Yeah."

"I bet those were good, huh?"

"Yum!"

"Okay, but what happened before that at the hospital, hmm? Why were you there?"

"I got stitches." Eli toyed with the buckle of his overalls.

"Why did you have stitches? Did you have surgery?"

"Yeah." Now he was earnestly trying to remove one of the overall straps.

"Are you trying to take off your shirt so I can see?"

"Yeah."

"That's okay, Eli. You don't have to show me right now."

"Okay."

"Why did you have surgery?"

"So they could fix my heart."

"Right. And what happened in the surgery?"

"I went sleepy."

"I know you went sleepy. But what happened *after* you fell asleep?"

"I waked up and Mommy was there and you were there and they gave me the banana pudding with the crackers."

A grunt of frustration. "What about *before* the banana pudding? Do you remember what you told the nurse when you woke up?"

"She said I was a brave boy."

"Yes, you were very brave, Eli. But what did you tell the nurse? You remember?"

Eli squinted. He played with the buckle of his overalls.

"Come on, Eli. I know you remember."

Eli frowned deeply. He squirmed in the seat.

". . . about the angels?" Dad said.

"The angels?"

"Yes! Yes, the angels. Tell me about the angels, Eli."

"I saw the angels?"

"What did they look like?"

"They were . . . pretty?"

"Can you describe them? Did they have wings and halos?"

"Yes . . . no."

"Yes, wings? No, halos?"

"I don't know."

"Where did they take you, Eli? Did they take you to Heaven?"

"I don't know."

"Because that's what you told the nurse when you woke up. You said you went to Heaven. You remember?"

"Okay."

"It's important that you remember, Eli. You need to remember."

Eli started crying. There was the sound of a door opening, footsteps.

"Simon!" Mom's voice. "What are you doing? He's barely home from the hospital and you're out here grilling him about—"

The camera went shaky; there was a clicking noise, the video ended.

I switched the first tape for *Eli #2 (7/23/98)*. In this one I wore a red Vacation Bible School T-shirt.

"Okay," Dad said, again off camera. "Let's see it."

Eli lifted his shirt and turned to the side to show off his stitches.

"There it is! The battle wound. Does it hurt?"

Eli giggled. "No."

"All right," Dad said. "Put your shirt down."

Eli obeyed.

"Today I want to talk about what you did when you got to Heaven. Okay?"

"Okay."

"Good. Now who did you meet there?"

"Um . . . Jesus?"

"Jesus? You met Jesus! I knew it. What was he like?"

"He was big and he had a beard."

"What else?"

"He showed me Heaven."

"What did he show you?"

"The clouds."

"And were there mansions?"

"What's that?"

"A big house."

"Bigger than our house?"

Dad laughed. "Much. In John 14:2, Jesus says, 'In my Father's house there are many mansions . . . I go to prepare a place for you.'"

"Okay."

"So . . . did you see them? The big houses?"

"Yeah."

"And?"

"They're big."

"And?"

Eli tilted his head. ". . . you live with Jesus?"

"That's right! That's right, Eli. Just like the Bible says."

Eli beamed.

"Did you meet anyone else in Heaven?" Dad said. "Someone who died?"

"Yeah," Eli said.

"Who?"

"Um . . . in the picture."

"What picture? Wait." There was the sound of a chair scooting back. "I'll be right back. Just a sec." Footsteps. A door opening.

Little Eli, alone in the garage. He sat, looking around, swinging his legs in the chair, humming to himself. Then he climbed down with a mischievous look. He walked around the table and peered into the camera, his nostrils grown huge. The image jostled a little.

Footsteps again.

Eli scurried back to his seat.

"Did you just touch my camera?"

Eli shook his head, sitting on his hands.

For the first time, Dad stepped on-screen. He crossed his arms.

"You rascal." He ruffled Little Eli's hair. "Can't turn my back for a second, huh?"

"Sorry."

"That's okay. You can play with Daddy's camera later. But you can't lie to me, all right? It's very important that you don't lie. You hear?"

Eli nodded.

"Now. I brought you a few pictures Mom had hanging on the wall. You think you could tell me if one of them is the person you saw in Heaven?"

"Yeah."

He held up a photo of Pepaw, holding baby Abe in the hospital.

"Um . . ."

"It's okay. Take your time."

Eli shook his head.

"No? Okay. How about . . ." Next was the photo of Memaw in her garden on Easter.

Eli sighed. "I don't want to play questions anymore."

"Just a few more and then we'll take a break. Was Memaw there?"

"Yeah."

"She was? Did she look like this?"

"No."

"She didn't?"

"I don't know." Eli propped his head in his hand, elbow on the table.

"Wait a minute. Wait. A. Minute. She . . . of course!"

Sound of Dad hurrying back into the house, off camera. This time Eli didn't go for the camera. He folded his arms and put his head on the table like he was taking a nap. Dad soon returned with an old photo album. He dropped it on the table—Eli sat up, startled—and Dad began flipping through the oversize pages.

"Where is it? Where . . . is . . . it . . ."

Eli drummed his fingers on the table, a gesture of impatience he'd clearly picked up from an adult.

"Aha!" Dad peeled back the plastic wrap and unstuck one of the photos. He admired it for a moment, then showed Eli. "Is this who you saw?"

"Daddy, I'm tired."

"Last question, I promise. Is this the person you saw in Heaven? Is it?"

Eli looked at the picture.

I knew which one it was. Memaw's wedding photo. I watched my younger self struggle to remember. He didn't struggle for long. His blinks had grown longer and longer. He yawned and stretched. He nodded.

"Yes, Daddy."

"I knew it!" Dad was giddy. "I just knew it! *Known as you are known!*"

He bounced over to the camera and held up the photograph: Memaw in her wedding dress, age twenty-two. "Corinthians 13:12. 'For now we see through a glass, darkly, but then face to face . . . then shall I know even as also I am known.' This proves it. He would not have seen her as she died, but as she was *known*—in the prime of her life."

Dad went on elaborating, but I wasn't paying him any attention. Neither was my younger self, who slid sleepily off his chair, trudged through the door to the kitchen, and left Dad alone, ranting in the garage.

I skipped ahead in the stack: *Eli #13 (8/12/99)*.

This Eli was older. He wore a *Bible Tales* T-shirt and jean shorts. He no longer fidgeted in the chair, but sat waiting patiently, hands folded in his lap. The camera adjusted to center him in the frame. There were no questions this time.

"Okay, Eli," Dad said. "When you're ready."

"Hi," Eli said. "My name is Eli Harpo. I'm five." He waved his hand. Five fingers. "When I was four I went to Heaven. I had to go to the hospital, because of my heart. That's when I died and went to Heaven. The angels flew me up into the clouds. I met Jesus and lived in his mansion. My Memaw was there, too. But she was young and pretty, not old and ugly. I met my older sister, Dinah. Jesus told me it was time to go back and tell everyone about Heaven. So I woke up in the hospital and . . . and . . ."

"'And now I'm spreading the Word of God,'" Simon said.

"And I'm saying the Words of God," Eli said.

"Close enough. Also, make sure you say heart *surgery*. And you didn't live in Jesus's mansion. He gave you a tour of it, remember?"

Eli nodded.

"And don't call Memaw ugly. That's not very nice. Old is okay, but not ugly. Try it again."

Eli recited his testimony once more, but I didn't hear it this time, because Dad had thrown back the covers of his hotel bed and sat up. He covered his eyes to block light from the TV. "Turn it off."

"No," I said.

Dad put on his glasses, checked the alarm clock. "It's three in the morning."

I glared at him. "I've been watching your videos."

"You can watch them tomorrow."

He padded into the bathroom. I listened to him pee and let the tape keep playing. I just sat there, seething, holding my sore arms. I tried to think of what to say to him, but all rational thought had been swept away, first by shock and then by this cold rage. When he came back out he paused in front of the screen.

"Aww. You were such a cute kid." He turned it off.

The room was dark, but only for a second. I turned on the bedside lamp. Mom groaned in her sleep. Abe rolled over.

"What are you doing?" Dad said. "Go to sleep."

"You made me lie," I said.

"What are you talking about?"

"Heaven!"

Dad shushed me. "What's wrong with you? You'll wake the whole hotel."

Mom lifted her head. "Eli? What time is it?"

"Family meeting," I said, my voice quivering. "Time for a family meeting!"

"It's the middle of the night," Dad said. "In the morning."

"I want to talk *now.*" I shuffled around the room, turning on all the lights.

Dad watched me, bewildered. Abe put a pillow over his head. Jake slept on. Mom got slowly out of bed. My chest felt heavy and I was clutching it. Mom sat me down on the couch by the mini-fridge. Dad got me a cup of water and Mom sat beside me, rubbing my back. "Breathe . . . just breathe." I was having a panic attack.

Dad tried to be patient. "Tell us what's wrong."

"The videos."

"What about them?"

"You were—you were—"

I didn't yet have the vocabulary for what was being done to me in those videos. Years later, in Psych 101, we learned about operant conditioning. *Positive reinforcement*: The presence of a stimulus as a reward for correct behavior increases the recurrence of the behavior. As the professor went through her PowerPoint, I thought of Dad in those videos, praising me after each addition to my Heaven story. I had to leave the lecture hall before I was sick all over my notes.

"I was what?" Dad said.

"Telling me what to say."

"I was helping you remember."

"You were—putting ideas in my head."

"Ha!" From across the room, Abe threw a pillow at me. "What are you saying? Dad *brainwashed* you?" He crossed his eyes, held up his arms, and groaned like a zombie.

"It's not a joke, Abe," Mom said. "Your brother's upset."

"I'm sorry," I said. Maybe Abe was right. It sounded ridiculous.

Dad took my hand. "Did something happen with that atheist? Because I want you to know you can tell us."

"What? No. I mean, yeah. But that's not what this is about. Those videos—"

"Do you know why God chose you of all my children to visit Heaven?" Dad said.

"God didn't choose me."

"I've thought about this a long time. Why not Abe, my eldest, a natural-born leader? Or Jake, with his sense of humor, his capacity for wonder? Wouldn't their skills be useful to the Calling?"

Mom cleared her throat. "We don't play favorites, Simon."

"I never knew why until now. And it's become so clear to me."

I didn't want to hear this. "Please, Dad."

"Let's go back to bed," Mom said.

"It's because you're our doubting Thomas, Eli. Did Thomas believe the other disciples when they said Jesus had risen? No, he was reluctant. Until he had a firsthand experience. He had to touch the wounds! He had to put his finger right into Jesus's side and *feel*."

"Stop it," I said. "It's not true. I can't do this anymore."

"If Abe's the confident one and Jake's the funny one, then you're the clever one, Eli. God knew that. He knew Jesus couldn't win your heart with love alone. You required *evidence*. And He gave it to you."

"You're not listening to me!"

"I *am* listening to you." Dad pulled me into his arms, held me tight, and rocked me. "You're warring, son. You're fighting the good fight. Between faith and doubt. Light and dark. Good and evil."

"We love you." Mom kissed my cheek. "It's going to be okay."

Dad rested his hand on the back of my head, like he used to when I was a little boy. "I know you'll win the war for the right side."

As they held me I felt the tightness in my chest release. But it wasn't so much from the comfort they were giving me as from my dawning acceptance of what those videos meant. I'd told Bright I didn't know if I went to Heaven, but now I was sure—I *didn't*. It never happened. It was a story made up between Dad and me in those sessions he taped. And with that understanding came a strange euphoria: a letting go. I was free. I was no longer convincing myself I'd experienced something I hadn't. It felt *so good* to finally stop lying to myself.

But it was emotionally exhausting getting there and I could feel my body finally shutting down. I told everyone I was sorry for waking them and we all went to sleep.

✢

Early the next morning, when Dad woke me to exercise, I couldn't get out of bed.

"Come on, Eli. Let's get a move on. Those weights won't lift themselves."

It felt like the flu. After the roller coaster of emotion the night before, I'd crashed. I was trapped and depressed; I couldn't move if I'd wanted to.

Eventually, Dad gave up and let me sleep an extra hour. But even after Abe and Jake were up, I still hadn't budged.

Mom rested the back of her hand on my forehead. "You're not warm."

"I know you're tired," Dad said. "We all are. But these are the consequences to *your* actions. Waking everybody up in the middle of the night . . ."

"Maybe he should rest today," Mom said.

"You said it yourself. He's not sick."

"You can't keep pushing him."

"*I'm* not pushing him. If Satan's whispering in his ear—"

Mom held up her hand. "Enough."

She told Dad to take Abe and Jake down to breakfast in the hotel lobby. We'd be down in a few. Once we were alone, she sat on the bed next to me.

"I know you're struggling and I'm sorry." She hesitated, then asked, gently, "Is it . . . Chase?"

"What? No!" I rolled over and turned my back on her. As distracted and busy as we were on tour, I'd hoped she'd forgotten about my "friendship" with Chase. She hadn't brought him up since the night we played *Raptured!*

"Come on. Talk to me."

"I told you last night. It's the videos."

"Okay, okay, I know."

She sounded like she was backing off, but I buried deeper anyway, pulled up the covers. "Chase has nothing to do with it. Why would you even think that?"

"Oh, I don't know, Eli." She sighed. "Maybe because you've been mooning after him for months?"

"What!" That floored me. Was it that obvious? "I don't . . . *moon.*"

"I see you checking your phone after you text him. I see the way you look at him. I even saw you—" She stopped abruptly.

"Saw me what?"

"Can you please just tell me what happened between the two of you?"

"What? Nothing. I mean, we're friends."

"*Just* friends?"

My face and neck felt hot. "What else?"

"You tell me."

"Stop it. This is about Dad, okay? Those videos. You were right. I didn't go to Heaven. Dad thought I did, but I didn't. It's his fault I have to lie to everyone."

Mom sighed again. "Your father can be difficult, I know. I'll talk to him."

I sat up. "You'll get him to let me quit?"

"I didn't say that."

I fell back. "You're worse than him. At least he *actually* believes. All you care about is the money."

"All I care about is *my family.* Financial security for when I'm gone. You're too young to understand how important that is."

"Not too young to do all the work."

"Sometimes you have to do things you don't want to do for the people you love."

"I hate you."

"I can live with that. I won't have to for much longer."

"That's not funny."

"I know it's not. It's the truth."

"I want to go *home*."

"And we will. It's just one more week. For as long as you've been doing this, you can survive one more week. Now come on." She yanked the covers off.

Slowly, I rolled out of bed and dragged myself into the bathroom. Brushed my teeth. Showered. Every move was an effort. But I was grateful for the door between us. I couldn't look at her after she'd asked about Chase. *Mooning? Really?* I felt sick at the idea that some part of me I couldn't control, a part I hadn't come to grips with yet, was on full display to everyone else. I wiped steam from the mirror, practiced my *Heaven or Bust!* face. "And then I played with lions!"

How had I ever believed it?

✛

The first church in Atlanta was like so many on tour. They were beginning to blur in my mind. Greeted by the pastor, shake hands, shake hands. Wave to everyone as we walk down the aisle and take seats onstage. It was the same as it had always been—only it was entirely different. I was seeing through the charade now and I was determined to make it through by saying as little as possible. I sat with arms crossed, eyes downcast.

"Is he okay?" the pastor asked before the service started.

"Eli's a bit under the weather today." Dad squeezed my shoulder. He went on to present our book and talk about Heaven and the new realm at Bible World. The pastor and the congregants asked questions, but I hardly listened. Dad fielded them until—

"Are there animals in Heaven?" one little girl asked.

I sat up with an idea.

"There are unicorns in Heaven," I said before Dad could answer.

"Unicorns?" the pastor said.

"Dragons, too."

The audience went cold.

Dad chuckled. "He's joking."

I shook my head. "I'm not. I rode them. My wings weren't fully developed yet, so the dragons let me ride them. We played tag with the angels."

"Dragons." The pastor frowned.

The congregants shifted uncomfortably in their seats. Dad had gone red in the face. Abe was holding his head in his hands. Mom was suppressing a snicker in the front pew. Jake's eyes were wide with excitement.

"In Revelation, John has a vision of a dragon," Dad interjected. He sounded calm, but had gone rigid in his chair. "Seven-headed, wearing seven crowns."

"But that was Satan," the pastor said. "In one of his bestial forms."

"These dragons were nice," I said.

"Pet dragons," the pastor said dryly.

"And they only had one head."

"When you think about it," Dad said, "a dragon and a dinosaur are not so very different. And we know that animals that have gone extinct, like dinosaurs, are now in Heaven. So perhaps what Eli rode was less of a dragon and more of a . . . pterodactyl."

"No, it was definitely a dragon," I said. "It breathed fire."

Dad smiled and gritted his teeth. "Next question?"

✢

On the drive to the next church, Dad gripped the steering wheel so hard his knuckles turned white. "What the heck was that?"

Apparently, when the gloves came off, the curse words came out. This time I didn't flinch; in fact, I found it oddly satisfying.

Mom couldn't hold it in any longer. "Did you see their faces? And you—trying to—to cover *with dinosaurs*? Ha!"

"It's not funny." Dad looked really hurt. I'd shaken something in him.

"He just wants attention," Abe said.

Kill me, I thought. The last thing I wanted.

Dad knew that wasn't the case, too. "He has plenty of attention! His story is captivating enough without embellishments. Just tell the truth, Eli. That's all I ever asked of you."

"I tried! I told you last night—"

"Last night you said you didn't want to tell lies and now you're spouting off about riding dragons in Heaven. Well, I hope you're happy. I hope you're proud of yourself for making a laughingstock of this family."

"It's all made up anyway."

"If ever I heard Satan speaking through you . . ."

"It's not Satan. It's me, Dad. It's just me."

"You've got to fight it. That voice whispering in your ear, telling you what to say. No more dragons, you hear? And stop encouraging him, Debbie."

Mom turned in her seat and wagged her finger at me. "You heard your father. No more stories about dragons."

"Thank you," Dad said.

"Try vampires next time."

"Debbie!"

"I'm kidding! He knows I'm kidding. Cut him some slack. He's under a lot of pressure right now."

They broke into a fight. Dad accusing Mom of putting ideas in my head, Mom accusing Dad of being too hard on me. Abe put in his earbuds. I was untangling my own when Jake tapped me on the shoulder, leaned over, and cupped a hand to my ear.

He whispered, "What color was it?"

It took me a second to understand. He was looking at me with such awe, I didn't have the heart to tell him I was making it all up.

"Red," I said. "But kind of a burnt red. Maroon. The scales were slippery, but there was a horn on the back I could hold on to."

"Wow."

⁜

At the next church, I did as Dad asked. I didn't talk about dragons. I said there was a golden phoenix that perched on top of Heaven's gates and burst into flame when the archangel Gabriel fed it goldfish. I said the angels carried lightsabers and Jedi-dueled against invading demons in the courtyard of the Celestial Palace. I said there was a golden-brick road that led to a Diamond City with a chamber inside where God's head floated like the Wizard of Oz's—only it was white and shining on a cloud, instead of green and cloaked in smoke and fire. Making up lies about Heaven is harder than you might think. Especially when the whole point is to get your fundamentalist audience to see through them. The congregations we visited were either too gullible or too polite to contradict me. Like Fox Mulder, they wanted to believe. And so—frustratingly—they did, no matter what new absurdities I came up with.

Granted, there were awkward pauses. A few cleared throats. I always spotted the skeptics. The ones who frowned or rolled their eyes. But no one directly challenged me. They'd laugh like I was joking or exaggerating or speaking metaphorically, sometimes even scoff outright, but back down when Dad glossed it over with Biblical verses. Sometimes Dad would cut me out of the conversation completely, serve as my spokesman. Which was fine with me—I was sick of talking about Heaven. But to quit for good, to end it forever, I needed someone to call bullshit. Someone to stand and point an accusing finger. *Liar!* they'd shout. *You never baked a batch of snickerdoodles with a passel of wood elves in the Tree of Life!* And I'd hold up my hands defensively, like: *What can I say? You got me!* I'm embarrassed to say that it was a cowardly thing I was doing, hoping someone would do the dirty work for me, instead of coming clean myself. Where was Reuben Hawker when you needed him?

No one had the nerve to say anything in person, but after two days, word of my more mythical Heaven adventures spread. Someone recorded me saying, "The fairies in Heaven are more like Tinker Bell than Flora, Fauna, and Merryweather," and posted it online. Dad began getting calls from Gideon.

"I know, I know. I *never* told him to say that. Of course he made it up. That's not in the book! He's going through some kind of rebellious streak . . ."

Mom sat in her wheelchair; Abe, Jake, and I leaned against the van, watching him pace the church parking lot, phone to ear.

"I thought it was funny at first," Mom told me. "You needed to let off some steam. But you really should stop. You're upsetting him. And Gideon."

"I don't care."

Problem was—I did. Everyone thinks teenagers get a kick out of trying their parents, but that was never me. I hated the idea of losing the money and disappointing Mom. And I hated doing this to Dad. Seeing him take off his glasses and run a hand over his face after every church visit. Listening, repeatedly, to his lecture about Satan's seduction. Watching him scramble to quote Biblical verses to cover up my outlandish fairy tales. But I hated him more for what he'd done to me, and by making up stories about Heaven, I was finally beginning to feel like I could breathe again. Like the more I could control the lies—the more they came from my own imagination and not the black hole that was my childhood—the more I became myself and not what he'd made me.

Dad hung up and crossed the lot to us. He was clearly upset.

"Gideon's furious. He says that if he has to break our contract we get nothing. *And* I lose the rights to *Heaven or Bust!*"

"But that's *your* book," Abe said. "You wrote it."

"I signed the rights over to Gideon when they rewrote it."

"You could always write another book," Mom said. "A Bible study? You wouldn't need Eli—"

"Are you going to quit with these lies now?" Dad asked me, point-blank.

I crossed my arms. "Are you going to let me?"

Dad looked angrier than I'd ever seen him. For the first time in my life, I was afraid he might hit me, but instead he dropped to his knees, right there in the parking lot. It looked painful. He held out his hands, palms up, and I reluctantly gave him my own. "Please, God," he intoned, eyes closed, fingers squeezing. "Help Eli conquer the demons inside him. Help him fight the forces of darkness—"

I couldn't stand hearing this again. I yanked my hands away. He snatched my arms and pulled me back.

"Ow! You're hurting me!"

"Simon, stop!" Mom said.

Dad let go of my arms. A look of bewilderment crossed his face. He hadn't really hurt me, but I'd been frightened by the way he'd grabbed me. He'd never once raised his hand to any of us before. He took in our looks of alarm.

"I'm sorry, son. I'm sorry. I'd never . . ." His eyes filled with tears and he wiped his nose with the back of his hand. It was hard to watch.

"It's okay, Dad. Really. I'm fine."

Still on his knees, he hugged my waist, his tears staining my shirt. "I just want us to be good again."

This was more painful than the arm grab. "Me, too, Dad." I patted the back of his head. "Me, too."

But we weren't good again. It hurt to see Dad suffering like that, but it was also kind of powerful. For the first time, I had control of the narrative and I wasn't about to give that up. I could tell he thought his apology had convinced me to quit lying, but it had actually done the opposite. When we went into that church, I was more determined than ever.

"It's beautiful in Heaven. There are lots of forests. Jesus took me on a hike. The trees were as big as skyscrapers. Eventually, we came to a clearing with a lake and that's when I saw him. He was bent over, drinking. At first I thought it was an animal, but then he stood up. He was tall and hairy. He turned and looked right at me. It was Bigfoot—"

I expected Dad to do as he always did. Interrupt me with a passage from the Bible to cover up the farce. I even had an idea which one he'd use—a verse on the Nephilim, Biblical giants. But instead Dad stood up. As soon as the word *Bigfoot* left my mouth, he was out of his seat. He walked offstage. The pastor called after him, but he didn't turn back. Dad went right down the aisle and out the church doors.

I didn't know whether to continue or not. I'd planned to talk about the Loch Ness Monster next, rising out of the lake like some B horror movie, but that seemed silly now.

Abe got up and went after Dad.

"Eli," Mom said, releasing the brake on her wheelchair.

"I'm sorry," I said to the pastor, and pushed her off the stage.

In the church parking lot the van was gone.

"He left us?" I said.

"What'd you expect?" Abe shoved me. "Bigfoot!"

"Boys." Mom had her phone to her ear. "He's not picking up."

We dithered in the empty parking space.

"How are we supposed to get back to the hotel?" Abe said.

"I'll call us a taxi," Mom said.

We went back and sat on the stairs of the church, Mom in her chair on the sidewalk. Inside, the service continued without us, the muffled sound of singing drifting out. We visored our hands over our eyes, waiting to be picked up, lost in our thoughts, worried about Dad.

Jake scratched his head. "What's a Bigfoot?"

⸸

Dad wasn't back at the hotel after the taxi dropped us off. We watched TV and ordered room service. For several hours, I was tortured by the thought he'd left us for good and it was my fault. Eventually, he texted Mom to let her know he was okay, but needed time to himself. He'd be back later that night. We shouldn't wait up for him.

But I did. I lay awake, listening for the sound of the key card unlocking the door. I didn't know what I'd say when he came in. I wanted to tell him I was sorry and I loved him, but I was afraid if I did, he'd use it to make me be a good little Heaven Boy again. So I waited until everyone was asleep. Then I climbed out of bed, careful not to wake Jake, and snuck down to the pool.

The night was warm, the pool dark blue. I sat on the lounge chair and connected my iPhone to the hotel's Wi-Fi. I typed *Levi Livingston* into the YouTube search box. The first video that came up was called "Heaven Hoax Remix," a dubstep parody that already had more hits than the original video. I scrolled down the list of reaction and commentary videos—"Livingston Fibbingston!!!" and "HeavenKidGoingtoHell" and "Liar Liar Halo on Fire (Oh, Wait. Those Are Devil Horns . . .)"—until I found the actual video, which was simply labeled "Apology." I plugged in my headphones and played it.

A teenage boy alone in his bedroom, sitting in a wheelchair. His lap was covered by a red blanket; I pictured scrawny chicken legs beneath it. The walls behind him featured posters of Switchfoot and Relient K over his bed. He delivered his speech quickly and monotonously, reading off what must have been a script on his computer screen.

"Hi. My name is Levi Livingston and I was in a car accident when I was seven. When I woke up in the hospital I told my family that I died and went to Heaven. My dad wrote a book about it called *A Tour of Heaven*. That book was made into a movie. I'm posting now to let you know that none of it is true. I lied. I did not go to Heaven. I did it for attention. It was wrong and I'm sorry. Only the Bible tells the truth about Heaven. It is the Word of God. You should trust in it alone. In Jesus's name, Amen."

He pushed a button on the wheelchair's armrest and it moved forward. He leaned over his desk and reached out. The video shook for a moment, then went black.

That was it. Forty-six seconds. I played it again.

. . . *I'm posting now to let you know that none of it is true* . . .

And again. Over and over like a prayer.

When I was little I used to imagine my prayers traveling like beams of light, straight up to Heaven, where a secretarial angel sat at a desk, transcribing my message on one of those yellow legal pads Mom used to make grocery lists. Not all prayers were answered. But when it mattered most, the angel would tear off the page and rush it to the Big Guy.

. . . *I lied. I did not go to Heaven. I did it for attention* . . .

If it had worked for Levi Livingston, it could work for me.

I tapped into the iPhone camera and hit record. The first few takes were useless.

"My name is Eli Harpo. My dad wrote a book about my trip to Heaven.

I was really little when it happened and thought I saw something, maybe I did, but now I'm not sure—"

"My name is Eli Harpo. When I was four, I had heart surgery and said I saw Heaven, but now I can't really remember it and my dad has these, like, training videos, but he thought he was just helping me remember and . . ."

"My name is Eli Harpo and I don't know anything. I'm confused. Please disregard anything I've ever said. Thank you. Goodbye."

I let out a groan of frustration.

Levi's message was direct: I lied. I'm sorry. Why couldn't I do that?

Because I didn't feel like I *had* lied. I didn't feel like Dad had either. He still believed in our story, no matter what doubts I harbored. How do you say, *My dad conditioned me without knowing what he was doing and I've only now seen the light?*

You don't. That's not a sound bite.

The only way out of one lie was into another. Who knows what really happened to Levi Livingston behind closed doors? Maybe he hadn't lied either. Maybe it was all a misunderstanding. But if he wanted out, he could only play the Boy Who Lied for Attention. And I'd have to do the same.

I watched Levi's video again, pausing between sentences, memorizing the speech. I plugged in "heart surgery" for "car accident," "four" for "seven," *Heaven or Bust!* for *A Tour of Heaven.* I struck the line about the movie and mentioned the upcoming realm at Bible World instead. I recorded myself again. It went much smoother this time. I did several takes, rewatched them, chose the least embarrassing, and went to upload it online.

Once the upload started, I felt immediate regret. I stood up, left the iPhone on the chair, and paced around the pool to stop myself from chickening out.

That's when I saw Dad on the other side of the pool gate.

"Nice speech," he said.

"You're back."

He opened the gate and entered the pool deck. He went to the chair and picked up the iPhone. I thought he might toss it into the pool, but he just moved it aside and sat down.

"I'm sorry," I said. "I thought if I did what Levi did—"

"Shhh. It's okay. Come here." He waved me over.

I sat beside him and glanced at the iPhone, where the video was still uploading.

"I'm sorry I left," he said.

"Where did you go?"

He shrugged. "Drove around. I was mad and in need of some spiritual guidance. I did a lot of praying and God finally spoke to me."

"He did?"

Dad smiled and I could see the spark of his old self. "I know exactly what we need to do now."

"I don't know, Dad." I was relieved he'd come back to us, but my stomach dropped at the idea of a new plan from God. Whatever God had said to him, I had a feeling it wasn't to let me off the hook.

"He said you can quit. You don't have to speak about Heaven anymore."

I didn't believe him. "What's the catch?"

"You're officially sick. Summer cold. We'll do it without you."

"You can't do it without me. I'm the Heaven Kid."

"God would rather the next few churches hear from two Heavenly brothers than some crock about Bigfoot's Hula-Hoop-size halo."

I laughed. "That's pretty good. I should have used that."

"Here's the deal, okay? No more Heaven until Bible World. But you have to promise to be on your best behavior on Gideon's show. That means you tell the *true* story about visiting Heaven one more time. None of this fairy-tale nonsense."

"What about *after* Bible World?"

He shrugged. "We go home."

He picked up the iPhone and held it out, but I just looked at it.

"And Hospice Duty?"

"I can do it alone. I was going to anyway, when you left for college. I'll just start a few years early."

"Abe could help."

Dad nodded. "His faith is strong. And I think it's time he stepped up.

It's like your mom said. It wouldn't have to be about Heaven anymore. What do you say?"

I thought about it. If I couldn't quit being the Heaven Kid without destroying Dad's hopes and dreams, I could at least see it through to the end. Dad would get a few minutes of fame on Gideon's show; Mom would be happy about the money and college; Abe would have Dad's full attention; Jake would have fun at Bible World. And I could finally move on. Everybody won.

I took the iPhone and canceled the upload.

Dad hugged and kissed me and thanked God for His guidance. It would all work out now, Dad was sure of it. One more gig, I thought. One more gig and then I could retire. Hang up my wings and halo. Permanently.

10

PFLAG

Whenever Eli was asked his favorite color, he'd cheat and claim all of them: "Wainbow, Daddy!" Rainbows, of course, are potent symbols from the Bible. In Genesis 9:12–13, God sets his bow in the cloud as a covenant with Noah and his descendants after the flood. In Revelation, rainbows are seen around the heads of angels and the Throne of God. Eli saw these in Heaven, too. He took pride in this, like Heaven had been designed especially for him. "It's bootiful, Daddy," he told me. "My favorite color's everywhere!"
—from *Heaven or Bust!*, "Flights & Sights," ch. 19, p. 107

DAD KEPT HIS PROMISE. EARLY the next morning, he woke Abe and Jake but let me stay in bed. It was the best feeling: snuggling down into the covers while my brothers complained how unfair it was I got to sleep in. It was my revenge for suffering through the diet and exercise routines they weren't forced to undertake. While Abe and Jake binged on junk food from hotel vending machines, Dad still wouldn't let me near anything salty, sweet, or processed. Mom made me snacks of carrots and celery sticks. Sometimes, if I was lucky, peanut butter crackers—but that was it. No sodas either. Green tea and water. At the hot breakfast each morning, I ate a banana, salivating over Abe's blueberry pancakes and Jake's chocolate chip waffles. Abe always piled on the bacon—just to rub it in. He never gained a pound. For the life of me, I'll never understand how our metabolisms were so radically different. I was doomed to be the husky Harpo and I sometimes felt like I deserved it. Like being fat was my punishment for doubting Heaven or being ungrateful. It was God's way of testing me. Dad's weight-loss regimens certainly didn't help my self-esteem.

Around ten, I rolled over and grabbed the TV remote. I was ready to hang at the hotel and channel surf all day, but as soon as I turned it on Mom moved in front of the TV.

"Upsy-daisy. We're going out."

"Dad took the van."

"I'm calling us a taxi. We're going on an adventure."

"Do we have to? It's my first day off."

"Please," Mom said.

We met the cab outside. The driver wasn't thrilled by her wheelchair, but managed to get it folded and into the trunk. Mom refused to tell me where we were going. All she said was we were playing hooky. As we drove through downtown Atlanta I predicted where she was taking me based on the pamphlets I'd glimpsed in the hotel lobby: the Georgia Aquarium, the Museum of Natural History, the World of Coca-Cola. Twenty minutes later we pulled up in front of a Methodist church.

I *knew* it. I knew Abe and Jake couldn't fill in for me. I was annoyed at losing my day off, but part of me also felt weirdly appreciated. I imagined Dad in front of a bored congregation, frantically texting Mom: Bring Eli! Hurry!

Mom paid the driver, but I refused to get out of the cab.

"Dad said Bible World would be my last time. We made a deal."

"Your father doesn't know I'm bringing you here and I'd rather you didn't tell him."

"I thought we were playing hooky."

"We are."

"In a *church*?"

"This has nothing to do with Heaven. I promise."

"I thought you meant like a museum. Or Putt-Putt."

"It'll take an hour, tops."

"Bowling or a movie . . ."

"I'll let you pick what we do next. Any of those things."

"Fine." I got out of the cab.

The driver unfolded Mom's wheelchair. I pushed her up the ramp to the church entrance. There was a yellow sign in the front window with an interlocked heart and triangle that said PFLAG: ATLANTA WELCOMES YOU! A Black woman came out to greet us. A boy my age held the door. They introduced themselves as mother and son, Grace and Derek.

"Audrey," Mom said. "And this is my son . . ."

"Oh, uh—Logan," I said, pleased at how fast on my feet I was.

Mom smiled up at me from her chair.

"Don't worry," Derek said. "You won't be struck by lightning."

"Pardon?" Mom said.

"It's the joke most people make when they enter the church," Grace explained.

"You know . . ." Derek looked up and struck a mock-terrified pose. "Smited by God. Or is it *smote*? I can never remember."

Derek's smile, when flashed in your direction, was its own kind of lightning strike. What a real Logan—confident, flirtatious, out—might have said: It's *smitten*.

"PFLAG is not religious-affiliated," Grace said. "The church is just a convenient meeting place for our chapter. We welcome people of all faiths. Or non-faiths."

She gave us name tags and a welcome packet, then directed us to the church basement.

"*Audrey?*" I said, when Mom and I were alone in the elevator.

Mom shrugged. "Sometimes it's fun to pretend to be someone else. At least that's what my son *Logan's* always telling me."

I wasn't sure what game we were playing, but I could humor Mom. I had no idea what PFLAG stood for either, but the families in the basement chatting around a table of breakfast (coffee, doughnuts) and snack foods (vegetable and cheese trays) clued me in: I knew a support group when I saw one.

When Mom was first diagnosed, Dad tried to take her to a meeting. He thought it would offer perspective, help stabilize her. There was only one cancer support group in Canaan and Mom's response to Dad's interest was always the same: "If I wanted everyone knowing my business I'd put up a billboard."

But we weren't in Canaan. Passing through Atlanta offered her anonymity, a low-risk chance to unburden herself. And apparently with an alias. Or at least that's what I assumed was happening.

There were two bald men—chemo, I figured—but no one looked as sick as Mom. She told me to park her in the circle of chairs, then bring her coffee and a doughnut.

It was all very Alcoholics Anonymous.

At the snack table, I reached for the last chocolate doughnut at the same time as a young woman in a headscarf.

"Go ahead," she said.

"No, you."

"Thanks." She took it. "You're new. What brings you here?"

I pointed across the room. "My mom. Stage four. Breast."

She frowned. An awkward silence stretched between us. I thought she was waiting for me to ask, so I said, "What about you?"

"I'm here with my aunt. My parents won't come to these meetings."

"I'm sorry."

She shrugged. "They're not the most tolerant of people."

"What do you have?"

"What do I *have*?" She laughed. "You make it sound like a disease."

My turn to be confused. "Cancer?"

She did a double take. "Excuse me?"

"Oh. I thought—" I gestured at her scarf.

"It's a *hijab*," she said bluntly. "I don't have cancer. I'm *Muslim*."

And she walked away in a huff. The back of my neck grew hot. Why was I so stupid? Her aunt must have been the sick one. I resolved not to talk to anyone else for the rest of the meeting. The best cure for foot-in-mouth syndrome: a vow of silence.

I brought Mom her doughnut.

"Making friends?" she said.

"No."

"That Derek seemed nice." She nodded across the room to where Derek was laughing with a blonde girl with streaks of purple in her hair.

"What are we doing here?"

"Well. You know I don't have a lot of time left."

"Mom. Don't."

"I want to make sure you're okay before I—"

"Stop. Please."

Was that what this was—grief counseling? She wanted me to mourn before she was even gone? Couldn't I do that without being stared at by a group of strangers?

"All right, everyone!" Grace clapped for attention. "Take your seats."

Last chance. "Can we just go?" I whispered. "Please?"

"One hour," Mom said.

"Before we begin," Grace said, "I'd like to remind everyone that you're in a safe space. We're all either members of this community or love someone who is. Now you've probably noticed: We have two new faces today. Everyone, please join me in welcoming Audrey and Logan."

She led the group in applause.

"When did you come out?" asked the girl with the purple hair.

"Kiera." Grace shook her head. "Let Logan share on his own, okay? Don't pry."

I was lost. "Out of what?"

Everyone laughed. The woman in the headscarf rolled her eyes. Derek hid his snicker behind his hand. I wanted to melt into the floor, but apparently the heat radiating from my face wasn't enough to do that.

"Aww," Kiera said. "He's adorable."

"Why don't we go around the circle and introduce ourselves?" Grace said.

It soon became clear that this was *not* the kind of support group I thought it was. Fatimah was a lesbian ("And *Muslim*, if that's not obvious");

Becca, a polyamorous dyke ("Loud and queer!"); Jamal, trans and bi; Tyler, genderqueer; Kiera, a pansexual vegetarian Green Party feminist ("Oh, and a Gemini"); and Greg, Justin, and Derek were gay ("Boring, I know. Just your average homo") The family members—mostly parents, but a few siblings, an aunt, a cousin—chimed in here and there with their support. For the first time, I took in the rainbow flag hanging from the snack table. I opened the welcome packet on my lap, flipped a few pages, and there it was: *PFLAG: Parents, Families, and Friends of Lesbians and Gays.*

Mom had brought me to a support group for homosexuals.

"You brought me to a support group *for homosexuals*," I hissed into her ear.

I was mortified. We were in the wrong meeting. Mom must have mixed up the rooms. Or churches. I imagined her looking up the cancer support group online, calling the cabdriver, confusing the address. I expected her to offer an apology ("So sorry, our mistake") and then we'd skedaddle, but when I sat back in my chair, she was looking at me not with embarrassment but with such worry and love—and that's when I knew. This wasn't an accident. There was no mix-up. She knew exactly what she was doing when she brought me here. All those fishing questions about Chase. She was sick of my evasions. I sat there, humiliated, while the meeting continued.

"Greg came out two years ago and we've been coming ever since."

Mom raised her hand. "How exactly does that work?"

"What?"

"The . . . out thing?"

"Coming out?" Kiera said.

"You mean publicly?" Grace said. "There's no one right way to do it. It's just a conversation with people you know. But some throw parties. Or post online."

"There's even a holiday for it," Tyler's father said. "It's in October."

"Greg first told us over dinner," Greg's mother said. "Then we went out for ice cream. We told people gradually after that. Honestly, it was such a relief. It's not like I didn't know. A mother knows."

"You didn't know," Greg said.

"Well, I suspected."

"You had no idea."

"It was like he could finally be himself. No more looming secret. No more black cloud over his head."

"It's not always easy after," Tyler's father said. "There's a lot of bullying."

"Family support is essential," said Greg's mother.

Mom raised her hand again.

"You don't have to do that," Grace said. "Talk whenever you'd like."

"Speak your truth," Derek said.

"Sorry, but . . . how do you get them to do it the first time?" Mom asked. "With their family?"

Eyes darted in my direction. I crossed my arms, looked at my feet.

"Wait," Kiera said. "You mean you're not—? You haven't—? Oh, that's fucked-up."

"Kiera!" Grace chided.

"What?" Kiera said. "It is."

Grace turned to Mom. "It's not up to you," she explained gently. "It's up to the person coming out."

"You can't just force someone out like that," Kiera said. "It's cruel."

"*Kiera.*" Grace sighed.

"What? What if he's not even queer? If my mom had dragged me here before I came out I would have killed her."

Several in the group murmured their assent.

"I'm sorry," Mom said. "I—I don't know what the rules are."

"They're not *rules*," Kiera said. "It's basic human decency."

"Mm-hmm," Jamal's older sister said. "Tell her."

"She obviously didn't know," Fatimah's aunt said.

"That's right," Grace said. "That's okay. We're all on our own journeys, at our own paces."

"But what if there's not enough time to wait?" Mom said.

The group went quiet. There was no answer for that. People shifted uncomfortably, eyes glancing off her wheelchair, her oxygen tubes.

"*Now* can we go?" I said.

"Logan?" Grace said. "Is there something you'd like to say?"

"No." I squeezed my arms tighter. "Yes. I don't even know why I'm here. I'm not . . ." I trailed off, but everyone kept looking at me. "I'm just not."

"He can't even say the word," Kiera said.

"Gay!" I yelled. "But I'm not, okay? And I don't like being talked about like I'm not in the room or being told I need to come out of anything or being tricked into a homosexual support group when all I wanted to do was taste sixty flavors of Coke!"

Silence. I got up to leave.

"Eli, wait!" Mom wheeled her chair after me.

Eli? The group murmured.

"I thought his name was Logan," Kiera said.

"I'm sorry," Mom said. "I knew I'd mess this up. I've been trying to talk to you, but I didn't know how and I thought this might help."

"Well, it didn't."

"Okay." Mom sighed. "Fine. Let's go."

"Wait." Grace got up and walked over. She put her hand on Mom's shoulder. "If you'd like to go, go. But I think you brought your son here for a reason. This is your chance to tell him."

"I'm worried," Mom said.

Grace nodded. "We all worry."

"What happens after I'm gone? It's going to be so hard for him."

"Tell *him*," Grace said. "Talk to your son."

Mom wiped her eyes and looked at me. "It's going to be so hard for you, with your father. And Abe. Whether you're—you know—or not. You're different from them. And I want you to know that's okay. But I don't think I can give you that. I thought if you met other people, people like you—but if you're not, that's fine, too. I'm sorry I assumed or . . . if I'm making you, um, *out* . . . I wish I could've waited, but I see you with Chase and I worry . . ."

I shook my head. "I told you."

"Eli. I *saw* you with Chase."

"We're friends."

"I saw you *kiss* Chase."

"*Dayum*," Kiera said. "She spying on him, too?"

"This just got good," Jamal's sister said.

"Would y'all hush?" Derek snapped.

"What?" I said. "When?" How could she have? We were so careful. Only in the closet.

"Outside the house, with your bikes. Maybe it was nothing. I'm sorry."

I remembered. It *was* nothing. Well, nothing and everything. It was after one of our later "practice" sessions. We usually parted ways at the church, but that one time Chase rode with me back to my house. I thought it very gentlemanly of him. We lingered with our bikes in the driveway and, as we said goodbye, an impulse came over me and I leaned forward, unthinkingly, and kissed him. Quickly. On the cheek. A goodbye kiss. A thank-you kiss. A see-you-later kiss. So small. But he recoiled like I'd stung him. Wiped at his cheek, looking up and down the street.

"Don't do that!"

"Sorry."

He rode his bike away angrily.

Mom must have been looking out the window at just the right moment. I would have done anything to take that kiss back.

"I'm sorry I pressured you," she said. "I love you. No matter what. No matter who you turn out to be."

Awwwww. The group softened at her words.

"That's beautiful, Audrey," Grace said.

"If that's even her name," Kiera mumbled.

Grace turned to me. "Would you like to respond?"

It didn't matter what I said. No excuse could backtrack us. And even if I came up with one, I felt too sick and ashamed to deliver it convincingly. So I didn't say anything. If I'd been a little older or a little more secure in myself, what would have happened? Would I have come out right then? Would it have been a cathartic experience that brought Mom and me closer, instead of one that hardened me against her?

Mom never got a chance to meet Will. She would have liked him, I'm certain of it. But I never got to bring a boy home to her. This moment was the closest I ever got to being myself with her and my shame ruined it. It kept me from seeing what she'd done for me. It wasn't until years later, almost a decade, that I understood. That moment, in the basement of a Methodist church in Atlanta, was a letter proclaiming her unconditional love. One she'd signed, sealed, and sent to my future self, so that I could open it and remember, after she was gone and I needed her most.

✛

I marched up the basement stairs, out of the church, and into the parking lot. Mom was slowed by her wheelchair and the elevator, so the first to catch up to me was Derek.

"Hey, Logan!"

"It's Eli."

"Okay—Eli. Sorry about that back there. I know we can be a lot."

"I'm sorry we lied," I said. "About the names."

"I hope you come again. Even if you're not gay. We could use some straight allies."

"I don't actually live in Atlanta. We're just passing through."

"Oh. That's cool. We can text." He took out his phone. "What's your number?"

I was dumbfounded. "Why?"

"You're cute." He smiled—flash of lightning, crash of thunder. I was struck right then and there, in that blistering parking lot, with not a cloud in the sky.

"I'm fat," I said.

He tilted his head. "Try not to hate yourself so much. I think they got it covered."

"Who?"

He grinned again and I was smitten—spot-of-ash-on-the-pavement smitten. "The haters."

✛

I sat on the curb while Mom called the cab. She hung up and wheeled over to me. "Want to go taste sixty flavors of Coke?"

"It didn't happen," I said. Instead of an excuse, I'd decided to go with flat denial.

"Okay . . ." She raised her eyebrows.

"I don't know what you saw, but it didn't happen. It didn't. It just didn't."

"Hey—stop!" She leaned out of her chair and swatted at me. "Don't do that, honey."

I'd been pinching my scar and hadn't realized it. I dropped my hand, turned away. "Leave me alone."

"Eli, please. Just listen."

I whirled around. "What!"

"Oh, sweetie. I'm sorry." She buried her face in her hands. "Ugh. Can we please forget I ever brought you here?"

I shrugged, noncommittal—but that was exactly what I wanted, too.

Mom held out her hand. "Will you ever forgive me?"

I sighed. "I don't know." But I took her hand. "Whatever."

"Hey. I have an idea." She hefted her Polaroid camera out of her bag. "Let's go to the aquarium and get a picture with a shark."

I shook my head. "Can we please just go back to the hotel?"

"Come on. Let me cheer you up."

But I didn't want to be cheered up. I didn't want to give her the satisfaction of seeing me have a good time, which felt impossible anyway. After a few more attempts to cajole me, she relented and we went back.

While Mom slept, I ate pizza and entered a TV coma. A few hours later, Dad, Abe, and Jake came bursting into the room, singing "Power in the Blood" all together.

Mom sat up in bed. "What's this?"

"Hello, my beautiful family." Dad kissed her on the cheek.

"Aren't you in a good mood. It went well?"

"The nicest churches and they *loved* us. You should have seen Abe up there, quoting Isaiah. He's a natural! And Jake did a solo on 'Jesus Loves the Little Children.' We have a little rock star on our hands."

"We got to eat cloud cake," Jake said.

"Yum," Mom said.

"The pastor said I had leadership potential," Abe said.

Dad pounded his shoulder. "A minister in the making!"

Abe beamed. "At first I thought, why would they want to hear from me? But then I started telling about how scared I was when Eli died and—"

"You were six," I said.

"So? That's Jake's age. You don't think he'd be scared if you died?"

Jake shook his head. "God sent Eli back."

"Anyway," Abe said, "I told them how Eli saw angels when I was in the hospital room."

"That never happened."

"It did. When we came to visit you. You said there was an angel behind me and I felt feathers brush my neck."

"You're making that up."

"I remember it!"

"Boys," Mom said.

"Mom, you should have been there," Abe said. "It was like the Holy Spirit was speaking through me. I felt it. There was this connection between me and them and God."

"It's called your ego," I said.

"Just because you never felt it doesn't mean it's not real," Abe said.

"Stop it, you two," Mom said.

I turned to Dad. "How'd you cover for me?"

"Summer cold, like we said. Worked like a charm."

"Honestly, it was easier without you there," Abe said.

"I wouldn't go that far," Dad said. "You can always come back."

I wanted to believe it was all a show to convince me to do just that. That Dad had coached Abe and Jake on what to say just to make me jealous.

That it had gone terribly without me. But the smug look on Abe's face said differently. Worse, it played right into Dad's hand anyway: I *was* jealous.

"What have you two been up to?" Dad asked.

"Oh, nothing," Mom said. "Watched some TV."

"Don't tell me you've been stuck in this room all day?"

Mom didn't bat an eye. "It was good to get some rest."

11

ORLANDO

*After Eli came back from Heaven he rattled off the names of all the
other kids he met there: Sammy and Janey and Molly and Kelly
and Susie and Timmy and Jimmy and Kimmy and so many more.
Unfortunately, he'd only learned first names, so it was impossible
for us to look up the families and let them know their children were
with Jesus.*

*But there was one name Eli spoke that stood out from the rest.
One very special girl, and when he said her name, Debbie gasped
and dropped the pan she was pulling from the oven.*

I rushed to her side. "Did you burn yourself?"

*She was unhurt, but shaking, and she went straight to Eli. "Where
on Earth did you hear that name?"*

Not on Earth, *I thought.* Not anywhere on this Earth.

*And as our son began to speak, my wife's mitted hands came to
rest, slowly, on her belly, and stayed there.*

—from *Heaven or Bust!*, "Soul Sister," ch. 17, pp. 96–97

ON THE DRIVE FROM ATLANTA to Orlando, the billboards on I-75 were
all of babies. Big eyes, bald heads, they called out to their mothers beneath
red cardiograms—*At 18 Days My Heart Is Beating!* When Jake wasn't playing on the Nintendo DS, he counted babies. He'd become obsessed with

car games. Abe and I indulged him through the alphabet game, twenty questions, and guess the verse. Baby counting was something he came up with on his own.

"Twenty-eight, twenty-nine, thirty!" Jake announced. "Thirty babies, Eli. I got thirty."

I looked out my own window, ignoring him. Dad was right: I was at war with myself. But it wasn't a spiritual battle between Good and Evil. Even more than the "practicing" with Chase, Mom's PFLAG stunt was what had finally cracked the closet door, and I was fighting to pull it shut. I couldn't stop coming up with things I could say to convince her she hadn't seen what she'd seen. It wasn't a kiss, but a secret handshake. It just *looked* like a kiss from where she was standing. Must have been a weird angle, and from so far away. A trick of the light. No, I remember now. I was actually trying to get something out of Chase's backpack. I was just reaching behind him and our faces came close . . .

"Good job," Abe told Jake.

The van passed another sign. A row of baby hands reaching up from the bottom. Above, in all caps: LET US LIVE!

Jake said, "Why are there so many babies in Florida?"

"Abortion," I said.

"Hey!" Dad yelled, and the van swerved. "I don't want to hear that word again."

The next one was of a lady, not a baby. She was holding a pregnancy test. The sign said, *Know Your Options*, with a phone number.

"What's abortion?" Jake whispered to me.

"Baby murder," I said.

"That's enough," Dad warned. "I mean it."

Everyone was quiet. Outside, the thrum of tires.

Mom said, "They shouldn't put signs like that up, where families on vacation can see them."

"It's cruel," Dad said. "They make me think of her."

Mom crossed her arms over her stomach and Abe and I looked at each other.

"Who?" Jake asked.

"Your sister," Dad said.

Jake laughed. "We don't have a sister."

"You do."

"Simon," Mom said.

"He's old enough to know," Dad said. "She was a preemie. That means she was born premature. It was too early for her to leave Mommy's tummy. She lived in the hospital for a few days. They tried to fix her, but God wanted her back, so she went to Heaven."

"She died," Mom said.

"But . . . why?" Jake said.

"Oh, honey," Mom said. "There's no reason why. Sometimes bad things just happen. It was before you boys."

"God called her home," Dad said. "She was too sweet for this world."

"I have a sister!" Jake said.

"That you do. Eli met her there, didn't you, Big E?"

Jake leaned toward me, eyes wide.

"*Dad*," I said. This was one part of the Heaven story I'd never been comfortable with.

"She was seven when Eli met her."

"That's one more than me," Jake said.

"Yes." Dad nodded. "And she had Mommy's red hair."

"So pretty," Jake said.

"Simon, please," Mom said.

"He knew her name," Abe said, nodding along with Dad.

"That's right," Dad said. "When he came back, he knew her name. Dinah. That's what we named her."

"You could have told me her name," I said.

"But we didn't. That's how we knew it was real."

"I could have heard it somehow. Kids hear things."

"Please stop," Mom said. "Simon, you know I don't like it."

Dinah was in *Heaven or Bust!*, but her story was one we didn't often tell. Even before I started doubting, my memories of Dinah were hazier than those of Memaw, and Dad knew that, like Mom, many church members had trouble hearing them. Even so, there were times Dad called upon Dinah's story to console other parents at Creation Baptist who'd lost children. Their babies were in Heaven, too. Now I was realizing that my memories of Dinah were probably foggier *because* I told them less often.

Jake yanked on my shirt. "What was she like? Was she nice?"

"What? No. I don't know."

"Of course she was," Dad said. "She's your big sister. She loves you. One day you'll meet her, too."

"We all will," Abe said.

"One day we'll all be together again, in Heaven."

"Mommy first," Jake said.

"That's right. Mommy will beat us there. She'll find Dinah and she'll wait for us to join her."

"Dad, stop!" I yelled.

Mom was heaving in her seat.

"Pull over," she said. "I'm going to be sick."

"What?"

"Just pull over!"

Dad put on his hazards and moved the van onto the shoulder. Mom threw her door open and retched onto the concrete.

Abe, Jake, and I unbuckled our seat belts and clambered forward to make sure she was okay. Dad came around the side of the van and gave her his handkerchief. He kept clean linen handkerchiefs in his back pocket. (I carry them now, too. On one of our first dates, Will suffered a sneezing fit. After I offered the handkerchief to him, he was delighted beyond measure: "Oooh. A gentleman!" He later told me this was one of the first moments he knew he could fall in love with me.)

Mom dabbed at her mouth. Dad rested a hand on her back, rubbing it in circles. We sat under a billboard with an enormous fetus, glowing in utero. *Every Child Is a Blessing from God.*

Mom sat back and breathed evenly, hand on her side. Dad held out the water bottle from the cup holder. She rinsed out her mouth and spat.

"Pain level?"

"Six."

He dug around in her purse until he found her pills. She swallowed one and he kissed her forehead. Mom stared at the billboard.

"You know I wish it were true," she said.

"Then let it be."

Mom waved her hand in front of her face. "Whew. It's so hot." Dad stepped back and closed her door. Mom cranked up the AC. "Let's get this show on the road."

✛

Two hours later, Jake had grown antsy and started kicking the back of Mom's seat.

"How. Much. Longer!" he demanded.

"Just four more *Bible Tales* and we'll be there," Mom said.

Four *Bible Tales*. Two hours. Only two hours stood between us and Orlando, land of vacation. Minutes later, the highway agreed: two Disney signs and, soon after, one for Universal Studios. The Bible World billboard came in between. It was smaller, with a larger-than-life-size Jesus in white robes, arms open, welcoming tourists.

COMING SOON! NEW BIBLICAL REALMS!

Jake bounced in his seat. "Did you see that! Did you! Did you!"

As much as I was dreading my final gig as the Heaven Kid, I felt a little thrill. It went through the entire van. Dad gave the horn a celebratory honk.

"Bible World, here we come!"

✛

That night, at the Orlando hotel, Mom laid out all our supplies for Bible World. Along with our khakis, button-downs, and ties for Gideon's show, there were three piles, one for each of her boys, color coded in the neon of highlighters—orange for Abe, yellow for Jake, green for me: matching fanny packs, visors, tank tops, swim trunks, beach towels, and sunglasses. There was also sunscreen and bug spray, water bottles, miniature battery-operated fans with misters, crackers and granola bars, bags of homemade trail mix—any and everything you could think of.

"We're going to an amusement park, not off to war," Dad joked.

He set up her wheelchair and oxygen tank by the door, then unzipped the backpack with my hand weights. "Okay, Big E. Three sets, teeth, then bed."

"Aw, really? Tonight?"

The last few days Dad had let up on making me do Heaven stuff, but not on the exercise regimen. My arms and legs were still sore from lifting weights up that morning's flight of stairs. Besides, tonight felt special, like Christmas Eve. I was determined to get the night off.

"Oh, let him go to bed early," Mom said. "We all have a big day tomorrow."

Dad wavered, then caved. "Oh, all right." He zipped the weights back up, then called Gideon to check in. We were to report to Bible World at nine sharp. We'd tour the park in the morning, then make our appearance on *The Charlie Gideon Hour* that afternoon.

That night I had another sex dream about Jesus. We were in the Meadow again. He wore a white robe with a purple sash. He held out his hand. When I reached out, Jesus guided my hand to the sash. Together we pulled, the knot came undone, and the robe opened.

Beneath, Jesus's chest was perfectly hairless. He must have worked out as well as waxed, because he had ropy arms, enormous pecs, and washboard abs. There was no cloud castle, no angels, no unicorn, just grass in every direction. I expected Jesus's beard to feel rough—scratchy—but it wasn't. When we lay together, the sky darkened. Lightning leapt overhead and struck fear in my heart. I tried to move away, but my body wouldn't obey. I tried to shove at his beautifully sculpted chest, push his broad shoulders, claw at the taut cords of his neck, but somehow, in the logic of dreams, I only clung more steadfastly to him. Jesus held me tight. He put his lips to my ear. The storm rumbled on, deafening.

"Let not your heart be troubled," Jesus whispered, and I woke.

✢

It took me a moment to remember where I was. Orlando, the hotel. The clock glowed red on the nightstand. I was in bed with Jake. My boxers were wet. I usually remembered to tuck a spare beneath my pillow, but that night I'd forgotten to get one from the suitcase. I slipped from the sheets as quietly as I could.

Dad snored from the bed opposite. Mom lay silent beside him. Groping in the dark, I tripped over the suitcase. I stopped, listened.

A concert of heavy breathing.

Finally, I fumbled out of my boxers and into dry ones. Behind me, the cot creaked.

"It's not a sin," Abe whispered, "if it's in your sleep."

I said nothing. I couldn't go back to bed, not with Abe knowing what had just happened, and the bathroom was no escape, so I opened the sliding glass door to the hotel's little balcony and stepped out into the warm Floridian night.

The interstate stretched below, headlights streaming, palms waving in the median. They didn't have trees like that in Kentucky. I'd seen my first earlier that day near the Georgia-Florida border. It looked exotic, like something out of a travel magazine.

Across the highway I could make out the tallest rides at Bible World. The mountainous silhouette of a roller coaster. The highest point in the park flashing red like a radio tower. For a long time, I stared at that light, trying not to think about tomorrow, or Mom sick on the side of the road, or Jesus in the dream, thinking instead about what Abe had said—a kind of guilt loophole. It's something I became used to doing as a kid: mental gymnastics to cope with my shame. *It's not a sin if . . . God won't mind because . . . It doesn't count when . . .* I've had to work hard to overcome such magical thinking and be more honestly forgiving of myself as an adult.

When I came back in, I was more careful, but still ended up stubbing my foot on something in the dark. It was a lot harder than the suitcase and hurt like the devil. I swallowed my *Ow!*, sat on the edge of the bed, and rubbed my throbbing toe until the pain eased. Fortunately, I hadn't woke anyone. Abe had fallen back asleep. I climbed in bed. That's when I noticed Jake was gone.

I checked the bathroom. Stuck my head out into the hall. Slid a chair over to hold the door open, then wandered down to the vending and ice machines. Had he taken the elevator down to the lobby? I wasn't too worried yet. Jake was prone to wandering off; something caught his attention and he'd follow it without thinking. He might have gone downstairs for one of the cookies they kept in the lobby. Or maybe he was still in the room, and I just hadn't seen him. He could've woken when I was on the balcony, gotten scared, and crawled in with Mom and Dad.

I went back in. He wasn't asleep between them. I turned on the light.

Dad covered his eyes with his arm. "Not this again."

"Jake's missing," I said.

"Did you check the bathroom?"

I had the nervous premonition you get when you might be overreacting— that as soon as someone else checked, the answer would be right in front of you, making you look like an idiot. So I tried again. Pulled back the shower curtain. Still no Jake.

Dad was grasping for his glasses now.

Mom was sitting up. "What's going on?"

I walked through the room and spotted what I'd tripped over: one of my dumbbells. I didn't know why but the sight of that was like ice down my spine. I went out to the balcony again. He still wasn't there either. I turned to head back in and that's when I saw him—down below, poolside.

I went over to the railing. He was dragging the black backpack with my hand weights.

"Jake!" I whisper-shouted. "What are you doing?"

He stopped, smiled, and waved up at me. Then he sat down on the edge of the pool and stuck his legs in. He slipped his arms through the straps of the backpack and buckled the belt. He scooted forward and the weight pulled his shoulders back. Then he slid into the water.

He sank like a stone. One second he was waving, the next he was under. I waited like an idiot for him to come back up.

"No." I rushed back in from the balcony.

"What's wrong?" Dad was pulling on sweatpants.

"He's in the pool."

"At this time of night?"

I didn't answer. There was no time. I was running. Down the hall, to the elevator. Pressing the button over and over. It was so slow! I took the stairs.

We were only on the third floor. Despite the exercise, I was still easily winded, but going down was easier than up. By the time I made it through the lobby, past the front desk clerk—"Hey!"—and out to the pool deck, he'd been under for several minutes. I was still half hoping to see him splashing around, goofing off—the whole thing a prank. Maybe Abe was in on it. But he was on the bottom, right where he'd gone in, the backpack rippling underwater like a black hole he was being sucked into.

I jumped.

I wasn't a very good swimmer. The water went immediately up my nose. I coughed and coughed. Took a breath best I could and dove down.

It wasn't very deep, only six feet or so. He was floating, serenely, pinned to the pool floor like a turtle flipped on its shell. I tried lifting him under the arms, but it was awkward and too heavy underwater. I had to resurface for breath.

The second dive, I worked on getting the straps off his arms, but the backpack was on too tight. I'd forgotten about the belt. I groped for the clasp at his waist and clicked it. I thought it'd slide off easy then, but it didn't, and I needed more air first.

Third dive and still it was a struggle, getting the straps off. Finally, finally, he was free and I was so tired, but he was weightless now. I wrapped an arm around his chest and he came right up with me.

Dad and Abe were suddenly there and went down on their knees at the side of the pool. They hauled Jake out and laid him flat on the concrete. I climbed out after. It took a few tries.

His face was white. His chest pale, unmoving.

Dad shook him, shouting. No response.

Abe called 911 on his cell.

Dad began CPR. But he didn't know what he was doing; he was just improvising from what you see on TV, pounding on Jake's chest. I knelt beside him, unsure what to do.

Abe gave instructions from the phone operator. "The airway. She says to check the airway. Tilt his head more. Eli, reach in with your fingers. Okay, now open his jaw. Two breaths, then thirty compressions. Lock your fingers, Dad. No, in the center—she says it needs to be over his breastbone—yeah, right there."

A wail from behind us. Mom in her nightgown, leaning on the night clerk's arm.

"Please, Lord," Dad was saying over and over. "Please, Lord."

After every thirty compressions, Dad gave me the signal and I blew twice into Jake's mouth.

"Squeeze his nose shut," Abe said.

Not even a hundred compressions in—less than two minutes, but it felt like two hours—I tasted a rush of chlorine. I pulled back just in time. On TV they cough up a bit of water, but Jake full-on vomited.

"Turn him on his side," Abe said. "You have to clear the airway."

We tilted Jake over, I dug my fingers into his mouth, and he gagged. More vomit. Rescuing someone from drowning is more *Exorcist* than *Baywatch*. This time—thank God—he coughed and spat and opened his eyes. Dad pulled him against his chest and sobbed.

"Thank you, Lord. Thank you."

Mom flung herself over the two of them. Abe and I joined the family huddle.

Jake was crying. "I didn't see her."

"It's okay, baby. You're okay."

"I didn't see Dinah."

✢

After the EMTs arrived and checked Jake over—alive, but with an extremely bruised chest—the story came out. How he woke in the middle of the night to an empty bed. How he'd changed into his swim trunks, tried to lift the backpack with the weights, removed one of the ten-pounders to lighten the load, and left the hotel room, all while I was out on the balcony. How he'd taken the elevator down to the first floor, dragged the backpack out past the lobby desk (where the graveyard-shift clerk had fallen asleep), and used the key card to access the swimming pool.

When asked why he'd tried to drown himself, Jake said, "To get to Heaven."

The EMTs exchanged looks of concern.

"But how were you going to get back?" Abe said.

"God."

"God?" an EMT said.

Jake pointed at me. "God sent Eli back."

I lost it then. All the adrenaline left me. I started hyperventilating. My vision went blurry. The EMT sat me down on a lounge chair and helped me take several slow breaths.

"You saved him," she said.

"But it's my fault."

"He's okay."

✢

After we got back from the hospital, I helped Mom gather up all the Bible World supplies and repack the suitcases. "We're leaving," she said. "We're leaving."

"We're all upset," Dad said. "But let's not do anything rash."

"He could have died!" Mom yelled. "He tried to *kill* himself!"

"I know. It was very scary. We've all had a shock. But the doctor said he's fine. Let's calm down and we'll—"

Mom shook her head. "I don't want to hear it. It's over."

Jake, who was resting in bed, started sobbing again. "But Eli did it."

"No, Jake. I didn't."

Dad sat down next to him on the bed. "Listen, Jakey. What happened to Eli was a miracle. It was God's Plan. But you don't go messing with God's Plan yourself. You don't put yourself in danger like that on purpose. God doesn't want that. He wants mommies and daddies to go to Heaven first. You don't skip the line."

"Would you listen to yourself!" Mom shouted. "God's Plan, God's Plan. Jesus Christ, Simon! Who are you to know the Will of God? Come here, baby."

Jake went to her, and she put her hands on his shoulders. "Forget what Daddy said. Dying is *forever*. There are no take-backs. Heaven's not real. You're real. I'm real. Your family's real. Understand?"

She was shaking him. Jake cried harder.

"You're scaring him, Debbie!"

"Good! He should be scared. It's our job to teach him to be scared. And we failed, Simon. We were supposed to keep him safe and we failed."

"Come here, Jakey." Dad held open his arms.

But Mom pulled Jake to her. "No. No more. We're going."

"Fine." Dad bent to pick up a suitcase. "I'll call Gideon from the car."

"No. You're not coming. *I'm* taking the boys back. Alone."

"You can't *drive*, Debbie. You're sick."

"Abe has his permit."

"I'm not going," Abe said. "I'm staying with Dad."

Mom whirled around. "Like hell you are."

Abe stood firm, but Dad deflated. "Do as your mother says."

"No. I want to go on Gideon's show with you."

"He's not *going* on Gideon's show," Mom said. "Not if he wants to stay in this family."

"I'll see you at home, son," Dad said.

We carried the bags down and loaded them in the trunk. Dad hugged each of us boys while Mom looked on, arms crossed, foot tapping. She held out the keys to Abe, but he wouldn't take them.

"Drive safe," Dad said.

Abe sighed and gave in. We piled into the van without Dad. Abe backed slowly out of the parking space and pulled out of the hotel lot. I turned in my seat and watched Dad watching us go. He lifted his hand in goodbye.

✛

This is how it should have ended:

We drove home to Kentucky without him. Back in Orlando, Dad broke the news to Gideon and I was finally able to give up being the Heaven Kid.

Mom wouldn't speak to Dad for weeks, even after he got home. Eventually, they divorced. I wanted to live with Mom; Abe wanted Dad. Jake was caught between. They decided on split custody.

Dad stayed on at Creation as minister to the homebound. He still told my story, but I was no longer involved and his sermons expanded to other Biblical topics besides Heaven.

Against all odds, Mom went into remission. The doctors called it a medical miracle—a term she was offended by ("Then what was all that *radiation* for!"). Turns out, I wasn't the first Harpo to graduate from college after all. Once she got better, Mom took online classes at Bluegrass Community and Technical College, then at the University of Kentucky; she got her bachelor's in communication, then her master's in library science; and she went back to work at Canaan's public library—as a full-time librarian.

Abe got married, had kids. He went on to manage a Chick-fil-A. (Okay, so maybe some things would play out the same.)

Jake was the third Harpo to go to college, after me.

I came out in college. It wasn't easy with Dad and my brothers, but Mom was there to support me. We had a good laugh about that PFLAG meeting in Atlanta. She got to meet Will and be a granny to Oliver. The Harpo family was broken, but in the end we were better off for it. We weren't exactly happy, but we weren't miserable either. That's as close to a happily-ever-after as I can imagine.

Sometimes it's much simpler, the wishful thinking:

Mom got better, Mom got better, Mom got better.

She didn't grimace and clutch her side in pain soon after we left Dad in the hotel parking lot. She didn't ask Abe, merging unsteadily onto I-75, to take the next exit and head back to the hospital. She didn't lean her head against the window, eyes closed, and chant under her rasping breath, "My boys, my boys, my boys . . ."

PART THREE
BIBLE WORLD

12

SHALOM!

Thank heavens for Google. Without the advent of the "image search,"
there would have been no way for Eli to make a positive ID of
Jesus. We clicked through painting after painting and it was no . . .
no . . . no . . . After about a hundred, he'd wiggle in his chair and sigh,
exasperated. I'd tell him to take a break and go play, but he wouldn't
budge from the computer screen.

"Just five more pictures, Daddy," he said. "Do five more."

It touched me how desperately he wanted to get this right. "Don't
worry, kiddo. We'll find him."

—from *Heaven or Bust!*, "Jesus Lineup," ch. 24, p. 144

AFTER WILL AND I HOOKED up, our relationship took off at breakneck
speed. It was fast-tracked by our mutual curiosities about each other—his
for my strange celebrity childhood; mine for what it was like to have a
boyfriend at all, to finally be loved by a man. In many ways, we were oppo-
sites. Him, extroverted; me, introverted. Him, right-brained, emotional,
artistic; me, left-brained, rational, scientific. Him, confident, relaxed; me,
self-conscious, nervous. He was always seeking the spotlight; I was always
avoiding it. I once joked that Will would have made an excellent Heaven
Kid for Gideon . . . had Will not thought the very idea of Heaven an insult
to the human condition.

But there was an imbalance to our relationship—part of which was real, the other just in my head. The gap in our experience was to blame. He was my first and I fell *hard*. I was paranoid about losing him. Will was popular and way out of my league. He always seemed to have guys crushing on him, waiting in the wings—David was just one of many. I was sure Will would grow bored of me eventually. I just *knew* he'd break up with me; it felt inevitable.

He later told me this had all been my own insecurity talking. He was just as into me as I was into him. But at the time, I always felt the need to keep him entertained. If ever I sensed him losing interest, I'd give him another piece of myself—an offering, new evidence of my unusual history, to captivate him all over again.

The "Heaven Boy Homo!!!!!!!" video on YouTube.

The white pocket Bible with Gideon's inscription.

The park map that showed my Biblical Realm.

Will wanted to hear all about what it was like meeting his hero, Gil Bright. I told him about flying the drone and my encounter with Bright's husband and daughter. About going to his memorial a few months later. Dad had understood how much it meant to me. He couldn't have been more opposed to Bright's life work, but he believed every person should be respected in death—Saved or not. What happened to you after was God's Judgment, not man's. Although it couldn't have hurt that there were numerous accounts of last-minute deathbed conversions, just like the Brights had said there'd be, many of which claimed *my* meeting with Bright had been his first step toward the Lord. Yeah, right.

The memorial was massive and held in the auditorium of a liberal arts college in North Carolina. Dad and I went alone; Abe stayed home with Jake. I couldn't imagine what an atheist funeral would be like—what would they sing? Read? Say?—and I was surprised to discover it wasn't much different from a religious one. Pop songs (Steve Winwood's "Higher Love," Whitney Houston's "I Will Always Love You," the Beatles' "Ob-La-Di, Ob-La-Da"—*life goes on, brah / la-la, how the life goes on!*), instead of hymns. Excerpts from literature (Percy Bysshe Shelley's "Adonais: An Elegy on the Death of John Keats," Shakespeare's *The Tempest*, E. B. White's *Charlotte's Web*), instead of Biblical verses. Eulogies from fellow scientists on Bright's work, instead of talk about Heaven or his soul. The focus was on what Bright did, how he lived. He'd done a lot of great things with his life and it made me wonder what I'd do with mine.

But with or without God, mourning was mourning was mourning. Laughter and tears. Food after. At the reception, I spotted Mel. She was the one who'd read the passage from *Charlotte's Web*, her favorite childhood book from Bright's nightly tuck-ins. But I was too anxious to offer her a sorry-for-your-loss. I was afraid she'd get mad at us for being there, lump Dad and me in with the evangelicals who'd damned her father to hell ("BRIGHT ENOUGH FOR YOU DOWN THERE?"). In college, Will certainly thought of Dad and my brothers like that. Homophobic stereotypes. I didn't correct him. I let him believe what he wanted about my family. It's only now, after years of therapy, that I understand this deceit as my misguided attempt to keep these two worlds I was inhabiting, these two parts of myself, these two halves of my heart, separate out of fear of their collision and implosion. Because if Will thought of my family only in the worst terms, he'd never want to meet them, right?

Instead of defending them, I found myself embellishing the stories. Will and I would be at dinner together, a lull in the conversation, and desperate to break the silence, I'd blurt—"Charlie Gideon once cornered me in a bathroom stall. He tried to touch me, but I got away." Or at the Halloween store, debating on our couple costume: "You should have *seen* the blood at the Crucifixion Reenactment. Buckets, like in *Carrie*. It was disgusting." Or after I caught him checking out a guy at our favorite bar: "My father used to make me memorize the Bible." It was always *my father*—never *Dad*. "All the verses about Heaven. We'd practice for *hours*. If I got it right, I got a cookie."

"And if you were wrong?"

"He'd . . . spank me."

Except for the one time in the church parking lot when he'd grabbed me, Dad never laid a hand on me or my brothers. But Will didn't know that. For authenticity, I read him the verse on corporal punishment—*He that spareth his rod hateth his son: but he that loveth him, chasteneth him betimes*, Proverbs 13:24.

"Hmm . . . does the Bible have a lisp?" Will said. He's always trying to make me laugh to cheer me up, likes to say his love language is *sarcasm*. When I told him about the Jesus sex dreams he'd waggled his eyebrows and said, "Should I grow a beard?" Later, he went to Party City and surprised me in the bedroom with a full-on Jesus costume: robe, sandals, wig, *and* beard. The whole shebang. My fantasy come to life. I tried, but I couldn't get into the role-play. I kept seeing the Throne Room. I made him take it off.

"Yeth," I replied. "The Gothpel of Jethuth Chritht."

It was a quieter performance, these memories retold. A one-man show with a one-man audience. I was still the Heaven Kid—not Gideon's version, but Will's. The child victim. He called it PTCS. Post-Traumatic Church Syndrome. It took a long time for me to find my way out of the web of lies I told him that first year we were together.

Will and I rarely fought. Growing up with two bickering parents had made me a conflict-avoidant type. Our first real fight came in the fall of my junior year. We'd been dating for over a year and were practically living together. I still had a dorm room, but only in name. More than half my things were in Will's apartment.

He was expecting me that night, but my organic chem lab was canceled—the TA had the flu—so I swung by Kroger and bought him a steak and some flowers. I was always buying Will flowers. I couldn't help myself. I'd never had anyone to buy flowers for. He acted like he didn't care for them—they were a waste of money—but I knew he secretly loved them. Sometimes he joked that if I put cash into a jar every time I had the urge, I'd be able to pay off my student loans before I graduated, with my flower money alone.

I planned on surprising him. I had a key to his place—I'd already begun to think of it as *our* place—so I let myself in. I took the grocery bags into the kitchen and put the irises on the counter. I was in the process of cutting the stems and transferring them to a vase of water when I heard Dad's voice coming down the hall.

". . . a-BOM-ination, I say . . ."

I froze, horrified, at the counter.

How had he found me? Why had Will let him in? The image of Dad in our bedroom, yelling at Will, flashed in my mind.

". . . a cor-RUP-tion of the flesh . . ."

I went shaking down the hall.

". . . for these shall be the wages of sin!"

I pushed open the door. Will, seated at his computer, leapt in surprise, fumbled with the mouse. The video froze on Dad's face—a Simon Says sermon.

"Jesus, E! You scared me."

"What're you doing?"

He started laughing. "God, I feel twelve again. Mom walking in, catching me with porn."

"What are you doing, watching my—my father . . ."

"Again with the flowers?"

I looked down. I held an iris in my hand. I threw it at him.

"You are a—a fuck." I was still new to cursing; I wasn't quite fluent.

"What?"

"A fucking—fuck. I thought he was here."

"Who? Your dad? Oh, shit. Sorry."

"I almost had a heart attack."

"Well, don't do that."

"What the heck, Will. Why are you looking him up online?"

"It's not a big deal. I was just curious."

"Had to check out the Jesus Freak. See just how freaky we are." Even as I was saying it, I knew it was hypocritical, but I didn't care.

"Hey, come on. It's not like that."

"I'm sick of you snooping into my life."

"I don't snoop. You share, I'm interested. So what? It's what boyfriends do."

"Why can't you just be happy with who I am now?"

"Because you're not happy, E! You're depressed. Or repressed. Or something. You have to deal with your trauma or—"

"Oh my God. If I have to hear the word *trauma* one more time."

"What do you want me to say? Wound? Damage? *Pain?* Call it whatever you want, it doesn't go away unless you confront it."

"What do you know about *trauma*, Mr. Perfect? Mr. Wonderful?"

"Stop. Just stop. You know my life is neither of those things."

"Close enough."

"I'm serious, E. Your family indoctrinated you. Your father used you. You can't just let this fester."

"Okay, Dr. Freud."

"I mean, it *is* kind of oedipal . . ."

"Shut up! Just shut up!"

What was he talking about, I wasn't happy? A second ago, I was standing in the kitchen with a bouquet of irises for him—*my gay lover*. How was that *repressed*?

"I think you should come out to your family," Will said.

"What? No!"

"Just listen. I'd be there to support you. We could do it at Christmas."

"That's *crazy*. You're crazy."

"Is it, though? I mean, how do they *not* know, after Bible World? That video . . ."

"We didn't talk about it, okay? Dad just thought I was hysterical or something. It was grief over Mom. Or the sun . . ."

"The *sun*?"

"I don't know. Sunstroke. Florida in the summer."

"Wow. He'd rather you brainfried than gay."

"I'm not coming out to them, okay? I'm just not."

"Okay, jeez . . . I'm just saying, they might surprise you. Who knows?"

I did, that's who. I knew exactly how it'd go. What verses Dad and Abe would spout at me. 1 Corinthians 6:9. 1 Timothy 1:10. Romans 1:27. How they'd pray with me—*over* me—for forgiveness. Lecture me about my "lifestyle choices." Will was always telling me stories of intolerant parents who flipped when their kid came out, overcame their biases, joined an LGBTQ-friendly church. It's easy to be prejudiced against people you deliberately other, but when it's personal? When it's *family*? Why couldn't Dad and my brothers rise to their better natures? Shouldn't I at least give them the chance?

No. Not when it was a test I knew they'd fail.

"Look," Will said. "I don't mean to pressure you—"

"*Really?*"

"Well, okay, maybe a little. I just think you can't keep compartmentalizing your life like this. It's unhealthy."

"You have no idea what you're talking about. It's the *healthiest* way. The only way."

"What about me? I want to meet your family, E. You want to meet mine, don't you?"

Ow—that hurt. Socked me right in the gut. Will was an only child. He talked about his parents, Jeff and Lois, all the time. He knew how badly I wanted to meet them. Saying I couldn't until he met mine felt like emotional blackmail.

"You know that's different," I said. "You're out to them. They're not— they don't—"

"Come on. *Please?* We could do Christmas at yours, New Year's at mine."

I shook my head. Nuh-uh. No way. It wasn't happening.

My eyes stung. He reached out to comfort me, but I pushed him away and left the apartment. I was mad at him, but I was far angrier at myself. It was unfair of me to expect him to bring me into his family when I wouldn't let him anywhere near my own. For the umpteenth time I thought, *It would have been so much easier if Mom were still here.*

The Saturday after Mom died, we woke early and got ready for Bible World. On a normal family vacation, we'd have fought over the hotel bathroom, elbow-sparring at the sink. But that morning we were calm and considerate. We took turns brushing our teeth. We slathered on sunscreen until our faces, necks, and arms glowed ghostly white. Dad, Abe, and Jake would all leave Florida with tans, but I had Mom's pale complexion—I'd roast.

We put on jean shorts and our color-coded neon tanks.

"Shouldn't we be wearing black?" I'd asked Dad, the night before.

He'd laid everything out, just as Mom had done a week—a lifetime—ago.

"Gideon's providing our suits. We'll change at the church, before the funeral."

When Mom was admitted to the hospital in Orlando, Gideon postponed the grand opening at Bible World. If he could have swapped me for another Heaven Kid, I'm sure he would have, but it was too late for that. After she died, he offered to host her funeral on his show before the big reveal of my new realm. Dad agreed, on the condition Gideon pay the expenses for a second funeral and the burial at Creation Baptist.

As if the fluorescent apparel wasn't inappropriate enough, Dad lined us up and handed out matching fanny packs.

"No way." I shook my head. "Nuh-uh. I'm not wearing that."

Dad cut to the quick. "Your mother picked them out."

I buckled the dumb plastic belt around my waist, the glow-in-the-dark kangaroo pouch hanging over my crotch.

Dad led us in prayer.

"Heavenly Father. We pray that You watch over us today at Bible World. Please show us the way to spread Your Word. We hope to Save as many souls as possible, so they can find—so they can meet—so Debbie—"

His voice broke. Abe put a hand on his shoulder. Jake crawled into his lap.

After days of waterworks, you'd think we'd be all cried out. I was exhausted, wrung dry, but the tears came anyway.

"Please don't cry," Dad said. "You'll make me start again."

"Dad," I said. "We don't have to do this."

But Dad had only one approach to grief. He cleared his throat, finished the prayer. "So they can join Debbie in Your Eternal Kingdom. In Your most precious and holy name, Amen."

A chorus of *Amens*.

"I want you boys to remember: Your mother might not be here in the flesh, but she *is* in spirit. She's looking down, watching everything we do today, and she wouldn't want us to be sad. So let's have fun, okay?"

⁜

The signs for Bible World were a majestic purple, featuring the park's mascots, a lion and lamb, gleefully counting down to the exit: Just *five miles! . . . three miles! . . . one mile away!* It was almost nine o'clock and the sun was bright on the van's windshield. The highway was mostly empty until the turnoff, where a line of cars was backed up at the parking tolls. We crawled to a standstill. Traffic put a crack in Dad's cheery facade. He was determined we have a good time for Mom, but after fifteen minutes of inching forward, he threw up his hands.

"This is ridiculous! Shouldn't they have a special entrance for us?"

Gideon had offered us a chauffeured car, but Dad, being Dad, insisted on driving us. Gideon promised a guide through Bible World, but he'd offered no instructions for parking. When it was finally our turn at one of the parking tolls, Dad rolled down his window, smiled, and told the Bible World employee who we were.

"Nineteen ninety-five," the cashier said. He was wearing a purple vest with little Bible World pins. "Thirty dollars flat for priority."

"You don't understand," Dad said. "My son is Eli Harpo."

"Okay." The man shrugged and repeated the price.

"No, but we're the family from *Heaven or Bust!*"

"What?"

Dad sighed. "*Charlie Gideon & the Heaven Boy!*"

He still wasn't getting it.

"We're the reason all these people are here. The new park attraction? That's based on my book."

"Okay, sir. But I'm still going to need you to pay before I can let you park."

"But—Charlie Gideon. Call Gideon. He'll tell you."

The toll operator picked up his walkie and called his manager. Meanwhile, the driver of the car behind our van laid on his horn.

"Dad," Abe said. "It's just twenty dollars. I can pay it, if you want."

"No. It's the principle. We're guests of the show. It's your mother's funeral, for goodness' sake!"

"Sir?" the cashier said. "Would you mind pulling over while we work this out?"

"Certainly."

We sat for nearly twenty minutes, watching cars pay and pass beneath the toll arm, trickling into the parking lot one by one. Jake couldn't sit still. Eventually Dad let him remove his seat belt and stand between the front seats, where he could peer through the windshield for a glimpse of the park. There was nothing to see but a topiary hedge on either side of the road, one in the shape of a lion, the other a lamb. Jake stared at them without blinking, like at any moment they might spring to life.

I rested my forehead against the window.

Outside, a bus pulled into the oversize-vehicle lane. It looked more like the luxury tour kind than a public school bus, but it was filled with children. The kids wore identical purple shirts and baseball caps. A church camp. One boy, with his cap off, sported the same summer haircut Mom gave us with the clippers she kept under the kitchen sink. She called it the Buzz. I always acted like I hated it: the wooden stool, towel draped over shoulders, hair snowing red on the kitchen tile. Real haircuts were done by professionals in salons or barbershops. This was yet another way my family cut corners to save a buck.

But secretly I loved it: the way she palmed my head in her hand like a melon, turning it this way and that, brushing off my ears and scalp. At the end, she whipped off the towel and blew on the back of my newly naked neck.

"*Voilà!* Mullet-be-gone!"

I touched the hair there now. It was overgrown, definitely mullet-worthy. Mom had been too sick to buzz us before the trip. Dad said the Buzz made us look like bald aliens and we'd be more photogenic with hair anyway. But it was so hot. I missed the summer cut, how light and cool it felt, how my spine tingled when she ran her hand over the bristles.

One of the boys on the bus, wearing his cap backward, had his head pressed to his window, too. I wiped my eyes, but he'd already seen. The boy placed the palm of his hand flat against the glass. I did the same.

✢

Once the Bible World cashier cleared it with his superiors, he apologized and waved us through the toll.

"They told me someone will be at the Welcome Arch waiting for you. Sorry again for the confusion. Have a blessed day!"

Beyond the lion and lamb topiary was a crowded parking lot, filled with not just cars but people, milling about in barricaded areas. At first I assumed they were waiting in line for the park. But as we drove past, I saw they were shouting and waving signs. A bearded man draped in a rainbow flag held up a banner: ALL UNICORNS GO TO HEAVEN! Next to him a young woman shook a picket sign with a photo of Charlie Gideon's face, green dollar signs Sharpied over the eyes. Her friend wielded the same photo, only hers was bordered by a collage of naked female body parts clipped from magazines. She'd drawn a conspicuous line of drool down Gideon's lips. A boy Jake's age wore a sandwich board in the shape of the Darwin fish, sprouting legs. His sister jammed a camel Beanie Baby at the eye of a long oversize needle. Their father stood close by with a plain, handwritten poster—MATTHEW 19:24—for context.

"They're having a party," Jake said.

"It's a protest," I said. It was a little scary, like Mom's Wall of Scandal had come to angry life.

"These people should be ashamed," Dad said. "They make the man out to be some kind of monster."

"They're just jealous," Abe said.

"Don't pay any attention to them," Dad said. "We won't let them ruin our day."

Just before Dad steered the van away, into the lane marked PRIORITY
PARKING, I glimpsed a sign and did a double take. It was the image of a small,
redheaded boy in a robin's-egg-blue suit. He was looking up toward the
sky, hands raised as if in prayer. The cover of *Heaven or Bust!* The protester
had blown up my picture and drawn over it. A black box with five vertical
bands. Prison bars. The message?

FREE THE HEAVEN KID!

✚

The priority parking lane curved away from the garages in the distance
and approached a massive stone wall circling the park. The Bible World
designers had made the wall look "ancient" in the way of a vaguely Egyptian
Indiana Jones set, like it had been fashioned from the same blocks used
to build the pyramids.

Even here the parking was atrocious. Dad drove up and down the aisles,
searching for a space close to the entrance, but to no avail. Half the lot had
been taken over by news vans with satellite dishes mounted to their roofs.
He eventually found a spot at the very back, almost to the chain-link fence
that separated the park property from the highway. In place of letters or
numbers, there was a Biblical book and chapter on a pole above our section
of the lot, to help you remember where you'd parked. We were Hosea 6.

We disembarked. Crossing the blacktop in matching tank tops, visors,
and fanny packs, I felt like a member of a cartoon trio, like Shem, Ham,
and Japheth, who, respectively, wear red, white, and blue swim trunks in
the episode of *Bible Tales* when Logan and Emma go tubing with Noah
and his family. I wished I could have gone tubing off an ark. Already the
parking lot was hotter than a desert; heat waves distorted the arched entry
to the park as we made our slow pilgrimage across the asphalt.

Halfway there, I caught sight of a figure in a white robe at the park
entrance. I rubbed my eyes, blinked. I was clearly hallucinating, because
this is what I saw: Beneath the Shalom! Welcome Arch, holding a sign
that read HARPO FAMILY in black marker, stood none other than Jesus
Christ Himself.

I stopped in my tracks. My family walked on.

Jake was the first to notice me lagging behind. "Eli?"

"What are you doing?" Abe called back.

"Come on!" Dad shouted. "We're late enough already."

I trudged forward reluctantly. The idea of encountering a real-life Jesus outside my dreams was more than a little unsettling. But the Meadow was coming back to me. The lightning, a robe opening. Something inside me was stirring. Something outside, too, I realized with alarm. Maybe the fanny pack wasn't such a bad idea, after all.

As we made our approach, I saw this Jesus wasn't *my* Jesus. This Jesus wasn't even the Jesus in the Bible World commercials or on the billboards. Those Jesuses had been supermodels. This Jesus was just an above-average-looking man with long hair and a beard. He was shorter, less built, and his eyes were a dull brown—not the intense shade of green that mesmerized me in my dreams.

"Harpo family!" Jesus called, arms wide. "Shalom!"

Dad stepped forward and shook Jesus's hand. "Good to meet you, um . . . Jesus?"

Jesus nodded. "Please, let me say, how deeply sorry I am for your loss." He turned to us boys. "But as I'm sure you know, your mom couldn't be in a better place than with Dad right now."

We looked at one another and then at Dad, confused. But then Jesus kissed two fingers and lifted them, and we knew which dad he really meant.

Next, Jesus bent down, hands on knees, to Jake.

"And you must be the famous Eli Harpo. You came to visit me in Heaven."

Jake frowned. He eyed Jesus skeptically. Then his hand shot out, snatched a fistful of beard, and gave a good yank.

"Ow!" Jesus jerked away, tripping over his sandaled feet.

"Jake!" Dad said. "That's not nice. Apologize to Jesus right now."

"That's okay." Jesus held his jaw. "I'm sure he was just playing."

"It's real," Jake informed us.

"I'm so sorry," Dad said.

"He did it to Santa, too," I said. "If it makes you feel any better."

"No, no," Jesus said. "It's an honor, really. Eli Harpo can pull my beard any day."

"I'm *not* Eli," Jake said. "I'm *Jake* Harpo. *That's* Eli."

Jesus's eyes shifted to me. His smile faltered.

"Of course!" Jesus smacked his palm against his forehead. He moved from Jake to me. "How could I forget? It's just you've grown so much since I last saw you."

He pulled me in for a hug. Jesus smelled like incense, olive trees, and Axe body spray. Up close, you could see he used bronzer and mascara. Blond highlights made his Jesus hair shimmer. I hung limply in his arms.

"Okay, Harpos! I'll be your guide for the day. *The Charlie Gideon Hour* shoots live at three this afternoon. That's when we'll have the funeral. After the service there'll be a ribbon-cutting ceremony and a tour of Eli's new realm. We have to get you into hair and makeup by one thirty, but until then you're free to explore the park. Even better, as guests of honor, Charlie Gideon has granted you Holy Orders, so you can cut to the front of any line. I know this is a difficult time, but let's do our best to have a fun and blessed day!"

Jesus moved from me to Jake to Abe, handing out Holy Orders—large VIP passes in the shape of a cross. They hung from gold lanyards.

"How about a picture?" Jesus said.

"Sure." Dad handed Jesus his iPhone.

We lined up beneath the Shalom! Welcome Arch. When we took family photos, we typically fell into a natural arrangement: Jake front and center, Abe and me on either side, Mom and Dad in the back. Dad stood at Abe's shoulder, Mom at mine. Posing without Mom, the arrangement was off-balance. Dad stood at Abe's side out of habit, leaving a gap behind me.

Jesus looked at us on the phone screen. "Why don't you slide a bit that way?" He waved Dad over to the middle. Dad did as asked and the composition became symmetrical. Jesus took several photos, then showed them to us for approval. None of them looked right. I thought of Mom's Polaroids. It wasn't the same.

Jesus beckoned for us to follow him into the park. Jake, who was bursting with excitement, ran ahead with him. Abe, trying and failing not to look too eager, was close behind.

"So," Dad said, nodding toward Jesus as we brought up the rear. "How's he look?"

"Not bad," I lied.

I did eventually find my Jesus. It was during an English class in college. We were doing an advertising unit to learn rhetorical analysis. My group did the famous 1984 Macintosh commercial. Another did a late-nineties one for Lumberjack Snacks!™, and when they played it for the class, there he was. Bearded with green eyes. Square-jawed, thick-necked, shoulders built. He wore red flannel, a black toboggan, suspenders. He looked more like a sexy caricature of a lumberjack than a real one, like a model in a camping catalog. He appeared after a little boy's Popsicle-stick log cabin magically grew to life size. *Chopping down trees sure works up a mighty appetite! Good thing I always carry some vittles on me!* The Jesus of my dreams tore open and tossed back a package of trail mix. At the end of the commercial Abraham Lincoln—stovepipe hat and all—stuck his head out the door. *Did somebody say Lumberjack Snacks?*

As soon as I saw it, I remembered it playing on CGN during the commercial breaks for *Bible Tales* episodes. I felt like a schmuck. I never told Dad.

"Sometimes the best you can hope for is an approximation," he said now. "Not everyone gets to experience the real deal."

Jake had grown impatient. Up ahead, he turned and waved for us to hurry. "Come on! What are we waiting for!"

And so we passed beneath the Welcome Arch and entered Bible World.

13

REALM TO REALM

Jesus loves me—this I know,
For to Bible World we go.
Mom and Dad will take us there,
Where we'll play without a care!

Off to Bible World . . .
Off to Bible World . . .
Off to Bible World . . .
You really gotta go!

Jesus loves me—loves me how?
Arks and harps and sharks, oh wow!
Shepherd leads, so be good sheep—
Hey, look, Mom! Tix are so cheap!

Bible World, the Most Spiritual Adventure on Earth!

—Bible World jingle, 2001

THE BIBLE WORLD PARK MAP, pinned to the corkboard in our bedroom, had boasted an array of attractions, with detailed drawings, color coded by Biblical Realm. But now that I was actually here, without Mom, and soon facing the biggest audience for my Heaven story yet, it was hard to muster up any feeling but dread. Abe and Jake pored over an updated version of the map at a stone table in Jerusalem Marketplace, the grand concourse just inside the Welcome Arch—tented kiosks, potted palms, and an Oasis Café with a view of the Lake of Crystal Waters. I looked over Jake's shoulder and tried to summon the excitement I used to feel at the idea of a vacation to Bible World.

"Okay, here's the plan." Abe traced the route with his finger. "First we do the Drop-Tower of Babel. Then Daniel in the Lions' Den in 3D."

"Don't forget Jonah's Whale!" Jake said.

"Jonah's is a water ride," Jesus said. "You might want to do the Drop-Tower after, to dry off."

"Or Sodom and Gomorrah." Abe tapped the spot in the Genesis Realm with two interconnecting roller coasters—one forward, the other back. That did look fun.

"Some of those might be a little too much for . . ." Jesus nodded toward Jake.

"Too much!" Abe said. "We're doing them all. Right, Dad?"

"Well, some rides have height requirements," Jesus insisted.

"Maybe we should start small," Dad said. "What can we all do?"

"Hmm . . . how about . . ." Jesus's finger landed on NOAH'S ARK, which wasn't a ride at all, but a petting zoo. "Ever pet a llama?" he asked Jake. "And right over here there's . . ." THE PARTING OF THE RED SEA, an aquarium in Moses's Realm.

Abe and I groaned. The kiddie realms?

Dad had his own agenda. His eye was on the Garden of Gethsemane, Crucifixion Corner, and the He Has Risen! Tomb replica—which all had live Biblical reenactments every three hours.

"Don't worry, boys," Jesus said. "We'll save the best for last." He tapped the map again, this time indicating the realm at the back of the park, coded white, with cartoon clouds and Pearly Gates opening onto a gleaming palace. It was labeled in gold calligraphy:

Eli Harpo's Adventure to the Afterlife

✢

A giant rainbow arch welcomed us to Noah's Ark with cascading water on either side of the walkway. Tourists entered the realm through a refreshing mist. A few kids from the tour bus earlier had climbed down off the path and were playing in the fountains. Their light purple shirts turned dark, wet fabric sticking to their chests.

The first thought I had when I saw the Ark was: *No way every species of animal could fit inside.* It was about the size of Creation Baptist and stood in the center of a clear pool. The water was low—ankle-deep—and the Ark looked more like a barn than a ship. Signs encouraged visitors to say prayers and throw coins into THE FLOOD WATERS.

A long line of tourists circled the pool, waiting for their turn to head up the wooden ramp and into the open bay. There was a sign: APPROX. WAIT TIME: 2½ HOURS.

"Don't forget." Jesus plucked the Holy Orders cross from Abe's neck and waved it. He led us straight into the throng. "Excuse me, excuse me. Very Holy Person coming through." Crowd members began to point and gawk. "It's Jesus! It's Jesus!" A man clasped Jesus's shoulder and called him a hero. Children swarmed him, clinging to his robes, beaming up with expressions of rapture. A woman with a stroller fell to her knees and kissed the back of his hand. "Now, now." Jesus helped her up and continued on. "Very Holy Person! Mr. Elijah Harpo! The Boy Who Went to Heaven! Coming through . . ." We moved in step with our guide and the crowd parted. No one said a thing as we cut the line, climbed the gangplank, and boarded the Ark.

✢

Inside, the Ark was three decks high and smelled of hay and poop. The first deck was the petting zoo, with animal stalls lining starboard and port. Signs outside each stall indicated the furry spectacles within.

"Hey, look." Abe pointed to a stall labeled KANGAROO.

I'd never been to a zoo before, never seen an animal more exotic than a Chihuahua. There was a line to enter the stall, but it was a small one—just three people waiting.

"Make way!" Jesus yelled. I cringed. He was really overdoing it. "Make way for the Boy Who Went to Heaven! And family."

Abe and Jake followed Jesus right into the stall. Dad and I aimed apologetic looks at the tourists we edged around.

The five of us barely fit. The stall's floor was covered in straw; sunlight entered through slats in the ship's wooden hull. Two kangaroos huddled in a dimly lit corner. A joey stuck his adorable little head out over the mama kangaroo's pouch.

I hesitated. I'd heard of kangaroo boxing. The cuteness was a deception; they were powerful, sometimes even vicious, creatures. And there was no cage between us and the animal to prevent it from attacking. Was this safe?

Abe wasn't afraid, though. He rushed the kangaroos, then let out a disappointed *awww!* and slapped the mama. The animal swayed with the force of the blow. It moved like a rocking chair—it *was* a rocking chair. I was supposed to have tumbled with lions in Heaven and now here I was, scared of a plaster kangaroo.

What was the point of a petting zoo with fake animals? I guess it was just meant to be one big photo op. We made the best of the letdown. Turned it into a game. Look at a sign on a stall and decide before entering: Real or Fake?

ELEPHANT. Obviously fake. They weren't even to size.

RABBIT. Real. A brown one and a white one. We looked, but couldn't tell the male and female apart.

GOAT. Real. Jake liked the little horns.

DONKEY. Real. We got this one wrong. They were fake.

HIPPO. Fake.

TIGER. Fake.

ZEBRA. Fake.

LLAMA. Real. But it was a cheat. Jesus had mentioned them.

PONY. Real. Wrong again. "What kind of petting zoo doesn't even have a pony?" Abe said. What a rip-off.

GIRAFFE. Fake. At least they had made them tall, their heads protruding through a hole cut in the floor to the second deck.

CAMEL. Fake. It did spit water, though.

MONKEY. Fake.

FLAMINGO. Fake. This was the only one we got wrong that was real. Two pink birds in a pen with a trough of water. You couldn't pet them.

TURTLE. Real? We couldn't tell. The shells (real enough) lay flat on the floor and were too heavy to lift. They were filled with *something*. Jake knocked, but the turtles (if they were in there) never came out.

Once we had our fill of plaster animals, we hiked up to the second deck, which was even more lame. A FLOOD TIMELINE and Bible verses ran across the walls. At least the third and top deck had a view of the park. Noah was there, speaking to tourists. He looked a lot like Jesus, except his beard was tinged with white and his cloak was red. "Shalom!" He waved us over. "Please, come join us. I was just telling these ladies and gentlemen how I managed to get the rhinos on board. Stubborn creatures, rhinos."

Dad, Abe, and Jake went to hear Noah's story, while Jesus attracted his own audience. I wandered over to the railing and looked out over the park. We weren't that high and you couldn't see much more than the line of people circling the Flood Waters, but at the bottom of the exit gangplank down below, there was a tableau of animals that had literally missed the boat. Most were dinosaurs: a stegosaurus, a triceratops, two velociraptors. The pterodactyl was a nice touch: perched on the tusk of a woolly mammoth, next to a saber-toothed tiger. The plaster creatures were all facing the Ark; they looked like they were reaching out to it with their little lizard hands, horns, and claws.

"Wonder what God had against velociraptors."

A boy in the church camp had walked up next to me. Purple shirt, purple cap. He looked about my age, maybe a year younger. The cap was backward. I recognized him from the bus—the boy who saw me crying through the window. I was nervous he'd bring it up, but he didn't.

"Adam and Eve used to ride them, with saddles and everything." He said this with a straight face, so I couldn't tell if he was joking.

"Like *The Flintstones*," I said, testing him.

He laughed. "Exactly. Your family drag you here?"

I nodded and pointed to them, taking photos with Noah. "You with your church group?"

I gestured at his shirt. It said *Angel Army*, with little halos over the *A*s. He shrugged. "Have you been on Sodom and Gomorrah yet?"

I shook my head.

"Wanna ride together?"

Did I ever.

"Eli!" Dad called. They were heading toward the exit.

"Ugh. I got to go."

"Ask your dad."

"I can't. Sorry."

I would have given anything to have gone with him, to freely explore the park with his youth group. All I wanted was to be a normal kid having a good time with his friends. But I knew better than to ask.

☩

The Parting of the Red Sea was a long, narrow aquarium. Two parallel tanks formed an alleyway of stingrays, eels, and parrotfish. The glass at the top of the tanks was curved to resemble the crests of waves. Spotlights gave the appearance of water moving overhead. In the middle was a strip of open sky. Moses stood at the entrance with his staff, swinging it this way and that, hefting it high overhead, then bringing it down dramatically to the ground between his feet. "Hurry!" He waved us inside. "The pharaoh and his army are coming!"

We walked through the parted sea and into blue light. Every few steps, Jake and Abe pressed their faces to the glass, looking for sharks. I lagged behind.

"You okay?" Jesus had been watching me since we exited the Ark through the gift shop, where it was stuffed animals galore. Jake bought a

T-Rex and Abe considered a jacket embossed with the Bible World logo, but I'd just stood there. The invitation from the kid in the church group had thrown my situation into stark relief. Every attraction we visited was just one step closer to me having to don my halo again. If only Mom were here. She'd have known exactly how to make fun of all this silly religious posturing. Everything was so much harder without her.

Before I could answer Jesus, Dad moved between us. "Hey, bud. What's going on?"

"I, uh . . . just miss Mom." I was fighting back tears.

"We all miss Mom," Abe said.

"Abe," Dad said. "Why don't you take Jake to look at the jellyfish?"

"I was just trying to help."

"Abe, please."

Abe rolled his eyes and steered Jake away.

Dad forced a smile at Jesus. "Would you excuse us?"

Jesus shrugged and trailed after them.

"Dad," I said, sniffing. "I can't do this."

"You haven't even tried yet."

"Mom didn't believe in Heaven."

"Of course she did."

"She didn't. She told me."

"Your mother was very sick. She wasn't in her right mind at the end."

"I know, but—"

Dad tapped under my chin, tilting my head back until I was looking straight up, past the aquarium tanks to the sliver of sky. It was a cloudless day.

"She's looking down on us right now. You see?"

I didn't. Not anymore. The tears came. At this rate, I'd be nothing but a puddle on Gideon's show.

"Hey, come here." Dad hugged me and gave me his handkerchief. Then he took my hand and led me over to a smaller, freestanding tank. Inside drifted little neon green question marks.

"Did you know the daddy seahorses carry the babies, not the mommies?" he said. "It's true."

I had only ever seen photos of seahorses. Mom did a marine biology unit with us when I was in fifth grade. They were much smaller and more lethargic than I'd imagined.

"I know you want Mom right now, but I can take care of you, too. Sometimes it's the dad who knows what's best. You have to trust me." He took me into his arms again.

Yes, I'd learned about seahorses before. I already knew that the males of the species carry the young, like penguin dads who take on egg-sitting duties. But I also knew that after a seahorse gives birth, he abandons his babies to mate again and make more. That's why seahorse litters are large: Like most fish, the fry are vulnerable to predators, and alone in the ocean, almost all of them die before reaching adulthood. I knew this, too, but pressed against Dad's chest, I didn't have the heart to tell him.

✛

Around eleven, we walked to Jerusalem for an early lunch. There was a Crucifixion reenactment at noon and Dad didn't want to miss it. On the way, we passed the Lake of Crystal Waters, where several kids in Angel Army shirts were playing in the water.

"Look!" Jake pointed. "It's a miracle!"

I didn't see what was so miraculous about a pond. Then I saw that the kids weren't playing in the water, but standing on its surface: walking on water. Only it wasn't a miracle. When you squinted you could make it out—an optical illusion. Just beneath the surface, a glass platform vanished to near invisibility.

"I wanna do a miracle," Jake said.

"It's not a miracle," I said. "It's just a glass platform."

"Is not."

"Uh, yeah."

Jake started to cry.

"Why do you have to do that?" Abe said. "Why do you always have to spoil his fun? Can't you just let him believe?"

"But it's stupid," I said. Not to mention reckless. Did I have to remind him of the last time Jake attempted a "miracle" in water? It might have felt like years ago, but it'd only been a week. I looked to Dad to say something, but he was oblivious.

"Stop fighting, boys."

Mom would have been livid. It was up to me to set him straight. "People can't walk on water, Jake," I said. "Only Jesus can. The *real* Jesus. No offense."

"None taken," Jesus said.

✟

At the entrance to Jerusalem was a cluster of three sad olive trees—the Garden of Gethsemane. Tourists knelt and prayed here as Jesus had with his disciples, the night before his Crucifixion. We approached and the visitors flocked to Jesus with cameras. He posed for photos, always polite to ask, "Don't you want a picture with the Heaven Boy, too?" None did. ("Who?") Cameras and phones were thrust into our hands; Dad, Abe, and I played photographer.

After fending off the last of the souvenir scavengers, Jesus led us into the Last Supper Restaurant. Inside, a replica of the famous Da Vinci painting was frescoed on the back wall. The air-conditioning felt like the answer to a prayer.

We were seated and ordered a Manna Bites appetizer and Water-to-Wines—grape soda that poured clear from the bottle but turned purple in the glass. This was actually pretty cool. For our meal we got the Fish and Loaves Family Platter.

"Sorry about all the photos," Jesus apologized. "I'm sure Eli gets enough of that."

I shook my head. "I'm not really famous."

"He gets his fair share," Dad said.

"One time," Jake said. "A man took Eli and there was a Bambi."

"Jake." Dad shook his head, chewing. "Not appropriate."

Jesus said, "Bambi?"

"He means Amber," Abe said. "You know, an Amber Alert."

"Boys," Dad warned. "Drop it."

"Wait." Jesus dropped his Manna Bite. "You were *abducted*?"

I shrugged. "It wasn't a big deal."

"Jesus Christ!" Jesus said.

"Language," Jake scolded, a near-perfect imitation of Mom.

"Sorry. But that's awful. I had no idea."

"He was *not* abducted," Dad said.

"Then what happened?" Jesus asked.

Dad sighed. "A member of our church borrowed Eli for an hour. He took him to the hospital to see his daughter and then he brought him right back. That's all. Debbie overreacted."

The daughter of the man who had kidnapped me had been only thirteen. She had some rare form of leukemia. She was scared to die. They were always scared to die. Even the ones who had faith their whole lives, the ones who had suffered in pain, who *wanted* to die, who were ready to go—they were all scared.

"Tell her," her father had said. So I told her.

"And you were how old when this happened?" she asked.

"Four."

"Uh-huh."

"You don't believe him," her father said, crestfallen.

"I want to." She took his hand. "I really do. Can't that be enough?"

Jesus left us halfway through lunch to prepare for the noon Crucifixion reenactment. It took place on Jerusalem's main street, cordoned off with rope. A crowd had already gathered. We found a spot on the sidewalk outside a strip of souvenir shops—King Solomon's Temple of Mementos, Mary's Perfumery, Martha's Kitchenware, and Esther's Makeover Emporium. There was a stage erected at the center of the street.

From behind a backdrop came Pontius Pilate, flanked by two Roman centurions. They carried shields and spears and wore costume armor:

breastplate, helmet, red woolen tunic. Pilate positioned himself center stage. He unrolled a piece of parchment with a flourish and addressed the crowd.

"The trial has concluded!" His voice was amplified by a conspicuous microphone headset and echoed from speakers hidden about the plaza. "The King of the Jews, known by his disciples as Jesus of Nazareth, has been found guilty! His sentence: Crucifixion!"

A few tourists yelled boos—a ripple of disapproval. A little girl next to me said, matter-of-factly, "I don't like that man."

"I can't see! I can't see!" Jake complained, hopping up and down.

Dad was watching the performance, rapt. Abe lifted Jake onto his shoulders.

The Roman guards began to pound the floorboards of the stage with their spears—the sound of thunder. "King of the Jews! King of the Jews! King of the Jews!"

It felt like a long wait, the crowd getting riled before the main attraction. The chanting and booing rose to a roar, and Jesus was finally dragged onto the stage. Roman guards dropped him at Pilate's feet. He made a show of cringing away and sweeping his robes back to prevent the King of the Jews from dirtying them.

Jesus cried: "Father, forgive them, for they know not what they do!"

Pilate ordered him stripped and the guards marched forward to obey. The crowd felt it—I did, too—every step of Jesus being manhandled, his arms lifted, the robes yanked from his shoulders, over his head. He was forced across the stage in his tasteful white loincloth and we were pulled with him. His hands were tied to a post and we felt the coarseness of the rope on our wrists. And when he was flogged, we winced at every lash of the whip— dramatized by a prerecorded *whoosh-thwack!*—feeling our own flesh rend.

I wasn't sure how they did it, if it was makeup hidden on the actor or dye in the leather prop whip, but there was blood. It stained Jesus's back, trickled down his ribs, and dripped at his feet. It was an unnaturally bright shade of red.

The crowd's reactions fractured between outrage and tears. Many continued to yell and boo. Someone threw a tomato—a *tomato*?—and it rebounded off a centurion helmet. Jake hid his face in his hands and Abe squeezed his dangling leg. The girl beside me was crying. Dad's eyes, too, were round and wet. But I felt little more than indigestion. When I cast around for the source of the tomato, I burped and tasted fish. A woman was wearing a box strapped to her neck, like a hot dog vendor at a baseball game. It was full of rotten vegetables—tomatoes, heads of lettuce, cabbages, broccoli, cauliflower. There was a sign: REFUSE FOR PELTING! A man in a Hawaiian shirt forked over a twenty for a sack of turnips.

Jesus was unbound. He collapsed. Pilate draped a purple robe over his body. He snapped his fingers and a guard came forward with the crown of thorns. Before taking it, Pilate put on a pair of thick leather gloves (a nice touch, I thought). Jesus's head was wrenched upward and held by another guard while Pilate lowered the crown, nestling thorns into scalp. Jesus flinched, but his face remained stoic. Too-red blood washed down his forehead.

Next came the cross. The Romans who carried it onstage exaggerated the weight of the prop: shuffling, straining, grunting with pretend effort. They dropped it like a stack of lumber and a pre-recorded *BOOM* rang out of the speakers.

"Pick it up," Pilate commanded.

Jesus didn't move.

"I said: Pick. It. Up." He punctuated each word with a swift kick to the ribs.

Jesus lay, groaning. The crowd howled. A deluge of leafy greens rattled Roman shields.

"Where's your God now?" Pilate cackled. The guards pounded their spears.

Jesus laid his palms flat against the floorboards of the stage. Slowly, dramatically, he pushed himself up, to his knees, then onto his feet. His legs shook, but he stood tall. He wore a look of triumph. The crowd cheered wildly.

Pilate spat in his face. Everyone gasped, but Jesus showed no anger. Instead, he calmly turned his cheek, moved to the cross, and lifted it. He stumbled the first time and nearly dropped it, as if he'd underestimated the weight. The second time he braced himself more fully and hefted the cross high enough to move under it, lowering it onto his back. He carried the cross down the stage stairs, Romans taunting him with every step.

He was on the street now, level with the crowd. He was nearly naked and bloody and hunched beneath the cross—but he wore sandals, I saw. The actor wouldn't go barefoot on the hot asphalt. Jesus approached the sidewalk, close enough for tourists to reach out over the rope and touch him. A few did, hands coming back red with paint. We weren't close enough, but Dad and Abe had their arms up in prayer and were swaying. Hundreds of phones clicked, cameras hanging from leather straps lifted to eye level.

"We love you!" A woman took a flower from her straw hat and tossed it.

"Scum!" An old man on a mobility scooter pitched an onion—hard and overhand, like a baseball. It hit a guard close to me dead in the leg, and I winced when it made contact.

"Ow!" The Roman dropped his spear. "What the hell, man!" To the guard next to him, he complained, "I thought the projectiles are supposed to be *soft*."

On the way to Crucifixion Corner, Jesus fell three times. Each time he was lashed. When he finally made it, he lowered the cross to the ground and lay exhausted.

Pilate had marched at the rear of the procession and now his shadow fell over Jesus. "Nail him."

Jesus's limp form was laid upon the cross. A guard lifted nails and hammer and went to work. They were far enough away I couldn't see the sleight of hand, but once again the sound effects drove the message home. *Bang! Bang! Bang!* timed perfectly with the actor's movements and with Jesus's screams, more earsplitting than ever.

"My God, my God! Why hast thou forsaken me?"

The crowd was hysterical. Fathers with beer bellies beating their chests. Mothers wailing over strollers. Children writhing on the ground as if possessed. Even Dad—Dad, who had always been restrained in his demonstrations of faith, who believed speaking in tongues was pure gibberish—he, too, was being moved by the Holy Spirit. Mumbling, *Jesus, Jesus, Jesus,* waving his arms overhead. Jake, still on Abe's shoulders, was opening and closing his hands, grasping at air. Abe was trembling.

I felt empty, apart from it all. Outside, looking in. Again, I wished Mom were here. Surely she'd make a joke of it.

The cross was hoisted between two others standing vacant in Crucifixion Corner. Red Velcro bands bound Jesus's arms and feet to the boards. There was a little ledge for him to stand on. His head hung heavy; his beard dripped with sweat. "I thirst," he moaned. "I thirst."

"This is what becomes of your Savior!" Pilate shouted. "Look long and hard at the Son of God. Blasphemy! Heretic! He will hang here till he rots."

The crowd surged forward. The rope separating spectators from spectacle had been either removed or trampled and a wave of tourists broke at the foot of the cross. It was tall enough to keep Jesus mostly out of reach, but children on the shoulders of their fathers could stretch just far enough to touch the foot of their Savior. Jesus beamed down at them.

"It is finished," he said. "Father, into your hands I commit my spirit."

And with that, he took his final breath.

A long moment of silence. Then a murmuring on the far side of the crowd. It parted, revealing a woman in a blue veil. The Virgin Mary. She approached, like a bride down the aisle, and knelt serenely at the base of the cross, clasping her hands in prayer. Until then I hadn't been moved by any of the pageantry, but seeing Jesus's mother reminded me of my own and my eyes filled.

"Take him down," Mary said. "He shall be buried in the Garden Tomb."

The Romans obeyed her request and draped a shroud over Jesus. They hefted the body and the crowd followed, not far, to a rock-hewn tomb. After Jesus was inside, an enormous boulder rolled into place in front of the opening, moved by some unseen mechanism.

Mary settled herself on a ledge outside the tomb.

"May He rest in peace." She bowed her head. "Resurrection will take place in half an hour."

✝

While we waited for the Resurrection—Dad insisted the thirty minutes symbolized three days, but I figured it was just enough time for Jesus to take a quick shower—we crucified ourselves.

Here's how it worked: The Roman soldier attendants draped a purple robe over your shoulders and performed a coronation with a crown of thorns—rubber, same as the ones in the gift shops. Then they bound you to a cross with red Velcro straps—there was a little foot ledge like Jesus's— and lifted the cross into place. There were ten stations total, so we were all crucified together, side by side.

Once I was up, I immediately felt the strain in my arms. Even with the straps to hold them in place, they tired quickly. So this was what it was like to be Jesus.

I was high enough to see the top of every head waiting in the line we'd skipped. The sun was merciless. Jesus didn't have sunglasses. I imagined the sweat dripping down my temple was blood. Next to me, Jake waved a pinned hand.

"Look, Eli! I'm Jesus."

"Me, too, Jake."

"We all are," Abe said.

"Boys," Dad said from his cross. "Take this seriously. This is a chance to experience what He experienced, to feel how He felt."

"We *are*," Abe said.

"Sure, Dad," I said.

There was a reverential silence, but only for a moment.

"I have to pee," Jake said.

Dad huffed. "Can you hold it for just a little longer?"

A Roman soldier photographer announced he was about to take our photo. He held up the camera and told everyone to smile and say, *Jeeesus!*

I laughed.

"Is this funny to you?" Dad said. "Our Lord and Savior dying for your sins?"

"No," I said.

"I *really* have to pee!" Jake whined.

"This is *nothing*," Dad said. "Nothing compared to what he suffered for us."

"Yes, sir," I said, hoping to prevent a lecture.

The photographer said we could purchase copies of our photo at King Solomon's Temple of Mementos. Dad was a skinflint when it came to such things; he thought souvenirs a waste of money. So I was surprised when, after we were de-Crucified a few minutes later and Abe took Jake to the bathroom, Dad headed straight to the kiosk.

Three screens displayed Crucifixion Corner photos, scrolling one to the next. We didn't have to wait long for ours to appear. Four crosses, all in a row. Dad, Abe, and Jake looked stoic enough, but the camera had perfectly captured the moment I'd laughed. My head was thrown back, mouth open. I was laughing, but I could have been screaming.

The photo came in a cardboard frame featuring the Bible World lion and lamb. For years after our trip to Bible World, it sat on our mantel, and when guests came over Dad told them the story of how, on the cross, I was overcome with the Passion. It was a kind of spiritual possession, he said. I'd cried out and Dad could hear the tortured voice of the Lord. He told this story so many times, to so many people, I have no doubt he believed it. Until one day, just before I left for college, I couldn't take it anymore, so I found the scissors in the kitchen utensils drawer, snatched the photo down from the mantel, and cut myself—*crrp crrp crrp!*—right out.

14

GREENROOM

Death is but a doorway. This life but a waiting room for the next.
—from *Heaven or Bust!*, "Blink of an Eye," ch. 9, p. 48

IN A PREVIOUS LIFE THE Bible World megachurch had been an ice rink—home to Orlando's hockey team, the Solar Bears. It had since been renovated into a state-of-the-art Worship Center. This was where *The Charlie Gideon Hour* was filmed live every Sunday morning and Wednesday night. After his resurrection, Jesus led us to the parkside entrance, where we found Charlie Gideon in a sharp slate-gray suit, a bolo tie with a mother-of-pearl pendant, and white crocodile-skin boots. Hovering behind him was an entourage of CGN employees: an assistant in a short skirt, three cameramen and two boom operators, a makeup artist and stylist, park security guards manning the perimeter, and several people with headsets, walkie-talkies, and clipboards.

"Howdy, Harpos." Gideon wasn't wearing his cowboy hat, but he raised his hand as if to touch the invisible brim of one. "Good to see you again. Let me say, how deeply sorry I am for your loss. I hope your visit to Bible World will be a healing one. A chance for you to glimpse the Celestial Kingdom, where Deborah now experiences eternal life with Our Lord and Savior."

Dad thanked him. "It's good to be here."

"Hey there, Elijah." Gideon offered me his meaty hand. The cameras moved in. "How're you enjoying Bible World?"

I stared at the cameras. Gideon waved in their direction.

"Don't worry. We're not live yet. It's just behind-the-scenes footage. Excited to visit your new realm?"

"Yes, sir," I said.

"'Yes, sir?'" Gideon mugged at the camera. "So polite. Tell me. What's been your favorite Biblical experience so far?"

"Um . . ." I glanced at Dad. "The Ark?"

Gideon scoffed. "The Ark! That's a kiddie realm. Come on now. What about Sodom and Gomorrah! The Drop-Tower of Babel! You like roller coasters, don't you?"

"Yes, sir."

Gideon turned to Jesus. "I told you to take them on whatever they wanted."

"But they wanted—the youngest—" Jesus sputtered.

Dad said we'd enjoyed both the Ark and the Parting of the Red Sea, but Crucifixion Corner was the family's favorite spot in the whole park.

"Immersion facility," Gideon corrected. "You liked it?"

"Phenomenal," Dad said. "Just phenomenal. What a blessing to experience that."

Gideon was pleased to hear it. He insisted on giving us a tour of the Worship Center. The first stop was the baptismal font, a mosaic pool in the middle of the atrium. Dad nodded appreciatively at the fountain. Gideon said he'd performed over two thousand baptisms there. Next he led us into the auditorium. It was freezing inside. I wondered if this was a holdover from the building's ice-rink days or if they just kept the AC blasting too high. It seated sixteen thousand and was mostly empty except for early arrivals. I had a feeling it was going to be a much smaller crowd than we were used to seeing on the show. After all the scandals, especially the sexual harassment ones, Gideon had lost a lot of followers. The Heaven Realm was supposed to attract new congregants and bring many back into the fold. Even so, it'd still be the biggest audience Dad and I ever had.

Gideon explained about the ceiling's lighting effects—they could project images of the sky and make it look like a sunset, a thunderstorm (complete with flashes of lightning for parables featuring God's wrath), or the peaceful blue of a spring day. The pulpit was fashioned of frosted glass. It looked like an enormous paperweight. Overhead, the stained-glass windows rendered the image of a cowboy, kneeling before Jesus, beaming down on him from the cross. I recognized most of the building's features from watching the show, but the window was new.

"Is that . . . you?" Abe asked Gideon, although there was really no need. The likeness was obvious—and ridiculous.

"Isn't it beautiful?" Gideon said. "Had it commissioned by a Dutch glass artist."

"It's very . . . bold," Dad said.

"Thank you."

On a platform at the base of the stage was Mom's casket. Gideon had splurged on the Ambrosial Ivory. Big as a Cadillac, gleaming like a tooth extracted from the mouth of God Himself. The service was open casket. Gideon beckoned us forward to see how well the embalmers did.

Dad, Abe, and Jake went ahead, but I couldn't take another step. I turned and stared at her photo, blown up to movie-poster size, mounted on a tripod beneath an arch of white flowers. It was the one from her thirty-fifth birthday party. I wanted to remember her like this, not how she looked in the box.

They were all huddled around the casket, peering down, like at a baby in a bassinet.

"Isn't she beautiful?" Gideon said. "I think she came out nicely."

"That's not her," Jake said.

Dad shushed him. "It is, honey."

"No, it's not."

"It's makeup," Dad said, gently.

"Actually, Jake's right," Gideon said. "It's not Debbie. It's just her earthly shell. She's with Jesus now."

I tried to imagine Mom in Heaven, looking like she was in the photo. Known as she was known. But no matter how hard I tried, it felt like pretending.

"Eli," Dad called. "Come and pay your respects."

I didn't budge. I was shaking, pinching my scar, trying not to cry.

"He doesn't have to," Gideon said. "We all grieve in our own way."

Dad relented and Gideon handed us off to his assistant, who showed us to the dressing rooms. "No, not you, Eli." She stopped me at the door my family passed through. "You have a room of your own. An extra-special dressing room for an extra-special star. Follow me."

I glanced in my family's direction.

Dad waved me away. "Go on. It's okay."

Chosen One, Abe mouthed silently behind the assistant's back.

"Don't worry," she said. "You'll join them in the greenroom."

The room she led me into was ablaze with lights and mirrors. It might have been my imagination, knowing it had been remodeled from hockey locker rooms, but under the scents of lotions, hair spray, and talcum powder was a sour note—BO, athlete's foot, jockstrap. A costume designer was waiting for me. I turned to ask the assistant if I could have something to drink before we began, but she was gone. I'd been handed off again, without so much as a goodbye or good luck.

The costume designer, a petite woman with a black bob, clapped her hands and waved me over to a clothing rack. An all-white suit hung from the metal bar.

"Ta-da!"

"What's that?"

"Why, your suit."

"Shouldn't it be black?"

"Lovely, isn't it?" She stroked the jacket. "Seersucker. Breathes easy. Like wearing a cloud."

"But—my mom died."

"I know, dear. Sorry for your loss."

"It's a funeral."

"It's also a TV show. And Gideon likes this one."

"I'm not wearing that. I'll look like Colonel Sanders."

"Who?"

"Colonel Sanders. KFC? The fried chicken guy."

"Don't be silly. You'll cut a dashing figure. Southern chic!"

"I want a black suit."

The costume designer bit her lip. "Gideon really wants you in this one. He wants to celebrate your mom in Heaven. You know what it's like—you were there!"

"It's disrespectful."

"How 'bout this? Why don't we try it on and see how it feels? If we don't like it, we'll find something else, mmkay?"

What was this *we* business? Last I checked, *I* was the one being made to dress like the member of a barbershop quartet. *We* weren't doing anything. But before I could protest again, she ducked out of the room.

For a while I just stood there, arms crossed. I held a staring contest with my reflection in the makeup mirror, which was so well lit I could make out every acne scar, every freckle. My face was a lunar landscape, a palimpsest of blackheads and spots.

I refused to give the wardrobe artist the satisfaction of popping her head back in and seeing me all decked in white, so I sat down in the makeup chair and waited. The suit hung on the rack beside me. I reached out and touched it. She was right. It *was* soft. It was the softest article of clothing I'd ever touched. There was a white dress shirt and a white satin tie. White patent-leather shoes, white dress socks, a white pocket square. There were even white suspenders. I'd never worn suspenders in my life. I didn't know how to put them on. Three presents sat on the makeup counter in front of me, each in a white box with a white ribbon.

I opened the smallest of the three—a ring box. Inside: mother-of-pearl cuff links in the shape of crosses. The next box held a glasses case. The glasses matched my prescription; the frames were white plastic. The largest box held a white pocket Bible, my name in gold on the cover—ELIJAH JAMES HARPO. I picked it up and ran my fingers over the embossed words, fanned through the pages. The dominical words, spoken by Jesus, typically printed in red letters, were in gold in this version. They glittered in the light. Pretty, but difficult to read. Inside the front cover was a dedication:

> For Eli,
> > The Boy Who Went to Heaven . . . and brought a piece back.
> > Always a fan,
> > > Charlie Gideon

I remembered my promise to Mom in the hospital.

Fine. I took the suit off the hanger.

After I undressed, I studied my scar in the mirror. It was red and inflamed from all the pinching I'd been doing the past few days. I tried not to touch it, but every time I thought of Mom, my hand drifted to my chest. My boxers were bright green and I was worried they might show through the pants. They didn't. They were the only splotch of color on my body and they remained my secret. The pants and shirt were a bit tight. So was the jacket.

I examined myself in the full-length mirror on the back of the dressing room door. With my back to the makeup counter, the lighting was more forgiving—but still not enough. I looked like a fat penguin with its tuxedo sneezed off.

The door swung open and I leapt back to avoid getting hit.

"Don't you look dapper," said the blonde woman who entered. She was chewing gum and wearing a leopard-print muumuu, and was not the costume designer.

"You're not the costume designer."

"No, love. I'm not. I do makeup."

"Where's the other lady? I told her I can't wear this."

She gave me the once-over. "You already are, handsome. And you look *great*. The girls'll be crawling all over you."

She sat me down in the chair in front of the mirror, then stepped back and examined my face from every angle, tilting my head this way and that, my chin pinched between her fingers. How could she get anything done with those acrylic nails of hers? She smacked her gum, then ran a talon over my top lip.

"Honey, we're going to have to do something about this peach fuzz." She dug around in a drawer and came up with a pink razor. "You care for the honors or should I?"

I was secretly proud of my mustache. Some guys in Lambkins already had beards. It had taken me months to grow the hair she whisked off—didn't even bother with shaving cream, just wet the razor under the faucet—in seconds.

"There you go! They want you baby-faced for the camera." She pinched me, like a great-aunt. "Those cheeks!"

The next ten minutes or so were spent holding still while she artfully dipped and dabbed here and there to hide the worst of my acne and freckles. After she was done it looked like my entire face had been photoshopped blemish-free. It was remarkable. And she was right. I looked younger. Maybe not exactly baby-faced, but I could pass for a fat ten-year-old.

Next came the hair. She squirted half a tube of gel into her hands and went to work. "You've got a lot of cowlicks." She struggled to get it flat. Once it was good and gelled, she ran a comb through and parted it down the middle. I'd never done it that way; it felt unnatural, the midline of my scalp exposed. I scratched it and she slapped me away playfully. "Don't touch." Finally, she sprayed me down with hair spray. By the end of it, I felt like I was wearing a helmet.

"There." She spun me around in the seat and gazed at her masterpiece. "Not a hair out of place." She un-Velcroed the cape she'd used to protect the white suit and—"*Voilà!*" I heard in Mom's voice—spun me back for the grand unveiling.

"I look like the Pillsbury Doughboy."

"No, love. You look *divine*."

✢

She took me to the greenroom, which wasn't green, but beige like the dressing rooms. It smelled strongly of Hawaiian air freshener. Comfy chairs were scattered about and snack tables lined one wall. Opposite that, a row of monitors displayed the stage, where Gideon was opening the show. Dad, Abe, and Jake were all seated watching the TVs, dressed in black suits with black ties. The moment Abe saw my outfit, he burst out laughing. It was a full-on fit of hysterics. He pointed and guffawed and even after Dad got him to quiet down, his face was frozen in a rictus of hilarity, tears streaming, laughter shaking soundlessly in his gut.

Dad tried to say something encouraging. "Don't you look"—he groped for a word—"bright."

"Oh, it's bright all right." Abe snickered. "It's *blinding*. They going to give everyone sunglasses before you come onstage?"

"Abe," Dad warned.

"What? He looks like he's ministering to polar bears."

Dad couldn't hold it in: He snorted.

"Can't I wear a black suit, too?" I begged. "I don't think Mom would like this."

"Sorry," Dad said. "Gideon told me he was giving you a new image. It's what they do in TV. Makes you unique. It's iconic."

"It's *mor*-onic," Abe said.

"Soft." Jake petted the jacket.

"Is there anything to drink?" I pulled on the too-tight collar.

"Not in that suit," Dad said.

"Please. I'm thirsty."

Dad handed me a bottle of Aquafina. A tech guy came forward to mike me. After he was done we sat together as a family and watched Gideon on the monitors, the stained-glass version of himself beaming down a kaleidoscope of colors.

"Can you believe that window?" Abe said.

"I'm looking right at it and I still can't believe it," I said.

"Like, false idol much? I mean, who does something like that?"

"Charlie Gideon."

"Apparently."

✢

In our visits to other churches, we had been seated in pews at the front so that we could participate in the service before being called upon for the interview portion. But Gideon was partial to grand entrances, and for the first part of *The Charlie Gideon Hour* we remained hidden in the greenroom, watching the show on monitors. It began with a lot of singing as the congregation filtered in. Dressed in their Sunday best, women in floral-patterned dresses, men in suits and khakis, all sang hymn after hymn as the Worship Center filled. It took nearly an hour.

It felt so wrong to me to see all these strangers in the audience for Mom's funeral. They didn't seem baffled by her photo, the open coffin, her name in the program. They took it all in stride. Maybe in a congregation this size, they were used to attending the funerals of people they barely knew. That incensed me to no end. I knew we'd have another—a *real* funeral—at Creation Baptist before her burial, but that only made this fake-funeral-slash-televangelist-show even more infuriating.

Gideon's taste in interior design might have been gaudy, but his flashy preaching style really took the cake. He hardly used the pulpit, instead paced the stage in his crocodile boots. The podium's very presence seemed to serve the purpose of emphasizing that he was constantly going off script. When Gideon spoke of a Biblical passage, he did not turn to it in his Bible to explicate it, as Dad did, but instead unholstered and waved the book overhead like a flag—his was oversize, sheathed in worn brown leather— brandishing it triumphantly at the audience as a magician would a scarf or playing card pulled from a top hat. I can't believe I used to think that move was so cool I'd practiced it with Abe. On that episode of *The Charlie Gideon Hour* Gideon was, of course, talking about Mom and Heaven, about her eternal reward that was the afterlife. Up until that moment, some part of me had held on to it, the belief I'd see her again. But coming out of

Gideon's mouth, it had never been clearer that it was all a bunch of crock. I couldn't stand to hear him talk about her like they'd been friends. Like he knew anything about her.

A stage manager stuck his head in the beige greenroom and signaled— five minutes.

"Come on, boys," Dad said, and we huddled up for one final prayer. "Heavenly Father. We ask that You grant us grace today on *The Charlie Gideon Hour*. Help us do Debbie proud in celebrating her life spent on Earth and her new, eternal one with You." I pinched my scar, hard. Dad was still praying: ". . . and if You see it in Your Will to impress upon Gideon that we're ready for the next phase of our journey, we'd be honored to take that step with Your Blessing."

"Wait," I said. "What do you mean, next phase?"

"Yeah, what are you talking about?" Abe said.

"Nothing." Dad shook his head. "I'll tell you after the show."

"Tell us now," I said.

"Dad?" Jake was frowning.

"Okay." Dad nodded. He was excited. "Gideon said that if the show goes well today he might have something more permanent for us."

"Permanent?" I said. The casualness of this betrayal, it was almost a physical pain in my gut. "You promised this would be the last time."

"That was before. Gideon's offered us a segment. 'Ask Eli,' or maybe 'Eli's Hotline to Heaven.' We haven't got the name yet."

"Won't that be a lot of . . . driving?" I was reeling, not making sense of what this meant.

"We'd move, doofus," Abe said.

"Yes," Dad said. "We'd move to Florida."

"Cool," Abe said.

"Are we going to live on the beach?" Jake said.

"But we can't," I said. "We can't just leave."

"It could be good for us. Now that your mom . . ." Dad's voice cracked. He shook his head. "It would be a new start."

"What about Lambkins? What about my . . . friends?"

Abe snorted. "What friends?"

The stage manager had reappeared.

"We'll talk about this later," Dad said.

We were ushered through the door. The stage manager held up his hand when it was my turn. "Not yet. You're last."

"Good luck, Marshmallow," Abe called. "Don't get roasted."

The door shut and I was alone again. I went to the monitors and watched Gideon welcome my family with great fanfare. The congregation stood and clapped. Stage lights flashed and their faces were blown up huge on the backdrop screen. Gideon yanked Dad's arm and hugged him. He hugged Jake and ruffled his hair. He hugged Abe and squeezed his shoulder. Then he gestured for everyone to sit on the couches to the left of the pulpit.

As I watched them, I was starting to panic. I couldn't stand the thought of having to do this forever. It was hard enough listening to Gideon and Dad babble on-screen about Mom, talking about her death like it was a blessing, speculating about what she might be doing in Heaven at this very moment. I was broken inside at losing her, no longer consoled by the idea of her living on in an eternal paradise. And now I might have to perform indefinitely on a show called *Charlie Gideon & the Heaven Boy!*?

No. No way. Not happening. Did this mean I could break my promise to Mom? She hadn't foreseen this in the hospital. She thought it'd be over after the opening of my realm. Would we still get paid if I did only the show today? But what if it went well and they wanted me to stay on? Surely, she wouldn't want that. How could I do this for her without getting stuck doing it forever? It seemed like no matter what I did, I'd be letting someone down.

The stage manager stuck his head in and beckoned. "You're on, kid."

15

THE CHARLIE GIDEON HOUR

At how many funerals, broadcast live to millions from the state-of-the-art Worship Center at Bible World * *in Orlando, Florida, had I spouted the consoling platitudes we've all come to expect:* She's in a better place *or* He's looking down on us *or* You'll see them again. *I always believed what I was saying with my mind, but I couldn't quite feel it in my heart. Until Elijah showed me the way.*

---

*Go to www.bibleworld.com for tickets, discount rates available for CGN club members; follow us on Twitter @BibleWorld; enter SWEEPSTAKES contest at www.bibleworldsweepstakesextravaganza.com for your chance to win Holy Order passes for the whole family! (restrictions do apply); for a quote on scheduling a celebrity officiant for a family member's or your own funeral, please contact heavenhelpers@cgn.com; if planning or officiating a funeral yourself, consider checking out other CGN titles such as *Charlie Gideon Puts the FUN Back in Funeral* and *Lasso Writes: Charlie Gideon Wrangles the Eulogy . . . and You Can Too!*

—from *Charlie Gideon & the Heaven Boy!*, "Epiphany by Elijah," p. 33

I FOLLOWED THE STAGE MANAGER into the wings, where we could look out and see Gideon in his overstuffed armchair, talking with my family on the couch by the pulpit. I moved toward them, but the stage manager yanked me back.

"Not your entrance," he whispered. He passed me off to a crew member, who led me around behind the giant wall of LED screens. There was no door here. I could still hear everything—"She truly was a wonderful woman," Gideon was saying, "and I'm sure it gives you great comfort, knowing what you know about Heaven, from your son . . ."—but I could see nothing. The crew member pointed to a metal ladder. I looked up. It ascended to a scaffolding at the top of the screen. Once, while I was helping Dad get Christmas decorations down from the attic, a rung on the rickety folding ladder broke beneath me and I almost fell. I've had a thing about ladders ever since.

"You want me to climb *that*?" I said—too loudly.

"Shhh!" The crew member held a finger to her lips. She spoke into my ear. "Turn on your mike once you get to the top." She showed me the switch on the pack clipped to my suit's waistband.

"I don't—"

"There's a door at the top."

"Can't I just *walk* on?"

"Shhh!"

I lowered my voice. "How am I supposed to get down?"

"Stairs. You'll see."

"Please," I said, but she was waving for me to hurry up.

Gideon's voice boomed from the other side of the wall. "What do you say? Would you like to meet Eli Harpo, the Boy Who Went to Heaven?"

Applause, cheers, a whistle of encouragement.

I stepped up onto the lowest rung. *It's metal*, I told myself. *It won't break.* But I wasn't moving fast enough for the crew member, and I felt her hands on my backside, pushing. Three rungs up and my legs started to quiver.

"Why don't we bring him out, huh?" Gideon said.

"That's you!" the crew member whisper-shouted. "Move!"

I climbed. After what felt like thirty rungs, I looked down and saw my ankles were still level with the crew member's head. She rattled the ladder below me.

"What are you doing! Get up there!"

"Eliiiii," Gideon called. "Come out, come out, wherever you are."

The congregation laughed.

I wrapped my arms around the ladder. I couldn't move. I didn't want to climb this stupid ladder and I didn't want to go on this stupid show and I hated everything and everyone.

"Boy must be shy," Gideon said. "That's okay. Remember—it's the meek who shall inherit the Earth."

Murmurs of assent. An "Amen!" or two.

"Kid flies to Heaven, but can't climb a fricking ladder," the crew member grumbled. "Come on! You can do it. Take it one step at a time. Just reach up—"

With some coaxing, I did it. Grasped the rung above me, stepped to the next, and steadied myself. Grasped, stepped, steadied.

"Really, Eli?" Gideon teased. "Surely we're not *that* scary."

"Don't look down," she called. I'd made it to the top. "Just pull yourself up onto the walkway there. Yes! Great job!"

I collapsed on the scaffolding and lay flat on my back. I was hyperventilating. My hands were shaking. Rivulets of sweat coursed from my forehead into my ears. The crew member scaled the ladder quickly—she made it look easy—and stepped off next to me.

"No time for a breather. The door's right there." She was pulling my arm now, trying to pick me up. I was too heavy, of course.

"Five minutes," I begged.

It's what I asked of Mom every morning when she came into our bedroom and snatched off our blankets to get us up for homeschool. If I could just have five more minutes, the world would be a much kinder place. Five minutes and my breathing would return to normal. Five minutes and I could work out exactly what to say to Charlie Gideon and Dad so we didn't have to move to Florida, so I wasn't stuck being the Heaven Kid forever. But I didn't have five minutes. I never did.

I moaned and rolled to my knees. She lifted under my arms.

I wobbled and took hold of the metal railing.

The crew member hugged me—a weirdly intimate apology—then I realized she was reaching around to turn on my mike.

"Red rover, red rover, send Eli right over," Gideon chanted. A note of impatience had crept into his voice.

The crew member was moving lightning quick now. She pushed a bar on the back of the wall and a door swung open.

I was blinded. It was like looking through a portal to the sun. There was a shove at my back. I stumbled into the light.

✢

It took a few seconds before the splotchy afterimages faded from my eyes and I could get my bearings. I was on a small balcony, fog machines sputtering wisps of white at my ankles. I was standing in the "clouds." There was a fanfare of trumpets, and CGI doves flew across giant LED screens. They were followed by angels—footage clipped from Bible World commercials and *A Tour of Heaven*. Rays of light sparked off the balcony.

"Is it a bird? Is it a plane?" Gideon called below. "No! Praise be! It's the Boy Who Went to Heaven! Eli Harpo, at last!"

I clung to the balcony railing, stunned by the force of the applause. Gideon held his arms out, smiling. My family gawked up at me.

Gideon motioned for quiet and the audience simmered down.

"I know it's a whole lot of fun up there in Heaven, Eli. But you think you might come down and grace us with your presence?"

More laughs. What a riot. They all loved him.

A flight of gold stairs descended to the stage. I focused on not falling on my face. It was a slow, agonizing process. With the stage lights shining on the too-white suit, I felt radioactive.

Finally, I reached the bottom. I crossed to center stage. Gideon pulled me in for a hug.

"Get your shit together," he whispered.

It took me a moment to understand what he'd said. The curse was so mismatched to his body language. He withdrew from the embrace with a nod and a wink. To the viewers it must have looked like he'd said something charming, avuncular. I stood there, confused, then upset, and a little scared. No one had ever cursed at me like that.

Gideon's hand moved to his mike pack. He switched it back on.

"Praise the Lord! Praise Jesus!" he yelled. "It is a glorious and blessed day to have the Heaven Boy in our midst. Why don't you have a seat, Eli."

I moved toward the far end of the couch, but he made everyone scoot down a cushion to free up the spot closest to his armchair. The whole setup was less church, more talk show.

"That's some suit," Gideon said once we were seated and the applause had died down. He whistled. "Sharp."

"You picked it," I said.

Gideon laughed, clapping his hands on his knees. "I must have good taste. What do y'all think of Eli's outfit?"

The congregation cheered.

"Now, Eli," Gideon said. "I know this is a very painful time for you and your family. Your dad and brothers were just sharing memories of your mom. But you in particular had a special relationship with her. Why don't you tell us about that?"

I shrugged, determined to be as uncharismatic as possible. If I could get through the show but not be *good*, then maybe I could keep my promise to Mom *and* stop *Heavenly Chats with Eli*—or whatever—from happening. "She was my mom," I said bluntly.

Gideon laughed. "Of course she was. But because you went to Heaven, you must've had a unique perspective at the end of her life, right?"

"I guess."

"Did you tell her about Heaven?"

"I tell everyone about Heaven. That's all anyone wants to talk about."

Gideon straightened his already-straight bolo tie. "And what do you think Debbie's doing in Heaven, right now?"

"You want me to say she's watching us, right? She's tuning in to your show on some big ole TV screen in Heaven. Popping popcorn with Jesus."

Dad coughed. "In Hebrews it says we are 'surrounded by a cloud of witnesses.' Debbie could certainly be—"

Gideon held up a hand and Dad fell silent. "No, Eli. I thought she might be doing any number of the things you did in Heaven. Why don't you tell us about them?"

"My mom didn't even believe in Heaven."

"I'm sorry," Dad said. "He's just nervous. Of course she did."

"She's not flying around with angels," I said. "Or touring her very own mansion with Jesus. Or feeding lions."

"You don't know that," Abe said. "She could be."

"She's in that coffin. Right there. Dead."

That last word echoed out into the stadium. The congregation was quiet.

Did I even believe what I'd said? Mom did. It was like Gil Bright said. No one knows. Not really. You had to decide for yourself. And I'd decided to believe only what I knew to be true. And that was that Mom was gone.

I could feel tears rising. I pinched my scar to push them down.

Dad reached over, took my hand, and returned it to my lap. He left his hand on mine and squeezed.

"All right." Gideon slapped his knees and stood up. "Let's take a look, then." He held out a hand to me.

Strange thing, when you're on TV in front of a live audience. All that attention, all that pressure. Even when you know what you want to say or do, you're not in control. You find yourself being moved about, doing what is expected of you, giving in. I took Gideon's hand and he led me across the stage and down the stairs to the Ambrosial Ivory casket.

"Tell me that's her," Gideon said.

He was right. Jake was right. It wasn't her, the body lying there. Her skin looked like it was made of rubber. I shook my head and moved away, but her face was on all the screens. I felt dizzy. Gideon caught me before I fell. He sat me down on the stairs.

"We all know that's not Debbie," Gideon said. "We honor her body, but her spirit's elsewhere." He was prattling on and I couldn't stand it. "Don't think of her in the past tense, Eli. It's not 'Deborah Harpo *lived*,' but 'Deborah Harpo *lives.*'" *Shut up, shut up, shut up!* "She lives on in that beautiful place you visited. What a blessing to have seen—"

"Only I didn't!" I shouted. "I didn't go to Heaven, okay?"

I expected an intake of breath. A gasp from the audience. A protest from Dad or Abe. But there was nothing. A confused silence.

"You miss her," Gideon said.

"Of course I miss her."

"Your grief is giving you doubts."

"What? No."

"We all have doubts, Eli. We're all vulnerable to the temptations of the devil. Even those of us closest to God. Even those who've met Jesus personally, like you."

"I'm not *having doubts* and it's not the devil. I'm telling the truth. She's gone, okay? Poof! She's gone and she's never coming back." I was crying, but that wasn't helping. It was playing right into Gideon's grief narrative.

"It's all right, Eli. Let it out." He tried to hug me again, but I pushed him away.

I wiped my eyes, then turned and spoke directly to the nearest camera. "I have proof. There are these videos my dad made, from when I was little."

"Yes. Good. The videos. Let's show those now."

The church suddenly went dark. The screens counting down: 5 . . . 4 . . . 3 . . . 2 . . . 1 . . . and then there I was. Five years old, in a robin's-egg blue suit, holding up five fingers to tell my age, then talking about Heaven. It was a Simon Says video I hadn't seen. From later in the series, after I'd been better rehearsed. They'd cut Dad's questions out, spliced in other footage of the family. Abe and me swinging in the backyard. Jake picking up Easter eggs. The three of us opening Christmas gifts, buried in wrapping paper. And then there was Mom. She looked so young. She was beautiful, she was alive.

"What Eli saw is nothing short of miraculous," she said.

Then there she was again, in the hospital. And there I was, at her bedside.

✢

I'd visited more deathbeds than I could count. But no matter how many you've been to, none of them prepare you for your own mother's. She lay in the bed with an IV in her arm. Her chest flat beneath the paper gown. I remember, when she came home from the hospital after her mastectomy, she'd smiled at me and said, "Now we both have scars."

When Dad came in, everything that had happened after Jake's attempted drowning was erased. Mom held out her arms and he went to her.

"Simon." She pressed her face into his chest. "I'm so scared."

"I know, Debs. I know."

They were together again. *We* were together. Those days in the Orlando hospital were the last time we were a family.

After initiating the prayer chain back home, Dad called Gideon. The next day, he came for a visit—with cameras. A cameraman, boom operator, and makeup artist all crowded into the hospital room to get footage of us by Mom's bedside.

"There he is!" Gideon said when he saw me. "Our little Heavenly Adventurer."

"You can't be here," I said. "You're not family."

"We're all family in Christ."

"Dad," I begged. "Make them leave."

Dad sighed. "It's up to your mother."

"Mom? Please."

Mom sat up in bed. "I'd like to talk to Mr. Gideon. Alone."

Dad picked Jake up. Abe followed them out into the hall.

I stayed by Mom's side. "But we quit. We're going home."

"Let me talk to him," Mom said. "Go on."

Dad took Abe and Jake down to the cafeteria, but I said I wasn't hungry. I stayed right outside her door. Ten minutes later, Gideon came out smirking. He said she'd like to speak with me next.

"Remarkable lady, your mom. Truly remarkable."

I brushed past him into the room.

Mom waved me over. "Come here, sweetie."

I sat on the bed beside her.

"God, I hate hospitals," she said. "The scariest day of my life was the day you were in the hospital. They rushed you to surgery so fast I didn't think I'd get to say goodbye. I kept thinking, *I'll never see him again, I'll never see him again*."

"Don't die," I blurted. "Please don't die."

"Now we get the chance for a proper goodbye."

"I won't do it." I crossed my arms. "I won't go on his show."

"Listen. Gideon has agreed to pay for *all three* of you to go to college. He's going to cover your tuition and your brothers' on top of the advance and royalties."

"What? Why would he do that?"

She puffed with pride. "I made a deal with him."

"Seriously? What did you do?"

"It's nothing. They're just going to film us in the hospital a little."

I didn't believe her. "Really? That's it?"

"Well, yeah." She shrugged. "And add a new part to the show."

I sat up straight. "What new part?"

"Don't worry about it."

"Come on, Mom."

"I told you. It's nothing."

"Mom."

She rolled her eyes. "CGN is going to host my funeral, okay? That's all. So what? You'll have another, proper funeral back home and everyone will be happy."

I couldn't have been further from happy. "Are you crazy! You can't do that! You can't sell the rights to your—your—to that—that—"

"Eli." She took my hands. "It's okay. It's a *good* deal. College for *all three of you.*"

"I don't care about college."

"Well, I do. All three of my boys with degrees and good jobs. That's my Heaven."

"That's not funny."

"You're right. It's not. But think about your brothers. Think about Jake. What he did in that pool . . ."

"But he did it *because* of Heaven!"

"He did it because of your father." Mom sighed. "You know I love your dad. He means the best for you boys, but I can't—I don't . . . trust his judgment anymore. But I trust *yours*."

"Mom. I can't."

"You can. You can go to Bible World, you can get the money—not just for you, but for your brothers. You can leave Canaan and go to college. You can help Jake go, too. Keep him grounded. Show him the way out."

"What about Abe?"

"I'm going to talk to him. The money's *only* for college. That's part of the deal. I hope he'll use it."

"Mom, please. I don't want to do this. I want to go home."

"I know, baby. I'm sorry. Hate me all you want, but please. Do it for me."

I started to cry, but she wouldn't let up.

"It's just a game we play. It's just a game. It makes us feel better."

"But I don't want to play anymore."

"It's almost over. But you have to finish the game. Fight the unrapts, slay the Anti-Christ."

I smirked. "You mean Gideon?"

She laughed. "You said it, not me."

I hugged her.

"Promise me."

She slipped her fingers under my chin and lifted my head.

"You promise?"

This is the way it happened, to the best of my memory. She made me do it. Not Gideon, hoping we'd save Bible World from scandal. Not Dad, desperate to please God. Her. She did it. Then why, after all these years, is she still the only one I can't blame?

"I promise."

"Good. Now come here." She made me lie next to her, my head on her chest. She ran her fingers through my hair. "You say whatever you have to say, but remember none of it's real. This is our goodbye, okay? The real one."

She told me to close my eyes. I did.

"Okay, now picture this. You're at your high school graduation. Dad's going to enroll you in public school when you get back, so it will probably be at Canaan County. Do you see it? The bleachers in the gym? You with your black robe and mortarboard?"

"What's a mortarboard?"

"A graduation hat. Flat on top. With a little tassel that hangs down."

"Okay. I see it."

"Now they're calling your name. *Elijah James Harpo*. Everyone's clapping. You're crossing the stage. The principal hands you your diploma. You got it? Hold it up."

She raised my hand and jiggled it.

"You look out into the crowd and who do you see?"

"Who?"

"Me, silly. I'm there, cheering like crazy. Jumping up and down. Tears down my face. Mascara a mess. I look like a raccoon. I'm yelling, *That's my son! That's my son!* You see it?"

I did. I saw her in the crowd, waving madly.

"Now you're at your college graduation. The robe's a different color. Hmm, what's the color for Harvard? Maroon?"

"I'm not going to *Harvard*, Mom."

"Well, I'm there again. Doing my job and embarrassing you in front of all your college friends.

"Now you're getting married." I stiffened, bracing myself for her to fish again. But she didn't go there. "You're standing at the front of a church in a suit. Jake and Abe, groomsmen by your side. And I'm in the front pew, bawling like a baby. At your wedding reception we dance—what song do we dance to?"

"I don't know. Probably something by Phil Collins."

She laughed. "You're right. It'll have to be . . . oh, I know. 'You'll Be in My Heart.' That's a good one. Perfect."

She hummed the chorus. Sang a line or two. She could have gone on imagining, I'm sure. Babies and career milestones, birthdays and retirement parties. She'd pop up at all of them. She'd plant memories in my head, one by one, like Dad had done, only this time for the future.

"Keep singing," I said, and she sang the whole thing.

"Again." And she sang it again.

Before she could finish a third time, Dad poked his head in the room. "You ready?"

Mom kissed me loud and sloppy on the cheek. "Showtime."

✤

They played a montage of deathbed goodbyes, all the pretty lies I told Mom in front of the camera.

"The first face you'll see when you wake is Jesus's," I said. "He'll take care of you, show you around. Just like he did for me."

"I never could afford the jewelry you deserved," Dad said. "Even your engagement ring's glass. I always swore I'd buy you a real diamond. In Heaven you'll be surrounded by precious jewels. You'll lay handfuls of them at Jesus's feet. I'm sorry I couldn't buy you beautiful things in this life, but I'm glad you'll have them in the next."

"You'll be with Uncle Michael again," I said. "And Granddad and Grandma."

"Tell Baby Dinah hi," Jake said.

"She won't be a baby anymore," Dad said. "She'll be a young lady now. Almost eighteen. A full-grown woman! I'm so jealous you'll get to meet her first. I bet she'll look just like you. All that red hair."

"I don't mean to be sad." Abe wiped at his eyes. "I'm sorry. Jesus is calling you home. We should be happy. I *am* happy. I am. I will be."

"We'll come and join you in the mansion," I said. "Sooner than you think. It'll be like no time has passed. A year's like a second in Heaven. And we'll all be together again."

"I'm not afraid anymore," Mom said. "I can't wait to Cross Over into my Life Everlasting."

Gideon had been obsessed with capturing just that—the Crossing Over, the exact moment of her passing. With Mom's permission, he mounted twenty-four-hour cameras in the corners of her hospital room. I'm not sure what he expected. A ball of light rising out of her chest? A sudden Heavenly aura? Angels?

We waited for her to die for days, driving back and forth from the hotel across the street. She soon entered what doctors called the "active dying" stage. Once they had her on a morphine drip, she was often semiconscious, hallucinating.

When it finally happened, it was strangely uneventful. Gideon's fervor was infectious. It felt important that we were there for her last breath. Dad worried we'd be asleep at the hotel when she died, but we were all there in the hospital room. Only none of us noticed. There was no sudden gasp, no convulsion in her body, no sign of her soul drifting away.

We weren't holding her hand or telling her how much we loved her, although we'd done plenty of that for days on end. No, Dad was on the phone, updating the prayer chain; Abe was reading a fantasy novel; Jake was playing Nintendo; and I was looking out the window. I was watching a squirrel when Mom died.

The nurse came in to take her vitals. "Oh," she said.

That was it—that "Oh." When we realized. We all looked at one another, stunned. The shock slowly wore off and we moved closer to her. But it was too late.

"It's not uncommon not to notice," the nurse reassured us. "I'm sure she felt your presence in the room and knew it was time."

Gideon reviewed the video later. Dad got a copy and showed it to us. You can barely see her chest rise and fall, rise and fall, then stop. The footage was useless, which was why the "Crossing Over" scene that played in the megachurch at Bible World wasn't the real moment of her death. It was taken from one of Gideon's earlier visits. He sat by her side, holding flowers in his lap. We were posed around his chair. It was a few days into the morphine drip. One of her worst days.

Mom was asleep. The monitors beeped around her. She opened her eyes.

"It hurts," she'd said, but this had been edited out. She started fighting her sheets, kicking her legs. "No! No!" This too was silenced, her mouth gaping.

"She's seeing angels!" Gideon said. This had been added in post-production. You couldn't see his lips, because of the flowers.

You couldn't tell from their edit, but she'd started cursing then. Words I didn't know she knew. "Motherfuck. Shitting asshole. Cock and balls. Goddamn, it hurts!"

"Help her!" I remember shouting. "Help her!" What she needed wasn't a prayer chain or a speech about Heaven. What she needed was more morphine.

"You're going somewhere beautiful," Gideon said.

"Sometimes the transition can be painful," Dad said. "But the reward is eternal." This, too, was dubbed. Recorded from a separate interview with Dad. They'd timed it to when his back was to the camera. He was leaning over Mom to hit the button for the morphine drip. It looked like he was whispering to her.

Mom fell back on the sheets, spent; a look of peace crossed her face. There was a flash of light over her body. They'd added a fucking *flash of light.*

"You'll love it there," Gideon said. "Eli knows. It's so beautiful."

But they hadn't edited out the twitch of his nose—a split second, on all the screens: Gideon's pinched face—as the stench released from her bowels slowly filled the room.

16

THE THRONE ROOM

I raged and raged at God: "How can you do this? How can you take my son from me!" And then a quiet, little voice blossomed in my heart: For God so loved the world, that He gave His only begotten Son, that whosoever believeth in Him should not perish, but have everlasting life. *And I had a vision of God's son embracing my son and I knew if God could do it—and our sons could be together—I could, too.*

—from *Heaven or Bust!*, "A Father's Sacrifice," ch. 2, p. 13

BEFORE THE RIBBON-CUTTING FOR THE new Heaven Realm dedicated to me, we were hustled back to the greenroom for touch-ups. Four makeup artists circled us, dabbing and fussing and spritzing. We had to hold still and face forward, which was awkward but actually made it easier to be honest with Dad.

"Why on earth did you do that?" He sounded more disappointed than angry.

"We can't move to Orlando," I said.

"Dude," Abe said. "Stop ruining this for us."

"Hey, Dad?" Jake said.

"I know moving is scary," Dad said, "but it'll be good for us. You'll make new friends."

"It's not just that," I said. "I can't keep doing this. I can't. I won't."

The makeup artists exchanged scandalized looks.

"Um, Dad?" Jake said again.

But Dad was focused on me. "You promised your mother."

"She thought it was a onetime thing!"

"Daddy!" Jake yelled.

"What!"

"Where's Mommy?"

Abe shot me a look in the makeup mirror. "You know where she is, Jakey. She's in Heaven."

"Of course she is," Dad said.

Jake fidgeted in his chair. "Then why did Eli say . . ."

"We don't know where Mom is," I said. "No one does. Mom's gone."

Jake started to cry.

"No no no!" His makeup artist consoled him, patting under his eyes, shooting glares my way.

"Stop it," Dad told me. "Just stop it. I know it's been hard. And I know you're having doubts—"

"I'm not *having* doubts. I don't believe it anymore! It didn't happen!"

My own makeup artist took a step back, eyebrows raised. She didn't say anything.

"I get it," Dad said. "You're upset. But please—*behave.*"

Gideon came in then, fuming. He asked for privacy and the makeup artists scurried from the room.

"Oh man." Abe leaned over. "You're gonna get it."

"What the hell was that!" Gideon barked.

"I'm sorry," Dad said. "It won't happen again."

"What is it with you Heaven Kids! All you have to do is stick to your story. How hard is it?"

"He—he had stage fright."

"Don't give me that." Gideon brushed Dad off and came at me. "It's your mom, isn't it?"

"Yes," Dad said. "It's like you said. He's grieving."

"She put you up to this?"

"No," I said. "She wanted me to go through with it. *I* did it."

Gideon grabbed my arm. "I will *not* let you mess this up for me."

"Ow!" I tried to pull away, but he held firm.

"Hey!" Dad pushed Gideon back. "Don't touch him."

Gideon stepped away, hands raised.

Dad jabbed a finger into Gideon's chest. "Don't you ever do that. You hear me?"

"Hey now," Gideon said. "We're all pals here."

"I'm not your *pal*," I said, rubbing my arm.

Dad squeezed my shoulder. "Are you okay?"

I nodded. It hurt no worse than when Dad had grabbed me in the parking lot to pray, but I made a show of clutching my arm to my chest.

"Listen," Gideon told Dad. "I didn't mean to hurt him. I just need to know he can go back out there without embarrassing me."

"He can. He will."

"I won't," I said.

"You little . . ." Gideon moved to grab me again, but Dad stood his ground between us. He put up a fist. I'd never seen Dad punch anyone before. I didn't think he had it in him. But in that moment, I believed him capable.

"Whoa," Abe said. "*Dad.*"

If the fist was a bluff, Gideon didn't call Dad on it. He took a step back, but locked eyes with me. "The only words I want to hear out of your mouth are *Heaven* and *beautiful*, got that?"

Then he whirled on his heel and stormed out.

Dad bent down to my chair and hugged me. "Are you sure you're okay?"

"Please can we go now?"

He sighed. "Haven't you ever had a dream, son? This is all I ever wanted. It might be my only chance to bring our story to this many people. It's what God wants, too. We can't hang up on the Calling now! Let's just get through today. Maybe we can find a way for you to quit later, but for now could you just try? If not for your mom, for me?"

✣

We were no longer live, but Gideon wanted promotional footage of the ribbon-cutting ceremony and the first tour of Heaven. It wasn't a far trek, only one realm over, but in the afternoon heat our progress was unbearably slow.

As we marched, I tried to come up with my next move. I'd thought, naively, that telling the truth on *The Charlie Gideon Hour* would be enough, but no one was listening. Gideon had used my grief and the doctored footage of Mom in the hospital to drown me out; he'd painted a picture of my faith being tested, then becoming stronger for it. How do you break free of a lie everyone *wants* to believe?

"Look." Dad pointed ahead. "There it is."

The Celestial Palace in the new Heaven Realm was a castle to rival Disney's—with courtyards and drawbridges and turrets on turrets. It was protected by a golden fence with large, ostentatious gates as white as Mom's casket. The walkway to these, the Pearly Gates, was bottlenecked with tourists. We came to a standstill. Gideon sent his goons ahead to clear a path.

Once we made it through, I saw a purple ribbon stretched across the base of the gates, looming closed to visitors. At the top, in gold calligraphy:

Eli Harpo's Adventure to the Afterlife

To the right was a podium and a line of people, seated in chairs. Reporters milled about, interviewing guests in anticipation of the ribbon-cutting. We were led to our seats. My spot was dead center, directly behind the podium. In my white suit, I couldn't be missed. Gideon stepped up to the microphone.

"Hello and welcome to Bible World!"

He waited out the crowd's cheers.

"I'm so happy to have you all here on this blessed day, the opening of my favorite—and what I'm sure will soon be your favorite—Biblical Realm. We've had many additions to our Biblical immersion facility over the years, but this is the first realm based on a living figure! Elijah Harpo, the Boy Who Went to Heaven! Get on up here, Eli!"

Dad patted me on the back and I trudged up to the podium. Gideon flung his arm around my shoulders and told me to wave. I waved.

I thought he might have me speak, but he'd learned better than to let me near a microphone. "In a moment, Eli will cut the ribbon, open the gate, and lead us all into Heaven!" Applause, applause, applause. I thought it would never end. "But before he does, I'd like you to meet our other special guests at Bible World today. We have here our very own Angel Army! Come on up, kids!"

Suddenly, the stage was flooded with kids in purple shirts.

Gideon adopted a somber tone. "For those of you who don't know, the Angel Army is a nonprofit I formed for children with terminal illnesses. The kids here today are being treated for various medical conditions like cystic fibrosis, muscular dystrophy, and childhood leukemia. They were nominated by their doctors to receive a trip to Bible World so they could have an advance tour of Heaven. It's my hope that it brings comfort to all their families."

It took me a moment to understand what Gideon was saying. The kids in the Angel Army were sick. No—they were dying. Their heads weren't shaved for summer: Their hair had fallen out from rounds of chemotherapy. The kids looked happy. They were on vacation in Florida. They were going to be on the news. But when I looked closer I saw they were also pale, moonfaced, their bodies skin and bones. They looked exhausted; they were smiling, but their expressions sagged, their eyes were jaundiced. Beneath their delight was the fatigue I'd seen in Mom at the hospital. In so many terminal patients. I noticed the boy with the backward cap from the Ark. He was staring. I turned away.

A reporter had asked me a question. I'd missed it. He asked again.

"What would you like to tell the Angel Army, Eli?"

Gideon reluctantly ceded me the mike.

What would I like to tell them?

"Um," I said.

"Go on," Gideon said. "What awaits them in Heaven?"

The sun was beating down on us, not a cloud in the sky. Sweat dribbled in my eyes, but I felt suddenly cold—a chill. The kids were watching, waiting for my answer. I couldn't look at the boy from the Ark. *What do I say to him?*

The reporter tried a new tactic. He asked the Angel Army if they had any questions for me, about Heaven. They sure did.

"What do you do for fun there? Do they have video games?"

"What have they got to eat? Is there no chicken nuggets, because dead chickens are alive in Heaven? What about cows?"

"Why don't you fall through the clouds?"

"Will I get wings, like Archangel in *X-Men*?"

"Who takes care of us while we wait for the mommies and daddies?"

"Well, Eli?" Gideon said.

The lies lined up in my head, a neat row of them. But these kids didn't want to hear about Jesus in the Meadow. Or seeing Memaw young again. I could have spun them a fantasy out of lions and unicorns. And maybe they'd feel better. All they wanted was for me to tell them they would be safe. That dying wasn't such a big deal. It was going to be okay.

But it wasn't okay. Mom was dead. We'd lost her. And it wasn't fair. It wasn't fair that they made me do this. It wasn't fair that these kids, most of them younger than me, would be dead before their first kiss. They were the victims, not me. It was selfish to think otherwise. Then why couldn't I bring myself to say what they needed to hear?

"I'm sorry." I was saying it to all of them, but I locked eyes with the boy in the backward cap. "I don't know."

☦

Exasperated with my performance, Gideon distracted everyone with a photo op. We moved from the stage to the Pearly Gates and the cameras gathered round. I stood at the center with my family and Gideon. On either side was the Angel Army.

Through the whole photo shoot, I felt sick. Maybe if I threw up I wouldn't have to go in. Or if I fainted? I could just sit down, right here, at the foot of the Pearly Gates, and pretend to pass out. They'd carry me on a stretcher to Bible World's first-aid station, where I could wait out the rest of the day, eating animal crackers and sucking down juice boxes. And then we could all go home. We'd never have to move to Florida or perform as Christian celebrities or deal with Charlie Gideon ever again.

"Now where are those scissors?" Gideon made a motion like he was trimming an invisible topiary. A woman came forward with a velvet pillow on which rested a pair of enormous silver scissors.

"There they are! Okay, Eli. Cut that ribbon!"

I took the scissors. They were huge. Heavy, too.

More photos. My hands were shaking, the silver handles slippery with sweat. Gideon nudged me. I didn't understand what he wanted. He nudged me again, making a motion with his hands. I opened the scissors. The blades slid apart.

I was dizzy. Maybe I'd faint for real. I wouldn't even have to fake it.

I turned to Abe. Held out the scissors. "You want to be the Chosen One? Here. Take it."

Abe hesitated, his eyes glinting on the silver. He reached out—

But Gideon swatted his hand away. "You're the Heaven Boy," he told me. "Not your brother."

"I'll do it!" Jake bounced up and down. "Please! Please! Please! Let me do it."

"Those scissors are too sharp for little boys," Gideon told him. He gave Dad a look like, *Get your kids under control.*

Dad took Jake's hand. "Gideon's right. It's Eli's job."

I stepped up to the ribbon and cut it with little fanfare. Then I dropped the scissors at Gideon's feet. The blades fell well in front of his boots, and I'm sure that crocodile skin was too tough to puncture anyway, but he still leapt back. He gritted his teeth at me, nostrils flaring;

then, remembering the cameras, he clapped his hands, raising his arms for attention.

"For Yours is the kingdom and the power and the glory forever!" he announced as the Pearly Gates opened dramatically in front of him, admitting us all to Heaven.

Beyond the entrance, there was a long, winding path for the line to the Holy Roller, a silver coaster that sent tourists through a reenactment of my Heaven story, ending with a panoramic view of Heaven and the Celestial Palace. I wanted to go with Jake, preferably in the back, but Gideon insisted I sit in the front car with him while the camera crews filmed us boarding the ride. Dad, Abe, and Jake sat behind us. Angel Army kids and their parents filled in the rest of the seats. We pulled down the safety bars and buckled in.

The coaster rolled slowly out of the station and everyone cheered.

We started uphill. *Clink-clink-clink.* On other coasters it might have been scary—the world at a diagonal, the excruciating rise before an inevitable descent—but I knew that the Holy Roller was a family ride. No drops, loops, or corkscrews.

Howdy, pardners! came the recorded voice of none other than Charlie Gideon, over the speakers embedded in the headrest.

You have just boarded the Holy Roller, on your destination to the holiest place of all—Heaven! Now sit back and enjoy the ride while I tell you a little story about the Boy Who Went to Heaven . . .

Elijah James Harpo was born on June 30, 1994, to Simon and Deborah Harpo, of Canaan, Kentucky. When he was just four years old, he suffered from a heart attack, due to a congenital heart defect.

"It wasn't a heart attack," I told Gideon. "It was just a palpitation."

Eli's parents called 911 and he was rushed to the hospital in an ambulance.

"That part's not true either. Dad drove me."

But Gideon wasn't listening. He was enjoying the sound of his own voice.

At the top of the hill, the coaster entered a tunnel with a flashing red sign over the entrance that said HOSPITAL. We jerked to a stop in a mock operating room. An animatronic nurse was setting out instruments on a table.

Eli had to have an emergency surgery to fix his heart.

An animatronic nurse wheeled in a gurney with an animatronic red-headed boy on it. Two seats behind us, Jake pointed and yelled, "Look, Eli! It's you!"

During the surgery Eli's heart stopped.

A dramatic scene unfolded. There was an enormous screen that showed the heartbeat of the boy during the operation and when it flatlined (*beep! beep! beeeee . . .*) the nurses shook in a panic. The animatronic doctor shocked the boy with paddles. Nothing. He shocked him again. Nothing. But already the Holy Roller was moving on and Gideon's narration was saying, *Where did Eli go? What happens after we die?* and we swooped into a dark tunnel, a terrifying blackness.

For those who love Jesus . . .

The speakers in the car went dead, cutting off the atonal ring of the EKG flatline. We all sat waiting in the dark—ten seconds, twenty, thirty—long enough that it started to become clear there was something wrong. A glitch in the ride.

"Hey—what's going on?" a passenger called from behind us.

"This isn't funny."

"Let me out of here!"

"Mommy!"

Gideon cleared his throat. "Everybody stay calm! I'm sure it's nothing."

"I don't like this."

"I can't see anything."

"Is this even safe?"

"Our engineers are working out the kinks, that's all!"

"Kinks?" someone yelled. "Kinks!"

"Help! Somebody! Anybody!"

"It's okay! These things happen on opening day! It'll just be a moment."

I closed my eyes. Behind me someone moaned in fear. We were all together, sitting in the dark, but it was almost like we weren't anywhere at all.

And then the Holy Roller shot forward, speakers blaring the ethereal music of a harp, and we went around the tunnel bend and out into the bright light of day.

. . . you have nothing to worry about! trilled Gideon's narration. *Welcome to Heaven.*

✢

The Holy Roller circled the Celestial Kingdom for the panoramic view. The Palace was constructed out of "cloud," a lumpy kind of plaster that made the castle slightly amorphous, painted blindingly white with silver glitter in the mix. Beneath the Orlando sun, it was almost too bright to look at directly; when you did, you got the impression of a child's school project, fashioned from toothpicks and marshmallows, half-melted. Spotlights of various colors were projected onto the white crenellations to look like rainbows. Once the coaster had completed a full revolution, it dipped down gradually, then came to a smooth stop at the arrival platform. Gideon's narration told us to watch our step when exiting, then said goodbye, wishing us all a Heavenly experience.

We'd been trapped in the tunnel for only a few minutes, but it had felt like hours and spoiled the panorama experience. Angel Army kids and their parents unbuckled their seat belts, yanked safety bars up, and clambered out of the coaster in a slowly ebbing panic.

"I don't like that ride!" Jake was crying. Dad hugged him.

"Me neither," Abe said.

Gideon got off in a huff. He looked more shaken than he'd sounded in the tunnel.

"What *was* that?" Dad said.

"Just a small glitch." Gideon smoothed his hair down. "Don't let it ruin our good time. Shall we?"

He beckoned and we followed hesitantly, out of the train station to the foot of a drawbridge. The camera crews were waiting for us there to shoot footage of us crossing over a sad little moat—a creek, really—and entering the castle.

Fog machines were hidden around the Celestial Courtyard, spurting out sporadic wisps of white. There were signs leading to the 𝕮𝖍𝖗𝖔𝖓𝖊 𝕽𝖔𝖔𝖒 and the 𝕬𝖓𝖌𝖊𝖑 𝕿𝖔𝖜𝖊𝖗. Food stands sold cotton candy clouds and star-shaped Popsicles. The Angel Army kids tossed coins into the Fountain of Wishes. Animatronic angels, with halos and wings that really flapped, floated above on zip lines, strumming gold harps. Jake was completely agog. We all were.

"What do you think?" Dad asked me.

"It's . . . something," I said.

"Just like you remember?"

"Dad."

"You can't re-create the spiritual dimension, of course. It's an impossible task."

"Right."

"But maybe it's close?"

He clearly hoped the park might jog my memory. But standing in that realm convinced me more than ever: I'd never been to a place remotely like this.

As we toured the Courtyard, Gideon kept prompting me for the cameras—"Isn't this just like what you saw? We took this straight from your testimony!"—but I gave him nothing.

We entered the Throne Room.

Inside, down a long purple rug, Jesus was waiting for us. We hadn't seen him since the Resurrection in Crucifixion Corner. He sat on a golden throne on a dais at the head of the hall. At his right hand was an even larger throne—an enormous throne, God's throne—but that throne was empty. It was like looking at the seat of the Lincoln Memorial without Lincoln in it.

The reporters from the ribbon-cutting ceremony were already gathered round the base of the dais, which was cordoned off by a purple rope. They must have been led through a back entrance while we were on the ride. As soon as we entered, they perked up, waving cameramen into place, tapping earpieces. Bible World security, in their light blue polos and silver badges, were posted around the purple cord. The Angel Army kids and their families gathered here, taking photos of Jesus on his throne. It was all too much for me, not just all the people—although that was plenty—but the ridiculous room itself. If this tacky fairy-tale land was what the *real* Heaven was like, I'd turn back at the gates.

Gideon marched down the aisle and up the stairs to the dais. He clapped his hands for attention and the room quieted. "Welcome! Welcome to His Most Celestial Palace! I am so moved to see all of you here today. As it says in Revelation, those who come out of tribulation, who have washed their robes and made them white in the blood of the Lamb, they shall not fear death, for the Lamb at the center of the throne shall be your shepherd"—he gestured toward Jesus—"and you will join Him in the Kingdom of Heaven. I hope this brings the Angel Army and their families comfort. And the Harpo family, too, knowing Deborah's here." There was an awkward pause. Gideon cleared his throat.

"That's right!" Jesus shot up from his throne, as if remembering a cue. "I've welcomed her to our Celestial Home. And now I welcome all of you. Come, children." He beckoned and the producers directed the Angel Army kids past the purple rope, to sit on the stairs leading up to the dais and at his feet for yet another photo op. I hated watching that, all these dying kids posing with Jesus, the younger ones enthralled, the older politely bored or embarrassed. It was all so desperately sad, the fantasy they were being sold to ease their minds—and their parents' minds—about the cruelty of an abrupt, untimely end.

"Blessed be the children, for theirs is the Kingdom of God," Jesus said. "Now where's my special friend Eli?" He held a hand to his brow until he spotted me. "There he is! Why don't you come join me on the throne? You can be the first to lay your head in my lap."

Dad pushed me forward.

I stood frozen. The cameras hovered.

Jesus held his hands out to me. "Eli? Come to me, my son."

I dragged myself down the purple rug, past the reporters. I picked my way up the stairs, around the seated Angel Army kids, and approached Jesus.

"Sit on his lap," Gideon said.

"What? No."

Jesus sat down on the throne and patted his lap. "It's okay. Come, child. Rest."

"I'm too old for that."

"You're never too old for Jesus's love."

Before I knew it, hands were on me and I was being plopped down onto his lap—Jesus went *oof!*—and the cameras moved in.

"Wow, Eli. You've grown since I last saw you." Jesus shifted as if in pain.

Angel Army parents aimed their cameras. Reporters circled with their microphones, volleying questions:

"What's it like to be back in Heaven, Eli?"

"Is it just like you remember?"

"How do you feel seeing Jesus again?"

I said nothing. It was too overwhelming. I was exhausted. I'd given up on trying to correct them. My hand went to my scar—

But I didn't pinch it. I had an idea. If I couldn't recant honestly and I couldn't break the lie with dragons or fairies or Bigfoots, then I'd have to tell them something true *and* shocking. Something I could never come back from.

"Oh, he's visited me before," I said.

"That's right," Jesus said, adjusting his legs.

"I mean *after* I went to Heaven. He took me back. We'd meet in the Meadow."

"Sure did," Jesus agreed.

"He told me he loved me."

"Uh-huh."

"And we'd lie down together in the grass."

"What now?"

"I'd open my robe and show him my scar and he'd touch it."

"Um . . . I don't think . . ."

"He'd open his robe and let me touch him, too."

Jesus did a double take. The Angel Army kids looked confused. The reporters' faces showed alarm. Gideon was moving in to shut me up.

I didn't plan what happened next. Honestly. If you watch the "Heaven Boy Homo!!!!!!!" video, it looks like I knew exactly what I was doing, but I was only acting on impulse.

Before Gideon could intervene, I reached out, took Jesus by his long flowing locks, and kissed him. It was not at all like the dream. His beard was scratchy and he tasted of garlic. Our lips remained closed and it was very brief. But it had a dramatic effect.

Jesus recoiled. "What the hell!" He shoved me off his lap and leapt to his feet. I fell to the ground, hard. "Not cool, man." He spat and wiped his mouth. "I don't get paid enough for this." He stormed off the dais and out a door marked Employees Only.

The reporters were speechless, but soon recovered. A hubbub filled the room.

Dad was suddenly there. He looked stunned but bent down to help me up.

It was chaos. The reporters were all pushing forward, trying to get at us for quotes, photos. They wanted reaction shots, sound bites about what had just happened. Angel Army parents were screaming, collecting their kids from the stairs of the dais.

Meanwhile, Gideon was conferring with his security team. They rounded us up, Abe and Jake joining Dad and me, light blue polos on all sides, barricading us from the reporters. At first I thought they were protecting us, but then Gideon said, "Please escort the Harpos out."

It was the flat tone of his voice. He was done. I could tell. It was over. Everything was wild around us, but in that moment, all I felt was an immense rush of relief.

"Please," Dad begged. "It was just a joke. He was just joking—"

The security officers hesitated, glancing at their boss.

Gideon finally blew. He flung his arms, spittle flying. "I said get these people out of my park!"

"It's a Biblical immersion facility," I said as we were led out.

✢

They frog-marched us out of Heaven, back through Bible World, all the way out to our van in the parking lot. We weren't in handcuffs, but it sure felt like it, what with park security flanking us on either side. And it wasn't just reporters snapping our photos, but tourists, too. Bystanders gawked as we were thrown out, speculating about what terrible thing we'd done to be forcibly removed.

"Just a misunderstanding," Dad told the people we passed. "A misunderstanding, that's all."

"Oh my God." Abe's gaze never left his feet. "This is *so* embarrassing."

"Bye-bye, everybody!" Jake waved.

It's hard to feel triumphant when you're being ejected from a Christian theme park by what basically amount to a bunch of glorified mall cops. Gideon could have snuck us out the back, but he deliberately made a show out of it. He was already distancing himself from the Harpo family. He wanted to broadcast our shame by casting us out.

But despite all that, part of me felt victorious. *Goodbye stupid ark with your stupid fake animals! Goodbye megachurch stage with your gaudy stained-glass cowboy! Goodbye lumpy cloud palace with your tacky throne room and false promises! I won't be back.* Sure, it was humiliating. But who cares? I was finally free.

PART FOUR

EXODUS

17

IT GETS WORSE

For those suffering from anxiety and depression [and family estrangement], *try practicing the art of mindfulness. Mindfulness is the state of being fully present in the moment, whether by meditation, breathing techniques, or coping mechanisms for stress* [such as the crippling guilt of dashing your father and brothers' hopes and dreams].

Remember: Being mindful is the first step toward good mental health [although there is no guarantee it will cure loneliness, heal childhood trauma, mend relationships, recuperate lost faith, prevent self-recrimination, or ward off the existential despair of daily living in a late capitalist society]. *You got this!*
—UK Counseling Center's "Mental Health & Mindfulness" pamphlet

MY JUNIOR YEAR OF COLLEGE, I went home for winter break. It'd been nearly two years since I'd been back for a visit, but it was time.

The evening I arrived, the house was empty. Everyone was at church for Wednesday-night service. After all those years, Dad's room still smelled like Mom: an olfactory miracle, or maybe a hallucination, given he'd donated all her things to Goodwill years ago. Her vanity was still there. Instead of perfumes, it was topped with a bottle of cologne and a change dish—a chunk of misshapen clay that was supposed to be Noah's ark, a Sunday school art project. The drawers were filled not with scarves but with handkerchiefs. His closet was half-empty.

I went to the kitchen—same counters, same stools, same fridge covered in Bible magnets. I stood at the sink and drank a glass of water. Texted Will to let him know I'd arrived safely.

We'd made up after he apologized. He said I should come out on my own time and he was sorry for pressuring me. He was already home with his family and sent me a photo of him and his parents gathering pinecones for their "pagan-ass Yule Altar." Every year Jeff and Lois did some kind of ridiculous winter solstice ceremony. They planted a tree, lit a bonfire, then proceeded to get drunk. The night ended with an inebriated sun dance, to re-lengthen the daylight. It sounded like a scene out of *The Crucible*. It sounded lovely.

I wouldn't have even considered coming out if Will hadn't suggested it. I wanted to coast through Christmas—drink eggnog, sing carols, share stocking stuffers. I wanted to watch *The Bible Tales Christmas Special* with Jake, the one where Logan and Emma have to hunt down the thieves who steal the frankincense and myrrh and return the gifts to the wise men in time for Jesus's birth. The only verses I wanted to hear from Dad were Luke 2:1–20, the Christmas story, which he read aloud to us every year.

But I did it. I came out to them a week later on Christmas, after seeing Chase and his pregnant wife at Carpenter's. I don't know what it was exactly, after all that. Seeing Chase and thinking *that could have been me*—stuck forever in Canaan, if I'd never left for college? Sitting in church, wondering if I'd ever get the chance to dance drunkenly around a bonfire with Will's ironically pagan parents? Feeling guilty for even dreaming of such a thing, because how could I ever expect him to introduce us if I couldn't be honest with my own family about who I loved? Whatever it was, we went back to the house to open presents and I just couldn't hold it in anymore. I don't want to revisit the nitty-gritty of what happened after. Let's just say it went about as expected. Dad quoted the verses I predicted. Jake was mostly quiet, but words were exchanged between Abe and me. I will say, as painful as it was, it was worth it.

Dad didn't ask me to leave, but I couldn't stand staying in that house for another night. So I packed my bag. Will came and got me and I spent the rest of the holiday with his family. You'd think I'd have been thrilled—I'd just been wishing I'd get to meet them—but I was too upset with my own family to enjoy getting to know his. It was a bizarre Christmas, with strangers who didn't even believe in, as the saying goes, *the reason for the season*. But for the first time I spent it with people who knew and accepted the real me.

Will was right: I should have done it ages ago. I wish I'd been able to when I first had the chance, after kissing Jesus at Bible World.

✝

The car ride back to the hotel was excruciating. When Abe tried to bring up the kiss—"I can't believe you did that. That was so *gay*!"—Dad shut him down. "Stop it. I don't want to hear about it." His eyes caught mine in the rearview mirror.

I looked away. Jake reached over and took my hand.

At the hotel, Dad ordered pizza and we ate silently, with the TV drowning out any need for conversation. We went to bed early.

I couldn't sleep. None of us could. We all just lay there, breathing in the dark, pretending. The word *gay* perched inside my chest like a bird. I knew how Abe meant it, but it didn't feel like a sin to me anymore. I thought of Bright and his husband and *gay* made me feel happy, warm. For the first time it felt like this wasn't going to be my life forever. Things were going to change. They were already changing. And that thought was what helped me finally drift off.

Dad rose early the next morning. Showered, ironed his clothes, dressed. Abe got out of bed, but I just sat up and hugged a pillow to my chest. Jake snored on. Dad gave Abe instructions before leaving. "Stay in this room until I'm back. Jake can watch as many *Bible Tales* as he wants. But no pool. I mean it. Here's money for pizza—"

"We had pizza last night," Abe said.

"Then get Chinese!"

Abe and I flinched at the shout.

Dad took a breath. "Order whatever you'd like. I'll be back tonight."

"But where are you going?" Abe said.

"I'm going to talk to Gideon and get our show back."

Abe raised a skeptical brow. "How are you going to do that?"

But Dad was already out the door. He hadn't addressed me once that morning or the night before, and I was surprised to find I was perfectly fine with that. I wasn't even worried about his last-ditch effort to salvage *Heaven or Bust!* I'd seen how Gideon looked after the Jesus kiss. There was no coming back from that.

I got out of bed and put on my swimsuit.

"Dad said no pool," Abe said.

"No. Dad said no pool *for Jake.*"

"Seriously? You just ruined all of our lives and now you're going to go and hang by the pool? Like you're on vacation?"

I gathered my sunscreen, beach towel, and a book.

"Gonna catch a few rays, huh? Take a little dip. Go on. Get a nice tan. Like you didn't just tank Dad's career. Lost him the rights to his own book."

"Eli?" Jake was awake now, rubbing his eyes.

"It's okay, Jake," I said. "Go back to sleep."

"What you did was sick," Abe said. "Perverted. That's what you are, a perv—"

I slammed the door behind me. Exiled myself down to the pool, face burning. I tried to hold on to that feeling of relief, even hope, from yesterday, but I just felt terrible. I laid out my towel on one of the lounge chairs. Tried to read. Slept some. Floated in the water when it was too hot. It was nothing like a vacation. I was miserable and lonely. But I couldn't be in the hotel room with Abe. I didn't even eat lunch with them, just starved myself until Dad came back.

He brought back McDonald's for dinner. He looked wrecked, said he hadn't been able to get hold of Gideon, but he was going to keep trying. I wondered what he'd done all day. I had this image of him pacing back and forth outside the Bible World gates, demanding to be let in. His phone rang while we were munching on cold fries and he leapt up to take the call out on the balcony. We tried to eavesdrop, but you couldn't make out anything but muffled shouting through the sliding glass door.

"He'll never forgive you for this," Abe said.

I ignored him, chewed my burger. I'd been so hungry, but everything tasted like Styrofoam.

"Why'd you do it?" Jake said. "Why'd you kiss Jesus?"

I couldn't look at Abe. "I had to."

"But why?"

"I just . . . it was too much pressure." The first of many excuses. *Too much pressure. A panic attack. Sunstroke.* I didn't know how to explain it away.

Dad came back in. He looked shell-shocked. Before, he'd been upset, but determined. Now he was deflated, wan.

"What'd Gideon say?" Abe said. "Is he giving us a second chance?"

More like third . . . fourth . . . fifth, I thought.

"That wasn't Gideon," Dad said. "It was Zeb."

"Oh." Abe gulped. "Are we in trouble?"

Dad slumped down onto one of the hotel beds. "I got fired."

"What!" Abe rushed over to him.

Jake started to cry. "No, Daddy! No."

"Gideon told Zeb he's pulling his donation. Zeb said all of Creation saw the videos of Eli and . . ." He waved his hand, unable to say it. "It's all online." He dropped his head in his hands. "It's over." They were all together on the bed. Abe with his arm around Dad, Jake in his lap. I've never felt worse in my life.

Dad finally looked at me. "What happened, son? What's going on with you?"

"I'm sorry." I didn't know what else to say. My throat went dry and I felt tears climbing their way up. I left the room and went back down to the safety of the pool.

Dad followed. Or I thought he was coming after me, but instead of passing through the gate to the pool, he went out to the van in the parking lot and drove off.

I didn't return to the room until I was sure Abe and Jake were asleep. Dad still wasn't back. I woke two hours later, to him stumbling around in the dark. The clock radio read four in the morning. He sat next to me on the bed, petting my head and praying. He smelled like a keg of beer, which was more than a little disturbing, because Dad didn't drink. He slurred his words, many of which I couldn't make out. But I definitely heard this: "Please, God. Help my son. I don't know how to fix him. Please, Jesus, please. Save him."

I played possum until he finished his prayer and passed out next to me.

Dad was too hungover to drive the next day, but he was finally ready to leave. He nursed a coffee from the hotel lobby and tossed his keys to Abe.

The car ride home was the longest of my life. Everyone upset and grieving and hating me. What would I say to comfort my younger self, staring out the window, on that twelve-hour drive? "It gets better"? That uplifting project wouldn't start for another two years, in 2010, but I needed to hear it then.

Even if I could have heard the words, I don't know if I would have believed them. Sure, it might get better over time, but sometimes it gets worse first. Sometimes everyone blames you for blowing your family's chance at fame and fortune. Sometimes you go home and can barely show your face at your new high school because you've made a disgrace of yourself on TV and the internet. Sometimes your father's ministerial career is reduced to a Simon Says YouTube channel no one watches and, though he never says it, you know it's your fault—his gay Jesus-kissing son—that no other church will hire him.

Would I have kissed Jesus and freed myself had I known the pain that would follow? That Dad would lose not only his deal with Gideon, his rights to *Heaven or Bust!*, and his job, but also any chance of being a minister again? That he'd have to go back to the misery of telemarketing to make ends meet? That in the years after Bible World, Abe would find every opportunity to guilt-trip me with a fantasy of what our life might have been like in Orlando: "We could be drinking coconuts on the beach right now." Not to mention the financial disaster of losing our chance at free college tuition. Mom would have been so disappointed.

But I don't want to dwell on the bad things. Because in college it *did* get better. I found my people; I met my husband. I started over.

After the Christmas I came out, I cut ties with my family completely. I didn't hear from any of them until more than a year later, when Jake came to my graduation. During that time, I kept turning this word—*estranged*—over and over in my mind . . .

I am *estranged* from my family. We are *estranged*.

Thankfully, I wasn't alone. Will was there for me. He supported me through the depression that followed that spring. Got me out of bed and to class, made sure I ate, sent me links to articles on mental health and religious trauma. He set up appointments for me at the Counseling Center. The therapist I saw there was overworked, often overbooked, but a good listener. She offered canned coping techniques—deep breathing, slow counting, grounding with the five senses—to help students manage stress and anxiety. Nothing earth-shattering, but I was glad Will made me go. He kept me sane that year. I don't know how I would have survived without him.

All of that was ahead of me. Will was ahead of me; Oliver was ahead of me. That's what I would have told myself on that interminable car ride home to Kentucky. They're there, in your future, I promise. Sometimes you have to lose one family to make another.

18

GRADUATION

Nothing's hotter than Kevin Bacon angry dancing in an abandoned warehouse.

—Debbie Harpo, circa 2004

IN THE END, I DIDN'T quite lose them after all.

Jake was thirteen going on fourteen, the same age I'd been at Bible World. It'd been only a year and a half since I'd laid eyes on him, at what I now thought of as Our Last Family Christmas, but I barely recognized him when he slouched off the Greyhound.

"Jake?"

"Eli!" He threw his arms around me, practically lifted me off the ground.

"Holy shit! Jake!" His hair was much longer. Shaggy, but it suited him. And he'd had another growth spurt. Must have shot up a full foot. "You're taller than me now!"

Jake beamed.

I just stood there and admired him. My baby brother, all grown up. We fought over his duffel. Eventually, he let me carry it the few blocks to the apartment.

He was in awe of everything we passed, things I took for granted: the trees on campus, the wildcat statue outside the university bookstore, the duplex off Rose that Will and I rented. I liked impressing him. It was his first trip away from home on his own.

"You could live somewhere like this when you go to college," I said when we dropped off his stuff.

He glanced around the living room. "You live here with your—uh, partner?"

"Boyfriend. Will. He's not here right now."

"Oh, okay," he said, unable to hide his relief.

"But he'll be back for dinner." My face was hot, but it felt cowardly to drop the subject, so I said, "He's looking forward to meeting you."

Jake nodded, clearly uncomfortable.

I started to say more, then stopped myself. I didn't want to push too hard.

I'd sent home three tickets for my graduation. Will made me do it. I told him I didn't care if Dad or my brothers were there, but he insisted I invite them: "You're the first in your family to graduate from college! You should at least give them the chance to come. They might surprise you." Jake was the only one I'd heard from. He'd bought the bus ticket and texted me the time he'd arrive all on his own.

I feigned nonchalance about his visit, but the truth was I desperately wanted Will and Jake to hit it off. I loved Will. Things were going great with us and I was beginning to suspect that, like Dad, who'd only ever dated Mom and always proudly declared himself a one-woman man, I might be a one-man man, too. Chase hardly counted. But it's difficult for one person to be your everything, and as upset as they made me, I missed my family. Jake's visit was a shot at reuniting the two halves of my life and I didn't want to mess it up.

We went to Tolly-Ho for lunch. We ate our burgers in silence for a while. It was awkward. I hadn't expected it to be so hard to make conversation. I didn't want to ask, but I couldn't *not* ask. "So. How are things . . . at home?"

"Fine, good. Dad and Abe send their congrats."

"No, they don't."

"They do. In their way."

"Yeah, okay."

"It's true. They're proud of you. I can tell."

"I thought I was *brainwashed*."

"Oh, you are. According to Abe at least. But Dad *is* proud. I can tell. He knew how badly Mom—" He swallowed the rest.

"I know."

"He wanted to come, I swear. But he worries about you."

"If he's so worried, why haven't I heard from him?"

Jake sighed. "He's worried *for your soul*. He thinks if he stays away, you'll come around. He's giving you space to find your way back to the Lord."

I scoffed. "Well, you can tell him that's never going to happen."

Jake frowned, but didn't say anything.

"What about you? Are *you* worried for my soul?"

"No." He shifted in his seat. "I don't know. I know it was hard for you, at home."

"Yeah, no shit."

Jake flinched at the curse. I had the impulse to apologize, then didn't. Will once told me there was a study done that showed people who used profanity were more honest. I didn't think that was always true, but I'd been finding my way to that more honest place.

✝

When Will came home from work—it was his first year at the *Herald-Leader*, in the mail room—he tried to kiss me hello in front of Jake and I panicked and turned my cheek. His lips landed on the corner of my mouth. Jake was looking pointedly at his phone during Will's arrival, so he missed the botched greeting.

Will gave me a hurt look.

I ignored his wounded expression and made introductions. I was, perhaps, a little too chipper. "Will, Jake! Jake, Will!"

"So this is the famous Jake Harpo," Will said, shaking Jake's hand.

"It's nice to meet you," Jake said, a little stiffly.

"Thirsty?" Will grabbed beers from the fridge. He pointed a bottle at Jake. "How old are you again?"

Jake turned to me in shock. "You *drink* now?"

"Just beer," I said.

"And a little weed," Will said.

"Will!" I slapped his arm. I'd deliberately hid our bong in the closet.

Jake's eyes bugged. "You do . . . *drugs*, too?"

I shrugged. I was kind of enjoying him seeing me in a new, more adult light. "Just a little. For stress relief. You know who else did weed?" I had such a clear image of her—in bed with her box of Polaroids. "Mom."

Jake rolled his eyes. "Yeah, right."

"It's true."

"So can he have a beer or not?" Will said.

"No thank you," Jake said politely. "I've tried beer before." He made a face. "It's gross."

Will chuckled. "It's an acquired taste."

"Wait," I said. "When did you try beer?"

Jake smirked. "You're not the only rebellious one in the family."

"Ha!" Will guffawed. He jabbed a thumb in my direction. "Rebellious? This guy? The man *irons* his handkerchiefs."

Jake looked confused. "What's wrong with that? Dad does, too."

"Wow, babe. You make *so* much more sense to me." Will tried to slip his arm behind my back. Jake's eyes widened. I moved away.

"Chips and salsa," I said, opening the pantry. "We need chips and salsa."

Will dropped his arm. He didn't try to show me any affection in front of Jake again. I felt bad about being so self-conscious, but also grateful for Will's discretion. I eventually loosened up. The beer helped. The rest of the evening went surprisingly well. Will put on a Fleetwood Mac record. He was into vinyl, showed Jake how the player worked. ("You mean, like, with an actual *needle*?") We talked about Abe's new girlfriend, Becca Stepka, who Jake thought was a bit of a goody-goody. Perfect for Abe, I thought. Will asked if Jake had a crush on anyone in his class and Jake turned bright red.

"Sorry," I said. "I'm trying to teach him tact."

Now it was Will's turn to roll his eyes. "Always with the *tact*. Sometimes it's okay to be a little assertive."

"By 'assertive,' he means blunt. It's rude, Will."

"No, it's *direct*. So what?" He turned to Jake. "It's okay. You don't have to answer, if you don't want to."

"Her name's Rachel," Jake blurted, then covered his face.

"Ooooh," Will said. "*Rachel*. She sounds pretty. Do tell."

And Jake did. Rachel was in his European history class. He showed us her Facebook page, which said she liked One Direction and Bagel Bites. She had long brown hair and braces. She didn't look like anything special to me, but Will whistled when he saw her profile picture. "I knew it. She's a looker."

Jake smiled bashfully. "You think?"

Maybe it shouldn't have been such a shock to me how easily he opened up. Will had this kind of effect on people. He knew how to draw them out. I'd seen him work this magic before—it's what made him a good journalist. If it weren't for him, I'd never have gotten Jake to admit he liked someone, much less who.

After dinner, we made a bowl of popcorn and watched *Footloose* in honor of Mom. Jake didn't really remember it, so I told him about her thing for Kevin Bacon. I totally get it now.

I thought we'd go to bed right after, but instead we stayed up late, chatting. We made plans for lunch after the ceremony.

"You proud of your big brother?" Will asked.

"Course," Jake said. "I can't wait to see him get that diploma."

I hadn't realized how badly I'd needed to hear that until Jake said it. "Thanks for coming," I said. "It's good having you here."

"So you're going to be a drug dealer, huh?" Jake winked.

"Ha. But, yes, a pharmacist."

"Why'd you choose that?"

"I liked my chemistry classes. And it seems like a good way to help people. What do you think you'd major in?"

"Oh, I don't know." Jake looked down into the empty popcorn bowl. "I don't like school like you do."

"What do you mean?"

Jake glanced at Will, then shrugged. "Nothing."

Will took the hint. He stood up and stretched, said he'd hit the hay. While he was in the bathroom brushing his teeth, I asked Jake again what he'd meant.

"Craig said he could get me a job at the Jiff when I turn sixteen."

"Craig Goodin? Doesn't he work at a tire shop?"

"The Jiffy Lube."

"Wow. Seriously, Jake? You want to do oil changes for the rest of your life?"

Jake shrugged. "He showed me around. Didn't seem so bad. I like cars."

"No." I shook my head. "You've got to get out of that place."

"It's not like that for me."

"The world is so much bigger than Canaan."

"So what? I *like* Canaan. All my friends are there, our church is there. I don't want to move."

"What about your education? It's what Mom wanted—"

"For you, maybe."

"For all of us."

"Why should I go into debt when I can start making money now?"

"It's an *investment* in your future. You'll make more later."

"Doing what? I'm not going to be a doctor or a lawyer or whatever."

"You don't know that. Unless you try."

Jake sighed. "Maybe." He yawned pointedly. "I'm tired. I'm going to bed, too."

"Wait. We should talk about this. If you don't get out for college, you'll be trapped there for good."

"Good night, Eli. Thanks for dinner." He went to the guest bedroom and closed the door.

I sat on the couch a little while longer. I wanted to go after him but couldn't. What more could I say? I saw his future so clearly. Under a car hood in a grease-stained jumpsuit. Married, with kids. Plopping down in front of ESPN on Friday nights. Mowing the lawn on Saturdays, church potlucks on Sundays. Why did this horrify me so much? It's not dissimilar to my life now. Varies only in the specifics. Lab coat for jumpsuit. Novels, instead of sports. No more churches—never again—but I find community in other places: a queer book club, dinner parties, the Pride Center. I was wrong to judge Jake by my needs. College saved me, but it isn't for everyone. I eventually came around, but I was so disappointed then. Maybe this was the real reason: I was lonely. I'd been admitted to UK's pharmacy program, which meant I'd be in Lexington for another four years, if not permanently, and I'd imagined us in each other's lives again when Jake came for college.

"I'm sorry, honey," Will said, holding me in bed that night. "He could still change his mind. He's just a kid."

"Yeah," I said. But Jake never left Canaan. And I never moved back.

✢

The next day, Will and Jake sat together in the crowd and watched me walk across the Rupp Arena stage in my UK blue robe. I'd envisioned that moment a lot before it actually happened. I thought I might look out and imagine Mom cheering next to them; I might burst with pride for being the first college graduate in my family. And although it wasn't quite like the future-memory Mom described at the hospital—it wasn't at Harvard and I didn't see her crying, raccoon-eyed, waving madly from the stands—I *did* feel her within me. And I *did* feel proud. And I knew she'd have been proud, too.

We met up after and Will took pictures of me tossing my mortarboard overhead while holding the flowers he'd bought me. Then we got tacos and went to a movie at the Kentucky Theatre. Soon it was time for Jake to catch his afternoon bus. He wanted to make it back that night so he could attend church the next day. Will said his goodbye at the apartment and I walked Jake to the station.

"Your friend's nice," Jake said, on the way.

"Boyfriend," I said.

"I know," Jake said.

"You don't seem to have any problem calling Becca Abe's girlfriend."

"You're right. I'm sorry. Let me try that again. I like your *boyfriend*, Eli."

"Thanks, Jake."

"I *am* proud of you, you know."

"I know."

"And Dad and Abe will come around. It just takes time."

"Sure," I said. But I was skeptical. "Come back and visit us, okay?"

"Of course," he said. "I'll be back soon."

But Will and I didn't see him again for another three years, until our wedding. And I didn't see Dad and Abe again until two years after that, at Jake's own wedding, where I finally met Abe's son and newborn daughter. Dad and Abe were polite but restrained around Will. We didn't start seeing them regularly again until after Oliver was born. Kids really do change everything. Will and I ultimately decided that we wanted my family in Oliver's life in some capacity, if limited, and Dad wanted to be a grandfather to Oliver. Jake was instrumental in bringing us all back together. He started inviting Will, Oliver, and me to Canaan every holiday season. We went at least twice a year, for the Fourth of July and Christmas, and we had everyone to Lexington for Oliver's birthdays. It was Don't Ask, Don't Tell when we saw one another. Not just about our being gay, but also our refusal to go to church. Whenever we could, we planned our visits to Canaan for a Thursday through Saturday to avoid the expectations that came with Sunday mornings and Wednesday nights.

It wasn't perfect, but it was much better than the years of silence that came before. There was a tacit agreement about the things we couldn't talk about. We couldn't talk about the harm that had been done to me by being the Heaven Kid; or about that disastrous family road trip to Bible World; or about how Charlie Gideon had wrecked us; or any of it, really—and I thought that's what I wanted. For the past to remain in the past. We'd come together again, we'd made our peace, we'd moved on—or so I'd assumed.

Why on earth would we ever go back?

HEAVEN HOAX REDUX

WHAT I DON'T EXPECT, WHAT I wouldn't have guessed, not in a million years—is that going back to Bible World would be *fun*. Except for a few shalom!-ing employees in Jerusalem Marketplace, we have the park to ourselves. Dad, Rachel, and Becca take Oliver with my nieces to the kiddie realms, so my brothers and I finally get to ride all the rides we missed out on while I was busy being the Heaven Kid. Even better—there are no lines.

We ride Sodom forward, Gomorrah backward. Then Jake rides Sodom and I ride Gomorrah and we air high-five when the coasters *woosh!* past each other. We switch and do it again. Four times we ride those coasters, exiting past the giant pillar of salt labeled Lot's Wife, and each time we make faces at the camera that snaps our photos mid-ride. Even my nephew, Chris, who pronounced Bible World lame from the get-go, has a blast doing that. Only Abe is sour, glaring at Will and his camera crew as they follow me, lining up shots.

Next, we do David's Slingshot twice, then cool off in Daniel in the Lions' Den in 3D. By the time we board the Drop-Tower of Babel, Will's looking nervous. It's almost noon and the only footage he has is of me screaming in delight, hands above my head. I'm having the time of my life. This does not a documentary make.

"You feel *nothing* being back?"

"You said I shouldn't force it."

"You shouldn't. I'm just . . . surprised."

"What do you want me to say? It sucked then, it's fun now."

The Drop-Tower's a giant red pillar in the middle of the realm, with seats that rotate as they rise, so you can look out over Genesis and beyond. We pull down the safety harnesses, buckle in, and dangle our feet.

Swift, pneumatic jolt—and we're lifting. A sultry female voice narrates the parable over the speakers in our headrests:

In the beginning, everyone on Earth spoke a common language.

Up, up, up. Past the metallic struts that form the mountainous Sodom and Gomorrah. Above the bright orange and yellow water slides undulating in Jonah's Realm. The Whale, perched atop its pinnacle, regurgitates rafts one by one.

But the Lord came down to see the city and the tower, which the children of men had built.

We make out Noah's Ark and the Red Sea Aquarium. They look puny from up here.

And the Lord said, Come, let us go down there and confound their language, that they may not understand one another's speech.

In the distance I catch sight of what had been my own realm. Pearly Gates flung wide, Holy Roller strewn like a silver ribbon, the Celestial Palace gleaming at the center.

Radio static in the speakers.

Y dijo el Señor, Ahora pues, descendamos, y mezclemos allí sus lenguas, que ninguno entienda la lengua de su compañero.

Static again.

Alors Il dit, Eh bien, descendons et brouillons leur langage pour qu'ils ne se comprennent plus entre eux.

It does it again. Static and then the same line spoken in a new language. German. Chinese. Arabic, Hindi, Italian. Russian, Polish, Portuguese. With each language, the ride whirls faster and faster, spinning like a plate on a stick. The languages mix, the static intermittent, cutting between words like radio channels coming in and out of frequency. The barrage of tongues soon reaches a fever pitch, a roar of nonsensical syllables: alphabet soup.

Then suddenly we jerk to a stop.

Silence.

"Oh God," Chris says. "Oh God, oh God, oh God."

"This is it," Jake says. "We're going to—"

"Aaaaaaaaaahhhhhhhhhh!"

Wind slaps my face. The park's a blur. A crescendo in my ears, pressure all about my head, my temples squeeze as if they're going to pop and then—

It's over.

The ride slows and the seductive female voice speaks again in English.

So the Lord scattered them abroad over the face of the Earth, and they ceased building the city. Therefore, its name is called Babel.

On the platform below, Will signals for his camerawoman and boom operator to shoot us leaving the ride. "Hey! How was it?"

"Crazy!" Chris says.

"Wicked," Jake says.

"Sick." Abe yanks the harness off and stumbles out. "I'm going to be sick."

I don't leave the seat. "You can film me while I go again."

☩

A lunch interview while we eat Fish and Loaves at the Last Supper restaurant.

"I don't know." I shrug. "It's fun. I never got to do the park like this."

"What'd you do before?" Will asks.

"The kiddie stuff. That and the megachurch. But it's closed."

Dad frowns. He doesn't like the term *megachurch*. Finds it derogatory. "We saw their Passion Play. It was quite good."

"What's that?" Will asks. "Some kind of sermon?"

"Crucifixion reenactment," I say. "But I don't want Oliver watching that. Let's go to Jonah's Realm. We can do the Whale."

"Becca and Rachel can take the kids to the water park. We're doing the Jesus-on-the-Cross thing. You've got to relive your experience."

But when we get there, there's a sign on Jesus's cross announcing the shows are off. Indefinitely.

"Damn." Will stomps in frustration.

Dad winces at the curse. I can tell he's disappointed, too, but for other reasons. This was always his favorite part of the park.

"Sorry," I say. "They probably can't afford to pay the actors anymore." I'm really only apologetic as far as Will's concerned. I've had my fill of actors playing Jesus.

"Come on," Will says, trying to keep it together for his camera crew. "We're going to Heaven."

"I thought you wanted to save that for last?"

"Let's go."

✝

The Heaven Realm is no longer 𝕰𝕝𝕚 𝕳𝖆𝖗𝖕𝖔'𝖘 𝕬𝖉𝖛𝖊𝖓𝖙𝖚𝖗𝖊 𝖙𝖔 𝖙𝖍𝖊 𝕬𝖋𝖙𝖊𝖗𝖑𝖎𝖋𝖊, but simply 𝕬𝖉𝖛𝖊𝖓𝖙𝖚𝖗𝖊 𝖙𝖔 𝖙𝖍𝖊 𝕬𝖋𝖙𝖊𝖗𝖑𝖎𝖋𝖊. My name struck from the marquee with ease. While we wait at the Pearly Gates for Becca, Rachel, and the kids, I finally relent a little and open up for the camera. I show Will where I stood at the ribbon-cutting. I explain about the Angel Army. How terrible I felt, unable to answer their questions. How I couldn't bring myself to lie about Heaven.

"Wow," Will says. "Couldn't have been easy bearing the weight of everyone's existential dread." I can tell he rehearsed it. A line for the doc.

But he's right. It *was* hard. All of those kids are probably dead now. I remember the boy with the backward cap on the Ark and I wonder if he—if any of them—might have had a miraculous recovery and survived. I hope so.

Dad looks pained hearing all this, but he doesn't interrupt or correct me like he did when I was a kid. I can feel him wanting to intervene, give his version of events, but when Will prompts him—"Anything you'd like to say, Simon?"—he just shakes his head.

The wives and kids arrive. Jake's daughters excitedly recount getting drenched on Jonah's Whale. This must be why they all sport souvenir T-shirts from Joseph's Coat of Many Colors, the Genesis gift shop.

"Look, Daddy!" Oliver points to the Bible World logo on his new purple shirt. It's gold and features the lion and lamb mascots. I'm not thrilled seeing him dressed in that. Becca and Rachel must not have found the change of clothes we'd packed in his bag. I imagine burning it later.

We pass through the Pearly Gates and head up the long, winding path to the loading platform for the Holy Roller. On the ride, my story has been replaced with a generic deathbed scene: a generic grandfather in a generic hospital bed surrounded by generic grandchildren. A doctor and nurse stand next to a cardiograph machine that flatlines (*beep! beep! beeeee...*) and the Gideon-narrator asks the eternal question: *What happens after we die?*

This time the coaster sweeps straight through the tunnel—no glitch— the darkness lasts only a second and then light.

The moat, the drawbridge, the Celestial Courtyard. All as empty as Jerusalem Marketplace. Heaven's a ghost town. In the Throne Room, Jesus's throne sits empty. Oliver and the rest of the kids race ahead to the dais to be the first to climb on God's giant gold chair. Becca and Rachel follow to supervise.

"Can you tell us what happened here?" Will says.

"I didn't plan it, honestly. It was an impulse, an act of desperation."

"He was caught up in the moment," Dad says. "It was an emotional time. Debbie had just left us for her eternal home—"

"Died," I say. "She *died*, Dad. Say the word."

"Sorry," Dad says. "Okay, yes. She'd just . . . died, and went to Heaven, and—"

"You don't know that," I said.

"I do. Where else would she be but with our Lord and Savior?"

"Would you look around?" I gestured at the purple rugs and tapestries, the gaudy gold furniture. "It's a fairy tale, Dad."

"Hey." Abe butts in. "Don't talk to him like that." He holds up a hand to the camera. "Could you call them off for one flipping second?"

Will waves the crew away.

Abe glares at me. "You might not believe it anymore, but that doesn't mean you get to mock us for it. Show some freaking respect."

I look around at Dad, Abe, and Jake—staring at me with pity. They all still believe. It makes life easier, not harder, for them. Nothing I say can change that.

"Ethan Silva," Abe says. "He lie, too?"

"Who?" I feign confusion, but I know exactly who he's talking about. I've seen the boy and his father's book, *Half an Hour in Heaven*, topping the bestseller lists. The trailer for the movie played in the theater Will and I frequent for date night. There's a dramatic scene of a boy skating on a frozen lake, then falling through cracked ice. Watching it, I felt like I was the one drowning.

Abe starts in about the Silva family being guests on *This Christian Life*, his favorite podcast. He would have killed to be invited on it. I've often thought of his anger toward me as petty jealousy, but listening to him now, I'm reminded it goes deeper than that. He'd been devout his whole life, and according to what we'd been taught, he should have been rewarded for it. And yet *I* was the one who'd been Chosen. I'd been given everything Abe ever wanted, everything he felt he'd earned by his faith, and then I'd spat in the face of it and left.

"Hey, Abe," Jake says. "Chill out."

"No, it's okay," I say. I don't know if I'll get through to him, but it feels important to try. "Listen, Abe. I know you think I was Chosen, but I wasn't the one who did the choosing. You have to stop blaming me for it."

Something flickers in Abe's face. A slight crumpling.

"If it'd been up to me," I tell him, "I would have chosen you."

Abe swallows and nods. "You're right." For a moment, I think he's going to apologize for the way he's treated me all these years, but then he says, "It totally should have been me."

It takes me a second, and then I laugh, mostly at myself, for expecting more. "Yeah, it definitely should have."

Abe punches my arm, then ambles off to be with his kids.

"Don't listen to Abe," Dad says. "What happened was meant to happen."

"Thanks, Dad."

"It was God's Will."

It takes everything in me not to roll my eyes.

"Really, Simon? No regrets?" Will, who'd been eavesdropping nearby, is now back with his crew.

"No," Dad says, glancing at the camera, which is rolling again. "It wasn't right for Eli, so it wasn't right for the family." My eyes sting when he says that. How many years have I waited to hear it? But then he adds: "I forgave him a long time ago."

"*You* forgave *me*?"

Dad nods. "It was hard at first. I couldn't understand why you, you know . . ."

"Why I what? Kissed Jesus? Sabotaged Gideon? Came out?"

"Any of it. All of it. When you were a kid, we were so close, then you started acting out and I didn't know how to handle it. I always thought we had a special bond and I didn't want to lose that."

When he says "special bond," I can't take it anymore and surprise myself by bursting into tears. Because we *did* have a special bond. Even if all the Heaven stuff had been fake, that was real. Dad and me, out Saving the world, one *Heaven or Bust!* book at a time. He'd never been prouder of me than when I was the Heaven Kid—*his* Heaven Kid.

Dad reaches for me, but I turn away, blurry-eyed, toward Will. "Can we please stop?"

I expect him to convince me to keep going, but he moves immediately in front of the camera—no questions asked. "Cut!"

"Seriously?" His camerawoman peers around the lens. "Now? This is the good stuff."

The boom dips and the operator frowns. "Yeah, isn't this what we came for?"

"I said *cut*." Will shoos them off. He ignores their looks of baffled annoyance, pulls me aside, and hugs me. "You okay?"

I sniff into his shoulder. "I don't want to do this. I can't do this."

"It's okay. You don't have to."

"I know I said I would, but it's not fair of you to ask me—"

"Eli. I said it's okay. We'll stop."

For some reason, this still doesn't register with me. "Wait. What?" It can't be that easy. "What about the grant money?"

Will shrugs. "Screw it. I'll give it back if I have to."

"Really?" I don't know why I thought it'd be so hard to get him to call it quits. Will wasn't Dad and I wasn't thirteen anymore.

"Of course, babe. I'm not going to make you do something you don't want to do. This was obviously a bad idea. I'm sorry."

I hug him again. "Thank you. I love you."

"I love you, too. Don't worry. Just talk to your dad."

Once we're alone off camera, Dad gives me his handkerchief. "Sorry, son. I didn't mean to upset you."

"It's okay." I wipe my eyes, watching the rest of our entourage pose for family photos around God's Throne. The kids take turns in the seat. Jake's girls, Leah and Ella, fit together and he throws up bunny ears behind their heads.

Dad's also watching. "I love seeing our family together."

"Me, too."

"One day we'll all be together again, with Debbie and Dinah."

"Dad. Please."

He looks up. "They're watching. I can feel it. Don't you want to see Mom again?"

"Of course I do. I miss her, too."

In twenty years, Dad has never remarried, never even dated. Despite pressure from my brothers and me, he's remained obstinately single out of loyalty to Mom. He doesn't want to be unfaithful before he's reunited with her in Heaven. Will always thought this was kind of sad and pathetic. I mostly agreed, but then again I also saw Dad's dedication to Mom as tragically romantic. She's been gone for so long now, and, though I can't believe I'll see her again like Dad does, part of me remains dedicated to her, too.

"You saw it," he says. "I know you did. You can go back."

"Dad. Come on. Still?"

"Please, Eli. I need you there with us."

"I'm here now. Your family's here now."

"I'll be next. Then you and your brothers."

"And Will and Oliver?"

"It's not too late for them. They only have to take Jesus into their hearts."

"I don't want your Heaven if they're not there. I won't go."

He clutches my hand, pulls it to his chest. "Yet so as by fire."

I pull free of his grasp and hug him instead. He'll believe what he needs to believe and I'll just have to love him for it. We stand there together, holding each other in God's Kingdom, neither of us wanting to be the first to let go.

✠

"*As by fire?* Sounds like he said you're going to hell." Will checks on Oliver in his car seat. He's still asleep. It's been a long day.

We're in the Bible World parking lot, about to head back to the hotel. The others have already left, but Will had to help his crew load the camera equipment, which took longer than expected. They'd argued with him about scrapping the doc, but Will reassured them they'd still be paid, even if it came from our own personal funds.

"The opposite," I say. "It's like this. The Bible says we're all builders. Our life's work is the house. It can burn, it *will* burn, but when it does the foundation is still laid."

"The foundation being . . . Jesus?"

"Right. In the end, even in flame, we are Saved. *Yet so as by fire.*"

Will gets in and starts the car. "So the fire's a good thing?"

"It's not good or bad. It's a test, a metaphor. You could build your house of gold or stone or wood, depending on how you live your life. And when it burns, some of your life's work might still be standing and you'll be rewarded for it."

"Sounds like a messed-up version of 'The Three Little Pigs.'"

"And if it *all* burns, if you lived your life in sin, even then, if you have Jesus in your heart, you will be Saved. But just barely and with little reward."

"Like you'll make it to Heaven, but only by the skin of your teeth?"

"Exactly. Once Saved, always Saved. But only by His grace." Dad had always been good at finding just the right verse to ease his mind. He'd damn my husband and son in one breath and reclaim me with the next. *Yet so as by fire* was his way of saying not to worry—no matter how I sinned, I'd still make it to Heaven because I'd been Saved as a child. When our family was reunited, I'd be there, too. He couldn't bear to have it any other way.

"I guess that's his way of apologizing?" Will says.

"Yeah. He admitted what happened wasn't right for me and he's sorry for putting me through it. He loves me in his own misguided way. You can't be loved by my dad without Jesus in the mix. It's just not going to happen."

"It *was* big of him to agree to the doc."

"*Huge*. The doc was a terrible idea, but you were right about one thing. I needed to come back here. I'm glad I did."

"Good," Will says.

In the back seat, Oliver murmurs in his sleep. I reach back and check on him. "You know he asked me about Heaven?"

"What? When?"

"When we were coming out. Jessie told him that's where you go when you die. Where Grandma Debbie is. And he asked me."

I've dreaded this question from Oliver for a while now, but I didn't panic like I thought I would. I thought I needed to prepare an answer, but once he asked, I realized I don't have to have one. It's not my job anymore.

"What'd you tell him?"

"I told him the truth. I said nobody knows. Some people believe there's an after. Some don't. He has to decide for himself."

"Perfect. I couldn't have said it better."

"Hey, Will."

"Yeah?"

"Can we please get the hell out of here?"

He smiles. "With pleasure." He backs the car out of the parking spot. The sunset has cast the sky a vivid pink. Our last glimpse of Bible World is a black silhouette.

"I'm glad they're tearing it down," I say.

"The animatronics are being stripped and sold to the Creation museum in Petersburg," Will says.

"Ugh. Really?" It's an hour and a half from where we live. "I wonder what they'll build here, after it's gone."

"It's commercial real estate. So probably a strip mall."

"I hope they build a gay bar."

"Ha!" Will cackles. "Yes. I can see it now. Mary Magdalene drag queens lining the block. Twinks in Jesus loincloths. A Leather Daddy Last Supper."

"I mean, it's basically built for a Pride party. They already have a giant rainbow."

We play this game all the way back to the hotel, inventing names for Biblically themed gay bars—the Flaming Sword, the Hairy Samson, the Semen on the Mount.

At the hotel I unbuckle Oliver, lift him gently out, and carry him to bed. Will and I undress, brush our teeth, then move together beneath scratchy hotel sheets. After, he's out like a light. He always drifts off before me. I'm a fitful sleeper, but when it comes tonight I know my sleep will be perfectly dreamless. No unicorns. No Jesus. No meadows. Until it does I'm content to lie still and wait, listening to Will's steady breath next to me and, across the room, Oliver's softer wheeze. I lie there, listening, and as I slowly drift off, my thoughts turn to Dad, to what he said about our special bond.

I don't feel special anymore. Not to him or to the public. I'm just a drugstore pharmacist now, one among many. I remember my white coat ceremony. Dad hadn't been there, but I'd thought a lot about him. I expected it to feel silly, childish even, donning an article of clothing and reciting an oath. But when I said that pledge, part of which went, "*I will consider the welfare of humanity and relief of suffering my primary concerns*," it struck me that I'd found, on my own terms, a way to honor the Calling, Dad's desire to take away some of the world's pain.

I think about this, less and less frequently, but still on occasion, while I'm counting pills, stocking shelves, updating patient files. Like so many jobs, it's mostly drudgery. Long hours on your feet. Headaches beneath fluorescent lighting. Disgruntled customers.

But there's still a moment at work that feels almost holy: the rattle of pills in the bottle, the stapling of the little paper bag, the reach across the counter. A ritual, an offering, a gesture of goodwill. The closest these days I come to prayer.

"Here you go," I say. *Take this. It will make you better.*

"Have a good day," I say, but what I really mean is, *Be well.*

AUTHOR'S NOTE

As an atheist from a Catholic family, I have, to say the least, a complicated relationship with religion. This is further complicated by my wife's upbringing as the daughter of a Baptist minister in small-town Texas. I could not have written this novel without her insights into the evangelical perspective and religious trauma, and I did my best to write from a place of empathy for Eli and his family. Much of *Eli* came out of conversations we had about religion and how it affected each of us and our relationship.

There are several other sources of inspiration for Eli's story. While neither Eli nor his family members are based on any real individuals, the novel itself was inspired by the many works in the heaven tourism and near-death experience genres of Christian literature. I also visited a number of Creationist museums and Christian theme parks. Lexington, Kentucky, where I'm from, is only an hour's drive from the Creationist Museum and the Ark Encounter, and I also toured the Holy Land Experience in Orlando, Florida—all models for Bible World.

More than religion, though, this book is about fathers and sons. And I became a father to a son while writing it. I was lucky enough to be raised by a wonderful father, and I hope to raise my son as my father raised me, as Eli intends to raise Oliver: to think for himself, to question everything, and to live a good and moral life on his own terms.

ACKNOWLEDGMENTS

THANK YOU TO:

Abby Muller, my editor extraordinaire who taught me not all adverbs are evil, fine-tuned my sense of humor on the page, and brought out the heart of this book. Why be anything else when you can be a *unicorn*?

The Overlook team: Andrew Gibeley, Sarah Masterson Hally, Eli Mock, Lisa Silverman, Jamison Stoltz, Christian Westermann, and Deb Wood for all their hard work designing and promoting the book.

Copyeditor Logan Hill for his deft hand at polishing my prose.

Joy Tutela, my agent at David Black, who was invaluable in guiding me through this process and is always there for a good chat about TV shows.

Rachel Ludwig. Eli's first champion! He never would have made it this far without you.

Writer friends CJ Hauser, Dan Hornsby, and Anne Valente and writer heroes Chelsea Bieker, Garrard Conley, Jonathan Evison, Annie Hartnett, Paul Russell, Shelby Van Pelt, and Kevin Wilson for your kind words on the book.

My Florida State dissertation committee: Elizabeth Stuckey-French, Mark Winegardner, Diane Roberts, and Lisa Ryoko Wakamiya for reading an early draft and providing much-needed encouragement.

Alice McDermott and Jeffery Renard Allen and the members of their fiction workshop at the 2017 Sewanee Writers' Conference for helpful feedback on early chapters.

The Virginia Center for the Creative Arts, Ragdale, Vermont Studio Center, and Hambidge for writing time and support.

My colleagues at the University of Memphis: Mark Mayer, Courtney Miller Santo, Emily Skaja, and Marcus Wicker. And the English Department Chair, Terrence Tucker. All of whom have made a literary home for me in Memphis.

My friends: Audrey Bowlds, Kate Kimball, SJ Sindu, and Anna Rose Welch.

My family: Jim and Phyllis Schlich; Pamela, Kevin, Elsie, and Alice Steinmetz; Maggie and Ross Micciche; Gene and Paige Ramsey; Aden, Sujin, and Hayoung Ramsey; Amy Mckenzie and Sam Holley. I love you all.

My everything: Jade and Ender.